Cavalier of Old South Carolina

Cavalier
of Old
South Carolina

WILLIAM GILMORE SIMMS'S CAPTAIN PORGY

Edited with an Introduction by

Hugh W. Hetherington

THE UNIVERSITY OF NORTH CAROLINA PRESS · CHAPEL HILL

TO THE MEMORY OF

Alice Hetherington Hedges
(1876-1955)

who showed that the Lady
of the Southern Legend could
exist in the Reality

Preface

This book was made possible because the University of Wyoming granted me Sabbatical Leave for a whole academic year so that I could write it. Some of the time was spent in Laramie, some in Tucson.

First came weeks of rather leisurely perusal or reperusal of the six of Simms's romances wherein Captain Porgy can be expected to appear more or less frequently. I always eagerly awaited his entrances and regretted his exits.

Then I collected the Porgy scenes and composed the preludes, interludes, and epilogues covering as briefly as I could the portions of the book not blessed with the presence of our hero so as to offer the complete story of his career. It was, as we say in the West, a "panning out the gold" and fashioning it into an ingot containing only so much of baser metal as was needed to make the whole structure cohere.

Next I commenced what was to be a brief "introduction" to try to tell why I admired Porgy so much, and thought him important for all who wished to understand our Old South, and indeed our whole nation as it was and even as it is today. I kept finding more and more materials to support my defense of Captain Porgy as an interesting and significant figure, until my little introduction was approaching book proportions in itself. Fears that some editors might require severe excisions from this introduction finally proved unfounded, thanks to the gracious staff of The University of North Carolina Press. This portion of the book is now called "A Reappraisal of Captain Porgy."

The many months I spent with Captain Porgy were good ones, and I greatly enjoyed his company. For many of the characters of the fiction of the 1960's I cannot say as much. One can become weary of being expected to admire the "art" with which recent novelists have risen to fame for depicting figures who, though as persons obviously detestable, are "brilliant portrayals of men and women confronting their own frustrations and confusions."

How different is Porgy! He is nothing less than the chief ornament and epitome—in fiction—of our old southern aristocracy. He had his hard knocks, too: seven years of fighting through the American Revolution without pay; a return to find his beautiful plantation ruined by the Tories; and even, though hilariously described, misfortune in love. Yet Porgy triumphs, because he is a master of a rare art, the art of living. His attainments are impressive. In many things he is the very best: the finest equestrian; the master most beloved by and most devoted to his slaves; the planter most conversant with belles-lettres; the gourmet most discerning; and above all, the patrician indubitably incomparable in hospitality. He also excels in avoirdupois, being about one hundred pounds overweight. To complete the accounting of his merits, I must resort to adjectives. He is charming, kindly, brave, witty, relaxed, unselfish, and gallant.

It is quite impossible for me to imagine such a portrait of a gentleman placed in any other frame than that in which Simms has placed it, the world of our ante-bellum South, the world of the Southern Legend. Simms himself implies also that the frame could have been fabricated only in South Carolina.

I may be confusing aesthetic judgment with, perhaps, friendship; but I cannot help confessing that I just happen to like Captain Porgy better than any other personage in American literature. In an era when the new novels are so full of disagreeable people, it has been a joy to have been allowed the time to be so much in the company of a man so entertaining and gracious. And I once did, I am happy to say, visit Charleston.

Acknowledgments

Major help in the preparation of this book has come from two persons. My first and greatest debt is to my wife, Grace Irvine Hetherington, for two somewhat different reasons. As a retired professional librarian, she did the preliminary spade work on the bibliography. Yet even more I am obligated to her for her continuing enthusiasm for Captain Porgy, as well as for her wholehearted concurrence in my conviction that he is a wonderful comic creation. Indeed she was the discoverer of some of the Porgy passages, as, even before I did, she read two of the books he adorns.

The second of my major debts is to Charles D. Froome, who, at my suggestion and under my direction, prepared a Master's thesis dealing with Simms's reply, especially in *Woodcraft,* to *Uncle Tom's Cabin.* He did a splendid job, and it has been of great value to me.

To Dr. George Duke Humphrey, President Emeritus of the University of Wyoming, and Administrator of the William Robertson Coe School of American Studies of that University, and to Dr. T. Alfred Larsen, Director of that School, go my thanks for a generous subsidy. Dr. Herbert Dietrich, Dr. William R. Steckel and Dr. Morton Ross, also associated with that School, have aided by their approval. Dr. Robert Bruce, Dean of the Graduate School, has provided expense funds. I appreciate the labors of my proofreaders, Dr. Tom Francis, Frank Welles, Eleanor Edgerton, my wife, and especially, Mary Welles.

I wish to express my gratitude to the late Dr. Gregory Lansing Paine, of The University of North Carolina at Chapel Hill, and Dr. Ruth Hudson, of the University of Wyoming, for originally arousing my interest in the literature of our South. Finally, for more than a dozen years, my morale has been kept up by many students in my course in the Literature of the South here at Wyoming, who have listened, with apparent interest, to my praises of Captain Porgy, Cavalier of Old South Carolina.

H. W. H.

The University of Wyoming
Laramie

Contents

Cavalier of Old South Carolina

1. A Reappraisal
of
Captain Porgy

The Fame of Porgy

Honor came to Captain Porgy in 1951 through the selection of Chapters XLIII, XLV, and XLVI from *The Forayers* by the editors of *The Literature of the South*, by far the best anthology of southern writers, as their chief offering from the works of William Gilmore Simms.[1] These chapters give us Porgy in his most resplendent hours, as he prepares and serves triumphantly his great feast "for the captains" and for the Governor of South Carolina as guest of honor. The editors could not have made a more judicious choice. In these chapters I met Porgy and became his advocate. Without conscious guidance, though perhaps unconsciously recalling some critic's remark, I leafed through some of Simms's many volumes to discover, to my delight, that there was a whole book—*Woodcraft*—about this charming character. Before I encountered Porgy, of Simms I had read, as had many others, his only book in print, a romance about Indian wars, *The Yemassee*, and the volume of short stories, *The Wigwam and the Cabin*.

1. Richard Croom Beatty, Floyd C. Watkins, and Thomas Dixon Young (eds.), *The Literature of the South* (New York, 1951), pp. 288-312.

Another dim recollection, however, guided me back to my Parrington, to find the eloquent paragraph he had written:

The creative masterpiece of the valiant Porgy was a notable banquet which he proffered General Greene and his staff in their swamp headquarters. His infinite resourcefulness in this great affair, his huge inventiveness, elevate the dinner to the rank of a culinary epic. The swamp frogs that he speared by moonlight, and the young alligators that he took by subtle stratagem, were transmogrified into delectable dishes served to his guests under the alluring names of *alerta* and *lagarta*. The scene is done with a gusto that only the worshipper of fleshpots could achieve. There is good fare for those who sit at table with the fat humorist of *The Forayers;* the ready talk does not lack the salt of wit.

Parrington declared, rightly, that the Porgy of *Woodcraft* scarcely came up to all this; for he was "less redoubtable as a wooer than as a warrior; nevertheless there is excellent humor to be enjoyed at Glen-Eberly [the name of Porgy's plantation is correctly spelled Glen-Eberley] and some extraordinary pranks."[2] Yet fine as may be the Porgy of *The Forayers,* he appears in these three chapters only; while he is the dominating figure of *Woodcraft.*

In 1961 came the reprinting of *Woodcraft,* thus signalizing the tardy recognition that it is as a whole Simms's best work of fiction, as Richard Croom Beatty in his Introduction emphatically indicated.[3] Among the various reasons for assigning *Woodcraft* such rank the chief is that it is centered around Porgy.

Then I found that Porgy comes into five of the other novels, or romances as Simms often called them, of the series of seven depicting with bravura and sweep, but also with some prolixity, the last two years of the American Revolution as fought in the South, especially in South Carolina. Partly for convenience this series will be referred to as the "Revolutionary Saga," or simply the "Saga," terms which it does not altogether fail to deserve. They have higher value than has been realized, though they contain stilted love-making and conventional melodrama enough; and the brightest pages are always, for me at least, those in which the portly and jovial Porgy appears. The romances average

2. Vernon L. Parrington, *The Romantic Revolution in America* (New York, 1927), p. 132.

3. *Woodcraft,* with Introduction by Richard Croom Beatty (New York, 1961), p. xv.

over five hundred pages of fine print, of which all too few, aside from those in *Woodcraft,* are about Porgy.

Really to know Porgy, one must meet him as he is seen not only in *Woodcraft,* but also in *The Partisan* (1835) and *Katharine Walton* (1851), written before *Woodcraft* (1852); and in *The Forayers* (1855) and *Eutaw* (1856), written afterwards. The two novels in which he is given the most space, aside from *Woodcraft,* are *The Partisan* and *Katharine Walton.* As for the other two novels of the Saga, Porgy gets a very few pages in *Mellichampe* (1836), and none in *The Scout* (1841). Donald Davidson has said justly that Porgy can irradiate and make more convincing a romance beyond the pale of his actual presence;[4] and hence it is probably not a matter of chance that the violently melodramatic *The Scout* is the poorest book in the Saga; while one critic assigns that position of dishonor to *Mellichampe.*[5] At any rate, I think, Porgy is worth meeting every time he comes on the scene.

The case of Simms and his Porgy is nearly unique, at least in American literature. Is there elsewhere a character, clearly its author's most inspired creation, appearing importantly in as many as six full-length novels, and by a writer of at least Simms's stature? For the moment any claims as to the vividness and significance of this character may be set aside.

Of course there are some examples where an author, equal or superior to Simms, has evoked one figure admittedly greatly outranking all his others. There is Huckleberry Finn; but to know this wonderful boy one has only to read the less than four hundred pages of large type of the book that bears his name, with a few glances at the inferior Huck of the shorter *Tom Sawyer.*

There is the Yoknapatawpha Saga; but it is debatable which is the greatest character in the Saga. Is it Isaac McCaslin, or Quentin Compson, or Tom Sutpen? Ike is made nearly complete for us in *Go Down, Moses;* Sutpen in *Absalom, Absalom!* though referred to sometimes elsewhere; Quentin in that novel and in *The Sound and the Fury.* None of these books by Twain or Faulkner is as long as those by Simms. Porgy, as Parrington said, "runs through the Revolutionary romances as a sort

4. Donald Davidson, "Introduction," in the *Letters of William Gilmore Simms,* eds. Mary D. Simms Oliphant, Alfred Taylor Odell, T. C. Duncan Eaves, 5 vols. (Columbia, S.C., 1952-56), I, xlviii. This work will hereafter be referred to simply as *Letters,* with the appropriate volume number.

5. Jay B. Hubbell, *The South in Literature, 1607-1900* (Durham, N.C., 1954), p. 575.

of comic chorus."[6] He keeps coming into five of the books, and briefly into a sixth, always to make a real impact, and often to reveal a hitherto-undisclosed facet of his complex personality.

The case most like that of Simms and Porgy is that of Cooper and the Leatherstocking. The idea for *Cavalier of Old South Carolina* came to me from the book Allan Nevins did, *The Leatherstocking Saga*.[7] Herein the prominent historian presented in one large volume the passages pertaining to Natty Bumppo in the five romances in which he appears. Nevins gave the passages about Natty in the order of the events of the Saga, as I do in the present edition. Both Nevin's book and mine have in common the reason for their preparation a difference between the order of the events in the story and the order of the publication of the books. It is true that the disjunction is more extreme in Cooper, who almost was making Natty younger as he grew older. *Cavalier of Old South Carolina* has an added justification, however, which *The Leatherstocking Saga* had not, because, unlike five of Simms's containing Porgy, all of the five Cooper romances containing Natty are in print.

Hence I planned *Cavalier of Old South Carolina*. It consists of those passages depicting Porgy and those referring to him, along with connecting summaries of what has happened between, in the six romances, together with a little explication and commentary. The existence of a study of Captain Porgy is justified, as has been implied, by the assumption that Simms was somehow able to create one character who is immensely superior to all the others in his voluminous narrative writing. He published eighty-two volumes, including thirty-four of fiction. Without my edition, to know this character one would have to read not all thirty-four but six of the Revolutionary Saga—a formidable enough task.

In the books containing Porgy, except *Woodcraft*, all the passages depicting or concerning him are given *in toto*. None of these is in print, and the total number of pages in them about Porgy is not great. *Woodcraft* posed a difficult problem. At first the alternatives seemed to be to include almost the whole book, or leave it out altogether. Its omission might be defended by the arguments that *Woodcraft* is now in print, and that surely every scholarly student of American Literature will read it. I decided on a compromise: to give complete only the best

6. Parrington, *Romantic Revolution*, p. 131.
7. Allan Nevins (ed.), *The Leatherstocking Saga* (New York, 1954).

passages about Porgy in *Woodcraft,* and to cut or summarize the rest. Thus I could make *Cavalier of Old South Carolina* complete, or complete enough. At any rate the cut version of *Woodcraft* is humbly offered for what it is worth.

The passages are given in *Cavalier of Old South Carolina* in the order of the occurrence of the events in the Saga, and thus also in the life of Porgy. The books of the Saga were not written entirely in the order of the chronological sequence of incidents of the story. Another justification is that in it the reader will have conveniently at hand the whole tale of Porgy in the order in which his adventures took place. Porgy's years in the army are depicted in *The Partisan* (1835), *Mellichampe* (1836), *Katharine Walton* (1851), *The Forayers* (1855), and *Eutaw* (1856). For these books, the happenings in the Saga are indeed in the same order as the publication; however *Woodcraft* (1852), published between *Katharine Walton* and *The Forayers,* gives the story of Porgy after peace has come and he has left the army. In *Cavalier of Old South Carolina,* the passages about him in *Woodcraft* will be given last, as they tell the last part of his story. In one section of this introduction, "The Progress of Porgy," I shall discuss the appearances of the character in the books in the order of publication and consider whether there were reasons why Simms's last-written accounts of Porgy show him, in disregard of chronology, back in the army.

Porgy has not been without his admirers. Porgy had his *aficionados* when he made his first bow to the world. When *The Partisan* had been out about five months, Simms wrote in 1836 to his northern friend James Lawson that Henry W. Herbert did "not appreciate those portions of the Partisan which belong to humble life and were intended to be humorous. This I foresaw; but you have no idea how popular Porgy is with a large majority. He is actually the founder of a sect."[8] The *Southern Literary Journal* for January, 1836, said Porgy was "one of those happy conceptions of humor which will ever please one, though it produces no downright laughter."[9]

Porgy had already become a controversial figure, as he had displeased Poe. In 1845, Simms wrote to Evert A. Duyckinck "Poe is no friend of mine. He began by a very savage attack on one of my novels the Par-

8. *Letters,* I, 82. Herbert had reviewed *The Partisan* for *The American Monthly Magazine* for January, 1836.
9. *Ibid.,* p. 83.

tisan."[10] Poe had in 1836 declared the Porgy of *The Partisan* "an insuffer-able bore," but he had condemned all the other fictitious characters in the book also, and found the hero Singleton and his uncle "non-entities."[11] He did admire the historical parts of the book and was more compli-mentary to some of Simms's later novels.

William P. Trent, in the first biography of Simms, in 1892, pro-nounced him only a talented, not a great writer. Yet he did regard Porgy with some favor. "None of the characters," of *The Partisan,* he declared, "can be called fascinating unless it be Lieutenant Porgy." He thought Porgy was taken from real life, to some extent Simms him-self, rather than copied from Falstaff. "Porgy is in many respects a typical Southerner, brave, high talking, careless in money matters, fond of good living, and last, but not least, too frequently inclined to take his own commonplaces as the utterances of inspired wisdom. It cannot be denied that Simms at times overdraws this favorite character, who is introduced in many succeeding volumes"—Trent did not say which. "But he is better drawn than most of the high-born gentlemen that figure in Simms's romances."[12] The "Reconstructed" southerner Trent's violent bias against everything about the Old South could not keep him from admitting somewhat unwillingly there was merit in Porgy.

Trent was so evasive about which of Simms's novels was best, that his praise for *Woodcraft* seemed comparatively warm: "Both for its interest and for its truth of history, the romance deserves to be read." He conceded that the "humor which for a wonder, Simms succeeded in putting into" this book "is not of a high order." Trent even re-gretted that the proposed sequel "The Humors of Glen-Eberley" was never written.[13] Though he did not mention Porgy, that man is so much the center of *Woodcraft,* that here—as with other critics—approba-tion of that book may be taken as essentially applicable to him.

Until 1962, Trent's remained the only biography of Simms; and since he did have access to letters, and also to oral materials no longer avail-able, the critics who accepted his seemingly authoritative declarations that Simms was of humble origin and was rejected by the elite of Charleston, may be judged with some leniency.

Parrington's re-evaluation of some southern writers was based on

10. *Ibid.,* II, 42.

11. *Southern Literary Messenger,* II (January, 1836), 117-21.

12. William P. Trent, *William Gilmore Simms* (Boston and New York, 1892), p. 109.

13. *Ibid.,* pp. 202-3. Toward the end of *Woodcraft* Simms says, "It may be that we shall someday depict these happy times, the 'Humors of Glen-Eberley' " (p. 509).

intensive reading and was original and stimulating, and frequently took us to the heart of books which had been long overlooked. His chapter on Simms was an example, despite his having been so far misled by Trent as to call the Charleston writer a "plebeian."[14] Parrington pronounced Simms "by far the most virile and interesting figure of the Old South"—one "endowed with a rich and prodigal nature, vigorous, spontaneous, creative."[15] He saw the Revolutionary romances were Simms's finest work. "The best of Simms is not in *The Yemassee*, but in those stirring tales of Marion's men. . . ."[16] he said most justly. He is to be credited with the discovery of Porgy for us today.

Of Parrington's eighteen paragraphs about Simms, two were entirely about Porgy, the only one of his characters he took time to analyze. After a paragraph contending that in "easy outpourings of picturesque speech," having Elizabethan antecedents, Simms "was without rival in his generation," he turned to Porgy:

The Elizabethan influence comes out strikingly in the character of Lieutenant Porgy, the spoilt child of his imagination. . . . Porgy is a South Carolina Falstaff, quite evidently done with a close eye to the original. He is a very mountain of a fellow, with a huge paunch . . . the most amusing and substantial comic character in our early fiction. . . . The copious stream of his speech runs on in an endless flow, sometimes roily but never stagnant. A pat aphorism is as succulent to him as Carolina terrapin. When philosophy fails he stoops to horseplay, but his practical jokes are carried off with theatrical splendour, with colossal assurance.[17]

Clearly for Parrington, Porgy was Simms's best character, and indeed a magnificent evocation.

In his few paragraphs about Simms, Russell Blankenship said *The Forayers* "shows the great Porgy at his best."[18] Others, including Parrington, have agreed that Porgy is at his finest in this novel.

Despite some biographical misconceptions resulting from following Trent, Van Wyck Brooks offered original critical comments on Simms, some of which have later been quoted approvingly. Brooks declared "Simms is the greatest by far, save Poe alone of all the Southern writers" —this in 1944. Was he ranking Simms above Glasgow, Warren, and

14. Parrington, *Romantic Revolution*, p. 125.
15. *Ibid.*, p. 127.
16. *Ibid.*, p. 134.
17. *Ibid.*, pp. 131-32.
18. Russell Blankenship, *American Literature* (New York, 1931), p. 236.

Faulkner? Simms was "the living emblem in letters of all that made one love the South, its spendthrift energy, its carelessness, lavishness, and warmth."[19] From Brooks seems to have come the first unequivocal pronouncement of the superiority of *Woodcraft* as a whole to any of Simms's other novels, a judgment which has not been challenged by any subsequent critic.[20] Brooks was an admirer of Porgy, also. "Captain Porgy kept reappearing [in the Saga]. This once rich planter who had drunk, eaten, and talked away all but his horse, his good sword and his negro servant" appealed to Brooks. *"Woodcraft,* the finest of these books, a tale of the days that followed the war, was certainly the best historical novel that was written anywhere in the South, or anywhere else, for that matter, in the country. Here Simms' talent for the picaresque and his feeling for comedy came to the fore in the episode finally involving Captain Porgy and the blackguards and outlaws who swarmed through the state, brought to the front by the war. These types had a peculiar appeal for Simms' realistic eye, and in fact it was his realism that kept the work of Simms alive when readers lost their taste for other romances."[21]

Alexander Cowie was not so sure that, as compared with Simms's two first popular successes, *Guy Rivers* (1835) and *The Yemassee* (1835), his Revolutionary romances were his best. They lacked a "good focus of the reader's hopes and affections." True, there were many effective major and especially minor characters, but "no single character" of the caliber of Natty Bumppo.[22] Obviously, it is the aim of *Cavalier of Old South Carolina* to show that such a focus does exist. Cowie did, nevertheless, relish *Woodcraft* considerably, saying, "It gives prominence to Simms' best comic character, Lieutenant [actually then Captain] Porgy, whose misadventures in courtship delightfully recall the Falstaff of *The Merry Wives of Windsor.*"[23] Cowie added that "in those respects in which Porgy differs from his prototype he is apparently a combination of Simms in self-portrait and of Simms' ideal of a South Carolina gentle-

19. Van Wyck Brooks, *The World of Washington Irving* (New York, 1944), p. 299.
20. Except somewhat tentatively by Holman, who still seemed to prefer *The Yemassee.* C. Hugh Holman, "The Status of Simms," *American Quarterly,* X (Summer, 1958), 181-85.
21. Brooks, *Washington Irving,* p. 314.
22. Alexander Cowie, *The Rise of the American Novel* (New York, 1948), p. 235.
23. *Ibid.,* p. 234.

man."[24] In 1950, C. Hugh Holman referred to "Porgy, the character who was Simms' most successful creation."[25]

The first volume, appearing in 1952, of the five-volume collection of Simms's letters was prefaced by two very valuable essays, one by Alexander S. Salley, State Historian of South Carolina, and possessor of many Simms documents, and the other by Donald Davidson, well-known southern author and critic. Salley proved conclusively that, despite Trent, Simms was from an excellent Carolina family, and was far from being rejected by the literary and social leaders of Charleston. His points were fully substantiated in the letters themselves.

In what may well be the best of the critical studies of Simms, Davidson clearly implied Simms's major accomplishment was the Revolutionary Saga, and was emphatic about the exalted status of *Woodcraft,* "which is Simms' highest achievement. Certainly it stands, *sui generis,* a book apart, without a rival in its day and time, and hardly excelled or even paralleled later in its peculiar vein." It was the first significant treatment in our literature of the subject of "soldiers' pay." But the "dominance of Captain Porgy distinguishes *Woodcraft* from all other post-war novels." He and his followers return to a ruined plantation, forgotten by officialdom; but "their philosophical resourcefulness and good-humored gallantry are so characteristically American that it would be very hard to find anywhere, I believe, a better representation of our supposed national temperament and principles."[26] Davidson confessed it was a relief, after too much of the gallants and their refined ladyloves, to rejoin Porgy and his comrades in the forest.[27]

Jay B. Hubbell, in 1954, asserted "Simms' best work is probably to be found in his seven Revolutionary Romances . . . *Woodcraft,* which Van Wyck Brooks regards as the best, is perhaps most likely to interest the modern reader. . . . The seven romances constitute a kind of epic of the American Revolution. . . . Simms' best character, Captain Porgy, who has a certain resemblance to Falstaff, plays a leading role in *Woodcraft.* . . ."[28] Yet Hubbell thought Simms had "failed . . . to create any one great character comparable to Cooper's best."[29]

24. *Ibid.,* p. 790.

25. C. Hugh Holman, "Simms and the British Dramatists," *PMLA,* LXV, 4 (June, 1950), 355.

26. *Letters,* I, xlv.

27. *Ibid.,* p. xlvii.

28. Jay B. Hubbell, *The South in American Literature, 1607-1900* (Durham, 1954), p. 589.

29. *Ibid.,* p. 597.

Edd Winfield Parks, an authority on southern literary criticism, in his 1961 book on Simms as a literary critic twice praised *Woodcraft.* "In 1852 he published his best novel"—*Woodcraft,* said Parks.[30] And again, "The quieter concluding novel, *Woodcraft,* reveals Simms at his best; more than any other of his works, with the possible exception of *Border Beagles,* it deserves to be reprinted and to be read."[31]

Warren D. Taylor, in his *Cavalier and Puritan* in 1961 emphasized Porgy as an important example of the Cavalier. He analyzed Simms's creation perceptively:

Porgy's genius lies in his capacity to be the opposite of what he seems. His character tends to be rendered in a series of antithetical statements. Although he is described as a wastrel who "ate and drank everything away," Simms later comments that "Porgy was a man nearly as full of prudence as plethora." . . . Even his eating is done in moderation. . . . Despite the fact that he adopts the motto, "Never hurry," and seems the most pacific of men, it is said of him that "he rides like the devil, and fights like blazes." Whimsical, witty, and benign, he is nonetheless capable of decisive and brutal action. . . . For Porgy somehow compounded sensuality and intelligence, reflection and action, imagination and common sense—every quality which the planter appeared to need.[32]

It is surprising that Taylor, after giving such an essentially complimentary dissection of Porgy, went on to argue that in *Woodcraft* he failed both as wooer and planter; and, in disagreement with most critics, including Davidson and Ridgley, to declare that a "mood of pessimism and foreboding hovers over the narrative from beginning to end."[33] If he had not overlooked entirely the Porgy of *The Forayers* and *Eutaw,* which he does not even mention, Taylor's interpretation might have been less negative. Such an oversight will be less likely with *Cavalier of Old South Carolina* available.

Joseph V. Ridgley in his *William Gilmore Simms* in 1962 offered a far more positive interpretation of the role of Porgy. This was the first biography since Trent's and the first based on the true facts of the subject's life, as well as on a real examination of his major novels and many

30. Edd Winfield Parks, *William Gilmore Simms as Literary Critic* (Athens, Georgia, 1961), p. 7.

31. *Ibid.,* p. 9.

32. William R. Taylor, *Cavalier and Yankee: The Old South and American Yankee Character* (New York, 1961), p. 286.

33. *Ibid.,* pp. 287-91.

minor ones also. He said that the Revolution was "an almost perfect motif for Simms to hit upon,"[34] and certainly implied by the space he gave them that the books of the Revolutionary Saga were Simms's finest. He called Porgy the "character who had been cited as Simms's most striking individual creation,"[35] and who, though "eminently a gentleman" was nevertheless the "relaxed aristocrat." *Woodcraft* was "fundamentally the story of one person, that true son of the Old South, Porgy. And it is the rotund Porgy's unflagging wit and good nature that sets the tale's major mood."[36]

Ridgley was the first to show that *Woodcraft* was Simms's reply to *Uncle Tom's Cabin,* and as such quite effective. He saw Simms as planning in this book "a positive rendering" of the South as a "responsible society. . . . In carrying out this aim, he produced what is his most cogent work of fiction."[37] Ridgley admired Porgy as a planter, once a "high-liver," but now reformed and willing and able to take his part in the perfecting of the southern system. Thus the theme of *Woodcraft* was "Porgy's rise to self-knowledge and responsibility."[38]

There has been, as I have shown, nearly unanimous agreement as to the pre-eminence of Porgy among Simms's characters. Some would not rank him as high as I do as compared with portraits found in other American authors. A number have, however, regarded him as an engaging embodiment of the culture of the South. Indeed, it has been suggested, that Porgy is the most adequate example of the ideal gentleman of the Southern Legend. The telling of the tale of Porgy was an important contribution to the formulation of that Legend or Myth.

The term Southern Legend is surely somewhat self-explanatory and recognizable as referring to the Old South as shown in song and story. Although some aspects of the Southern Legend have been since further elaborated upon, thirty years ago Francis Pendleton Gaines offered the first and still one of the few actual definitions of what he called "The Plantation Tradition," which was virtually the same thing as the Legend.

Against a background of a white-porticoed mansion, according to Gaines, the Tradition envisioned gentlemen who were gallant, chival-

34. Joseph V. Ridgley, *William Gilmore Simms* (New York, 1962), p. 60.
35. *Ibid.,* p. 65.
36. *Ibid.,* p. 98.
37. *Ibid.,* p. 104. As will be explained in Section V, Ridgley had previously published an article about this.
38. *Ibid.,* p. 102.

rous, cultured, skilled as horsemen, a bit high-strung when honor was in question, inept in business, hospitable. The ladies were lovely, sparkling in repartee, but gifted in supervising complicated households. Race relations were perfect. Which was greater, the devotion of master to slave or of slave to master? The Negroes were satisfied, as they were lavishly fed, tolerably housed, and had time for singing and dancing.[39] Although his province was the Tradition, not the actuality, Gaines did conclude that the actual was surprisingly in harmony with the tradition, the main difference being that in the actual the race relations were unruffled more because of custom than because of self-conscious mutual devotion.[40] Ridgley said of Simms: "Certainly better than any other creative writer of his era and region he managed to capture the essence of the Old South dream."[41]

Virtually all the aspects of the Legend as just outlined appear in the story of Porgy and the picture of his household, with a special emphasis on an aura of the comic spirit, surrounding Negroes and master alike.

39. Francis Pendleton Gaines, *The Southern Plantation* (Gloucester, Mass., 1962, reprinted from the original edition, 1924), Chapter I.
40. *Ibid.*, Chapter VIII.
41. Ridgley, *Simms*, p. 130.

Porgy's Progress in the Saga Romances as Published

The first book of the Saga, *The Partisan* (1835), opens in July, 1780, when the American cause in the South seemed doomed. It is a romance of considerable effectiveness. Outside of *Woodcraft,* the longest Porgy sequences are here and in *Katharine Walton.*

In *The Partisan,* we are introduced to Lieutenant Porgy, who has just decided to join the partisans, and thus become one of Marion's men. He is, therefore, in on the start of the revival of the American spirit, which centers around the gallant leadership of the Swamp Fox. Porgy had, however, been "fighting from the very beginning of the war";[1] the chance to do his part for the winning of independence had given him a new purpose in life.

He is notable in *The Partisan* mainly for his culinary activities. Soon

1. *The Partisan,* p. 98.

after his arrival in the camp, he begins preparations for an excellent feast. As the main dish is an artfully seasoned terrapin stew, the repast is a trial run for the supreme one in *The Forayers*. It is a comparatively minor affair, as it is for the partisans only; and through no fault of Porgy's is rather ill-timed, as his detachment receives marching orders while he is in the midst of his project. He has to hurry—always a trial for a real *cuisinier,* and even has to do coaxing to get some of the men to linger to sample his concoctions. Most of those who do taste are converted.[2] He has not yet, however, established the tremendous reputation as host and *gastronome* which he has by the time of the events in *The Forayers,* two years later. He asserts that the stomach is more important than the brain in winning wars.

As to his retinue, he has already acquired two, Dr. Oakenburg and the poet George Dennison, but he has his first meeting with a third, young Lancelot Frampton.

In *Mellichampe* (1836), which is somewhat less in the main stream of the events of the Saga, Porgy's entrances are only two, both brief. Yet they reveal a new facet of his personality, his great love for his horse Nabob, who is big enough to carry easily his huge master. We hear of his concern at the illness of Nabob;[3] and then of his deep grief at the horse's death; and of the fine bay sent as a replacement by Porgy's immediate superior, Major Singleton.[4]

There is thus very little of Porgy in *Mellichampe* and no Porgy at all in *The Scout*—originally entitled *The Kinsmen* (1841). Alone in the Saga, it is set in an area commanded by Sumter instead of Marion; is without various characters who are elsewhere in the Saga; and is thus even more of an excursion than *Mellichampe.* In *The Scout,* the most humorless, the most Gothic of the seven books, it seems the genial Porgy cannot breathe, and can exist so briefly in *Mellichampe,* only somewhat less conventionally romantic. Ten years later, in the rather more realistic *Katharine Walton* (1851), Simms returns to the central matter of the Saga, reintroduces the main figures of *The Partisan,* including Porgy, and continues the action commenced in that novel into the fall of 1780.

The aspect of Porgy emphasized in *Katharine Walton* (1851), as well as the slant of much else in the book, was determined by the con-

2. *Ibid.,* pp. 361-62.
3. *Mellichampe,* pp. 151-54.
4. *Ibid.,* p. 172.

ditions of its publication. Mrs. Sarah Josepha Hale, editor of *Godey's Ladies Book* had rejected Simms's *Vasconselos* for her magazine because it contained too much low life and crime. He, therefore, sent her *Katharine Walton,* "to which I pledge you no exception will be taken."[5] He no doubt thought the fair readers would be pleased by a book in which a lovely southern belle is the title character and is finally happily married; in which in contrast with the first two books of the Saga with their rural settings, the doings of Charleston society, gay despite the war, are given many pages; and in which the gentlemanly Porgy gives his theory of matrimony and shows the first symptoms of considering it, though he stays away from Charleston. Also stressed is the real establishment of Porgy's friendship with Lance Frampton, disciple and later retainer.

The portly officer voices preference for a widow, as already well-trained, if she has had a good husband. He wants a wife who can cook and keep house, and above all has a due reverence for her husband's authority. The continuity of the Porgy thread is here illustrated; as the reason the "Widow Eveleigh" will give in *Woodcraft* for rejecting Porgy is that she feels he wants to dominate his wife. She is not mentioned here or elsewhere before *Woodcraft,* but Porgy, along with Lance, is sent to carry official condolences to Mrs. Griffin when her soldier husband is killed. Porgy had admired her, and on this journey thinks of her as a possible spouse. He conveys to her the sad news in a wonderfully tactful manner, however;[6] and is far too much of a gentleman to reveal his amorous intentions until a seemly interval has passed, some years later in *Woodcraft.*

The titles of the other romances of the Saga are reasonably appropriate, but that of *Woodcraft* is surely inept. The uninitiated might even imagine the book dealt with carpentry. "Woodcraft" is the art of seeing without being seen, of shooting before one is shot, when snaking through the heavy southern woods. Simms thought the American proficiency in this art helped importantly in the winning of the last phase of the Revolution in southern forests and swamps; but here there is more of it even after the end of the war in *Woodcraft.* The "woodcraft" part of the novel occupies only about one third of its pages, fortunately.

The title the book bore in its first or 1852 edition was *The Sword*

5. *Letters,* II, 560.
6. *Katharine Walton,* p. 376.

and the Distaff, a better title as it does at least pertain somewhat to the central subject, and better than the alternate title used in the original magazine publication, *Or Fair, Fat, and Forty.* For the second or 1855 edition the title was *Woodcraft, or Hawks About the Dovecote.* This second alternate title refers to the main subject fairly well. Why did Simms change the title? Was he really convinced that the public preferred to the main matter, the "woodcraft" part, which is not too unlike the later "horse opera" and perhaps had as wide a popular appeal?

None of these titles, unfortunately, indicates explicitly that the work is mainly about Porgy, and not about him as an exemplar of "woodcraft," in which he does have some ability. It is Porgy's book, and he should have been in the title. It might have been named *Captain Porgy's Homecoming* or *Captain Porgy's Return.*

Woodcraft has two parts, Porgy's journey home from war, and his life at home. Running through both is the subplot of the intrigue of the Scotchman [*sic*] M'Kewn and his restive tool the squatter Bostwick against Porgy. These villains are poor whites, but M'Kewn has become rich by trafficking with the British.

On his way home Porgy gallantly rescues Mrs. Eveleigh and her son, also going home from Charleston, from a gang led by the masked Bostwick. It is indeed a chance for a chivalric gesture. He seems less knightly as he remains long undecided which of two attractive widows he wants to marry. For delay, he has sensible reasons, however, his debts, his lack of decent clothes, his run-down plantation.

He weighs the advantages and disadvantages of each. Mrs. Eveleigh is a landed proprietor, and has imposing good looks, competence, intellectuality, and sophistication. Her wealth tempts him, but he asks himself whether he loves her for herself or her possessions, and refuses, despite his overseer's prodding, to propose to her while he is poor. On the other hand, her efficiency is almost masculine, and her very accomplishments and assets are somewhat formidable. Sometimes he objects to being so dressed up and on good behavior as seems requisite in her mansion, and—amusing note—he finds her rather too plump.[7]

Mrs. Griffin attracts by her more feminine prettiness, her pliability, her soft domesticity, and her ability to cook excellent meals herself; yet she repels by her poor education and dull conversation.[8] Though he

7. *Woodcraft,* p. 399 and *passim.*
8. *Ibid.,* p. 400 and *passim.*

hardly confesses it to himself, he is probably deterred by her not quite belonging to his social class.

Porgy does not entirely resist his overseer Millhouse's repeated insistence that Mrs. Eveleigh greatly desires him. At any rate, she appears to be his first choice, as he does propose to her before approaching the other.

Mrs. Eveleigh tells Porgy clearly why she will not marry him: "I have been too long my own mistress to submit to authority . . . and you . . . have a certain imperative mood which would make you very despotic, should you meet with resistance."[9] Why not take her at her word? Other reasons she does not give at the time might include the problem of how to get rid of his bachelor retainers, especially the crude and tenacious Millhouse; and her son's intermittent resentment at seeing his father's place taken by another.

As he is forestalled by Mrs. Eveleigh's overseer Fordham, Porgy never proposes to Mrs. Griffin. Probably she would have, however, taken a landed gentleman rather than an overseer. Porgy's hesitating between two widows is realistic in an almost fiftyish bachelor, as is also his easy reconciliation to not marrying at all.

The main concern in *Woodcraft,* however, is not with Porgy's love affairs, but with his plantation. On his way home he has moments of dejection. When he thinks of the difficulties he must face when he reaches his ruined home, he wishes the war was still on, and even dreams of having died heroically leading a charge as a way out of his present dilemmas. He has, however, "moral resources which kept him from basely cowering and whining beneath the cloud."[10] He pulls himself together and resolves to build a new life.

He has two very loyal white helpers, Lance Frampton and Sergeant Millhouse. Lance is completely sympathetic with Porgy, but marries and leaves Porgy's household, and Millhouse remains his chief employee. Porgy had saved Millhouse's life by resolutely amputating his battle-shattered arm, and aroused in him great gratitude.[11] Unsolicited, he announces he will be Porgy's overseer. Millhouse's long-winded discourses on the value of money can be trying; but Porgy has compensations, for with the energetic overseer on the job, he has plenty of time himself for hunting, socializing, and reading.

9. Ridgley is surely wrong in saying she rejects Porgy "because she knows that immediate convenience and not love has prompted" his proposal (*Simms,* p. 102).

10. *Woodcraft,* p. 102.

11. *Ibid.,* p. 50.

True, Porgy needs his overseer's concentration on business; but equally important are Porgy's having the personality to attract the financial and legal aid of influential friends, especially in his fully successful struggle against his ruthless and criminal creditor M'Kewn.

An example of Porgy's ability to keep Millhouse in hand is his outwitting him by making a full and probably exaggerated confession of his early faults. By this sweeping admission, he forestalls the sergeant's intention to drag out of him, item by item, and painfully, acknowledgments of his various weaknesses in business.[12] Porgy lets Millhouse think he is more the boss than he really is.

Aided by Tom, Porgy leads Millhouse on to make a fool of himself by his belief in ghosts. When Millhouse, right at Mrs. Eveleigh's dinner table with Porgy, makes the egregious *faux pas* of openly urging her to marry the stout captain, she just laughs at him, but Porgy silences him with a military-style order.[13] Afterwards Lance severely reprimands him: "Even her son, Arthur, thought you was insulting his mother, and I had to tell him that you was a very foolish sort of person . . . talking about things you don't understand."[14] Next Porgy calls him down, declaring he thinks he can instruct everybody, even to teaching the angels how to fly, and that if he ever makes love for Porgy again, "by the lord that liveth, I will fling you from the windows."[15] And Mrs. Eveleigh never invites the sergeant again.

At Lance's wedding, Porgy overrules Millhouse when he tries to prevent the darkies from dancing into the night.[16] Millhouse loudly maintains that the useless Dennison and Oakenburg must not be invited as house guests. He even assures his crony Fordham, "I ain't gwine let the cappin waste himself . . . upon sich wagrants."[17] Porgy, nevertheless, declares he will invite them, and he does, and they come, and "much to the disquiet of Millhouse, become portions of the establishment"—for good, apparently.[18] Millhouse's biggest setback is the collapse of his pet project of marrying Porgy to the rich widow, his own conduct

---

12. *Ibid.*, p. 207. Taylor saw Porgy as "virtually the prisoner of his overseer" (p. 289). Ridgley, however, was probably nearer the truth in speaking of the "clash of personalities" of Porgy and Millhouse, and "the resultant benefits to both men" (p. 102).

13. *Woodcraft*, p. 359.

14. *Ibid.*, p. 363.

15. *Ibid.*, p. 366.

16. *Ibid.*, p. 397.

17. *Ibid.*, p. 287.

18. *Ibid.*, p. 508.

having alienated her son and helped to deter her. He cannot be muzzled, but he is more and more put in his place.

The account of Porgy's career thus takes him into peacetime and ends with him quite happy at home among adoring Negroes and congenial friends. The author, however, decided to turn back the clock, and in *The Forayers* (1855) and *Eutaw* (1856) to continue his portrayal of the Revolution from near the end of 1780, where he left it in *Katharine Walton,* to the last months of 1781, and so to show Porgy again as a soldier. The Porgy passages occupy a relatively small portion of these two novels, but greatly enrich our conception of his character.

In the earlier books, even in *Woodcraft,* Porgy had been caught sometimes in undignified postures, although never so as to be the object of the laughter. Now, however, in the final two books written, Simms seems to want to ennoble him further. Between *Katharine Walton* and *The Forayers,* the next novel in the sequence of the tale, he is promoted from lieutenant to captain, and especially in *The Forayers,* but also in *Woodcraft* and *Eutaw,* his high social status is stressed.

Although from the beginning it is clear Porgy is well-educated, in the final three books of the Saga, his intellectual attainments are revealed to be greater than had been supposed. In *Woodcraft,* his familiarity with literature and music is stressed, and he comes to be a leader in humanistic interests in the parish. His discourses are actually more learned in the two books yet to be written. Spiced with retorts courteous and with entertaining literate allusions, his conversation is at its finest in *The Forayers.* His hitherto undisclosed insight into military tactics is shown in *Eutaw.*

Throughout the Saga runs the theme of the importance in the war of the South Carolina partisans—a theme dramatically embodied in Porgy himself. As *Woodcraft* does not deal with the war, the theme is given its greatest emphasis in *The Forayers* and *Eutaw,* rising to a crescendo in the two last-composed works. In *The Forayers,* the theme is given in the gay variation of Porgy's ultimate triumph in hospitality; in *Eutaw,* in the serious variation of his acumen as military theorist. In each area Porgy emerges as the master—supreme both as host and critic of tactics.

By making his forest dinner party such a success, Porgy shows the ingenuity of the partisans and their social equality to the other branches of the army. Who else could provide such food, such wit, such warmth of welcome as does the Porgy of *The Forayers?*[19] By his analytical review of two battles, the Porgy of *Eutaw* shows how admirably the partisans had fought, and also shows his own gifts in military theory are superior to those of the high command.[20] Porgy emerges in these two novels both as the persuasive advocate of the partisans, and himself the image of what made their contribution so invaluable to the winning of American independence.

If the portrait of this southern gentleman had ever been even slightly tinged with touches of the ridiculous, it is no longer so in *The Forayers* and *Eutaw*. In the former, Porgy is at his most charming as well as masterful, and still the humorist; in the latter, he is at his most impressive. Visualizing him in this sterner if more imposing guise, Simms wrote his last pages about his Porgy.

19. *The Forayers*, pp. 539-53.
20. *Eutaw*, pp. 360-66, 526-35.

Porgy and Falstaff

Practically everyone who has written about Porgy has been reminded of Falstaff. Some have declared the similarities unimportant; while others have found them highly significant. Curiously enough, those critics who have admired Porgy most have usually been the ones who have found the Falstaffian echoes most vital. No one has accused Simms of any slavish imitation of Shakespeare's character. The matter is surely worth more consideration than merely saying that Porgy is like Falstaff in "certain ways"; or that the resemblances are "superficial." I propose, first, to show there is verbal and other evidence that Simms in creating Porgy did have Falstaff in mind; and then to examine carefully the ways in which the two figures and their situations are alike, and the ways they are unlike.

That Simms must have often recalled Falstaff is shown, in the first place, by a number of references he makes to the knight by name in his letters.

The earliest is probably the most significant. It comes in a long "Note" to an already long letter Simms writes on August 12, 1841, to Philip C. Pendleton, poet, and editor of *Magnolia,* a magazine issued first in Savannah and later in Charleston.[1] Pendleton had been severely censured by a correspondent signing himself "A Puritan" for the supposed immorality of "The Loves of the Driver," a story by Simms he had published in his magazine. This letter and its appended note constitute a truly eloquent statement of the case for honest realism in literature, and a rejoinder to the hypocritically prudish. Simms points out that "Your Homers, your Shakspeares, your Chaucers, your Beaumonts, your Fletchers, your Shirleys, your Massingers, your Scotts, your Byrons, —in short all the great portray man's deadly sins as foils to his 'living virtues.' "[2] Indeed he almost anticipates Henry James's argument in *The Art of Fiction* that to exclude from the province of the novel as immoral certain areas of life is simply to say that life itself is immoral.

Simms finally offers a rebuttal to the attack on his own story: "Any reader who is curious will find a very strong case of parallelism in the materials of the 'Loves of the Driver'—that very immoral story—and Shakspeare's 'Merry Wives of Windsor'—Falstaff pursues the same course with Mingo, and the same results happen precisely. The virtue of the woman goes thro' the furnace unsmerched [*sic*]. Falstaff gets pinched and tumbled into the Thames—'slighted into the river with as little remorse as they would have drowned a bitch's blind puppies, fifteen i' the litter,'[3] and Mingo gets the horse-whip and a broken head, not to speak of degradation from his high place of authority. The language quoted in inverted commas is Shakspeare's. Let your people of very nice moral nerves make the most of it. Had it been ours, Mr. Pendleton, we should have been in the stocks ere this."[4]

This passage reveals Simms had a special interest in Falstaff's adventures in *The Merry Wives;* and also suggests that some of the differences between Falstaff and Porgy may result from his unwillingness to fly too recklessly in the face of the Victorian tastes of his readers. Simms's vigorous defense of the coarseness in his tale by calling attention to the similar earthiness in the basket incident in Shakespeare's comedy supports the probability that it suggested to him that scene in *Woodcraft* in which Mrs. Eveleigh and her son ride up on horseback unexpectedly

1. *Letters*, I, 254-66.
2. *Ibid.*, p. 259.
3. *Merry Wives of Windsor*, III, v.
4. *Letters*, I, 264.

to visit Mrs. Griffin, only to discover on her front porch Porgy tangled with her in the yarn he is helping her to unreel.[5]

In a letter Simms writes on or about February 24, 1845, to congratulate young George Frederick Holmes on his marriage, he remarks, "You were, never, I believe, a positively wicked person. Evil lay in your way as rebellion in that of Falstaff, and you did nothing about it."[6]

Again Simms thinks of Sir John when, on January 7, 1846, he writes to upbraid his northern friend James Lawson for writing answers to his letters in his office, while the letters themselves were at his house: "The result is that you answer nothing, but go on prattling like Falstaff in the bedclothes."[7] Simms is here surely recalling the famous description of Falstaff's death. Naturally enough the dying man, rather than replying to the questions of his friends or heeding their admonitions, "babbled of green fields," called on God, and to use Simms's expression, went "on prattling."[8] That Falstaff's "prattling" included mutterings about wine and women, Simms ignores or forgets.

To Evert Duyckinck on September 11, 1850, Simms writes, "Lawson, like Falstaff grows fat, and forgets his friends."[9] In a letter to William Porcher Miles, probably in 1856, Simms says, "Approaching that physical condition when a citizen incurs the risk of being made an alderman, I—in Falstaff's mournful language—'lard the lean earth as I walk along.' "[10] Actually it is Prince Hal who says this about Falstaff, using the third person.[11] Although Simms here refers specifically only to his resembling Porgy in avoirdupois, there may well have been back of the comment a tendency to identify himself in other ways with the fat knight, whom he surely did resemble in robust conviviality.

In the Saga, Simms mentions Falstaff several times by name and verbally associates Porgy with Falstaff. There is a use of the knight's name in the paragraph giving Porgy's very first entrance, in *The Partisan*. Porgy was "not a mere eater. He amused himself with a hobby when he made food his topic, as Falstaff discourses of his own cowardice without feeling it."[12]

5. *Woodcraft*, p. 515.
6. *Letters*, II, 34.
7. *Ibid.*, p. 131.
8. *Henry V*, II, iii.
9. *Letters*, III, 62.
10. *Ibid.*, V, 328.
11. *I Henry IV*, II, ii.
12. *The Partisan*, p. 110. *I Henry IV*, IV, ii.

In the same book the partisan corps of the Swamp Fox come into the camp of General Greene, who had collected a small army of continentals or regulars. Lieutenant Porgy is among these partisans, who are subject to the "unmeasured jest and laughter of the continentals," because, though they are well-mounted, they are "in wretched attire." After various jibes from several of these continentals, one "more classical, borrowed a passage from Falstaff, and swore he should at once leave the army, as he wouldn't march into Coventry with such scarecrows; but a fourth said that was the very reason that he should stick to it, as Coventry was the only place for them." Porgy and his comrades are thus compared with Falstaff and his ragged recruits.[13]

Then Porgy himself has to endure a rude personal insult about his equipment from Colonel Armand, a foreign mercenary on the American side. Armand is emaciated, and Porgy, cooly tightening his ample belt, eyes him "with contempt," telling him he has the "body of a sapling" along with the "voice of a puncheon," and that he intends to feed him generously so as to increase his bulk, and to flog him, so as to "diminish his voice." Says Porgy, "Your jaws are thin, your complexion mealy, and your belly—what there is of it—is gaunt as a grey-hound's. I'll help to replenish it. Tom, bring out the hoecake and that shoulder-bone, boy."

This repartee may well have been suggested by the passage in which, after Prince Hal calls Falstaff "this bed-presser, this horse-back-breaker, this huge hill of flesh," he replies, " 'Sblood, you starveling, you elk-skin, you bull's pizzle, you stock-fish. . . . You Tailor's yard, you sheath, you bow-case. . . ."[14]

Falstaff is really just in fun, and actually is expressing teasingly his affection for the Prince, while Porgy is being satirically angry at the impudent foreigner. Earlier in *The Partisan,* Porgy had been, however, mainly joking in calling that attenuated eel-eater, Dr. Oakenburg, not to his face, "a crane-bodied cormorant."[15] Falstaff ridicules as underfed a man he really disdains, in declaring Justice Shallow could be thrust with room to spare into an eel-skin or treble hautboy.[16] The more bawdy metaphors in Shakespeare are symptoms of differences between Falstaff

13. *The Partisan,* pp. 439-41. *II Henry IV,* III, ii. In the *Cosmopolitan Art Journal* for December, 1860, Orville James Victor published an article "Falstaff Reviewing His Ragged Regiment." Simms was interested in this article, and promised to review it, although there is no evidence that he did so (*Letters,* IV, 286).

14. *I Henry IV,* II, iv.

15. *The Partisan,* p. 365.

16. *II Henry IV,* III, ii.

and Porgy which reflect the differences in the centuries wherein each flourished. Simms does contrive, however, to give considerable saltiness to Porgy's sharp thrusts of wit.

In *The Forayers* also, comment is made on Falstaff's mongrel recruits. The whig Willie Sinclair is explaining to his tory father that Lord Rawdon has taken into his service the very rascals, including Hell-Fire Dick, who are at that moment besieging the Sinclair Barony. The father, who greatly reveres the British, cannot believe that Lord Rawdon would "employ such scoundrels." Willie replies, "Nay, his lordship is not in a situation to scruple at any qualities in his levies. He is only too well pleased to fill the gaps in his regiment with any sort of cattle. His lordship thinks with Falstaff, that, if good for nothing else, they are at least excellent food for powder."[17]

In *Eutaw*, Porgy himself alludes to Falstaff. He is trying to explain to the tory Colonel Sinclair that it was easy for the Americans to capture the Irish recruits, not because they are cowards, but because they have "little love for British rule." He goes on: "Do you remember how the fat knight of Eastcheap conquered Sir Colville of the Dale? We felt on taking our raw Irishmen as Falstaff did in that conquest, and said to them—almost in his language—'Like kind fellows ye gave yourselves away, and I thank ye for yourselves.' We did not have to sweat for them any more than Sir John, for his prisoner."[18] Falstaff easily gets the lukewarm rebel Sir John Coleville to surrender to him; his exact words are ". . . thou, like a kind fellow, gavest thyself away gratis; and I thank thee for it."[19]

In *Border Beagles*, Tom Horsey, Shakespearean actor in Mississippi, refers four times to Falstaff, twice using the knight's last name.[20]

Before presenting the similarities between Porgy and Falstaff, I should say that I agree with Parrington[21] and Holman[22] that Simms has drawn not just on Falstaff but on Elizabethan drama in general in fashioning his characterization. Edward P. Van Diver thought that Simms took hints from Cooper's Captain Lawton in *The Spy*. As Van Diver said, both are southern gentlemen serving as officers in the American army;

17. *The Forayers*, p. 150.
18. *Eutaw*, p. 351.
19. *II Henry IV*, IV, iii.
20. *Border Beagles*, p. 43, inaccurate reference to Falstaff and Shallow; p. 55, to *II Henry IV*, iii; p. 60, to *I Henry IV*, iv; p. 98, to Falstaff's eating less than drinking.
21. Parrington, *Romantic Revolution*, p. 130.
22. Holman, "Simms and the British Dramatists," *PMLA*, p. 359.

both are large; both are gourmands; and each has a physician to tease. Van Diver said Lawton talked more about food than did Porgy, and in this was more like Cooper's Captain Polworth in *Lionel Lincoln*. Although there is no verbal evidence Simms had these characters in mind, and the only external evidence Van Diver offered was Simms's high opinion of *The Spy*, it is, of course, still possible that Simms took some hints from Cooper.[23]

Porgy is in many ways like Falstaff. First and most obvious is their corpulence. Falstaff's "stuffed cloak-bag of guts"[24] is matched by Porgy's "excessive development of the abdominal region."[25] Prince Hal asks Falstaff how long since he saw his knee.[26] Colonel Sinclair calls Porgy "a mountain on horseback."[27] Both manage, nevertheless, to be very active. As we have seen, both are much given to clever ribbing of skinny men.

Neither is regarded as any longer young. Falstaff is older, though in his self-portrait he is rather evasive, giving his age as "some fifty, or by'r lady, inclining to three score."[28] In *Woodcraft*, it is definitely stated that Porgy is forty-five, considered by the author to indicate he has passed middle age.

Both are military men, with the rank of captain, though Porgy, when we first meet him, is a lieutenant. Falstaff's being a knight is paralleled by Porgy's owning a large plantation. The possession of such a plantation does probably place Porgy higher in the American hierarchy than being "Sir John" places Falstaff in the English nobility; but there is Falstaff's intimate friendship with the Prince of Wales to give him a kind of special elevated standing. Though not so close to Major Willie Sinclair, of one of the very best Carolina families, as Falstaff is to Prince Hal, Porgy is still a good friend of the young major, who greatly admires him.[29] Porgy is on excellent terms with the impressive Governor of South Carolina, John Rutledge, and General Marion, and as host wins the hearty approbation of many officers, including General Greene.

23. Edward P. Van Diver, "Simms's Porgy and Cooper," *MLN*, LXX (April, 1955), 272-74. Ivor Winters had declared that Polworth "must beyond question be the prototype of William Gilmore Simms' Porgy." (*Maule's Curse*, Norfolk, Conn., 1936, p. 45.) Polworth is a Briton. Winters did not develop his case further.
24. *I Henry IV*, II, iv.
25. *Woodcraft*, p. 49.
26. *I Henry IV*, II, iv.
27. *Eutaw*, p. 247.
28. *I Henry IV*, II, iv.
29. *The Forayers*, p. 175 and *passim*.

Both are in the technical sense—which still had meaning in our old South—"gentlemen." All in all, there is a virtual equivalence in their social status, though toward the end of their stories, Falstaff goes down while Porgy goes up.

They are both denoted "gourmands." Porgy is described as a "sentimental gourmand."[30] In his rejection-of-Falstaff speech, the newly-crowned King Henry V urges the "surfeit-swelled" old man to "Leave gourmandizing."[31] Parrington said that it was true that in some ways Porgy was a "model of southern chivalry"; but that "in the far greater matters of the belly, he is strikingly Falstaffian. He is not so much a valiant trencherman, as artist in food and drink. He lived to eat and to speculate on the virtues of a good dinner. . . . 'He took philosophy with him to the table, and grew wise over his wine' (*Woodcraft*, Chapter XVIII). He is an epicure of words, a gourmand of wit."[32]

Although while Porgy offers a whole doctrine of the physical and mental benefits to be derived from good eating, and Falstaff says little or nothing in justification of his intense love of food, both do present philosophical defenses of strong drink. Falstaff ascribes the "sober-bloodedness" and lack of a sense of humor of Prince John of Lancaster to his refusal to drink wine. He says that these demure boys are cowards; and that sherris-sack produces both wit and courage; and that his brother Prince Hal has warmed his cold Lancastrian blood and become "hot and valiant" by "drinking good and good store of fertile sherris."[33]

Porgy likewise contends that strong drink stimulates courage; but, although he does love Madeira, he believes whiskey or Jamaica far better than wine in developing valor. Neither the Tuscan nor the "Falernian" wine of the Romans would "rank today with the juices of the common corn" prepared by the American process, if a battle needs to be fought. "Whiskey or Jamaica could have saved Rome from Gaul and Vandal. The barbarians, be sure, drank the most potent beverage."[34] Porgy's "feast for the captains" must be "spiritualized" not only by Dennison's poetry but also by correctly-made Jamaica punch. Only this poet can

30. *The Partisan*, p. 175 and elsewhere.
31. *II Henry IV*, V, v.
32. Parrington, *Romantic Revolution*, p. 131.
33. *II Henry IV*, IV, iii.
34. *The Forayers*, p. 537. Willie evidently misunderstands Porgy's opinion about the effect of whiskey (*The Forayers*, p. 177).

be trusted to compound the punch properly, by using the right proportions of lemons, sugar, and "spirit"—the rum.[35]

Both Porgy and Falstaff are jovial and companionable in the highest degree. Each has a gift for surrounding himself with a group of congenial male comrades, to enjoy life together, and, if necessary, to fight all enemies. Falstaff has Prince Hal, Bardolph, Pistol, Poins, and Peto; Porgy has Lance, Millhouse, Dennison, Dr. Oakenburg, and the Negroes Tom and Pomp. Falstaff's gang includes at times, as Porgy's does not, two women, Mistress Quickly and Doll Tearsheet. These are the inner circles; each has an outer circle also: Porgy, first, other and brave partisans, and later his other slaves; and Falstaff his wobbly recruits.

In each case the inner circle constitutes a sort of retinue or band of courtiers around a king of mirth; and each circle includes deeply devoted followers. Bardolph says to Justice Shallow, "My captain, sir, commends himself to you; my captain, Sir John Falstaff, a tall gentleman, by heaven, and a most gallant leader."[36] Actually Bardolph's lavish compliment is truer of Porgy, as we shall see, but does reveal his great faith in the fat knight. Parrington thought Porgy's poet Dennison much like Bardolph.[37] Sergeant Millhouse can be exhaustingly critical of Porgy, but would fight to the death for him, and really does admire him. Lance's worship of Porgy is the most perceptive as well as intense, among the whites;[38] and his adoration is perhaps exceeded by that of black Tom.[39] Millhouse's outspokenness to Porgy is somewhat paralleled by that of the Prince to Falstaff, though the Prince is more in jest. Porgy is more devoted to his followers, with the exception of the Prince, than is Falstaff; but Porgy is just as fond of Lance, who is an officer, as Falstaff is of Hal.[40]

And certainly it can be said for Porgy what Falstaff says for himself: "I am not only witty in myself, but the cause of wit in other men."[41] The less boastful Porgy would not have given tongue to such a claim, but he has the right to. His own wit scintillates in many of his discourses, and he causes wit in others again and again. He does arouse wit in Millhouse, even if it has a sort of cloddish quality, and the

35. *The Forayers*, p. 538.
36. *II Henry IV*, III, ii.
37. Parrington, *Romantic Revolution*, p. 132.
38. *Woodcraft*, p. 336 and *passim*.
39. *Ibid.*, p. 183 and *passim*.
40. *II Henry IV*, V, v.
41. *Ibid.*, I, ii.

sergeant often becomes the butt, but the repartee between him and Porgy can be most amusing. Porgy even strikes a few sparks from the sincere and serious young Lance. Porgy arouses the wit of Tom several times, notably in the hilarious scene in which the Negro cook quickly catches the cue and collaborates with Porgy to convince the superstitious Millhouse that no old Negress had been in the house last night to embrace him, and that he must therefore have seen a ghost. Porgy's childhood nurse had indeed come and in the darkness put her still strong arms around the burly sergeant imagining he was her beloved Porgy.[42]

There is some parallelism, perhaps intended, between the well-known rejection of Falstaff by the newly-crowned King Henry V and the rejection of the partisans, including Porgy, at the time of the reoccupation of Charleston by the American army. The reasons for the two rejections have something in common. The King feels he must turn away from his former self, the self of his dissipation and roistering with Falstaff. The partisans are rejected ostensibly for their disreputable appearance, they being "nigh to utter nakedness" in their rags; but actually because it was supposed that these irregular troops, after having their great contribution unrecognized and unrewarded, might at least seek "to do justice" for themselves.[43] Simms insists there was no possibility they would misbehave, as Marion had them, then as always, under perfect control. Still they were not allowed to appear at the ceremonies and to receive pay; nor have historians, Simms contends, given them their just deserts.[44] The outcomes are very unlike, as Falstaff dies of a broken heart, while Porgy sets out bravely to restore his plantation and to rebuild his life.

Porgy and Falstaff both are and remain bachelors, though for very different reasons. When Justice Shallow politely asks Bardolph how Sir John's "wife doth," he replies, "Sir, pardon, a soldier is better accommodated than with a wife," a comment which is almost a theme of *Woodcraft*. Porgy does indeed try to win a wife, while Falstaff wants only to cuckold the two husbands; but certainly he, no less than Porgy, can reconcile himself to the absence of a marriage bond for himself. Porgy is mainly sincere in his final words to his retainers, "I have determined to live a bachelor for your sakes."[45]

42. *Woodcraft*, p. 323.
43. *Ibid.*, pp. 46-48.
44. *II Henry IV*, III, ii.
45. *Woodcraft*, p. 513.

As everyone knows, *The Merry Wives of Windsor* was traditionally written for Queen Elizabeth, who wanted to see Falstaff in love. Was *Woodcraft* likewise a command performance for some reigning South Carolina belle who had a similar wish about Porgy? Whether or not thus motivated, Simms like Shakespeare obliged with a story of how his autumnal wooer also, vacillating between two mature but attractive women, loses both. There are various differences, and the love plot does not occupy the whole of *Woodcraft*. In the sequence of the events of both stories, the love games come after the military service of the portly captain is finished. Kittredge said, "the incidents in THE MERRY WIVES fit the biographical interval between his repudiation by the King at the end of 2 *Henry IV* and the onset of the 'burning quotidian tertian' that the hostess describes in *Henry V*,"[46] wherein Falstaff dies. Thus, just as *The Partisan, Mellichampe, Katharine Walton, The Forayers,* and *Eutaw,* giving Porgy's war years, are Simms's the two parts of *King Henry IV, Woodcraft* is in some ways Simms's *The Merry Wives of Windsor*.[47]

In view of the allusions to Falstaff in Simms's letters and of the actual couplings of the names of Porgy and Falstaff in the Saga—as well as some of the objective resemblances I have pointed out—it is somewhat difficult to know just what to make of Simms's condemnation of the attempt to create "a Falstaff" in a play which has been ascribed to Shakespeare. Simms edited a collection of Shakespeare Apocrypha, entitled *A Supplement to the Plays of Shakspeare,*[48] wherein in his introduction to *Sir John Oldcastle,* he said:

Sir John Wrotham, who is meant to be a Falstaff, with the additional virtue of courage, might have been successful, but that Falstaff stood in his way. Whether drawn by Shakspeare or another, the character of Sir John Wrotham fails only as it reminds us we have known Falstaff. It was this knowledge that paralyzed the effort to repaint the character under another name, and with additional attributes. "Our sweet John Falstaff," "kind John Falstaff," "true John Falstaff," "valiant and plump John Falstaff," is already sufficiently perfect; and an accumulation of more virtues in his character

46. George Lyman Kittredge (ed.), *The Complete Works of Shakespeare* (Boston, 1936), p. 63.
47. The Charleston *Mercury,* April 23, 1856, said: "His chain of historical novels which 'Eutaw' completes will be to after generations the history of South Carolina, in the same degree that the historical plays of Shakespeare are the history of England for the period they embrace." Quoted, *Letters,* III, 426.
48. New York, 1848, p. 89.

might only withdraw him in some degree from our sympathies. Sir John of Wrotham is a failure; but we can see what he might have been, but for the overwhelming excellence of his predecessor.

Holman, who is to be commended for discovering this passage, argued that "those qualities which seem most essential to Porgy appear not at all in Falstaff."[49] Setting aside the question of how "essential" to both characters is their love of good living and conviviality, it may be admitted there is some truth in Holman's statement. There does appear, however, to be some disjunction between Simms's theory and practice, as it simply cannot be denied that Porgy does at least "remind us"—and has reminded most critics—that "we have known Falstaff."

Simms wrote his censure of Sir John Wrotham in 1848, twelve years after he had published the only two novels he had so far written containing Porgy, *The Partisan* and *Mellichampe*. He said "more virtues" in the character "might"—not would inevitably—"withdraw him from our sympathies." I wish to suggest that Simms became very ambitious and resolved to succeed where the author of Sir John Oldcastle had not. He may have felt some qualms about the Porgy of *The Partisan*. The real enrichment of the portraiture began with the next book *Katharine Walton,* and goes on with mounting effectiveness in *Woodcraft* and *The Forayers,* revealing a determination to complete a characterization which "additional attributes"—even admirable ones—did not spoil. It is not so much to claim for Simms that he could succeed better than the obscure Elizabethan dramatist; in fact, probably considerably more than that can be claimed for his Porgy. At any rate, there are certainly many ways in which Porgy and Falstaff are not alike, as I shall now show.

The major difference between Porgy and Falstaff in their basic natures stems from their immensely different concepts of courage. Prince Hal's first speech introduces Falstaff and consists entirely of twitting him about his addiction to old sack.[50] Despite Falstaff's later stated theory that alcoholic drink produces courage, it certainly fails to do so in his case. At Shrewsbury, Falstaff is forced into combat with the Earl of Douglas and saves his own life by falling down as if dead. He continues to sham death even while Prince Hal speaks words of lament and discusses the disposal of the corpse.

Immediately after the Prince's exit, Falstaff rises up and justifies his

49. Holman, "Simms and the British Dramatists," *PMLA*, p. 347.
50. *I Henry IV*, I, ii.

conduct by his famous soliloquy in which he says, "The better part of valor is discretion; in which better part I have saved my life." He fears this "gunpowder Percy"—whom the Prince has just really killed may be counterfeiting too and may rise to injure him, and stabs him with the intention of claiming the honor of having dispatched this enemy leader.[51] Of course, nothing could be less probable than that Hotspur, whose valor is the antithesis of discretion, would resort to such behavior. Could anti-courage be carried farther than it is here by Sir John?

Major Willie Sinclair does tell his father Colonel Sinclair that "Porgy asserts no man is absolutely a coward or absolutely brave; that all depends on training; that we are all, more or less, the creatures of circumstance . . . that every man, even the most brave, has moments of fear." Simms has a footnote that this "was subsequently the opinion of Napoleon and Wellington." Porgy goes on with the peculiarly Porgian doctrine that the "stomach has more to do with it than the brain or heart." These ideas are the only aspect of Porgy the Colonel does not like, and he says he himself has never known the "sentiment of fear in his life." Willie cleverly reduces the Colonel's boast to absurdity by telling little Lottie, his sister, she is about to tread on her papa's foot. The old man screams at the child, even though she has never moved, and is laughed at for thus revealing he has boasted too much.[52]

Porgy, however, whether in battle or elsewhere, never acts with anything but the highest courage. Before he has met Porgy, Major Singleton says such a fleshy man would "never do for a dragoon." Dick Humphries defends Porgy ardently, saying "he rides like the devil, and fights like blazes . . . and is a mighty smart fellow."[53] Thus in this, our introduction to Porgy, is struck the keynote of his martial character.

Simms finally presents Porgy as a military theorist, something entirely beyond Falstaff's range. Porgy "was wont to say that half of the battles he had ever lost, were lost by a petty *finessing,* when plain honest, direct, up and down fighting, was all that was essential." Such tactics are clearly those requiring the maximum bravery.[54]

Several episodes exhibit him as an effective as well as a valiant combat soldier, although often with humorous overtones. Although on foot, he does not hesitate to fight the mounted Lieutenant Meadows. "Lieutenant

51. *Ibid.,* V, iv.
52. *The Forayers,* pp. 179-80.
53. *The Partisan,* p. 83.
54. *Eutaw,* p. 345.

Porgy . . . with an audacity quite inconsistent with his extreme obesity, advanced with sword uplifted to the encounter with the British lieu-tenant." Porgy downs his foe, and the amusing note comes in as he throws his "gigantic bulk" on the enemy, and stretches out on him to subdue him. He remains good natured until Meadows calls him an elephant, and thus causes him to pummel the Briton soundly; but he is mollified when Singleton comes and says Meadows is referring only to Porgy's "power" as "comparable" to that of the "mighty animal."[55]

In more romantic vein is the prime example of his chivalry, his rescue of a lady in great distress. When he learns that Mrs. Eveleigh has been ambushed and captured by a gang of bandits, he gives his men snappy orders for effecting her deliverance, and himself dashes forward on his horse "with a spirit and celerity that seemed scarcely consistent with his great bulk." Throughout this mission Porgy exhibits the great-est bravery, as well as skill in "woodcraft," the art of woodland scout-ing and fighting. Once he becomes the "chief pursuer" of one of the outlaws, who knows Porgy's "fierce headlong valor, the power of his arm, the fleetness of his steed."[56]

Porgy gives his soldier's creed: "Danger is part of the contract! It is to be counted on, but not considered. He who stops to consider the danger never goes into battle! No wise man, embarking in such an amusement as war, ever considers its mischances as likely to occur in his own case. He knows the fatal sisters have singled out certain favor-ites for Valhalla, but he always takes for granted that they have over-looked *himself!* He relies, always, on his peculiar personal star, and goes into battle—not to be killed, but to kill!"

Indeed Captain Porgy frequently behaves like the "Berserkers." He dashes "with a sort of frenzy, into the worst of dangers, totally heedless of them all, as if bearing a charmed life—and only seeking to destroy." Simms argues that such a "practice . . . is very apt to carry with it its own securities. A rage that blinds the champion to all dangers, and makes him totally unconscious of all fears, is very apt to inspire fear in the enemy. . . . The onset of Porgy was well calculated to inspire such feelings."[57]

Could Porgy's conduct and beliefs mean Simms was recalling another

55. *Katharine Walton*, pp. 181-82.
56. *Woodcraft*, p. 128.
57. *Ibid.*, p. 127. To his son, a cadet at the Citadel, Simms writes in 1861, "The less you fear for yourself, the more your security." *Letters*, IV, p. 379.

character in the first part of *King Henry IV,* one of the most famed for headlong valor in the annals of England, "Harry Percy, surnamed Hotspur"? South Carolina was often called the "Hotspur State."[58] Simms's—and Porgy's—theory that courage can actually be a sort of protection in battle seems almost an echo of words of Hotspur's, when he is commenting on a letter he had received from a defecting and cowardly ally: "Let me see more. 'The purpose you undertake is dangerous,'—why that's certain; but I tell you, my lord fool, out of this nettle, danger, we pluck this flower safety."[59]

Lady Percy enters, to complain that her husband has been fighting "iron wars" in his slumbers, has "spoken terms of manage" to his steed, has cried " 'Courage! to the field.' "[60] Porgy is too sound a sleeper to have such dreams, but the Lady's report depicts a Hotspur who resembles him in battle ardor.

Porgy as an equestrian combatant is much like Hotspur as he envisions himself in exclaiming:

> Come, let me taste my horse,
> Who is to bear me like a thunderbolt
> Against the bosom of the Prince of Wales:
> It is of course true that the mammoth American cannot, like Hotspur,
> Rise from the ground like feather'd Mercury,[61]

into his saddle; but when Porgy is at last there, it is no exaggeration to say of him, as Vernon says of Hotspur, that he does "witch the world with noble horsemanship." Porgy's superb riding is often referred to in the Saga, besides in the passages just quoted about it. Fortunately for him, this huge man, who is understandably not very agile on foot, is an accomplished horseman and is in the cavalry in a phase of a war which was fought chiefly on horseback—the Revolution in the Carolinas. Hotspur is more impetuous in formulating battle plans, than is the more prudent Porgy, but once the bugles have sounded, their actions are surprisingly similar.

Curiously enough, Hotspur also has a physical handicap, though of a very different kind. In praising her husband after his death, Lady Percy says it is "speaking thick, which nature made his blemish," but

58. Trent, *Simms,* p. 29.
59. *I Henry IV,* I, iii.
60. *Ibid.,* II, iii.
61. *Ibid.,* IV, i.

that he was so much the model for "all the chivalry of England" that they even imitated his very speech defect.[62] No one seems to want to acquire an abdomen like the dashing Porgy's; but Porgy does indeed want to fatten the skinny, and there is the amusing implication that those who continue to enjoy Porgy's cuisine may put on flesh.

That the more high-keyed heir to the Earldom of Northumberland does have a sense of humor is shown in the two scenes in which he affectionately teases his wife.[63] Hotspur's brand of humor is not very Porgian, it is true; one cannot imagine the courtly American southron speaking so sharply to any lady whatever. In the first scene, however, Hotspur is making his wife obey him; and Porgy does believe a wife should have "a due and reverent sense of her husband's authority."[64] Although Porgy never tells Mrs. Eveleigh this in so many words, she shrewdly senses his opinion; and gives as her chief reason for refusing his marriage proposal that she has "been too long" her "own mistress to submit to authority."[65]

Simms may have been thinking a little of Prince Hal too, who is much more a joker than the basically serious Hotspur. He, unlike Hotspur, has been exposed often to Falstaff's wit-producing powers; and his jests have something of the quality of Sir John's own. After the Prince reforms, he becomes a noble leader, and as such probably was something of a pattern for Simms's patrician officers. Ridgley pointed out that Major Singleton's going around his camp with words of personal encouragement to his men echoes Henry V's similar action before Agincourt.[66]

Falstaff is the anti-hero or un-hero; while Porgy is just as much of a hero as Shakespeare's two young Harrys and as Simms's two young majors, Singleton and Sinclair. Of these two leading gallants in Simms's Saga, Sinclair does have some of the comic spirit, as shown especially in his great sympathy with Porgy. Even if not everyone finds as many resemblances between Porgy and Hotspur as I do, surely Simms used the master dramatist as a guide in his endeavor to blend the principle of heroism and the principle of humor. The two English Harrys and the two Carolina majors are after all primarily heroic; the most jovial

62. *II Henry IV*, II, iii.
63. *I Henry IV*, II, iii; III, ii.
64. *Katharine Walton*, p. 368.
65. *Woodcraft*, p. 513.
66. Ridgley, *Simms*, p. 64. *The Partisan*, pp. 355-56. *Henry V*, IV, i.

of the four renounces the spirit of comedy when he is crowned.[67] Simms boldly sought to fashion a character in which there would be a perfect equipoise between derring-do and laughter, and so wrought his Captain Porgy.

In contrast to Falstaff's, Porgy's humor is without bawdiness. Yet it has at times a down to earth quality, reflecting army and camp life, and a plantation household without white women. Simms did feel restrained by reader prudery; though even in actuality the eighteenth-century southern gentleman's talk probably lacked renaissance freedoms.

Critics have pointed out that while Falstaff is a rogue, Porgy is not, a valid distinction if by roguery is meant actual thievery or dishonesty.[68] It is inconceivable to imagine the honorable Carolinian and patriot stooping to the tactics of Falstaff, who fills his purse by letting the able-bodied recruits buy themselves off, while he retains the weaklings for the king's service. Yet there is in Porgy a penchant for comic deviltry which he thoroughly enjoys as long as it can be exercised to defend himself against an opponent who is passing as respectable but is really a criminal.

The prime illustrations are the three frustrated attempts of the sheriff or his deputy to serve the foreclosure papers. M'Kewn does have a mortgage on Glen-Eberley, and in a narrow technical legal sense has a right to foreclose. But he has no real ethical right to do so. If Porgy had been paid for his seven years in the army, he might have been able to pay his mortgage. M'Kewn rejects Mrs. Eveleigh's plea that he be lenient with such a worthy patriot.[69] He is morally and even legally worse by far than Porgy, as he had become rich by treasonous trafficking with the British during the war, and had even tried to steal Porgy's slaves.

Thus, as he is really in the right, he can be free to get all the fun he can out of defying the sheriff and agents, and can indulge his love of practical jokes and clever "kidding." On the sheriff's first visit, Porgy soon realizes that Colonel Blank is the sheriff and enjoys the antics of his retainers, especially Millhouse, who do not know this. Thus he plays the colonel and the sergeant off against each other. By a combination of threats and hospitable offering of good food and drink, and con-

67. *II Henry IV*, V, v.

68. Hampton M. Jarrell, "Falstaff and Simms' Porgy," *American Literature*, III (May, 1931), 204-12.

69. *Woodcraft*, p. 389.

viviality, Porgy subdues the gentlemanly sheriff, so that he leaves without having served the papers. Porgy can laugh at the discomfiture of the blustery Millhouse, when he tells him, after the colonel's departure, that he really was the sheriff. "The joke is a good one on which I can feed fat with laughter for a month,"[70] says Porgy. Porgy is a "rogue" playfully, not actually unethically. As he says, he has not acted illegally because the sheriff had not declared himself as such.[71]

Another salient difference between the roles of the two humorous captains is emphasized especially in the foreclosure attempts—Falstaff is typically the butt of the jests, particularly in *The Merry Wives,* while Porgy is typically not. It is the sheriff, and later the deputy, who are the butts, and here, and elsewhere, the bumptious Millhouse.

Prince Hal's brother, his father, and himself as Henry V, and Hotspur, all regard Falstaff as a bad influence. Falstaff's speech accusing the Prince of having made him "one of the wicked" is purest irony.[72] Porgy's influence is clearly good. His efforts to impart a little humanistic culture to Millhouse make only a slight impression; but the sergeant does work hard for him. Porgy gives a deserving poet and scientist a home, inspires his cook, and guides in virtue and wisdom his disciple Lance.

The contrast between the attitudes toward women is obviously great. One cannot imagine Porgy after another man's wife! Falstaff, however, has no qualms about extracting money from Mistress Quickly.[73] Doll Tearsheet is "blubbered" as she bids him farewell on his leaving for war, but she can playfully revile him.[74] As for Porgy, it is never disclosed whether his prewar "profligacy" involved women; he is obviously too busy during the war to think of them. He does borrow money from a woman, but as a business deal, and it is repaid.[75] He hesitates between the two widows, but does not, like Falstaff, try to woo them both on the very same day. He waits to propose to the rich one until he is financial-ly solvent.[76] She would probably not have had him in any case; but the fact that he loses the other mainly because he procrastinates until another man had been accepted seems an echo of Shakespeare's comedy.

70. *Ibid.*, pp. 449, 451.
71. *Ibid.*, p. 440.
72. *I Henry IV,* I, ii.
73. *Ibid.*, III, iii.
74. *II Henry IV,* II, iv.
75. *Woodcraft*, p. 347.
76. *Ibid.*, p. 510.

Porgy undergoes, as of course Falstaff does not, a virtual reformation. The war gives Porgy's life meaning; he becomes a dedicated fighter for independence. He likes army life, and is proud of his ability to help with the food problem. True, he does not get as high a rank as he thinks he deserves. But who ever does? Actually his army career is quite successful—in terms of honor, though not in terms of pay. He is so much the military man that it is hard for him to get going after the war; but he pulls himself together and finally becomes more successful than he had been before the war.

Porgy's attitudes toward women and toward his job as planter embody aspects of the Southern Legend as Simms interprets it, with his special emphasis on the southern patrician's sense of obligation to preserve and improve the way of life of his region. The southern gentleman as Simms sees him has not only Hotspur gallantry but also the capacity for assuming responsibility in civilian life. Naturally it is the Hotspur qualities of the young aristocrats that are stressed, although it is implied they will carry on with probity after the war; but it is only Porgy who is actually exhibited doing so.

Thus I have finally come to the ways in which Porgy is least like Falstaff; yet the similarities are sufficient to have provided for Simms an inspirational basis and given to the personality a relaxed quality he would not otherwise have had. At least some of the differences seem to involve an almost deliberate variation from Falstaff; and there has been an intentional fusion of the qualities of the South Carolina patrician with those of Sir John. Also in the Saga, and in Porgy himself there are echoes of other characters in those of Shakespeare's plays which introduce Falstaff.

Porgy and *Uncle Tom's Cabin*

Woodcraft is Simms's major reply to *Uncle Tom's Cabin*. His ardent advocacy of the southern way of life strongly motivated him to outdo himself and produce as effective as possible a novel of rejoinder to Mrs. Stowe. This drive may well have been the chief reason the usually hasty Simms proceeded with more control and made *Woodcraft* his most unified novel; and is one of the reasons Porgy especially in this book and later in *The Forayers* is so superior to his other characterizations, as the personality and conduct of Porgy are the very essence of his answer.

Simms's admiration for the achievement of another leading southern novelist perhaps gave him the idea of writing a novel of his own to refute northern attacks on slavery. On May 12, 1851, less than a month before the first chapter of Mrs. Stowe's novel appeared, he wrote to John Pendleton Kennedy, "I am glad to hear that we are to have a new edition of Swallow Barn [1832]. Its genial & natural pictures of Virginia life, are equally true of Southern life generally among the old & wealthy families, and are in fact the most conclusive answer to the abolitionists (if they would be answered) that could be made. But they are not a people to need or tolerate an answer. They will not listen any more than Pilate to the truths, which they profess to solicit."[1] This comment reveals Simms as ripe for action, with the plantation life of his own state as illustration, just before *Uncle Tom's Cabin* hit the nation like a bomb. The central figure of Kennedy's novel, genial and articulate Frank Meriwether, who is on such good terms with his slaves, keeps them happy, and strongly disapproves of the breaking up of Negro families by the selling of slaves,[2] very likely suggested to Simms the plan of using his already-created Porgy as a representative southerner, who is equally harmonious with his Negroes and refuses to sell any of them.

There is direct, incontrovertible, if brief, external evidence that Simms did intend *Woodcraft,* which he had finished in little over a year after writing this letter to Kennedy, to be a reply to Mrs. Stowe's book. To his friend Hammond, then former Governor, Simms wrote on December 15, 1852, that "My last Book, 'The Sword & Distaff' [the first title of *Woodcraft*] had not been named by a single Carolina Press, though it is probably as good an answer to Mrs. Stowe as had been published."[3] Simms, always pessimistic about the reception of his books in the South, had overlooked a notice of his book in October in the Charleston *Courier,* which was favorable if it did not recognize he was thinking of Mrs. Stowe.[4] On May 1, 1853, Hammond wrote to Simms referring to minor blemishes in his novel, but recognizing his polemic thesis and for the

1. *Letters,* III, 122.
2. *Swallow Barn,* Chapter 46.
3. *Letters,* III, 222.
4. *Ibid.,* p. 213n.

most part commending his accomplishment: "Still on the whole I think it fully equal to any of your novels, & that you have admirably defended our 'Institution' & elevated it in some respect."[5]

The dates of the serial publications of the two books are also indicative of Simms's intention. *Uncle Tom's Cabin* was published serially in the Washington, D.C. *National Era* from June 5, 1851 to April 1, 1852, and in book form on March 20, 1852.[6] Simms actually began to write, or at least to publish, his book before all of Mrs. Stowe's had appeared. He had the forthcoming publication of *The Sword and Distaff* announced in the December 20, 1851, issue of the Charleston *Southern Literary Gazette,* and his book came out in semi-monthly supplements to this journal during the earlier months of 1852.[7] As will be demonstrated shortly, he had finished reading her novel by July 1, 1852. He had completed writing the last installment of his own by August 18, 1852, according to a letter on that date to Hammond.[8] His book was published in book form in September, 1852.[9]

There is one verbal item in *Woodcraft* which surely ranks as objective evidence Simms had Mrs. Stowe's title character in mind. The first night a meal is served in Porgy's still unfurnished mansion after his return, Tom the cook is ordering Pomp, fiddler and cook's helper, to spread a tablecloth. The bewildered Pomp replies: "I no see clot' uncle Tom." Tom tells him to use a blanket. Pomp possesses himself of one but "still stands vacantly looking around."

"Well," quoth our major domo, "Wha' you 'tan' [stand] for sucking in de whole room wid your eyes?"

"I no see any table, uncle Tom!"

"Don't you uncle me, you chucklehead! Lay de table on de floor. Who could b'lieb dat a pusson could lib so long and grow so big, and nebber l'arn nutting."[10]

During the very weeks he was writing the last part of *Woodcraft,* Simms was also engaged in attacking *Uncle Tom's Cabin* through direct argumentation, as well as through the medium of fiction. In "The Morals of Slavery," having a preface dated July, 1852, Simms belligerent-

5. Quoted in *ibid.,* p. 243.
6. Joseph Sabin (ed.), *A Dictionary of Books Relating to America* (New York, 1933-34), XXIV, 45.
7. *Letters,* III, 185.
8. *Ibid.,* p. 193.
9. *Ibid.,* p. 213.
10. *Woodcraft,* p. 179.

ly advances such standard southern doctrine as that the slaveholders had the "moral and physical guardianship of an ignorant and irresponsible people" and hence are "great moral conservators." He then turns to *Uncle Tom's Cabin* and puts his finger on what is surely its greatest weakness as argument against the southern mores, its author's placing Simon Legree in such an isolated location. "She shows that *he resides in a remote and scarcely inaccessible* [accessible surely is intended] *swamp region, where his conduct comes under no human cognizance. How is society answerable for his offenses?*" [The italics are Simms's own.] How can he be considered a representative slaveholder? Then she makes this "brutal specimen" a Yankee. We have a right to "refer his responsibilities back to his native parish."[11] Simms's allusion to Tom's final owner, Legree, shows he had finished reading Mrs. Stowe's book by this July.

In 1853, Mrs. Stowe brought out her *A Key to Uncle Tom's Cabin,* in which she aims to show that, though the book is fiction, it is based on "facts and documents" and first hand observation. She had actually done little research, according to Joseph C. Furnass, who said "the text exploits her one foray across the Ohio as few trips so short have ever been worked."[12] Simms wrote a long and acrimonious review of *A Key,* in which he first attacks the novel itself, and then the *Key.*[13] A complete summary of his attack is hardly needed here, but a few of his points may be given. He begins by accusing her of "charging on an institution, what are the defects and virtues of humanity at large." He declares she has been uncritically biased in selecting the cases on which she bases her defamatory generalizations. She has not chosen typical or representative planters and wives at all, but has amassed atypical and

11. "The Morals of Slavery," in *The Pro-Slavery Argument* (Charleston, 1852), p. 274. This essay had first appeared in the *Southern Literary Messenger,* III (November, 1837), 641-57, as a critical review of Harriet Martineau's book *Society in America* (1837). The essay was reprinted as a pamphlet in *Slavery in America* (Richmond, 1838), and in a form revised so as to include discussion of *Uncle Tom's Cabin* in *The Pro-Slavery Argument.* Joseph V. Ridgley, "*Woodcraft:* Simms' First Answer to *Uncle Tom's Cabin,*" *American Literature,* XXXI (January, 1960), 422.

12. *Goodbye to Uncle Tom* (New York, 1956), pp. 26-27.

13. *Southern Quarterly Review,* XXIV (July, 1853), 227-54. S. P. C. Duvall proved that this unsigned review was by Simms, but unfortunately regarded it and not *Woodcraft* itself as Simms's first and main retort to Mrs. Stowe. "W. G. Simms's Review of Mrs. Stowe," *American Literature,* XXX (March, 1958), 107-17. Simms's review of *A Key* will be cited hereafter as the "*Key* Review."

horrible exceptional cases so as to make them seem typical. Herein she is guilty of a fallacy, and her logic is false.[14]

Nor is her book defensible as a work of art, which a romance must be, according to Simms. He condemns her for violating the very nature of the "romance," to which "class of writings Mrs. Stowe's story belongs." "The attempt to establish a moral argument through the medium of fictitious narrative is, *per se,* a vicious use of art and argument."[15] Simms may here seem to be disqualifying his own *Woodcraft* as art, since it does attempt to answer the moral attack in her book.

Charles D. Froome argued well that Simms is really not guilty of such inconsistency:

> Moreover, although *Woodcraft* contains what may be broadly termed "a moral argument," the quality of the novel is evidence that art was Simms' central consideration. Mrs. Stowe attacked slavery through the story of Uncle Tom, numerous "pictures" external to her plot, authorial comments inserted into the text, and didactic sermonizing. Simms replied to *Uncle Tom* only on the first level, the narrative itself; he was concerned to present rather than to argue, to tell an illustrative story . . . not to interpolate passages of noncontextual rhetoric. . . . The general reply of Simms is implied, not asserted, through *Woodcraft's* specific characters and actions. The overtones of the novel, only, suggest that Simms knew, in coupling fiction and a moral rebuttal, "art is paramount."[16]

Simms's method, indeed, contrasts with that of Kennedy in *Swallow Barn,* wherein the narrator, a fictitious visitor from Maryland, who had come to the plantation prejudiced against slavery, finds the Negroes so happy he condemns emancipation; and proprietor Meriwether, although admitting slavery is theoretically wrong, argues it is benign as practiced in tidewater Virginia.[17] Simms, however, eschewing virtually any direct words of defense of slavery from the author or from Porgy or any other character, conveys his assumption the "peculiar institution" is admirable merely through a softly glowing evocation of its functioning under the tolerant Porgy.

How different is the tone of *Woodcraft* from the spirit of bellicose

---

14. *"Key* Review," 214-15.

15. *Ibid.,* pp. 216-17.

16. "William Gilmore Simms' Reply to *Uncle Tom's Cabin*" (Master's Thesis, University of Wyoming, 1962), p. 102.

17. *Swallow Barn,* Chapter 46.

controversy of Simms's various direct defenses of slavery, including the "*Key* Review," wherein he maintains that family ties are really less binding among Negroes; that cases of painful family separations are uncommon anyway and by no means avoided among the oppressed if free people of areas where there is no slavery; and that the South has done much to improve the lot of the Negro.[18]

Since Simms, particularly in the "*Key* Review," reveals a determination to offer direct polemic rebuttal to her book, it is not surprising that, because he was a fiction writer, he had already chosen to answer her by an entirely different method, the positive one of presenting his idea of the undistorted picture of southern plantation life. So he had written *Woodcraft* as the antithesis of *Uncle Tom's Cabin.*

Ridgley has given the best summation of Simms's conception of the South. Simms, he said, saw the life of the South as a unique and ordered society with integrated class responsibilities. There was a hierarchy, with aristocrats, lower class whites, and the Negro slaves. Ridgley quoted from Simms's "The Morals of Slavery": "He is a freeman, whatever his condition, who fills his proper place. He is a slave only, who is forced into a position in society below the claims of his intellect."[19] The master must, however, assume his responsibilities, and guide and care for the slaves. The South had its faults, but was on the way to perfecting its social order if only let alone. Porgy illustrates this process.

In *Woodcraft,* after getting Porgy home, Simms settles down to the main subject of the book, stated by Ridgley as "the restoration of the plantation way of life."[20] Porgy had neglected his plantation before the war which completed its ruin. He courageously sets out to do the job. True, he must have help—the help of friends, of Mrs. Eveleigh, to donate supplies, and to lend him money on a mortgage. He must have the help of an astute lawyer, Pinckney. He must have the help of his workers, black and white. Millhouse, his overseer, and also Mrs. Eveleigh volunteer their aid. Yet it is Porgy who has the personality and status as a gentleman to attract and warrant all this assistance. This is right, as in such a society all can and must work together, to rebuild, and to foil the criminal poor whites M'Kewn and Bostwick, who aid by destroying each other, and by both making deathbed confessions of their nefarious deeds.

18. "*Key* Review," 247.
19. *Simms,* pp. 22-23.
20. *Ibid.,* p. 100.

In contrast with the remoteness of Legree's plantation from any center of culture, Porgy's is on the Ashepoo River only some thirty miles from Charleston. Legree is a lone wolf; Porgy functions as an integral part of the society of his comparatively very civilized parish.

A typical southern gentleman, Porgy has limitations as a business man; and he realizes he must employ the efficient if sometimes irritating Millhouse. The crops become good, and Porgy is at last able to liquidate his debts. Thus finally Glen-Eberley presents to the world "the condition of a well-managed household in which the parties were all at peace with themselves and one another."[21] As an ultimately successful planter, he is a contrast to Mrs. Stowe's Augustine St. Clare, who had been so inept on the plantation that his brother, to get him out of the way, let him live a luxurious life in the family town house, where he does evince some of the personal attractiveness of the southerner.[22]

Porgy, however, besides being a pretty good administrator in knowing how to delegate tasks to those best suited to perform them, embodies also far more adequately than St. Clare, the charm of southern culture. He is highly charitable, collaborating with Mrs. Eveleigh in caring for the family of the poor white squatter Bostwick, who had, among other villainies, tried to kidnap the lady and steal the slaves of both. With his many interests, riding, hunting, gastronomy, literature, music, and conversation as an art, he is the southern patrician at his best. And so "Glen-Eberley became a sort of center for the parish civilization."[23]

Did Simms make Porgy an unmarried man so as to present a picture of a pleasant bachelor establishment as a contrast to the repulsive bachelor ménage of Legree? Legree gets little satisfaction out of his affairs with his slave girls. He fears Cassie because she supposedly dabbles in black magic, and sends her to work in the fields for later defying him.[24] She is to be succeeded by Emmeline, who is bought at the same sale as Tom, and is pretty but unwilling.

Simms might perhaps be accused of evasiveness in *Woodcraft* about the darkest shadow over slavery, the sexual relations between white master and slave girl. That he was well-enough aware of such situations, and severely disapproved of them is shown when he condemns "the

21. *Woodcraft*, p. 508.
22. *Uncle Tom's Cabin*, p. 286.
23. *Woodcraft*, p. 508.
24. *Uncle Tom's Cabin*, p. 452.

illicit and foul conduct of many among us who make their slaves their victims, and the instruments of the most licentious passions" in his review of Harriet Martineau's unflattering *Society in America* (1837).[25] Gaines pointed out that not only did interracial immorality exist on a large scale, but was not ignored in the Legend.[26] It is scarcely necessary to remind the reader of how extensively the dramatic possibilities of this have been exploited by many southern writers, notably Cable and Faulkner.

Since *Woodcraft*, however, was a reply to *Uncle Tom's Cabin*, Simms may have felt he was relieved of the necessity of dealing with a subject distasteful to him by the fact that Mrs. Stowe does not therein actually depict cases of southerners seducing Negresses but only shows the Yankee Legree thus occupied. In view of Simms's expressed strong censure of miscegenation, and of the absence of any reference in his voluminous letters to it as occurring in his own immediate circle, it seems only fair to conclude that it was not therein common or condoned. Here was another reason he could feel he was not compelled to bring it into *Woodcraft* or the rest of the Saga, wherein nearly all the masters and slaves who appear have backgrounds similar to his own.

There are a few amusing episodes in *Uncle Tom's Cabin*, but the predominant tone is one of piety or righteous indignation. Humor, however, serves to establish the main mood of *Woodcraft*. On his way home, Porgy is so depressed by the thought that his occupation as a soldier is gone, and that he will come home to a despoiled plantation, under mortgage to the ruthless M'Kewn that he even suggests that Lance might as well cut his jugular. But when he and his men stop for refreshments, his state of mind quickly lightens in due proportion to Tom's progress in making dinner preparations. After eating, Porgy is in a much better frame of mind, and Lance teases him as to the reason for the change. Porgy admits it: "Dinner, you dog, I suppose—dinner and drink . . . Well—I grant you . . . My soul was at the mercy of my stomach. But the wolf pacified, my mind acquired freedom. . . . Philosophy, my boy, appears once more to comfort me. . . ."[27]

Again humor brightens Porgy's threadbare poverty, yet with the effect of making one laugh with and not at Porgy, as members of his

25. *Southern Literary Messenger*, III (November, 1837).
26. Gaines, *Southern Plantation*, pp. 221-23, 234-36.
27. *Woodcraft*, pp. 108-9.

household busy themselves to find in his ragged wardrobe something to cover his nakedness as he goes to call on Mrs. Eveleigh. Tom has to warn him to move very carefully in the ancient garments "or de breeches will be busting out."[28] Porgy does then visit the rich widow, but will not propose until he has acquired some fine new clothes. Humor alleviates the desperate situations of the attempted foreclosures on Glen-Eberley. Humor is not only used in showing Porgy's gallantry in enduring his temporary poverty, but it sets the tone even for the reply to Mrs. Stowe about race relations. The topic, viewed so grimly for the most part by Mrs. Stowe, and by the majority of northerners then and now also, is handled in *Woodcraft* in a vein of diverting comedy.

The good feeling between Porgy and his Negroes is frequently exemplified in the book, and usually with most amusing touches. There is his joyfully tearful welcome home by the Negroes who have hidden so long in the swamp. There is his solicitude for their being given at once warm clothes. There is the fondling of Porgy by his old nurse Sappho, and the comic note comes in as the skinny old woman calls the huge fat man "my chile."[29] And herein, as throughout Simms, the aristocrats habitually avoid the use of the word "nigger," the use of which word by a Caucasian virtually brands him as a "buckrah"—lowest of poor whites.

The main illustration of race relations in *Woodcraft,* as in the rest of the Saga, is the extended study of the friendship and mutual dependence of Porgy and Tom. Between them is a jocular democratic give and take, with good-natured ribbing on both sides. In addition to the theme of their partnership in the gentle art of cookery, which I stress elsewhere, there is also the theme of their mutual proprietorship. After Porgy finally has a clear title to Tom, and can afford it, he offers Tom his freedom. The cook concludes his emotional speech of absolute refusal thus: "You b'longs to *me,* Tom, jes as much as me Tom b'longs to you; and you nebber guine get you free paper from me long as you lib."[30]

Although Ridgley established basically the case that *Woodcraft* is Simms's reply to *Uncle Tom's Cabin,* he said nothing about the problem of miscegenation, and he left other ground untouched. It remained for

28. *Ibid.,* p. 332.
29. *Ibid.,* p. 310.
30. *Ibid.,* p. 509.

Froome, starting from a suggestion of my own, to develop what we thought the "most important and telling factor in the reply—Simms' handling of the entire matter of the sale of slaves. . . . Hammered home time after time in *Uncle Tom's Cabin,* this is Mrs. Stowe's most vehement indictment of the South's 'peculiar institution.' " The main purpose of Froome's study was to "investigate Simms' answer in *Woodcraft* and *The Forayers* to Mrs. Stowe's sale argument and attack" in her immensely influential novel.[31]

Mrs. Stowe admits there are planters who are well-disposed toward their slaves and portrays two of them, Shelby and St. Clare. Neither of them, however, protects his slaves from the possible dire consequences of their being sold. Her attack is, nevertheless, not on southerners but on the "peculiar institution" itself. The very concept that human beings can be chattels is in itself bad enough, but it has the truly terrible consequence that these chattels can be sold for money. The very focus of her assault is thus on the sales. In the slave market auctions, repulsive enough in themselves, there is nothing to prevent a slave who may have had the kindest of masters from being purchased by a human fiend. William R. Taylor said, "Harriet Stowe's sharpest barbs are not finally aimed at either Northerners or Southerners as such, but at the ruthless masculine world of business enterprise. . . . In *Uncle Tom's Cabin . . .* commerce in slaves is represented as the ultimate in human exploitation. For in the slave trade as in no other, all human values are converted into pecuniary dollars and cents."[32]

Uncle Tom is sold twice, once by Shelby and once by Mrs. St. Clare after her husband's death. He does not fare too badly after the first sale, because he is bought by the benevolent if ineffectual St. Clare. The second time, however, his new owner is the inhuman Simon Legree.

Shelby, threatened with financial difficulties, decides to sell Tom and George Harris; he can get good money for both; because Tom is strong and hard-working, and notably pious and hence especially well-behaved; and because George, a mulatto, is young and strikingly handsome. Shelby swears grandiloquently to Tom: "I tell you solemnly, and before God, that I will keep trace of you, and bring you back as soon as I can command the money." A few months later, his determination has greatly weakened. Mrs. Shelby tells her husband she has a letter from Tom

31. Froome, "Simms' Reply to *Uncle Tom's Cabin,*" p. 17.
32. *Cavalier and Yankee,* p. 309.

asking when the redemption money is to be raised, and that he has not at all, as Shelby wants to believe, "become reconciled to a southern residence." Shelby replies, "I's sure *I* don't know. Once get business running wrong, there does seem to be no end of it. It's like jumping from one bog to another."[33]

St. Clare had intended to free Tom, but is killed in a duel before he actually does so. Before the sale of the estate Negroes takes place, Miss Ophelia—the New England cousin—reminds the widow of her husband's promise to Tom and expresses hopes she will carry out the necessary legal action for his freedom. Mrs. St. Clare replies sharply: "Indeed I shall do no such thing! . . . Tom is one of the most valuable servants on the place,—it couldn't be afforded, any way." So Tom goes up for auction![34]

Simms evidently senses the power in Mrs. Stowe's depiction of the possible horrible results of the sales of slaves and in her contention that there are many weak or callously indifferent slaveholders who can be induced to sell—all illustrated in the case of Uncle Tom. He, therefore, counters with his portrayal of the admirable conduct of Porgy and his friend, the kind and also competent Mrs. Eveleigh. Porgy, who says he has only eleven guineas in cash, is under far greater financial pressure than are Mrs. Stowe's Shelby or Mrs. St. Clare. M'Kewn has a mortgage on Porgy's plantation for a much larger amount than the place will sell for; but although M'Kewn has no lien on Porgy's Negroes, they would become liable for the rest of the debt to M'Kewn if the latter obtains judgment.

Mrs. Eveleigh proposes that he give her a mortgage on his Negroes so as to secure them from M'Kewn. If she forecloses *her* mortgage, Porgy's Negroes will thus pass into the hands of a trusted friend, who will be very good to them, and as she is a neighbor, will not be taking them far from their old home. She, however, gives Porgy her word of honor she will not foreclose, and Porgy, of course, believes her. He will thus actually be keeping his Negroes on his own plantation. It is she who raises the question of what her son might do in case of her death. Porgy is willing to trust the son; but she insists on setting up "legal security" which will protect Porgy even from her son.[35]

33. *Uncle Tom's Cabin*, p. 281.
34. *Ibid.*, p. 363.
35. *Woodcraft*, pp. 349-50.

Porgy cannot bear to have even this sort of friendly mortgage placed on his beloved Tom, and he does not include him in this mortgage. A little later, when it appears that the threatened foreclosure will engulf Tom, Porgy with great difficulty persuades Tom to let him sell him to Mrs. Eveleigh, with the understanding that Porgy can hire him for fair wages, and that she will ultimately sell him back for the same amount—one hundred guineas—she is paying for him.[36] Only to keep Tom out of the clutches of the ruthless M'Kewn will Porgy agree to this "sale," which is virtually no sale, but a gentleman's agreement between a southern gentleman and lady. Porgy's "sales" are not really sales, but ingenious legal maneuvers arranged between upper caste people of honor to keep the Negroes from being sold at all.

Thus the true and typical southern patricians, as Simms sees them, will, when one of them has a tough financial problem, find a way to collaborate to prevent the selling of slaves to anyone whatever, and especially to such a man as M'Kewn. M'Kewn is not actually shown mistreating slaves, but he is detested as a poor white by Tom, is utterly unscrupulous, and is not to be trusted. At best there could never be between Tom and him the perfect understanding that exists between Porgy the aristocrat and the Negroes who have always lived on his plantation, even if M'Kewn were a good man, as he is not. The thought of Tom's passing into the hands of M'Kewn is anathema to both Porgy and Tom, and to the patrician lady of the adjacent plantation.

How different is Mrs. Eveleigh from the affable Mrs. Shelby, who weakly and ineffectively opposes the sale of Uncle Tom; and from the heartless and self-centered Mrs. St. Clare, who is only too glad to get the money from selling him again! Mrs. Eveleigh is an important part of Simms's reply.

Unlike the self-excusing Shelby, Porgy carries out his promise and does buy his Tom back.[37] He finally has all of his slaves with him for good, as he pays off the mortgage on the rest of them to Mrs. Eveleigh. He could not have borne to part with any of them, nor do any of them wish to leave. Thus Simms completes his engaging picture of Porgy with his Negroes at Glen-Eberley, and offers to the pious New England woman the "soft answer that turneth away wrath." It was with real

36. *Ibid.*, p. 407.
37. *Ibid.*, p. 509.

justification that he said, in 1852, that *Woodcraft* was "probably as good an answer to Mrs. Stowe as has been published."

Yet the ultimate in the soft and sophisticated answer was still to come from our South Carolinian. Having in *Woodcraft* disposed of Mrs. Stowe's disconcerting charges, especially about the selling of slaves, Simms could in *The Forayers* three years later "relax and give his Porgy and Tom over completely to considerations of fun and food," as Froome put it. He is therein continuing to reply to her only in presenting the epitome of harmony between a white and a black. Froome said, "Simms' consummate dramatic skill in this book is his portrayal of Porgy and Tom, not so much as master and slave, but as fellow artists working together in close cooperation to create a masterpiece—Captain Porgy's dinner party. . . . Porgy's resourcefulness here is in direct contrast to the incompetence of Mrs. Stowe's Shelby and St. Clare."[38]

Porgy, along with Tom, more than fulfills the expectations of Governor Rutledge, who, in taking the liberty of inviting General Greene of Rhode Island and Colonel Lee of Virginia, says to Porgy that "your provision will not only be ample, but . . . the taste which usually presides over your banquets will give to our friends from Rhode Island and Virginia such a notion of the tastes of Apicius and Lucullus, as certainly never yet dawned upon them in their own half-civilized regions."[39]

Porgy has been the cause of wit in the rather stately governor! At a time when Simms himself had been actively crusading for secession,[40] which was widely approved in his state, he is content in *The Forayers,* to have Porgy as representative of that state praised for pre-eminence over other states in hospitality and gastronomy. Herein are various suave and indirect implications, such as that there is one state where the rapport between master and Negro is better than elsewhere; or a reminder that even Mrs. Stowe puts her pusillanimous Shelby in Kentucky, her callous Mrs. St. Clare in New Orleans, her sadistic Yankee Legree in the undeveloped Red River Valley in Louisiana, while Porgy, warm-hearted and captivating, is to be found in Simms's native South Carolina.

38. Froome, "Simms' Reply to *Uncle Tom's Cabin*," 110.
39. *The Forayers,* p. 535.
40. *Letters,* III, pp. 108, 121, 123, 133.

Porgy as Self-Portrait

The final and most important reason for the superiority of Porgy to Simms's other characterizations is that he is in many ways a self-portrait. A month after Simms's death, the poet Paul Hayne, who had known him intimately, wrote "Simms's genius *never had fair play!* Circumstances hampered him! Thus, the *man* was greater than his works,"[1] an opinion Trent[2] and others have subscribed to. If Simms was able to project in a special way his own self into this one figure, it might help to account for its looming so far above the multitude of his other figures. Van Wyck Brooks said, "A berserker in battle, a wit and buffoon, a bon vivant and gourmet, a philosophic humorist and great reader, this living relic as it were of the days of Queen Elizabeth reflected Simms' own overflowing nature."[3] Parrington declared, "Simms delighted in Porgy because he was himself something of a Porgy."[4]

Unfortunately Trent provided no footnote for this assertion: "Simms said that Porgy was a transcript from real life, and I have it on good authority that he intended Porgy to be a reproduction of himself in certain moods."[5] Trent's biography appeared only twenty-one years after Simms's death, and he was able to draw on conversations, and letters, of people who had known Simms in the flesh.

Before I present the many similarities between Simms and Porgy, I may note a few obvious differences. First is the variance in marital status. Porgy is a bachelor and will probably remain one.[6] Simms, however, was married twice, both times very happily. He was deeply grieved at the death of each wife; two of his letters revealed the shattering intensity of his sorrow when he lost Chevillette, his second.[7]

Second, Simms never served as a soldier, as Porgy does through the whole Revolution. Third, Porgy is not a writer, although his sometimes elaborate disquisition suggests he is a sort of potential author. Fourth, Porgy at last makes a financial success of his plantation, while Simms,

1. Quoted in Trent, *Simms*, p. 322.
2. *Ibid.*, p. 332.
3. *Washington Irving*, p. 132.
4. *Romantic Revolution*, p. 132.
5. Trent, *Simms*, p. 109.
6. *Woodcraft*, p. 518.
7. *Letters*, IV, 437-38.

as the years passed, seemed to be making less and less; for, in 1856, he wrote, "The plantation for 20 years has barely paid expenses."[8]

Among the numerous similarities between Simms and his Porgy are physical resemblances. Both were big, imposing, robust, attractive, energetic. According to Trent, Simms was described as being at the age of twenty-eight "a strikingly handsome and powerful man. . . . He was not far from six feet in height, and 'erect as a poplar,' with fine head set upon broad shoulders. Later in life he inclined to corpulency, but now his figure suggested strength and activity rather than heaviness. His brow was superb." His eyes were bluish-gray. "As he wore no beard in those days, the resoluteness and dogged determination of his heavy jaws and chin must have told upon the crowd."[9] Paul Hayne, when Simms was forty-one, saw him as "a man in the prime of life, tall, vigorous, and symmetrically formed," having a noble head with "conspicuously high forehead, finely developed in the regions of ideality, and set upon broad shoulders in haughty, leonine grace." He had a "massive jaw and chin which might have been moulded out of iron."[10]

Simms was thirty-one when in *The Partisan* he first imaged Porgy; and hence his ballooning his own then trim-waisted largeness into his character's enormous abdominal protuberance is to bring in the comic note, suggested by Falstaff, and involves some departure from literal self-portraiture. He may have been foreseeing that when he was past forty, as is Porgy, he might put on weight, although Hayne reported he had not at forty-one. He was forty-nine when he wrote *Eutaw*, containing his last depiction of Porgy, who is then forty-four.

Porgy, though huge in girth, is considered handsome. "Porgy was a good-looking fellow, spite of his mammoth dimensions. He had a fine, fresh, manly face, clear complexion and light blue eyes."[11] So we see him for the first time in *The Partisan*. He is a year older when he appears in *The Forayers* thus: "He was a fine-looking fellow, in spite of the too great obtrusion upon the sight of his abdominal territory. . . . His face was almost as the moon at full, of a ruddy brown, his head massive, chin large and prominent, eyes bright but small, and mouth eager with animation. His nose was decidedly intellectual."[12] Observe

8. *Ibid.*, III, 453.
9. Trent, *Simms*, p. 64.
10. *Letters*, I, lxxxix.
11. *The Partisan*, p. 111.
12. *The Forayers*, p. 507.

that both Simms and Porgy have salient chins. Even old Colonel Sinclair has to admit about Porgy: "His face is positively handsome."[13] Porgy's vigor and mobility on horseback are often noticed as remarkable for so heavy a man. He is not, however, to judge from their respective countenances, quite as forceful a personality as Simms.

Naturally enough both these large men enjoyed good eating. Trent told that the food served at Woodlands, Simms's beautiful plantation, excelled in both quantity and quality, and came mostly from the neighboring river, the Edisto.[14] In *The Forayers,* the author celebrates the catfish from this river: "You have never eaten the blue cat of the Edisto, gentle reader—or have you?—in either case you have something to live for. It must be eaten with butter only, so flavorful it is; but the red-belly perch of that river is properly eaten with sauces, as it requires strong condiments."[15] Simms can certainly sound like Porgy! In *Southward Ho!* Simms talks glowingly of the merits of the meat cooking at the St. Charles in New Orleans, the Pulaski in Savannah, and the Charleston Hotel, in contrast with the crude methods by which meat is practically ruined in frontier inns.[16]

According to Trent, "Simms prided himself on his gastronomic attainments, and in the person of Lieutenant Porgy once allowed himself to grow eloquent over the delicacy of a stew made of alligator terrapins." Some members of the "club" of young admirers of Simms decided to make a test. They procured one of the terrapin, made it into a stew, invited Simms to dinner, and served him a big helping. "At the very first mouthful he made a wry face, and exclaimed: 'For heaven's sake, boys, where did you get this rancid stuff?' 'That is alligator terrapin, stewed à la Porgy, Mr. Simms,' was the reply. All Simms could do was to declare there was some mistake in the recipe."[17]

Things turn out much better in the fiction. Trent is inaccurate, as it is not mere terrapin stew Porgy serves, but terrapin soup, and as *pièce de résistance,* a terrapin pie. They are eaten with relish by all present, except the undernourished Dr. Oakenburg, whose food preferences are deplorable.[18] This is in *The Partisan,* where the highest-rank-

13. *Eutaw,* p. 353.
14. Trent, *Simms,* p. 98.
15. *The Forayers,* p. 276.
16. *Southward Ho!* p. 401.
17. Trent, *Simms,* p. 237.
18. *The Partisan,* p. 361.

ing guest is only a major, and the number of other officer guests is small. Trent overlooked Porgy's masterwork, the feast in *The Forayers*. There two generals, many other officers, and the governor give Porgy, now a captain, immense satisfaction by preferring his *lagarta,* made of juvenile alligators, and his *alerta,* made of frogs, to the captured British hams and tongues which had been destined for the table of Lord Raw-don. Governor Rutledge himself pays the gourmet host the supreme compliment of asking for the recipes.[19]

Porgy enjoys himself tremendously functioning as epicurean host: by thus helping to keep up the morale of the officers; by preaching the importance of proper food in making an army successful; by working to procure it; and by illustrating what can be done with abundant but overlooked native materials, he makes a real contribution to winning the war. Gastronomy is more of a central interest and occupation for Porgy than for Simms; but it was an essential enough concern to the author to provide the basis for the fanciful and delightful elaboration of it in the characterization.

Connoisseurs of food are typically genial, and Simms and Porgy are no exceptions. Porgy is denoted a "jovial philosopher."[20] His convivial-ity has been illustrated in bringing out his resemblances to Falstaff. Paul Hayne told how Simms, with a bowl of punch before him, "shone in his lighter moods. Of wit, that bright, keen, rapier-like faculty, which frequently wounds while it flashes, he possessed, in my opinion, but little; but his humor—bold, bluff, and masculine—with a touch of satiri-cal innuendo and sly sarcasm, was genuine and irrepressible. . . . I can hear his voice rolling in jovial thunder above a murmurous sea of con-versation."[21] Benjamin Franklin Perry wrote of Simms: "He is a most genial and boon companion . . . is fine looking, and possesses fine manners."[22] Porgy too could show some inclination to dominate discus-sions, though when he is talking with gentlemen or ladies, he shows courtly restraint, but can "burst into an uncontrollable fit of laughter."[23] Porgy's jests are perhaps more often in the category of humor than of wit.

Simms believed that the English were not a humorous people, as

19. *The Forayers*, p. 548.
20. *The Partisan*, p. 110.
21. Quoted by Salley, *Letters,* I, lxxix.
22. Quoted in *ibid.,* I, cxxix.
23. *Woodcraft*, p. 427.

their essential genius was for tragedy. Even Shakespeare, Scott, and Dickens employed humor mainly as a foil. (Porgy is not intended to be, and surely is not, a foil.) With the English as their literary ancestors, the Americans started off at a disadvantage in their approach to humor. Paulding, Kennedy, and also Irving, like Addison, produced not humor but "pleasantries."[24] The only true humor Simms could find in our country was the rapidly-developing frontier humor, and the best work in this genre, he believed, was in Longstreet's *Georgia Scenes,* containing the finest specimens of a "rare, racy, articulate native humor."[25] This was original; whereas that from the seaboard cities was not. Simms was implying, without actually using the word, that Longstreet was folkish and hence good.

Since Simms had such admiration for *Georgia Scenes* (1835), it is not surprising to find places where he resembles Longstreet. Van Wyck Brooks said, referring especially to *Guy Rivers,* with its Georgia setting, "Sometimes Simms' racy scenes were quite in Longstreet's manner."[26] Davidson said that "'folkishness' is an all-pervasive quality in Simms' best fiction." Simms was at his best, Davidson was sure, with Porgy.[27] In a vein particularly recalling Longstreet are the rebuffs Porgy and his loyal henchmen give the three attempts of the sheriff or his agent to serve the foreclosure papers on Porgy's plantation. The vigorous defenders resort to unhorsings, fisticuffs, outwittings, and an ingenious gamut of slapstick tactics, many very funny.

Having much of the Longstreet flavor especially is the foiling of the second attempt, this time made by the really less formidable, though very self-important little deputy, Crooks. Porgy himself sets Millhouse to shaving off the deputy's treasured coppery-red beard, despite the small man's violent protests. After Crooks has violated southern hospitality unforgivably by refusing Porgy's excellent food and drink, Porgy has Millhouse carry out the appropriate punishment of forcing Crooks to eat the papers.[28] The pranks played on the deputy seem actually cleverer, yet not cut of entirely different cloth from "The Turnout," that "Georgia Scene" in which the boys barricade the schoolhouse against

24. Simms, *Views and Reviews,* II (1846), ed. Hugh C. Holman (Cambridge, Mass., 1962), p. 174.

25. *Letters,* I, xlix, li.

26. *Washington Irving,* p. 309.

27. *Letters,* I, lxxiii.

28. *Woodcraft,* p. 439.

the late-arriving master. After he breaks his way in with a log, they all jump on him at once, to compel him to declare a holiday, which he is actually quite willing to do after doing his duty of making a show of resistance.

The painter and piscatorial author Charles Lanman was a guest at Woodlands, in April, 1848. In a roseate description of Woodlands and the life there, he wrote of Simms: "Among his more intimate friends he is also particularly celebrated for his story-telling powers, and it does seem to me that he related more amusing stories within the past two days, than I ever before heard in my life."[29] Davidson is right in regarding Simms's "How Sharp Snaffles Got His Capital and His Wife" as probably the very best of all American tall tales.[30]

Flush Times in Alabama (1853) is admittedly superior to *Border Beagles* (1840), but Simms's book, thirteen years earlier than Baldwin's, does in its opening pages picture with some satiric effectiveness the "Flush Times" in Mississippi. For example, there is the bright young lawyer Harry Vernon's clever defense of Shippen, who had beaten up Watson. Vernon argues that Watson's meek failure to fight back, as it was accompanied by his constantly calling the attention of the bystanders to each blow, was a result of a deliberate intention to try to extract a money payment for each stroke when the assault case comes to court. The risibilities of the frontier jury are thus tickled, and Vernon gets his client off with a nominal payment despite the rather serious injuries he had inflicted on Watson.[31] The antics of Porgy's followers in resisting the foreclosures, as well as Porgy's own wise cracks in conducting the trial of the outlaw Norris,[32] are products of one who had no need to borrow from the "Southern Humorists," as he was born one himself.

Simms can give Porgy scenes a tone of robust and masculine humor, as when, rejecting false dignity, the mammoth lieutenant crawls in the dark to capture the terrapin for tomorrow's dinner.[33] Hearty farce appears in incidents involving the big man's trousers. Once he sits down in the woods and relaxes by loosening his belt. An unexpected bullet shot by the villain in ambush causes him to rise too hastily, and his

29. *Letters*, II, 405n.
30. *Ibid.*, I, lii.
31. *Border Beagles*, pp. 75-80.
32. *Woodcraft*, pp. 153-58.
33. *The Partisan*, p. 321.

pants fall before he can buckle his belt.[34] In similar vein is the amusing scene in which Porgy and his "family" have problems deciding which of his only two pairs of pantaloons, both in sad shape after his years of army life without pay, is less impossible for his going to call on the rich widow.[35] Here are hilarious descents to the ridiculous, and perhaps a kind of depiction of "low life," though not exactly what is usually meant by that term.

"Low life" as usually understood is often enough found in the Saga, in such chapters as that in which criminal poor whites are pitted against each other as Bostwick profanely extracts guinea after guinea from M'Kewn in return for promising to give him the papers which would "hang him," if disclosed.[36] Salley told how Simms "was noted for holding a company entranced by graphic description of low life." Simms can indeed picture "low life" in his fiction; yet there is no reason to believe he himself preferred it. Nor is it correct to say that Porgy prefers "low life."[37] Tom regards Millhouse as a "buckrah," and in the old South no one would speak with more authority about social levels than a house Negro. But Porgy's relationship with Millhouse is basically a business one of master and overseer; and he by no means prefers him to sensitive and refined Lieutenant Frampton and the poet Dennison, who are in no sense "low." Simms and Porgy alike could appreciate life, whether low or high.

Like Porgy, Simms was a member of the South Carolina aristocracy. Davidson has recently pointed out that Trent was wrong in considering Simms not of the South Carolina upper social stratum. Davidson said, "Simms was a native Charlestonian of highly acceptable origin and connections. That being so, his degree of poverty or wealth cut no figure. He belonged."[38]

Conclusive support for Davidson was provided by Salley and by the Simms letters. Simms's mother was a Singleton, and thus of a "well-known Charleston family." Her father had been an active and effective patriot, even lending money to the state Revolutionary government.[39] Simms's ancestral pride is shown dramatically by his giving the name

34. *Woodcraft*, p. 169.
35. *Ibid.*, Chapter XLVI.
36. *Ibid.*, p. 257.
37. As does Holman, "Simms and the British Dramatists," *PMLA*, p. 349.
38. *Letters*, I, xxxv.
39. *Ibid.*, p. lix.

Robert Singleton to the gallant hero of *The Partisan* and *Katharine Walton,* obviously very much the aristocrat.

A cousin of Anna Malcolm Giles, who became Simms's first wife, was the wife of James Louis Petigru, attorney general of South Carolina.[40] He was called "the ablest lawyer of his state" by Trent, who was evidently unaware that in "Simms' early career he and Petigru were rather closely associated," and that there was between them even this family tie.[41]

Any lingering doubts as to Simms's place in the best South Carolina society were dispelled by his second marriage, in 1836, four years after his beloved Anna died of tuberculosis. One of the young Simms's closest friends was Charles Rivers Carroll, who had great wealth and became a writer on the drama as well as a distinguished lawyer. Simms studied law in Carroll's office. The Simms and Carroll town houses were both on the "Neck" in Charleston.[42] The families attended the same church. To Carroll, Simms dedicated *Guy Rivers* (1834), his first important novel.[43]

After the death of his first wife, Simms and his little daughter were long-staying guests at one of the Carroll plantations, Clear Pond, from which he successfully courted a girl on a nearby plantation. She was Chevillette Roach, daughter of Carroll's first cousin, Nash Roach, who possessed a town house and two plantations, Oak Grove and Woodlands, encompassing nearly seven thousand acres. In all the Roach "establishments Simms felt equally at home," said Salley, who emphasized the mutual affection and understanding between Simms and his father-in-law.[44]

Even Trent admitted Simms met a warm reception from the first families of Barnwell County, where the Carroll and Roach plantations were located.[45] Fifty miles away was Silver Bluff, the plantation of James H. Hammond, soon to be governor, and then United States Senator. Few of Simms's friends received more frequent or more re-

40. *Ibid.,* p. cxxx. Anna's great-grandmother had been, before her great-grandfather married her, a widow, Lady Colleton.
41. Trent, *Simms,* p. 26.
42. *Letters,* I, cxxx.
43. *Ibid.,* p. xcvii.
44. *Ibid.,* p. lxxvii.
45. Trent, *Simms,* pp. 145-55.

vealing letters than did Hammond, whom he later called "my most confidential friend for nearly twenty-five years."[46]

George Herbert Sass, Charleston lawyer and poet and contemporary of Simms said: "The best people of Charleston that were worth knowing had Mr. Simms at their houses, and he certainly was as 'good' as the 'best' of them."[47]

One of the "distinguished Charlestonians" named by Trent as among those who "did not know" Simms was Joel Roberts Poinsett.[48] To him, however, Simms, in 1840, wrote regretfully declining, because of "a previous pressing engagement," an invitation which had been conveyed to him "under the envelope" of Poinsett, then Secretary of War. The invitation was to dinner—with President Van Buren![49] Certainly Simms had an entree into the highest circles. Many examples of his association with the "best" people can be found in his letters, even if he had no further chance to dine at the White House.

It is important to establish clearly Simms's patrician status, because it must be realized that, whatever may be the literary limitations of his portrayals of southern aristocrats, he is writing about his own class, and not giving an outside view as Trent maintained.[50] Simms saw the South in terms of his concept of "degree," insisting there was an "aristocracy" as distinguished from the middle and lower classes.[51] His work cannot be judged fairly unless he is placed correctly in the social scale.

His Porgy is likewise a patrician. Lieutenant Dick Humphries, in introducing him says, "He's been a rich planter in his time."[52] Glen-Eberley had once been, and again became, splendid. Simms says that his Charleston inheritance, chiefly from his mother, was quite ample but had been mismanaged by his grandmother.[53] Here is partial parallelism with the situation of Porgy, who in youth had got into money troubles, but by his own mismanagement mainly, though he places some blame on his father for not better teaching him how to work.[54] "Captain Porgy is a gentleman by birth and education," declares the rich and

46. *Letters,* II, opposite 258.
47. Quoted by Salley, *Letters,* I, lxxxiv.
48. Trent, *Simms,* pp. 20, 27.
49. *Letters,* II, 177.
50. Trent, *Simms,* p. 128 and *passim.*
51. Ridgley, *Simms,* p. 98.
52. *The Partisan,* p. 98.
53. *Letters,* I, lxi.
54. *Woodcraft,* p. 206.

highborn Mrs. Eveleigh.[55] Like Simms he moves with ease among scions of the leading families of South Carolina, is on the best of terms with the governor, certain other high officials, and, in Captain Porgy's case, generals. Major Willie Sinclair, of a "First Family" of South Carolina is an admiring friend of Porgy,[56] who is invited to visit at the Sinclair Barony by the Major's sister Carrie, seconded by her father, the colonel.[57]

So much in accord with the Southern Legend is the harmony between Porgy and his Negroes at Glen-Eberley that it may seem difficult to demonstrate that it reflects specifically the similar situation at Woodlands. Yet many instances of the affection between Porgy and his darkies do suggest he may be painting from the life on his own plantation, where the Southern Legend was not far from the reality. Two of the most glowing accounts of happy conditions at Woodlands are by northern partakers of Simms's Carolina hospitality. William Cullen Bryant enjoyed hearing the Negroes sing "with great glee" and seeing them dance with amazing energy at a husking bee.[58] The painter Charles Lanman delighted in making word pictures of the forest, birds, flowers, fruits, and mansion as a background for the "polite and happy slaves" and "white and black children frolicking under the trees," and for the "esteemed" Mr. Simms of Woodlands.[59]

Simms's own references to his Negroes in his letters tend to be those of a man to whom all this is somewhat a matter of course. Yet he could glow with satisfaction in telling of the mountains of luscious food he can still provide for them even in 1861, and exclaimed, "My negroes are all fat, and satisfied with the prospect before them. Briefly I have calculated the calibre of each portly paunch, and fancy that they will say at every sunset *quant. suff.*"[60] He told of sending an injured Negro to the city for the best surgery available. True, he could complain that the Negroes were irresponsible. But he could be deeply touched, as when telling Hammond that during the first burning of Woodlands the Negroes "worked admirably . . . with the most eager zeal & perfect devotion. That fact, my dear H., is to me full of consolation."[61]

At the wedding of Lance Frampton in *Woodcraft*, the Negroes in a

55. *Ibid.*, p. 389.
56. *The Forayers*, pp. 539-54.
57. *Eutaw*, p. 352.
58. *Letters*, I, 350n.
59. *Ibid.*, II, 405n.
60. *Ibid.*, IV, 326
61. *Ibid.*, p. 404.

hypnotized ecstacy dance the Juba and double shuffle to the tuneful fiddle of Pomp. When Millhouse tries to stop it as a waste of time, Tom denounces him as a "poor buckrah" who can't comprehend Negro nature, and tells him that when the Negro "dance he sweat all he badness." Millhouse is overruled by Porgy, and the whites dance on the piazza and the blacks under the trees until the midnight supper. This is not at Glen-Eberley, but at the home of Lance's bride; but Porgy is present, benign in a big chair, radiating approval.[62] It is a scene that might well have taken place at Woodlands, where Simms might have had a strict overseer who understood the Negroes less than the patrician owner.

The closeness of the ties between master and Negroes is shown in the warm reception they give Porgy after his seven years away at war. His old nurse Sappho almost overwhelms him as she embraces him with cries of joy. He is delighted to see her, but immediately expresses concern because her clothes are too thin to keep her warm. She soon brings with her seventeen others of his Negroes she has hidden these years in a swamp, and the air is filled with such exclamations as "De Lord be praised, maussa, you come home at last."[63]

A sense of security in the continuity of the associations of the same black and white families through many decades is felt at both Glen-Eberley and Woodlands. After describing the welcome given Porgy by the Negroes, Simms says, "But we need not multiply phrases . . . he who knows what a Carolina plantation is—one of the old school—one of an ancient settlement—where [Negro] father and son, for successive generations, have grown up, indissolubly mingled with the proprietor and his children for a hundred years, may . . . repaint the picture for himself."[64]

Woodland's best days were over, after two burnings and the end of the War Between the States. Simms's letters during his five postwar years told of the familiar woes of Reconstruction, especially the refusal of the freedmen to be hired for pay.[65] At last, adjustments were made, and his granddaughter Mrs. Oliphant could testify, even in 1962, that the continuity of association of the families of the two races was preserved. "Living at Woodlands today," she said, were the descendants

62. *Woodcraft*, pp. 396-97.
63. *Woodcraft*, pp. 309-15.
64. *Ibid.*, p. 325.
65. *Letters*, V, 528.

of the Negro families of her grandfather's times; for "Woodlands is their home, and they are a part of the very fibre of the place."[66]

In the novel, the terrible internecine war is long in the future. As for Porgy, "The piquancy of his society, was everywhere acknowledged," and he delights his guests with jests, and brilliantly delivered anecdote and philosophy.[67] Even as Simms was closing his novel by writing of these "happy times," certainly, despite the deaths of some of his children, there were days when Woodlands was for him, during the writing of the Saga, as satisfying as Glen-Eberley is for Porgy.

Simms believed he could help the cause of the South not only as politician but also as military theorist. Many of his letters present military proposals, some seeming very practical. As early as April 17, 1851, he was writing Nathaniel Beverley Tucker to lament that some southerners "build on the assumption that we are to be suffered quietly to leave the Confederacy [meaning the Union]. This is mere imbecility." He foresaw a blockade of Charleston harbor if South Carolina seceded, and outlined to Tucker plans for defeating and sinking "some of the blockade squadron." He complained that "we are making no plans for this that I can see—squabbling among ourselves & making bad blood by an insane desire to build a magazine for gun fire . . . in the very heart of Charleston."[68]

A decade passed, during which he published *Eutaw* (1856), but the defenses of Charleston remained in his opinion inadequate. His letters of early 1861 were full not only of recommendations about setting up a new nation but also about military preparations. On April 2, 1861, he informed his influential friend William Porcher Miles that he had been writing "almost nightly" to General Jamison, Secretary of War for South Carolina, to urge him to strengthen the land and marine batteries near the city. He made the surely sensible proposal that shore fortifications be faced with railroad irons. It seems that the ironclad battery of Cummins Point on Morris Island had actually been built according to his specifications, though he had not been given full credit, chiefly, he thought, because he was a civilian.[69] He may or may not have had much effect on actual constructions, but he did produce a great amount of propaganda, including, in 1861, many editorials in the Charleston *Mer-*

66. *Ibid.*, I, cli.
67. *Woodcraft*, p. 508.
68. *Letters*, III, 108.
69. *Ibid.*, IV, 354-55.

cury,[70] to arouse interest in better protection of the seaport. In his letters he made many other suggestions concerning the art of war.

Out of such thinking on his part must have come the impulse to give Porgy a new role in *Eutaw*, his main role in that book, that of brilliant military theorist whose advice is disregarded. Porgy is given space for extended analytical critiques of two battles after they have resulted in rather fumbled victories, the minor Skrimmage at Quinby,[71] and the crucial Battle of Eutaw.[72]

Simms precedes Porgy's disclosure of the American faults in the conduct of the Skrimmage at Quinby by a whole chapter in which he had shown complete and detailed agreement with what Porgy is to say. Whether such a procedure makes the book better as a work of fiction or not, it does make very clear that Simms and Porgy think alike about military tactics. Simms does not offer such complete support for Porgy's devastating revelation of the American blunders at the far more important Battle of Eutaw, but he does state he agrees with Porgy there "was no complete victory for the Americans" at Eutaw.[73] Apparently Simms thought Porgy's analysis of the Battle of Eutaw would carry its own weight, and be taken virtually as his own, first because it is so lucidly and cogently presented, and second it is actually sound—as is found if we turn to modern authorities.

A detailed demonstration of the validity of Porgy's explanation of why the American success at Eutaw could have been so much more complete, would no doubt exhaust the reader's patience, but could be offered. The great mistake, says Porgy, was placing the partisans, or militia, although they were grievously under-equipped and more useful for skirmishing, in the front lines at the very beginning. They did come through with immense credit to themselves, though with very heavy casualties. He thought the continentals, who were equipped with bayonets, as were the British, should have been placed in the front instead, especially if they were so much better soldiers, as the partisans are always being reminded they are. Also the victory was virtually won, when these continentals broke through the British line only to enter the tents and seize the rum and brandy.[74]

70. *Ibid.*, p. 374n.
71. *Eutaw*, pp. 360-66.
72. *Ibid.*, pp. 526-35.
73. *Ibid.*, p. 526.
74. *Ibid.*, pp. 526-35.

Essential agreement with Porgy is found in an authoritative recent work, Christopher Ward's *The War of the Revolution*: "The militia in Greene's front line stood up to their work manfully, advancing without hesitation, and firing steadily, although they were receiving the fire of the whole British line, double their number. Greene said their 'conduct would have graced the veterans of the great King of Prussia.' "[75] Ward said the strongest elements of the American army, the continentals, were not engaged until quite late in the battle.[76] When these were put into the fight, nearly all the British were in full retreat. "But in that moment of almost complete victory the discipline of the Maryland and Virginia continentals blew up and vanished. They and the militia halted. . . . In utter disorder, complete confusion, they looted the stores, ate the food . . . and drank the liquor until many were drunk. No efforts of their officers sufficed to bring them back to their duty."[77] Porgy's only mistake is in not admitting that his partisan friends participated in this looting! Ward did agree with Porgy that the American "victory" was quite unnecessarily a very partial one.[78]

Why had Porgy not been consulted before and during these battles about the strategy? Why are his valid objections given after the event, and thus without having had any actual effect? Of course, it can be said that hindsight is always better; but the actual explanation in the novel is simple and obvious—Porgy is only a captain and is therefore ignored by the high command.

Porgy justifies his censuring severely the superior officers, when Major Sinclair pleads for leniency, by saying that only by such ruthless and close examination of the mistakes of leaders can future errors be prevented, and perhaps necessary changes in command be made.[79] Porgy admits he could have ordered things better himself; but he really is arguing that General Marion should have been in charge. He thinks Marion had not been given the authority he merited; and Simms insists that, after the war was over, Marion was not even given recognition for all he, despite handicaps, had achieved.[80]

Simms says that "Captain Porgy is no mean authority" on military

75. Christopher Ward, *The War of the Revolution*, ed. John Richard Alden (New York, 1952), II, 830.
76. *Ibid.*, p. 831.
77. *Ibid.*, p. 832.
78. *Ibid.*, p. 834.
79. *Eutaw*, p. 528.
80. *Ibid.*, p. 533.

affairs.[81] Since he explicitly supports Porgy's censure of the American errors at Quinby, and implicitly, of those at Eutaw, Simms clearly intends Porgy to be his own voice in these matters. Only by creating a character who is "no mean authority," yet was not consulted about the plans, would he have a chance to give his own judgments about the tactics in the battles through the mouth of the character. Porgy, a projection of a part of Simms, acts as a safety valve for the author, a kind of catharsis. To Hammond, Simms wrote in November, 1861, that with such incompetents in charge of the defenses "I was fated like Cassandra to speak the truth with nobody to listen. My plans would most effectively have kept the enemy from breaking in at Port Royal."[82]—an event coming after the surrender of Ft. Sumter. Although this statement was made some time after the writing of *Eutaw,* it summarized the reception he thought his counsels about military matters had been getting for years. So he had, in the last incarnation he gave his Porgy, made him a little-heeded, yet penetrating military theorist, and thus added a few more brush strokes to Porgy as self-portrait.

Like both Porgy and Falstaff, Simms was the center of a group of admirers. He gathered around himself in Charleston a band of ambitious young men writers, mostly poets, at about the time he was completing his delineation of Porgy. "They formed a club and placed him at the head," said Trent. There was whist, as well as drinking. "Simms dominated and discoursed on anything and everything, in a voice that could often be heard for blocks."[83] To some of them, and perhaps to himself, he was a Dr. Johnson; it was difficult to confute him. They considered themselves the southern literati. Of them at least the poets Hayne and Timrod are still well-known. It was as brilliant a gathering as South Carolina could muster. They often met at Simms's house or "wigwam"; or, in the afternoon at Russell's Book Shop, where there was a special chair for Simms.[84]

Simms has been described by his granddaughter Mrs. Oliphant as at home "the household god, surrounded by a family circle so adoring that it savored of idolatry."[85] Porgy's circle seems a kind of fusion of the Russell Book Shop group and Simms's own family, and they are

81. *Ibid.,* p. 354.
82. *Letters,* IV, 385.
83. Trent, *Simms,* p. 227.
84. *Ibid.,* p. 229.
85. *Letters,* I, xlviii.

for him his family, or all the family he has. Porgy's group like Simms's includes Negroes. Trent says no one disputed Simms; Millhouse, though loyal, does dispute Porgy. Yet when Porgy, replying to Millhouse, defends the arts in something of the manner of a southern orator,[86] Simms may have been recalling himself in some similar outburst of eloquence to his disciples. In Lance Porgy has a surrogate son and a pupil. His poet Dennison and eccentric scientist Dr. Oakenburg may well have been suggested by some of the habitués at Russell's.

Although talented writers are usually avid readers, Simms's acquaintanceship with literature is of a remarkable extent. It is sufficient to make him, said Parks, "a good but not a great critic."[87] Though his formal schooling was very limited, he was precocious in his thirst for books. As the years passed, he was ranging from Aristotle to Schlegel, from Homer to Swinburne. Of his characters Porgy is the best projection of his love of literature. It would be neither possible nor desirable to have a character in fiction illustrate such a range as Simms's, but Porgy's own is considerable for a planter who is not, like Simms, also an author.

Porgy had a classical education. He tells Lance of having as a boy been stimulated by many floggings to become intimate with Cicero but not to make him love that Roman.[88] It is later indicated that most of his knowledge of letters came enjoyably, like Simms's, from independent reading. Before he entered the army, he "was well read in Shakspere, Milton, Dryden, and the best of the then current English writers." He had also "drank freely of fountains less undefiled; had dipped largely into the subsequent pages of the Wycherlys, the Vanbrughs, the Congreves, the Wilmots, Ethereges, and Rochesters, of a far less intellectual, and therefore less moral period." He realized the superiority of the former group, but could make excellent conversation out of the contrast.[89] In the same book he quotes from the Bible,[90] and compares himself with Shylock.[91]

Othello was one of Simms's favorite plays. He modified so as to apply to his own situation a line from it: "Othello's occupation is gone for the present," meaning that his occupation was gone because after

86. *Woodcraft*, pp. 281-84.
87. Parks, *Simms as Literary Critic*, p. 110.
88. *Woodcraft*, p. 172.
89. *Ibid.*, p. 369.
90. *Ibid.*, p. 115.
91. *Ibid.*, p. 434.

the war began there was no demand for his writing. "This phrase apparently haunted his mind, for he played changes on it in several other letters," said Parks.[92] Porgy too applies the line to himself: "A seven years' apprenticeship to war has left no resources in peace. Othello's occupation's gone—gone!"[93] The reference fits Porgy better than Simms, as Othello like Porgy is giving up the glory of taking part in war. Here is a specific bit of evidence that Simms tended to identify himself with Porgy.

Parks noted how numerous are the quotations and allusions in Simms's letters, and said, "The allusions are always appropriate and frequently humorous, but the quotations and ascriptions are not impeccable."[94] The same may be said of Porgy's except, I believe, he makes almost no errors.

In contrast to Porgy's judicious references are the pedantic and intruded ones of the affected Dr. Hillhouse in *The Scout*,[95] though Porgy does, like Hillhouse, exhibit some touches of euphuism. The spouting on every occasion of the bard's lines by the Shakespearean actor Tom Horsey is another sort of thing. Both of these other characters usually bore their associates by their incessant quoting; but Porgy's background in the drama especially and his "frequent happy quotations" are greatly enjoyed by the intellectual Mrs. Eveleigh and help much to make him welcome as her frequent dinner guest.[96] When Porgy talks about the arts, the philistine Millhouse is baffled, but receives it respectfully as part of his education, and Dennison listens appreciatively. At the great banquet Colonel Lee is glad to show he can complete the fragment Porgy gives from *Paradise Lost*.[97] One thinks of Simms at Russell's Book Shop, and of his allusion-studded letters to Bryant and Duyckinck, to senators and governors.[98]

Simms often claimed that his real forte was his poetry rather than his prose.[99] Dennison, poet of Marion's partisans, represents Simms himself in that his poetry is, of course, by Simms himself, and includes

92. Parks, *Simms as Literary Critic*, p. 77.
93. *Woodcraft*, p. 54. *Othello*, III, iii. Othello feels he must renounce "glorious war" if Desdemona be guilty. Another allusion to Othello is in *Woodcraft*, p. 436.
94. Parks, *Simms as Literary Critic*, p. 73.
95. *The Scout*, pp. 298, 300, 483, etc.
96. *Woodcraft*, p. 369.
97. *The Forayers*, p. 549.
98. *Letters*, IV, 549, and *passim*.
99. Parks, *Simms as Literary Critic*, p. 42.

"The Swamp Fox,"[100] his most famous poem and one of his best. When Dennison is extemporizing his "frogpondian chant," Porgy shows poetic gifts by contributing spontaneously a stanza in the same rhyme and rhythm.[101]

In his critical writings Simms emphasizes that the fine arts had civilizing power, and that in this sense poetry was "practical."[102] In a similar vein Porgy replies to Millhouse's charge that poetry is useless, by saying that the music of Dennison's poetry brings sunshine to his heart and is thus "very useful to me," as it is also so by destroying the "grubs and insects of the heart . . . its cares, its anxieties, its sorrows, its bad feelings, and vexatious passions."[103]

Porgy's most graceful and humorously suitable allusions are in *The Forayers,* where, before and at his big dinner, he finds occasion to bring in Horace, Milton, Homer, and especially aptly, Aristophanes. As he and Dennison are gathering the frogs for the feast, the frogs give a veritable "concert." Porgy wants to make "the music tributary to satire. The frogs should furnish a running commentary on the follies and vices of society as in Aristophanes, only adapted to our times."[104] No other character of Simms could suitably be given such lines.

Thus many of the features of Simms reappear in the lineaments of Porgy and make him so much a self-portrait—the large physique, the good looks, the gourmet inclinations, the devotion to literature, the frontier humor, the gift for military theory, the capacity for attracting convivial admirers, the kindliness of the South Carolina patrician who feels he is "owned by his slaves." All these factors tend to make Porgy seem also not just a figure back in the era of the Revolution, but one made vivid by his creator's knowledge of himself as he was only yesterday.

In *Woodcraft,* Simms speaks tentatively of plans for a sequel to tell more about the years of the satisfying way of life Porgy had at last established at his country home. "It may be," he says, "that we shall someday depict these happy times, the "Humors of Glen-Eberley."[105] Seven years later he was still mulling over this possible project, as he

100. *The Partisan,* pp. 238-40.
101. *The Forayers,* p. 512.
102. Parks, *Simms as Literary Critic,* p. 44.
103. *Woodcraft,* p. 284.
104. *The Forayers,* p. 513.
105. *Woodcraft,* p. 509.

wrote to the novelist John Esten Cooke in 1859: "I am anxious to write the 'Humor of Glen-Eberley,' but I am not *mature* enough for it. It will require three years more of life in solitude & in the growth of my own soul, to make the work that I design. For Porgy, in that work, is to become a Legislator, and he will probably close his career in its denouement. I must prepare him & myself together to drape our sunsets with dignity."[106] It is gratifying to find him assuming that the talented fellow-novelist was familiar with Porgy. The war which commenced before the three years had passed, and which Cooke depicted in a mood of ardent southern romanticism in *Surrey of Eagle's Nest* (1866), was quite enough to prevent the quiet soul growth Simms needed for the book that was never written.

Did writer ever feel more obligation to one of his characters or more reverence for him? Do we need further proof that Simms realized Porgy was something above and beyond, something far more important than his other creations? Does he not experience with Porgy more than a sense of brotherhood, indeed a realization of deep identity? And this is a writer of whom it was said that the man was greater than his work.

I am sorry he never wrote the proposed book, because I should like to have heard the rest of the tale of Porgy. Because, however, Simms had made "him" so much like "himself," and had kept him "together" with himself, ready for "sunset," I think that, in the Saga as we have it, he had not altogether failed "together to drape" their "sunsets with dignity." Perhaps for once, if once only, his work—Porgy—was as great as the man, because the man *was* Porgy. Perhaps for once Simms achieved a full demonstration of the "holy" creed, as enunciated by Henry James in *The Death of the Lion*, "The artist's life's his work."

106. *Letters,* IV, 169.

Porgy as Complex and Contemporary

A rather ambitious synthesis of eighteenth-century South Carolina gentleman and Falstaff, Porgy is a complex personality. He is far from simple enough to be merely, as has been maintained, a "humor" character after the manner of Ben Jonson.[1] If he ever approaches being one,

1. Holman, "Simms and the British Dramatists," *PMLA*, p. 369, argues that Porgy is essentially a Jonsonian "humour" character, supporting his case with quotations from *The Partisan.*

it is in *The Partisan,* the first Saga book; Simms greatly broadened the scope of Porgy later. Simms does have a penchant for drawing such "humor" types. The most completely provable cases are in *Border Beagles,* because the first chapter is headed thus:

> ------"I have got
> A seat to sit at ease here, in mine inn
> To see the comedy; and laugh and chuck
> At the variety and throng of humors,
> And dispositions that come jostling in
> And out."—Ben Jonson—*The New Inn.*[2]

In these lines in this play, mine host, known as Good-stock, who has been asked by his melancholy guest Lovel why he has chosen to preside over such a "sordid" place as an inn, tells of the compensations he has found there.

In this novel, the two prime examples of "humors" are in actor Tom Horsey, who spouts Shakespeare continuously, and even, while sleep-walking, acts Romeo; and in pious Methodist, William Badger, who preaches long actual sermons everywhere and every day, if he has even one listener. Each talks to little purpose; for Tom is unemployed; and Badger's own son is a leader of the "Beagles" or outlaws. Thus both Horsey and Badger misfire and invite derision.

Jonsonian "humor" figures in the Saga include the foppish Dr. Hillhouse in *The Scout;* the epigram-emitting Major Berry, and some other ornaments of Charleston society in *Katharine Walton;* and juxtaposed with Porgy, the snake-obsessed Dr. Oakenburg and the money-obsessed Millhouse. It seems that Simms is most successful with his "humor" characters when they serve as butts for Porgy's jibes.

Jonsonian "humor" figures exist to be targets of satire, it is usually assumed. Simms makes it clear he so regards them, by placing at the very beginning of one of his novels these lines of the host at the "New Inn" telling it is his happiness to "laugh and chuck" at the "throng of humors." Porgy is really not a "humor" character. No one "chucks" at him. Ridgley said that "while he is not a serious person, he is meant to be taken seriously."[3] Also he is far from being reducible to any one, or even two or three or four "humors."

---

2. *The New Inn,* I, iii, in *Ben Jonson,* eds. Herford and Simpson (Oxford, 1938), VI, 414. This scholarly edition reveals Jonson spelled it "humor" in this play.
3. *Simms,* p. 65.

To see how far Porgy is from being a Jonsonian "humor" type, look at him as he is contrasted with his overseer, who is one. There is not much they agree about, but they seem to come nearest to agreement about the importance of food. Millhouse says "that the great business of men on this earth is eating."[4] The agreement with Porgy, however, is more apparent than real. Although Porgy does believe an army fights on its stomach, he sees eating not as a "business" but as a fine art. He is actually more interested in preparing the food to please his guests than in himself eating. Good food can enhearten him; a superb dinner can make a day one to be remembered always; but he is one of the most temperate eaters in the world.[5]

Indeed it is not Porgy but Millhouse who is the glutton, as he demonstrates at Mrs. Eveleigh's dinner party by consuming many a "huge gobbet" of beef.[6] A big feeder, he sees eating as having nothing to do with art, but bluntly equates food with money, and money with food, and thus constantly argues that the pursuit of money is man's only rational activity, as man needs lots of food.

Millhouse's money-obsession colors his every remark. It determines completely his attitude toward women, whether it is a rich widow to be married for her riches, or a girl child pauper needing a few shillings. The property of the one must be clutched, the small requirements of the other be denied—all so Porgy—and he—can have more money. He becomes increasingly ridiculous, as he is laughed at openly by the widow, described as a fool by Lance to her son, and rebuked sarcastically by Porgy—all for words and deeds stemming from his money-madness. Porgy tries in vain to convince him there are other things in life besides money. Millhouse, however, remains to the very last sentence in the book "in his humor." On the other hand, Porgy's gustatory enthusiasms are presented to be admired, and do not distort his vision. He recognizes even his beloved gastronomy as only one of the numerous arts that humanity should cultivate.

Like Ben's host at the "New Inn" (who is a Lord in disguise),[7] Porgy can "chuck" at his guests and retainers, in Porgy's case, those

---

4. *Woodcraft*, p. 292.

5. *The Partisan*, p. 359.

6. *Woodcraft*, p. 356. Ridgley seems to have overlooked this scene, as well as Millhouse's avowed worship of eating, in arguing that he "counterbalances Porgy's sensual pleasure of gluttony" (*Simms*, p. 102).

7. *The New Inn*, V. v, p. 485.

in his house who are incapable of apprehending and enjoying life as fully as he can himself. In the intimations about the subsequent years of abundant life that are lived at Glen-Eberley, Simms says that "with the sergeant and Dr. Oakenburg as *foils* [the italics are mine], the humor of our captain of partisans was irresistible."[8] Here the word "humor" is used with American frontier connotations. There is, admittedly, an Elizabethan tone to Porgy. It may be suggested he is Elizabethan in approaching being the complete man in the Renaissance meaning, in contrast to the limited sergeant and doctor. Insofar as my case for the self-portraiture in Porgy has been convincing, it surely tends to confute any idea that Porgy is a mere Jonsonian "humor" vehicle, as Simms would not want to mirror himself as such an illustration of folly.

Porgy is also seen as the complete man in contrast to other characters who are by no means satirized—the serious young men Lance and Arthur, and the two main "heroes" of the Saga, Singleton and Sinclair. Simms indeed desires to cherish and preserve the heroic ideal, as an essential in the Southern Legend. As Davidson put it so well:

> His solution of the problem . . . was to secure tolerance and belief for it by setting it in a context of characters that move, on the whole, on the level of comedy rather than tragedy. The Singletons and Sinclairs, presented in isolation, would hardly convince a reader of their heroisms. But taken in association with Porgy, the seemingly unheroical philosopher and epicure who is nevertheless the essence of heroism, they become credible; and so does the story of the Singletons and Sinclairs, and the fabric of their society. Porgy is not, as some have thought, a mere foil to the gallants, imitated from Falstaff. He is, instead, the man the gallants would be if they did not have to be on parade as gallants.[9]

In Simms's interpretation, the ideal southern gentleman is certainly not possessed by a Jonsonian "humor." To exist and be believable, he must rather have "a sense of humor," be the one who laughs, not the one laughed at, must be a master of life. So Simms imaged Porgy, a cheerful "philosopher" in the sense of a maker of the best of things, and gourmet indeed, but also warrior, horseman, patriot, humanist, virtual father of Lance and Dory, successful planter, admirer of women as companions; and he placed this many-faceted figure in the spotlight in his dramatization of the Southern Legend.

8. *Woodcraft*, p. 508.
9. *Letters*, I, xlix.

It might seem that as a reply to *Uncle Tom's Cabin, Woodcraft* would have been more powerful if it had been literally contemporary, instead of being, as it is, virtually contemporary in many of its implications as viewed through a rather thin fictitious historical veil. The great popularity of the historical romance might appear to be almost a sufficient explanation for Simms's offering what purports to be a costume story. He was, however, forced to use the era of the Revolution by his decision to use his already-created Porgy, a soldier in that war and forty-five years old at its close. Porgy would be seventy-five in 1803, eighty-five in 1813, and one hundred and twenty-five in 1852! He was unable to invent another medium for his reply as effective as Porgy.

Even if he had not been thus compelled to employ a time some decades ago, there may well have been another cause for his selection of the period. He wanted to place his embodiment of the Southern Legend in an era before the resentment at the abolitionists and other Yankee meddlers had soured the temper of the South; in an era before the time when it became almost impossible for southerners to discuss their system without being on the defensive. He wanted to close his Saga with a depiction of a society which was allowed to and was able to deal with its internal enemies, and could assume itself to be justifiable and perfectible. He thought there had been such an era in the South, toward the end of the eighteenth century. Instead, therefore, of having to listen to acrimonious arguments in rebuttal to northern attacks, we are called on to admire what the South could evolve.

Woodcraft is hardly a historical romance or novel in the way in which the other books of the Saga are. Except that it starts with the British evacuation of Charleston, which it is done with in Chapter IX, and then deals with the soldiers' return home, it does not depict specific chronicled events. Except for one glimpse of Marion and a few of the lawyer Pinckney, it is virtually without actual historical figures. It contains a hint that Porgy is based a little on a certain man—not Simms himself—who actually existed, but as he is not named or otherwise known, this hardly makes Porgy a historical personage.[10] One reason *Woodcraft* excels is that it is, therefore, so much less a historical novel, and suffers much less from that excessive bondage to historical accuracy which Hol-

10. *Woodcraft*, p. 509. A basis in actuality for Porgy and his comrades is also indicated in the dedicatory letter.

man thought tended to injure Simms's historical fiction.[11] Thus in *Woodcraft,* and to some extent even in the other Saga novels when Porgy is on stage, Simms could have greater imaginative freedom in elaborating him.

Of course *Woodcraft* is historical in that it portrays literally a time some seventy years before the date of the writing. Yet in the last chapter there is a kind of extension of the story over an indefinite number of years. The "happy times" at Glen-Eberley "were well remembered by many thirty years ago" in the parishes between the Ashley and the Savannah Rivers. Thus the action of the book comes almost within Henry James's "visitable past" as he defines it in the Preface to *The Aspern Papers,* and illustrates it by the aged Jane Clairmont's recollections of her past with Lord Byron, and in the *nouvelle* by the equally aged Juliana Bordereau's passionate memories of her past with Jeffrey Aspern.

For various reasons Porgy is a figure who seems to exist as much in the nineteenth century as in the eighteenth. The rehabilitation of plantations can be necessitated by other things than war devastation. Insofar as he is the complete gentleman of the Southern Legend, which Simms reverently believed could be kept animate; insofar as he is a reply to the contemporary *Uncle Tom's Cabin*; insofar as he is a self-portrait of a living man, Porgy emerges out of the "biding and dreamy and victorious dust"[12] into Simms's present. Here is a summarizing explanation of why Porgy surpasses in interest and in verisimilitude the other figures in Simms's vast and sometimes dreary canvases. Since Porgy is less of 1783 than of Simms's present of 1852—a present that in the romance magically retains the serenity of an older South—in fashioning him Simms was unfettered by the conventions of historical romance, unrepressed by obligations to the details of recorded events of long ago.

Under the chandeliers of the now splendidly refurnished Glen-Eberley, Porgy is somehow still alive and waiting to welcome Chevillette and William Gilmore Simms as guests for dinner. As they know Tom is still in the kitchen, they ascend the steps of the stately veranda with the most agreeable expectations.

---

11. C. Hugh Holman, "The Influence of Scott and Cooper on Simms," *AL,* XXIII (May, 1951), 214.

12. William Faulkner, *Absalom, Absalom!* (Modern Library ed.; New York, 1936), p. 2.

A Note on the Text

Ridgley said: "In the 1850's the New York publisher J. S. Redfield (and later his successor W. J. Widdleton) published the only collection of Simms's writings. This included those works listed above under *Fiction* and *Poetry* [including the novels of the Revolutionary Saga]. Illustrations were by F. O. C. Carley. The stereotype plates were used for many reprintings during the remainder of the nineteenth century. Many large libraries have either the original or a reprint of this set, which contains Simms's own selection and revision of his best fiction" (*Simms*, 1962, p. 139). Since all nineteenth century copies were printed from these same original stereotype plates, I have assumed that any nineteenth century copies of these novels could be used.

Redfield published these revised editions of *The Partisan, Mellichampe, Katharine Walton, The Scout*, and *Woodcraft* successively during 1854 (*Letters*, III, 315). He published *The Forayers* in 1855 (*Letters*, III, 410), *Eutaw* in 1856 (*Letters*, III, 425), and apparently simply included them in the collection, probably without revision. "Redfield's house had failed and had been taken over by William J. Widdleton" by 1860. (*Letters*, IV, 240)

The copies of the Saga novels I have used are as follows:

The Partisan: Title page undated. Imprint W. J. Widdleton, New York. Publisher's advertisement states he has supplied readers with a "cheap" form of this novel [probably about 1860, not long after Widdleton took over].

Mellichampe: Title page dated 1890. Imprint Donohue, Henneberry & Co., New York.

Katharine Walton: Title page dated 1885. Imprint Belford Clarke & Co., Chicago.

The Scout: Title page dated 1885. Imprint Belford Clarke & Co., Chicago.

Woodcraft: Title page undated. Imprint W. J. Widdleton, New York. On back of the title page: "Entered, according to Act of Congress, in the year, 1854, BY J.S. REDFIELD." Type, format, and pagination of the text are identical with that of another copy I have which is of the 1890 reprinting.

The Forayers: Title page dated 1890. Imprint Donohue & Henneberry, Chicago. Blue cover with erroneous superscription "Border Romances" (Simms did not classify the Revolutionary Saga novels as "Border Romances," but the copies I have of *KW* and *S,* and my 1890 copy of *F* have this superscription). Identical in every respect with another copy I have, except that it has a gray cover with superscription "Caxton Edition."

Eutaw: Title page undated. Imprint W. J. Widdleton, New York. On back of title page: "Entered, according to Act of Congress, in the year 1856 BY J. S. REDFIELD."

In his letters (see especially *Letters,* I, 238), Simms often declares he was intensely desirous to have competent printers and proofreaders. As far as can be judged from his meaty but usually hastily-written letters (as available in the carefully edited *Letters*), he certainly needed aid for what he called *"literal* errors." He expresses humbly his gratitude to one proofreader employed by a northern firm—obviously one of his own publishers. This gentleman's work can hardly have been as impeccable as Simms thought (*Ibid.,* p. 239). Such considerations have led me and the publisher to correct what have seemed obviously errors of the first printers. There *have* been changes in approved spellings since the nineteenth century, and a case can be made for some of Simms's southernisms, and not just in the dialogue in dialect.

2. Porgy
in
The Partisan

In the first novel of the Saga, The Partisan, *Porgy makes an early entrance. He is presented in at least thirteen passages in all, interspersed with the other all too numerous affairs of the book. This novel is for the Porgy afficionado the third or fourth in importance in the Saga. It has freshness and momentum that make it one of the best.*

Porgy has just chosen to become one of the partisans—officially militia, sometimes referred to as forest rangers. Although, being as yet only a lieutenant whose actual military function is minor, he emerges almost at once as the most individualistic of them. He flourishes in the central matter of the novel, the beginnings of the gathering of the partisans around their inspiring leader, General Francis Marion, of the famous sobriquet, the "Swamp Fox." The first Porgy passages concern his arrival at the camp of "Marion's Men," superb horsemen, who in the remaining thirty months of the war, aroused respectful dread in the British, if they were never accorded due credit by the American high command, or, Simms insists, by the historians.

Porgy has joined the small detachment led by Major Robert Single-ton, a handsome young whig of high degree, serving under the "Swamp

*Fox." Singleton indeed, is "our hero," a winner in war and love, the
"Partisan" of the title.*

*As presented, the gathering of the partisans started in the "Royal
George" in Dorchester town in South Carolina. Old Holy Dick Humphries, "after the proverbial fashion of landlords" in all wars, "cared little
about who was king," and had put his George III sign in his garret, but
had now just restored it, a visible symptom of the low status of the American cause in the South in July of 1780. The British were triumphant
throughout the Carolinas; Charleston had fallen; half the American
army were prisoners; the very able Lord Cornwallis had assumed command; and many, especially of the elderly gentry, had taken "the protection," a pledge of neutrality in return for a British guarantee that
their plantations would not be molested. However, General Clinton had
just ordered those sheltered by the "protection" now to take up arms
for the King or to be treated as "rebels."*

*That in this nadir it was Marion's partisans who began the reanima-
tion of the American will to win is the main theme of* The Partisan;
*it is the main theme of the Saga that they, more than the continentals,
virtually won the Revolution in its southern and final phase. (According
to Christopher Ward,* The War of the Revolution, *ed. John Richard
Alden [New York, 1952], II, 661: The partisans "kept the flame of
resistance to tyranny alight in the South during the darkest days of the
revolution.")*

*Major Singleton had come to the inn to recruit, not disclosing his alle-
giance openly. He was joined by Lieutenant Bill Humphries, a sincere
whig, though son of the vacillating landlord. Leaving the inn, the Major
and Lieutenant and a few followers rode to the camp of the "outlawed
whigs," on an island in the Cypress Swamp. There Humphries, a re-
liable man, announced to Singleton that among those who had decided
to join their band was Doctor Oakenburg, a onetime horse doctor who
now aspired to prescribe for the horses' masters.*

"Well, the doctor will be here to-day with Lieutenant Porgy"—
"Porgy—an ancient and fishlike name."
"Yes, but Lieutenant Porgy is not a fish—though you may call him a
strange one. He is more fleshy than fishy; for that matter he has flesh
enough for a score of dragoons. He's a perfect mountain of flesh."
"He will never suit for a dragoon, Humphries."

"Well, Sir, if I didn't know the man, I should think so too; but he rides like the devil, and fights like blazes. He's been fighting from the very beginning of the war down in the south. He comes from the Ashepoo, and is a mighty smart fellow, I tell you. You'll like him. Lord, how he can talk. You'll like him, I know. He's been a rich planter in his time, but he's ate and drank and talked everything away, I reckon, but his horse, his nigger servant, and his broadsword."

"And he's one of our lieutenants, you say."

"Yes, he joined us, saying he had been a lieutenant from the beginning, with Harden and Moultrie, and he wasn't going to be less with anybody else. You'll like him, Sir, he's a man; though he's a mountain of flesh."

"Very good. I suppose you know him well, and now to other matters."

Porgy's first actual entry comes a few pages later:

Dr. Oakenburg was in the company—under the guidance in fact—of a person whose appearance was in admirable contrast with his own. This was no other than the Lieutenant Porgy, of whom Humphries has already given us an account. If Oakenburg was as lean as the Knight of La Mancha, Porgy was quite as stout as Sancho—a shade stouter perhaps, as his own height was not inconsiderable, yet showed him corpulent still. At a glance you saw he was a jovial philosopher—one who enjoyed his bottle with his humours, and did not suffer the one to be soured by the other. It was clear that he loved all the good things of this life, and some possibly that we may not call good with sufficient reason. His abdomen and brains seemed to work together. He thought of eating perpetually, and, while he ate, still thought. But he was not a mere eater. He rather amused himself with a hobby when he made food his topic, as Falstaff discoursed of his own cowardice without feeling it. He was a wag, and exercised his wit with whomsoever he travelled; Doctor Oakenburg, on the present occasion, offering himself as an admirable subject for victimization. To quiz the doctor was Porgy's recipe against the tedium of a swamp progress, and the fertile humours of the wag perpetually furnished him occasions for the exercise of his faculty. But we shall hear more of him in future pages, and prefer that he shall speak on most occasions for himself. He was attended by a negro body servant—a fellow named Tom, and of humours almost as keen and lively as his own. Tom was a famous cook, after the fashion of the southern planters, who could win his way to your affections through his soups, and need no other argument. He was one of that class of faithful, half-spoiled negroes, who will never suffer any liberties with his master, except such as he takes himself. He, too, is a person who will need to occupy a considerable place in our regards, particularly as, in his instance, as well as that of his master—to say nothing of other persons—we draw our portraits from actual life.

Porgy was a good looking fellow, spite of his mammoth dimensions. He had a fine fresh manly face, clear complexion, and light blue eye, the archness of which was greatly heightened by its comparative little-ness. It was a sight to provoke a smile on the face of Mentor, to see those little blue eyes twinkling with treacherous light as he watched Doctor Oakenburg plunging from pool to pool under his false guidance, and condoling with him after. The doctor, in fact, in his present situation and imperfect experience, could not have been spared his disasters. He was too little of an equestrian not to feel the necessity, while battling with his brute for their mutual guidance, of keeping his pendulous members carefully balanced on each side, to prevent any undue pre-ponderance of one over the other—a predicament of which he had much seeming apprehension. In the mean time, the lively great-bodied and great-bellied man who rode beside him chuckled incontinently, though in secret. He pretended great care of his companion, and advised him to sundry changes of direction, all for the worse, which the worthy doctor in his tribulation did not scruple to adopt.

"Ah! Lieutenant Porgy," said he, complaining, though in his most mincing manner, as they reached a spot of dry land, upon which they stopped for a moment's rest—"ah! Lieutenant Porgy, this is but unclean travelling, and full too of various peril. At one moment I did hear a plunging, dashing sound in the pond beside me, which it came to my thought was an alligator—one of those monstrous reptiles that are hurt-ful to children, and even to men."

"Ay, doctor, and make no bones of whipping off a thigh-bone, or at least a leg: and you have been in danger more than once to-day."

The doctor looked down most wofully at his besmeared pedestals; and the shudder which went over his whole frame was perceptible to his companion, whose chuckle it increased proportionably.

"And yet, Lieutenant Porgy," said he, looking round him with a most

wo-begone apprehension—"yet did our friend Humphries assure me that
our new occupation was one of perfect security. 'Perfect security' were
the precise words he used when he counselled me to this undertaking."

"Perfect security!" said Porgy, and the man laughed out aloud. "Why,
doctor, look there at the snake winding over the bank before you—look
at that, and then talk of perfect security."

The doctor turned his eyes to the designated point, and beheld the
long and beautiful volumes of the beaded snake, as slowly crossing their
path with his pack of linked jewels full in their view, he wound his
way from one bush into another, and gradually folded himself up out
of sight. The doctor, however, was not to be alarmed by this survey.
He had a passion for snakes; and admiration suspended all his fear, as
he gazed upon the beautiful and not dangerous reptile.

"Now would I rejoice, Lieutenant Porgy, were yon serpent in my
poor cabinet at Dorchester. He would greatly beautify my collection."
And as the man of simples spoke, he gazed on the retiring snake with
envying eye.

"Well, doctor, get down and chunk it. If it's worth having, it's worth
killing."

"True, Lieutenant Porgy; but it would be greatly detrimental to my
shoes to alight in such a place as this, for the thick mud would adhere—"

"Ay, and so would you, doctor—you'd stick—but not the snake. But
come, don't stand looking after the bush, if you won't go into it. You
can get snakes enough in the swamp—ay, and without much seeking.
The place is full of them."

"This of a certainty, Lieutenant Porgy? know you this?"

"Ay, I know it of my own knowledge. You can see them here
almost any hour in the day, huddled up like a coil of rope on the edge
of the tussock, and looking down at their own pretty figures in the
water."

"And you think the serpent has vanity of his person?" inquired the
doctor, gravely.

"Think—I don't think about it, doctor—I know it," replied the other,
confidently. "And it stands to reason, you see, that where there is beauty
and brightness there must be self-love and vanity. It's a poor fool that
don't know his own possessions."

"There is truly some reason, Lieutenant Porgy, in what you have
said touching this matter; and the instinct is a correct one which teaches

the serpent, such as that which we have just seen, to look into the stream as one of the other sex into a mirror, to see that its jewels are not displaced, and that its motion may not be awry, but graceful. There is reason in it."

"And truth. But we are nigh our quarters, and here is a soldier waiting us."

"A soldier, squire!—he is friendly, perhaps?"

The manner of the phrase was interrogatory, and Porgy replied with his usual chuckle.

"Ay, ay, friendly enough, though dangerous, if vexed. See what a sword he carries—and those pistols! I would not risk much, doctor, to say, there are no less than sixteen buckshot in each of those barkers."

"My! you don't say so, lieutenant. Yet did William Humphries say to me that the duty was to be done in perfect security."

The last sentence fell from the doctor's lips in a sort of comment to himself, but his companion replied—

"Ay, security as perfect, doctor, as war will admit of. You talk of perfect security: there is no such thing—no perfect security any where —and but little security of any kind until dinner's well over. I feel the uncertainty of life till then. Then, indeed, we may know as much security as life knows. We have, at least, secured what secures life. We may laugh at danger then; and if we must meet it, why, at least we shall not be compelled to meet it in that worst condition of all—an empty stomach. I am a true Englishman in that, though they do call me a rebel. I feel my origin only when eating; and am never so well disposed towards the enemy as when I'm engaged, tooth and nail, in that savoury occupation, and with roast-beef. Would that we had some of it now!"

The glance of Oakenburg, who was wretchedly spare and lank, looked something of disgust as he heard this speech of the gourmand, and listened to the smack of his lips with which he concluded it.

He had no taste for corpulence, and probably this was one of the silent impulses which taught him to admire the gaunt and attenuated form of the snake. Porgy did not heed his expression of countenance, but looking up overhead where the sun stood just above them peering down imperfectly through the close umbrage, he exclaimed to the soldier, while pushing his horse through the creek which separated them—

"Hark you, Wilkins, boy, is it not high time to feed? Horse and man—man and horse, boy, all hungry and athirst."

"We shall find a bite for you, lieutenant, before long—but here's a sick man the doctor must see to at once: he's in a mighty bad way, I tell you."

The casualty was a severely wounded tory captain, Clough. The doctor treated this patient, and then hurried off after a snake, as his main interest was really herpetology.

Porgy, who was busy urging the negro cook in the preparation of his dinner, cried out to the dealer of simples, but received no answer. The doctor had no thought but of the snake he had seen, for whose conquest and capture he had now set forth, with all the appetite of a boy after adventures, and all the anxiety of an inveterate naturalist, to get at the properties of the object he pursued. Meanwhile the new comer, Porgy, had considerably diverted the thought of the trooper from attention to his charge; and laying down his sabre between them, the sentinel threw himself along the ground where Porgy had already stretched himself, and a little lively chat and good company banished from his mind, for a season, the consideration of his prisoner.

Thus the prisoner, a worthless scoundrel, was killed by the maniac Frampton, who crawled in unseen under the cypresses. Frampton had been driven mad by the brutal murder of his refined wife by a band of degenerate adventurers from Florida who had attached themselves to the royal cause just for pay; and he had an insane compulsion to satisfy his need for vengeance by killing any tory he could approach. Frampton's son, Lancelot, then sixteen, later becomes Porgy's most devoted retainer.

After various skirmishes have occurred, Porgy, still in the Cypress Swamp, had his first meeting with Singleton.

There we find our almost forgotten friends, the sentimental gourmand, the philosophic Porgy, and the attenuated naturalist, Doctor Oakenburg; the one about to engage in his favorite vocation, and hurrying the evening meal; the other sublimely employed in stuffing with moss the skin of a monstrous "coachwhip," which, to his great delight, the morning before, he had been successful enough to take with a crotch stick, and to kill without bruising. Carefully skinned, and dried in the shade, the rich colours and glossy glaze of the reptile had been well preserved, and now carefully filled out with the soft and pliant moss, as it lay across the doctor's lap, it wore to the eye of Singleton a very life-like appearance. The two came forward to meet and make the acquaintance of the partisan, whom before they had not seen. Porgy was highly delighted, for, like most fat men, he liked company, and preferred always the presence of a number.

"There's no eating alone," he would say—"give me enough for a large table, and a full company round it: I can then enjoy myself."

His reception of Singleton partook of this spirit.

"Major Singleton, I rejoice to see you; just now particularly, as our supper, such as it is, is almost at hand. No great variety, sir—nothing much to choose from—but what of that, sir? There's enough, and what there is, is good—the very best. Tom, there—our cook, sir, he will make the very best of it—broils ham the best of any negro in the southern country, and his hoe-cake, sir, is absolutely perfection. He does turn a griddle with a dexterity that is remarkable. But you shall see—you shall see for yourself. Here, Tom!"

And rolling up his sleeves, he took the subject of his eulogy aside, and a moment after the latter was seen piling his brands and adjusting a rude iron fabric over the coals, while the epicure, with the most hearty good-will for the labour, busily sliced off sundry huge collops from the convenient shoulder of bacon that hung suspended from a contiguous tree.

The labours of Porgy were scarcely congenial either with the mood of Singleton or the quiet loveliness of the scene.

Singleton drew away somewhat from the "culinary operations," and sat down by young Lance. They heard sometimes the hissing fire and the "voice of Porgy." Suddenly Lance's huge mad father appeared. The boy, familiar with the nature of his father's insanity, allowed him to come near and stroke his hair. Singleton asked Oakenburg if this insanity case was within his province; but the frightened doctor declared it hopeless. Porgy, however, had a remedy, or at least an alleviation to propose:

At length having made all arrangements for the evening repast, the provident Porgy came forward with the lofty condescension of a host accustomed to entertain with princely bounty, and announced things in readiness. Singleton then spoke to the maniac, and endeavored to persuade him to the log on which the victuals had been spread, and around which the party had now gathered; but this application was entirely unheeded.

"He won't mind all you can say to him, major [said Porgy]; we know him, for he's been several times to eat with us; that's the way with the creature. But put the meat before him, and his understanding comes back in a moment. He knows very well what to do with it. Ah, Providence has wisely ordained, major, that we shall only lose the knowledge of what's good for the stomach the last of all. We can forget the loss of fortune, sir, of the fine house, and goodly plate, and pleasant tendance— we may even forget the quality and the faces of our friends; and, as for love, that gets out of our clutches, we don't know how; but major, I won't believe that anybody ever yet lost his knowledge of good living. Once gained, it holds its ground well; it survives all other knowledge. The belly, major, will always insist upon so much brains being preserved in the head, as will maintain unimpaired its own ascendancy."

As the gourmand had said, the meat was no sooner placed before the maniac, than seizing it ravenously in his fingers, he tore and devoured it with a fury that showed how long had been his previous abstinence.

After eating, the madman disappeared into the forest. Singleton delighted Lance by choosing him as sole comrade on a night mission, and the two were soon in the saddle. "Porgy waved a blazing torch over the creek, giving them a brief light at starting."

Now comes the longest and most amusing Porgy sequence in the book, wherein our fat officer discarded all dignity, as he was so gripped by his gourmet passion. He was still in the swamp camp, which had been enlarged for more recruits; and he has just naturally gravitated toward assuming direction of the meal preparations.

A partisan, young John Davis, was in love with the innkeeper's daughter Bella. His rival, the British Sergeant Hastings, whom Bella had encouraged a bit, was now Davis' captive. He decided to mount and free his captive, so they could ride out into the woods to settle the love rivalry by honorable single combat. He was approaching in the darkness to borrow one of the horses, when he came "unexpectedly upon no less a person than Lieutenant Porgy."

What was the fat lieutenant doing in such a situation? What was the nature of that occupation which he pursued by the precious starlight, and when most honest men are sleeping? Davis could not divine the answer to his own questions. It was enough that the lieutenant was greatly in his way. Had Porgy been sleeping? No! He was bright enough when he found himself disturbed. But he had certainly been in a state of very profound reverie when the unconscious footstep of Davis sounded in his ears. Rifle in grasp, and crouching low upon the bankside, looking out upon the dark water which glittered in spots only beneath the starlight, the philosophic epicure was as watchful as a sentinel on duty, or a scout on trail. Davis could not say at first whether he lay flat upon the ground, or whether he was on his knees. To suppose him to be crawling upon all fours, would be a supposition scarcely consistent with the dignity of his office and the dimensions of his person. Yet there was so much that was equivocal in his attitude, that all these conjectures severally ran through the head of the woodman. He started up at the approach of Davis, disquieted by the intrusion, yet evidently desirous of avoiding all alarm. His challenge—"Who goes there?" though given in very quick, was yet delivered in very subdued accents. Our woodman gave the answer; and the tones of Porgy's voice underwent some change, but were still exceedingly soft and low. They embodied a good-natured recognition.

"Ah! Davis, my good fellow, you are just in time."

"For what, lieutenant?"

"For great service to me, to yourself, to the whole encampment. But no noise, my good fellow. Not a breath—not a word above your breath. He is a fool who suffers his tongue to spoil his supper. As quiet as possible, my boy."

"What's to do, lieutenant?" was the whispered query of Davis, much wondering at the anxiety of the speaker, who seldom showed himself so, and who usually took events, without asking for the salt or sauce to make them palatable.

"What do you see?" he continued, as the eyes of Porgy were straining across the imperfectly lighted pond.

"See!—what do I see? Oh! Blessed Jupiter, god of men as little fishes, what do *I not* see?"

And as he spoke, he motioned to Davis to sink down, crouch close, and creep towards him. Davis, much bewildered, did as he was required, Porgy meanwhile, *sotto voce,* continuing to dilate after his usual fashion of eloquence—a style, by the way, that was very apt to bewilder all his hearers. Davis had never studied in the schools of euphuism; nor in any school, indeed, except that of the swamp. He fancied he knew the philosophy of the swamp as well as any other man; and that Porgy should extract from it a source of knowledge hitherto concealed from him, was a subject of very great amazement. He began, accordingly, to question the sanity of his superior, when he heard him expatiate in the following language:

"We live in a very pleasant world, Master John Davis. Nature feeds us in all our senses, whenever we are willing and wise enough to partake. You breathe, you see, you smell, you taste, and you ought to be happy, Davis; why are you not happy?"

"Well, I don't know, lieutenant; I only know I ain't happy, and I can't be happy in this world, and I don't expect to be."

"Oh! man of little faith. It is because you won't use your senses, John Davis—your eyes. You ask me what I see! Blind mote, that thou art! Dost thou see nothing?"

"I see you, lieutenant, and the dark pond and water, and the big cypresses, and the thick vines and bushes, and just above, a little opening in the trees that shows where the stars are peeping down. I don't see nothing else."

"And what were the stars made for, John Davis, but to show you the way to other things? Look for yourself now, and let me show you the pleasantest prospect, for a dark night, that your eyes ever hungered over. Stoop, I say, and follow my finger. There! See to the lagune just beyond that old cypress, see the dead tree half rolled into the water. Look now, at the end of the fallen tree,—there just where the starlight falls upon it, making a long streak in the black water. Do you see, man of little faith, and almost as little eyesight! Do you not understand now, why it is that I rejoice; why my bowels yearn, and my soul exults? Look, and feast your eyes, Jack Davis, whom they call of Goose Creek, while you anticipate better feeding still hereafter. But don't you utter a word—not a breath, lest you disturb the comely creatures, the dainty delights—our quail and manna of the swamp—sent for our blessing and enjoyment by the bountiful Heaven, which sees that we are intensely deserving, and mortal hungry at the same time. Hush! hush! not a word!"

Here he stopt himself in the utterance of his own raptures, which were growing rather more loud than prudence called for. The eye of Davis, meanwhile, had followed the guiding finger of the epicure, and the woodman nearly laughed aloud. But he dared not. Porgy was evi-

dently too seriously bent to permit of such irreverence. The objects that
so transported the other, were such as had been familiar to the eyes of
both from their earliest consciousness of light. The little lagune, or bayou,
on the edge of which they crouched, showed them, drowsing on the old
and half-decayed tree to which Porgy had directed his own and the gaze
of Davis, three enormous terrapins of that doubtful brood which the vulgar in the southern country describe as the alligator terrapin—an uncouth
monster, truly, and with such well developed caudal extremities as seem
to justify them in classing the animal in this connexion. The terrapins
lay basking, black and shining in the starlight, their heads thrust out,
and hanging over the lagune, into which the slightest alarm of an unusual nature would prompt them to plunge incontinently. Their glossy
backs yet seemed to trickle with the water from which they had arisen.
Their heads were up and watchful; as if preparing for that facile descent
into the native home, a region black as Avernus. Porgy continued—
now in a whisper—

"That's a sight, John Davis, to lift a man from a sick-bed. That's
a sight to make him whole and happy again. Look how quietly they
lie; that farthest one—I would it were nigher—is a superb fellow, fat
as butter, and sticking full of eggs. There's soup enough in the three
for a regiment; and now, my good fellow, if you will only be quiet, I
will give you such a lesson of dexterity and stratagem as shall make
you remember this night as long as you live. There never was a terrapin
trapper that could compare with me in my youth. We shall see if my
right hand hath lost its cunning. You shall see me come upon them
like an Indian. I will only throw off this outer and most unnecessary
covering, and put on the character of a social grunter. Ah, the hog is
a noble animal—what would we do without him? It's almost a sin to
mock him—but in making mock turtle, John Davis, the offence is ex-
cusable: a good dinner, I say, will sanctify a dozen sins, and here goes
for one."

"But, lieutenant, them's alligator terrapins."

"Well!"

"Well, nobody eats alligator terrapins."

"Nobody's an ass, then, for his abstinence, let me tell you; an alligator
terrapin is the very prince of terrapins."

"Well, he's the biggest."

"And the best! His meat is of the rarest delicacy, and with my dressing, and the cooking of my fellow, Tom, the dish is such as would tickle monstrously the palate of any prince in Europe—that is, of any prince born to a gentlemanly taste, which is not to be said of many of the tribe, I grant you. But, there's no time to be lost. Hold my rifle, and witness my exertions."

Here he forced the rifle into the hands of the Goose-Creek forester, and prepared for the proposed achievement; which we may venture to say, in this place, requires a degree of dexterity and painstaking which few can show, and which no one would attempt, not stimulated by tastes so exquisite and absorbing as those of our epicure.

Porgy's agility greatly belied his appearance. You have seen a heavy man move lightly, no doubt. It requires a certain conformation to show this anomaly. Porgy possessed this conformation. His coat was off in a jiffy. His vest followed it, and he was soon stealing away, along the edge of the hammock, and in the direction of his victims. Davis had become interested, almost to the utter forgetfulness of his own victim, Sergeant Hastings. He watched our epicure, as, almost without a sound, he pressed forward upon hands and knees, his huge form, in this attitude, appearing in the dusky light very like the animal whose outer habits he was striving to assimilate.

The terrapins were a little uneasy, and Porgy found it necessary to pause occasionally and survey them in silence. When they appeared quiet, he renewed his progress; as he drew nearer, he boldly grunted aloud, after the porcine habit, and with such excellence of imitation that, but for his knowledge of the truth, Davis himself might have been deceived. Porgy knew the merit of his imitation, but he had some scruples at its exercise: but for the want of fresh meat in camp, and the relish with which he enjoyed his stew of terrapins, he would have been loath to make an exhibition of his peculiar powers. Even at this moment he had his reflections on his own performance, which were meant to be apologetic, though unheard.

"The Hog," he muttered as he went, "has one feature of the good aristocrat. He goes where he pleases, and grumbles as he goes. Still, I am not satisfied that it is proper for the gentleman to put on the hog, unless on occasion such as this. The pleasures of a dinner are not to be lost for a grunt. He must crawl upon his belly who would feel his way to that of a terrapin."

Thus fortifying himself with philosophy, he pressed forward to the great delight of Davis, who had become quite interested in the performance, and grunt after grunt testified to the marvellous authority which his appetite exercised over his industry. The terrapins showed themselves intelligent. Alas! the best of beasts may be taken in by man. Porgy's grunts were a sad fraud upon the unsuspecting victims. At the first sound, the largest of the three terrapins, having the greatest stake (Qu? steak) of all, betrayed a little uneasiness, and fairly wheeled himself around upon his post, prepared to plunge headlong with the approach of danger. His uneasiness was naturally due to the importance of the wealth which had been intrusted to his keeping. His bullet head, his snaky neck, were thrust out as far as possible from beneath the covers of his dwelling. Like an old soldier, he pricked his ears, and stood on the alert; but he was soon satisfied. His eye took in the forms of his drowsy companions, and he saw no sign of danger in the unbroken surface of the stagnant pond. A second grunt from the supposed porker reassured him. He had lived in intimate communion with hogs all his days. The sow had made her wallow beside his waters, and reared her brood for a hundred years along their margins. He knew that there was no sort of danger from such a presence, and he composed himself at his devotions, and prepared once more to reknit his half-unravelled slumbers.

"Beautiful creature, sleep on!" murmured Porgy to himself, in tones and words as tender as made the burden of his serenade, in the days of his youth, to the dark-eyed damsels upon the waters of the Ashley and Savannah. He made his way forward, noiselessly—the occasional grunt excepted—until he found himself fairly astride the very tree which his unconscious victims were reposing on.

You have heard, no doubt, of that curious sort of locomotion which, in the South and West, is happily styled "cooning the log?" It is the necessity, where you have to cross the torrent on the unsteady footing of a spear,—or rather, where you must needs cross on a very narrow and very slippery tree, which affords no safe footing. In plain terms, out fat friend squatted fairly upon the log, hands and knees, and slided along in a style which John Davis thought infinitely superior to anything he had seen. Telling the story long afterwards, John always did the fullest justice to the wonderful merits of the lieutenant, in some such phrase as this:—

"Lord! 'twas as slick going as down hill, with the wheels greased up to the hub!"

"Greased up to the hub!"

Porgy, you may be sure, was never suffered to hear of the villanous comparison.

The anxiety of Davis, at this point of the adventure, made him fidgety and restless. It required strong resolution to keep quiet. But, though himself anxious enough, the stake was too great to suffer our epicure to peril its loss by any undue precipitation. He moved along at a snail's pace, and whenever the huge tree would vibrate beneath his prodigious weight, the cautious trapper would pause in his journey, and send forth as good a grunt as ever echoed in Westphalian forests. The poor terrapins were completely taken in by the imitation, and lay there enjoying those insidious slumbers, which were now to be their ruin.

Nigher and nigher came the enemy. A few feet only separated the parties, and, with an extended hand, Porgy could have easily turned over the one which was nighest. But our epicure was not to be content with less than the best. His eyes had singled out the most remote, because the largest of that sweet company. He had taken in at a glance its entire dimensions, and already, in his mind, estimated, not only the quantity of rich reeking soup which could be made out of it, but the very number of eggs which it contained. Nothing short, therefore, of this particular prize would have satisfied him; and, thus extravagant in his desires, he scarcely deigned a glance to the others. At length he sat squat almost alongside of the two—the third, as they lay close together, being almost in his grasp, he had actually put out his hands for its seizure, when the long neck of his victim was again thrust forth, and, with arms still extended, Porgy remained as quiet as a mouse. But the moment the terrapin sheltered his head within the shell, the hands of the captor closed upon him with a clutch from which there was no escaping. One after another the victims were turned upon their backs; and, with a triumphant chuckle, the captor carried off his prey to the solid tussock.

"I cannot talk to you for an hour, John Davis, my boy—not for an hour—here's food for thought in all that time. Food for thought did I say! Ay, for how much thought! I am thoughtful. The body craves food, indeed, only that the mind may think, and half our earthly cares are for this material. It is falsehood and folly to speak of eating as a mere animal necessity, the love of which is vulgarly designated an animal appetite. It is not so with me. The taste of the game is nothing to the pleasure of taking it—nothing to the pleasure of preparing it in a manner worthy of the material, and of those who are to enjoy it. I am not selfish, I share with all; and, by the way, John Davis, I feel very much like whipping the fellow who shows no capacity to appreciate. I am a sort of Barmecide in that respect, though I suspect, John, you know nothing of the Barmecides."

"No; I never heard tell of them."

"So I suppose! Well, I won't vex you by talking of fine people not of your acquaintance. Now, John, tell the truth,—did I not seem to you very peculiar, very remarkable, and strange—nay, something ridiculous, John, when you saw me crawling after the terrapins?"

"Well, to say truth, lieutenant, you did seem rather ridickilous."

"Ridiculous! do you say? Well, perhaps! I forgive you, Jack Davis; though there are times when to hint such a word to me, would insure you a broken head. A man of my presence ridiculous!"

"Oh! I don't mean no offence, lieutenant."

"To be sure not! Do I not know that! But, John, think of the soup that we shall get out of these terrapins. Think of our half-starved encampment; and do you not see that the art which traps for us such admirable food, rises into absolute sublimity? Some hundreds of years from now, when our great-grandchildren think of the sort of life we led when we were fighting to secure them an inheritance, they will record this achievement of mine as worthy of Roman fame. But you don't know anything of the Romans, John."

"Not a bit, lieutenant. Is it a kind of terrapins?"

"Yes, indeed! a kind of terrapins that crawled over the whole earth, and claimed it for their own."

"You don't say so!"

"True, every syllable; but the breed's died out, John, and such as are left hav'n't marrow enough in 'em for a stew for a single squad. But, John, it was not the soup only that I thought of when I trapped these beauties. Did you ever feel the pleasure, John, of chasing a fox?"

"Yes, to be sure: a thousand times. It's prime sport, I tell you."

"But you never ate the fox, John?"

"No, indeed! the stinking creature!"

"Well, even if I shouldn't taste these terrapins, the pleasure of their capture is a feast. I have exercised my skill, my ingenuity—I feel that my right hand has not forgot its cunning. That, John, is the sort of practice that proves the true nature of the man. He is never so well satisfied as when he is contriving, inventing, scheming, planning, and showing how cunning he can be. Whether it's red-fox or red-coat, John, it's a sort of happiness to chase, and trap, and catch, run down and cut up."

"I reckon that's true, lieutenant. I feel jist so when I'm on a scout, or a hunt, or anything like it"; and John Davis was reminded of his practice with respect to Sergeant Hastings. He began to be impatient of the long speeches of Porgy; but there was no getting him out of the way, except at his own pleasure.

"Talking of cutting up, John, brings up the terrapins to-morrow. You shall see what a surprise I shall give the camp. You shall see what a thing invention is! How beautiful is art! Now I shall dress each of these beauties in a different style. Steaks and soup you shall have, and enough to satisfy, in the old fashion. But I have some inventions—I thought of them as I neared the log; and when the cunning senses of that patriarch there almost found me out, a timely grunt silenced his doubt. With that grunt came the idea of a new dish. It was a revelation. That terrapin, I said, shall be compounded with the flesh of the porker that Joe Witsell brought into camp at noon. There shall be a hash that shall make your mouth to water. There shall be such a union of the forces of hog and terrapin as shall make them irresistible; and you will then learn the great truth—great to us at short commons in the swamp—that alligator terrapin is a dish worthy to be set before a king."

John Davis looked dubiously, but said—

"Yes, I reckon, lieutenant."

"You reckon! well, but whither do you go?" he asked, as he saw the other lay down his rifle and prepare to go.

"I've got to scout for two hours, out here on the skairts of the swamp."

"Very good! But before you go—have you a handkerchief about you?"

"A mighty old one, lieutenant."

"The very one for my purposes. Mine is a new one, John, and meant for great occasions, when I am entertaining some of the big bugs in epaulettes. Let me have it,—and—but—old fellow, won't you help me home with my captives?"

In one of the best Porgy passages in the Saga, Porgy the next morn-ing dominated the scene. Here was his first great triumph, his success in delaying the departure of the partisans to their next camp on the Santee long enough to do justice to his superb food. The partisans had not yet been exposed to the full Porgy culinary glories, or he would not have had to resort to so much verbal persuasion to get the men to linger the hour or two. His main problem was the impatience of the just-arrived Colonel Walton to get on the road. Walton, uncertain in his loyalties, had taken the "protection." When the end of this con-venient arrangement was imminent, his patriotic nephew Major Single-ton had persuaded him to choose the whig side.

Porgy began the new day by reliving gustily in imagination his suc-cessful hunt of the evening before.

Among those who rose early that morning, we must not forget to distinguish Lieutenant Porgy. But it would be a mistake to suppose that he was stirred into activity at the dawn by any mere sentiment, such as prompts youth, in its verdancy, to forego its pleasant slumbers, in order to take a farewell gripe of the hand of parting friends, and meditate, with no appetite for breakfast, on ruptured ties and sundered associations. Porgy's sentiment took a somewhat different direction. He had survived that *green* season of the heart, when it delights in the things which make it sad. His sentiment dealt in solids. He might be pathetic in soups and sauces; but never when a thinning camp increases the resources of the larder. He rose that morning to other considerations than such as were involved in Walton's departure; though, no doubt, the bustle of that evening had contributed to his early rising. His dreams, all night, had been a mixed vision of *terrapin.* It floated in all shapes and aspects before his delighted imagination. At first, his lively imagination re-enacted to his sight the scene in which he became the successful captor of the prey. There was the picture of the sluggish water, beneath the silent starlight. There, jutting out from the bank, was the fallen tree; and snug, and safe, and sweet in the imperfect light, there were the grouped victims, utterly unconscious, and drowsing to their doom, even as his eyes had seen them, some six or eight hours before. Nothing could seem more distinct and natural. Then followed his experience in the capture. How he "cooned" the log, slowly but surely wearing upon his prey, he again practised in his dreaming mood. How, one by one, he felt himself again securing them, turning them upon their backs, and showing their yellow bellies to the starlight; while their feet paddled ineffectually on either side, and their long necks were thrust forth in a manifest dislike of the fortune which put them in such unnatural position. Porgy experienced an illusion, very common to old fishermen, in being suffered to re-enact in his dreams the peculiar successes which had crowned his labours by day. As the angler then goes through the whole adventure with the cunning trout—beguiles him with the favourite fly, dexterously made to settle over his reedy or rocky retreat,—as he plays him from side to side, now gently persuades him with moderate tension of his line, now relaxes when the strain threatens to be too rude, and at length feels his toils crowned with victory, in the adroit effort which spreads his captive on the bank;—even so did the pleasant servitors of Queen Mab bring to the fancies of our epicure a full repetition of all the peculiarities of his adventure.

But the visions of our fat friend were not confined to the mere taking of his victims. His imagination carried him further; and he was soon busied in the work of dressing them for the table. The very dismembering of the captives—the breaking into their houses, the dragging forth of the precious contents—the spectacle of crowding eggs and generous collops of luxurious swamp-fed meat; all of these gave exercise in turn to his epicurean fancies; nor must we forget the various caprices of his genius, while preparing the several dishes out of the prolific mess before him. He awoke from his dream, crying out "Eureka," and resolved soberly to put some of his sleep devices to the test of actual experiment. Of course, he does not forget the compound of terrapin with pig, which he has already declared his purpose to achieve; but he has other inventions even superior to this; and, full of the one subject, the proposed departure of Colonel Walton, of which he hears only on awaking, provoked all his indignation. He grew eloquent to Humphries, from whom he heard particulars.

"To go off at an hour so unseasonable, and from such a feast as we shall have by noon—it's barbarous! I don't believe it—I won't believe a word of it, Bill."

"But I tell you, lieutenant, it is so. The colonel has set the boys to put the nags in fix for a start, and him and the major only talk now over some message to Marion and General Gates, which the colonel's to carry."

"He's heard nothing then of the terrapin, you think? He'd scarcely go if he knew. I'll see and tell him at once. I know him well enough."

"Terrapin, indeed, Porgy! how you talk! Why, man, he don't care for all the terrapin in the swamp."

"Then no good can come of him; he's an infidel. I would not march with him for the world. Don't believe in terrapin! A man ought to believe in all that's good; and there's nothing so good as terrapin. Soup, stew, or hash, all the same; it's a dish among a thousand. Nature herself shows the value which she sets upon it, when she shelters it in such walls as these, and builds around it such fortifications as are here. See now, Bill Humphries, to that magnificent fellow that lies at your feet. You should have seen how he held on to his possessions; how reluctantly he surrendered at the last; and, in the mean time, how adroitly, as well as tenaciously, he continued the struggle. I was a goodly hour working at him to surrender. To hew off his head cost more effort than in taking off that of Charles the First. No doubt, he too was a tyrant in his way, and among his own kidney—a tyrant among the terrapins. His self-esteem was large enough for a dozen sovereigns, even of the Guelph family. But if the head worried me, what should I say about the shell —the outer fortress? I marched up to it, like a knight of the middle ages attacking a Saracen fortress, battle-axe in hand. There lies my hatchet: see how I have ruined the edge. Look at my hand: see what a gash I gave myself. Judge of the value of the fortress, always, from the difficulty of getting possession. It is a safe rule. The meat here was worthy of the toils of the butcher. It usually is in degree with the trouble we have to get at it. It is so with an oyster, which I take to be the comeliest vegetable that ever grew in the garden of Eden!"

"What, lieutenant, the oyster a vegetable?"

"It originally was, I have no doubt."

"And growing in the garden of Eden?"

"And if it did *not,* then was the garden not to *my* taste, I can assure you. But it must have grown there; and at that period was probably to be got at without effort, though I am not sure, my good fellow, that the flavour of a thing is at all heightened by the ease with which we get at it. It's not so, as we see, with terrapin and oyster, and crab and shrimp, and most other things in which we take most delight—which are dainties to human appetite;—if indeed we may consider appetite as merely human, which I greatly question."

"Well," quoth Humphries, after a short fit of musing, "that does seem to me very true, though I never thought of it before. All the tough things to come at are mighty sweet, lieutenant; and them things that we work for hardest, always do have the sweetest relish."

"Yes; even love, Humphries, which considered as a delicacy—a fine meat, or delicate vegetable——"

"Mercy upon us, lieutenant, what can you be thinking of? Love a meat and a vegetable!"

"Precisely; the stomach——"

"Oh! that won't do at all, that sort of talking, lieutenant. It does seem to me as if you brought the stomach into every thing, even sacred things."

"Nay, nay, reverse the phrase, Humphries, and bring all sacred things into the stomach."

"Well, any how, Lieutenant Porgy, it does seem to me that it's your greatest fault to make too much of your belly. You spoil it, and after a while, it will grow so impudent that there will be no living with it."

"There will be no living without it, my good fellow, and that's sufficient reason for taking every care of it. What you call my greatest fault is in fact my greatest merit. You never heard of Menenius Agrippa, I reckon?"

"Never; didn't know there was such a person."

"Well, I shall not trouble you with his smart sayings, and you must be content with mine to the same effect. The belly *is* a great member, my friend, a very great member, and is not to be spoken of irreverently. It is difficult to say in what respects it is *not* great. Its claims are quite as various as they are peculiar. It really does all one's thinking, as well as——"

"The belly do the thinking?"

"That's my notion. I am convinced, however people may talk about the brain as the seat of intellect, that the brain does but a small business after all, in the way of thinking, compared with the belly. Of one thing be certain: before you attempt to argue with an obstinate customer, give him first a good feed. [It is amusing to note Porgy's anticipations of the arguments advanced by big business in the twentieth century which have led to the notorious expense account deductions.]

Bowels of compassion are necessary to brains of understanding, and a good appetite and an easy digestion are essentials to a logical comprehension of every subject, the least difficult. A good cook, I say, before a good school house, and a proper knowledge of condiments before orthography. It is a bad digestion that makes our militiamen run without emptying a musket; and when you find an officer a dolt, as is too much my experience, you may charge it rather upon his ignorance of food than of fighting. A good cook is more essential to the success of an army than a good general. But that reminds me of Colonel Walton. Go to him, Bill Humphries, with my respects. I know him of old; he will remember me. I have enjoyed his hospitality. If he be the gentleman that I think him, he will find a sufficient reason for delaying his journey till afternoon, when he hears of our terrapin. Be off and see him, lieutenant, and let him understand what he loses by going. Give him particulars; you may mention the dexterity of Tom, my cook, in doing a stew or ragout. And, by the way, lieutenant, pray take with you the buckler of that largest beast. If the sight of that doesn't make him open his eyes, I give him up. See to it, quickly, my good fellow, or you may lose him, and he the stew."

Humphries laughed outright at the earnestness of the epicure. Of course he understood that Porgy had a certain artificial nature in which he found the resources for his jests; and that he covered a certain amount of sarcasm, and a philosophy of his own, under certain affectations at which he was quite content that the world should laugh, believing what it pleased. Humphries found no little pleasure in listening to the shrewd absurdities and thoughtful extravagances of his brother officer; and he could sometimes understand that the gravity of Porgy's manner was by no means indicative of a desire that you should take for gospel what he said. But he was this time thoroughly deceived, and was at much pains to prove to him how utterly impossible it was for Colonel Walton to remain, even with such temptations to appetite as might be set before him.

"The fact is, lieutenant, I did tell the colonel what you had for him, and how you were going to dress the terrapin in a way that never had been seen before."

"Ay, ay! Hash, stew, ragout,—the pig. Well?"

"Yes, I told him all, as well as I knew, but——"

"Ah, you boggled about it, Bill; you couldn't have given him any just idea——"

"I did my best, lieutenant; and the colonel said that he liked terrapin soup amazingly, and always had it when he could get it; and how he should like to try yours, which he said he was sure would prove a new luxury."

"Ay, that was it. I would have had his opinion of the dish, for he knows what good living is. There's a pleasure, Humphries, in having a man of taste and nice sensibilities about us. Our affections—our humanities, if I may so call them—are then properly exercised; but it is throwing pearl to swine to put a good dish before such a creature as that skeleton, Oakenburg—Doctor Oakenburg, as the d—d fellow presumes to call himself. He is a monster—a fellow of most perverted taste, and of no more soul than a skiou, or the wriggling lizard that he so much resembles. Only yesterday, we had a nice tid-bit—an exquisite morsel—only a taste—a marsh hen, that I shot myself, and fricasseed after a fashion of my own. I tried my best to persuade the wretch to try it—only to try it—and would you believe it, he not only refused, but absolutely, at the moment, drew a bottle of some vile root decoction from his pocket, and just as I was about to enjoy my own little delicacy, he thrust the horrible stuff into his lantern jaws, and swallowed a draught of it that might have strangled a cormorant. It nearly made me sick to see him, and with difficulty could I keep myself from becoming angry. I told him how ungentlemanly had been his conduct—taking his physic where decent people were enjoying an intellectual repast—for so I consider dinner—and I think he felt the force of the rebuke, for he turned away instantly, humbled rather, though still the beast was in him. In a minute after, he was dandling his d—d coach whip [A snake], that he loves like a bedfellow. It is strange, very strange, and makes me sometimes doubtful how to believe in human nature at all. It is such a monstrous budget of contradictions, such a diabolical scene of conflict between tastes and capacities."

The departure of Humphries left Porgy to the domestic duties which lay before him, and cut short his philosophies. While the whole camp was roused and running to the spot where Walton's little command was preparing for a start, our epicure and his man Tom—the cook par excellence of the encampment—were the only persons who did not show themselves among the crowd. As for Tom, he did not show himself at all, until fairly dragged out of his bush by the rough grasp of his master upon his shoulder. Rubbing his eyes, looking monstrous stupid, and still half asleep, Tom could not forbear a surly outburst, to which, in his indulgent bondage, his tongue was somewhat accustomed.

"Ki! Maussa: you no lub sleep you'se'f, da's no reason why he no good for udder people. Nigger lub sleep, Mass Porgy; an' 'taint 'spec'ful for um to git up in de morning before de sun."

"Ha! you ungrateful rascal; but you get up monstrous often when its back is turned. Were you not awake, and away on your own affairs, last night for half the night, you might have found it quite respectable to be awake at sunrise. Where were you last night when I called for you?"

"I jist been a hunting a'ter some possum, maussa. Enty you lub possum."

"Well, did you get any?"

"Nebber start, maussa."

"Pretty hunting, indeed, not to start a possum in a cypress swamp. What sort of dog could you have had?"

"Hab Jupe and Slink, maussa."

"You will be wise to invite me when you go to hunt again. Now, open your eyes, you black rascal, and see what hunting I can give you. Look at your brethren, sirrah, and get your senses about you, that there may be no blunder in the dressing of these dear children of the swamp. Get down to the creek and give your face a brief introduction to the water; then come back and be made happy, in dressing up these babes for society."

"Dah mos' beautiful, fine cooter, maussa, de bes' I see for many a day. Whay you nab 'em, maussa?"

"Where you were too lazy to look for them, you rascal; on the old cypress log running along by the pond on Crane Hollow. There I caught them napping last night, while you were poking after possum with a drowsy puppy. Fortunately, I waked while they were sleeping; I cooned the log and caught every mother's son of them: and that's a warning to you, Tom, never to go to sleep on the end of a log of a dark night."

"Hah! wha'den, maussa! S'pose any body gwine eat nigger eben if dey catch 'em? Tom berry hard bittle (victual) for buckrah tomach."

"Make good cooter soup, Tom, nevertheless! Who could tell the difference? Those long black slips of the skin in terrapin soup, look monstrous like shreds from an Ethiopian epidermis; and the bones will pass current every where for nigger toes and fingers. The Irish soldiers in garrison at Charleston and Camden wouldn't know one from t'other. Tom, Tom, if ever they catch you sleeping, you are gone for ever— gone for terrapin stew!"

"Oh! Maussa, I wish you leff off talking 'bout sich things. You mek' my skin crawl like yellow belly snake."

"Ay, as you will make the skin of other people crawl when they find they have been eating a nigger for a terrapin. But away, old boy, and get every thing in readiness. See that your pots are well scoured. Get me some large gourds in which we may mix the ingredients comfortably. We shall want all the appliances you can lay hands on. I am about to invent some new dishes, Tom; a stew that shall surpass anything that the world has ever known of the sort. Stir yourself, Tom, if you would have a decent share of it. When you once taste of it, you rascal, you will keep your eyes open all night, for ever after, if only that you may catch terrapin."

"Hah! I no want 'em mek' too good, maussa, eider! When de t'ing is mek' too nice, dey nebber leabs so much as a tas'e for de cook. Da's it!"

"I'll see to it this time, old fellow. You are too good a judge of good dressing not to be allowed a taste. You shall have your share. But, away, and get everything in readiness. And see that you keep off the dogs and all intruders, bipeds and quadrupeds. And, Tom!"

"Sa! wha' 'gen, maussa?"

"Mind the calabashes; and be sure to get some herbs—dry sage, thyme, mint, and, if you can, a few onions. What would I give for a score or two of lemons! And, Tom!"

"Sa!"

"Say nothing to that d—d fellow Oakenburg—do you hear, sir?"

"Enty I yerry, maussa; but it's no use; de doctor lub snake better more nor cooter."

"Away!"

The negro was gone upon his mission, and throwing himself at length upon the grass, the eyes of Porgy alternated between the rising sun and the empty shells of his terrapins.

"How they glitter!" he said to himself: "what a beautiful polish they would admit of! It's surprising they have never been used for the purposes of manly ornament. In battle, burnished well, and fitted to the dress in front, just over humanity's most conspicuous dwelling-place, they would turn off many a bullet from that sacred, but too susceptible, region."

Musing thus, he grappled one of the shells, the largest of the three, and turning himself upon his back, with his head resting against a pine, he proceeded to adjust the back of the terrapin, as a sort of shield, to his own extensive abdominal domain. Large as was the shell, it furnished a very inadequate cover to the ample territory, at once so much exposed and so valuable. It was while engaged in this somewhat ludicrous experiment, that Lieutenant Porgy was surprised by Major Singleton.

Singleton laughed aloud as he beheld the picture. Porgy's face was warmly suffused when thus apprised of the presence of his superior.

"Not an unreasonable application, lieutenant," was the remark of Singleton, when his laughter had subsided, "were there any sort of proportion between the shield and the region which you wish it to protect. In that precinct your figure makes large exactions. A turtle, rather than a terrapin, would be more in place. The city has outgrown its walls."

"A melancholy truth, Major Singleton," answered the other, as he arose slowly from his recumbent posture, and saluted his superior with the elaborate courtesy of the gentleman of the old school. "The territory is too large certainly for the walls; but I am a modest man, Major Singleton, and a stale proverb helps me to an answer: Half a loaf, sir, is said to be better than no bread; and half a shelter, in the same spirit, is surely better than none. Though inadequate to the protection of the whole region, this shell might yet protect a very vital part. Take care of what we can, sir, is a wholesome rule, letting what can, take care of all the rest."

"You are a philosopher, Mr. Porgy, and I rejoice in the belief that you are fortified even better in intellectual and moral than physical respects. But for this, sir, it might not be agreeable to you to have to hurry to the conclusion of a repast, for which, I perceive, you making extraordinary preparations."

"Hurry, Major Singleton—hurry?" demanded the epicure, looking a little blank. "Hurry, sir! I never hurried in my life. Hurry is vulgar, major, decidedly vulgar—a merit with tradesmen only."

"It is our necessity, nevertheless, lieutenant, and I am sorry for your sake that it is so. We shall start for the Santee before sunset this afternoon. This necessity, I am sorry to think, will somewhat impair the value of those pleasant meditations which usually follow the feast."

Porgy's face grew into profound gravity, as he replied—

"Certainly, the reveries of such a period are the most grateful and precious of all. The soul asserts its full influence about an hour after the repast is over, and when the mind seems to hover on the verge of a dream. I could wish that these hours should be left unbroken. Am I to understand you seriously, major, that the necessity is imperative—that we are to break up camp here, for good and all?"

"That is the necessity. For the present we must leave the Ashley. We move, bag and baggage, by noon, and push as fast as we can for Nelson's Ferry. Our place of retreat here will not be much longer a place of refuge. It is too well known for safety, and we shall soon be wanted for active service on the frontier."

"I confess myself unwilling to depart. This is a goodly place, my dear major; better for secresy could scarce be found; and then, the other advantages. Fresh provisions, for example, are more abundant here than in Dorchester. Pork from the possum, mutton from the coon; these ponds, I am convinced, will yield us cat quite as lively if not quite so delicate as the far-famed ones of the Edisto; and I need not point you more particularly to the interesting commodity which lies before us."

"These *are* attractions, Mr. Porgy; but as our present course lies for the Santee, the difference will not be so very great—certainly not so great as to be insisted upon. The Santee is rich in numberless varieties of fish and fowl, and my own eyes have feasted upon terrapin of much greater dimensions, and much larger numbers, than the Cypress yields."

"And of all varieties, major? the brown and yellow—not to speak of the alligator terrapin, whose flavour, though unpopular with the vulgar, is decidedly superior to that of any other? You speak knowingly, major?"

"I do. I know all the region, and have lived in the swamp for weeks at a time. The islands of the swamp there are much larger than here; and there are vast lakes in its depths, where fish are taken at all hours of the day with the utmost ease. You will see Colonel Marion, himself, frequently catching his own breakfast."

"I like that—a commander should always be heedful of his example. That's a brave man—a fine fellow—a very sensible fellow—catches his own breakfast! Does he dress it too, major?"

"Ay, after a fashion."

"Good! such a man always improves. I feel that I shall like him, major, this commander of ours; and now that you have enlightened me, sir, on the virtues of the Santee, and our able colonel, I must own that my reluctance to depart is considerably lessened. At late noon, you said?"

"At late noon."

"I thank you, Major Singleton, for this timely notice. With your leave, sir, I will proceed to these preparations for dinner, which are rather precipitated by this movement. That rascally head there, major," kicking away the gasping head of one of the terrapins as he spoke, "seems to understand the subject of our conversation—of mine at least—and opens its jaws every instant, as if it hoped some one of us would fill them."

"He contributes so largely to the filling of other jaws, that the expectations seems only a reasonable one. You will understand me, lieutenant, as an expectant with the rest."

"You shall taste of my ragout, my dear major, a preparation of—"

But Singleton was gone, and Porgy reserved his speech for Tom, the cook, who now appeared with his gourds, and other vessels, essential to the due composition of such dishes as our fat friend had prescribed for the proper exercise of his inventive genius.

Attention for a few pages is shifted from Porgy to Singleton, as Simms seeks to reveal the secrets of the latter's success as a military leader. Singleton went the rounds of the camp, speaking with democratic friendliness and real interest to each man. Another aspect of his success was shown in the growing attachment to Singleton of the delightful young Lance Frampton, who felt free to tell the major of his own distress that his superior had been swearing and seeming to fight the enemy in his sleep. Lance's worship was sealed when Singleton gave him the gift of a dirk, with instructions for its use in fighting.

These humours of the camp! But it is time that we see what preparations for his feast have been made by our corpulent Lieutenant of Dragoons. Of course he was busy all the morning. Porgy had a taste. In the affairs of the cuisine, Porgy claimed to have a genius. Now, it will not do to misconceive Lieutenant Porgy. If we have said or shown anything calculated to lessen his dignity in the eyes of any of our readers, remorse must follow. Porgy might *play* the buffoon, if he pleased; but in the mean time, let it be understood, that he was born to wealth, and had received the education of a gentleman. He had wasted his substance, perhaps, but this matter does not much concern us now. It is only important that he should not be supposed to waste himself. He had been a planter—was, in some measure, a planter still, with broken fortunes, upon the Ashepoo. "He had had losses," but he bore them like a philosopher. He was a sort of laughing philosopher, who, as if in anticipation of the free speech of others, dealt with himself as little mercifully as his nearest friends might have done. He had established for himself a sort of reputation as a humourist, and was one of that class which we may call conventional. His humour belonged to sophistication. It was the fruit of an artificial nature. He jested with his own tastes, his own bulk of body, his own poverty, and thus baffled the more serious jests of the ill-tempered by anticipating them. We may mention here, that while making the greatest fuss, always about his feeding, he was one of the most temperate eaters in the world.

He has effected his great culinary achievement, and is satisfied. See him now, surrounded by his own mess, which includes a doctor and a poet. A snug corner of the encampment, well shaded with pines and cypresses, affords the party a pleasant shelter. Their viands are spread upon the green turf; their water is furnished from a neighboring brooklet, and Tom, the cook, with one or two camp scullions waiting on him, is in attendance. Tin vessels bear water, or hold the portions of soup assigned to the several guests. The gourds contain adequate sources of supply, and you may now behold the cleansed shells of each of the fated terrapins made to perform the office of huge dishes, or tureens, which hold the special dishes in the preparation of which our epicure has exhausted all his culinary arts.

He presides with the complacent air of one who has done his country service.

"Tom," he cries, "take that tureen again to the major's mess. They need a fresh supply by this time, and if they do not, they ought to."

The calabash from which Porgy served himself was empty when he gave this order. In being reminded of his own wants, our host was taught to recollect those of his neighbours. Porgy was eminently a gentleman. His very selfishness was courtly. Tom did as he was commanded, and his master, without show of impatience, awaited his return. In those days no one was conscious of any violation of propriety in taking soup a second time; and though the prospect of other dishes might have taught forbearance to certain of the parties, in respect to the soup, yet it was too evident that a due regard to the feelings of the host required that it should receive full justice at all hands.

Porgy was in the best of humours. He was conciliated by his comrades; and he had succeeded in his experiments—to his own satisfaction at least. He even looked with complacency upon the lantern-jawed and crane-bodied doctor, Oakenburg, whom, as we have seen, he was not much disposed to favour. He could even expend a jest upon the doctor instead of a sarcasm, though the jests of Porgy were of a sort, as George Dennison once remarked, "to turn all the sweet milk sour in an old maid's dairy." Dr. Oakenburg had a prudent fear of the lieutenant's sarcasms, and was disposed to conciliate by taking whatever he offered in the shape of food or counsel. He suffered sometimes in consequence of this facility. But the concession was hardly satisfactory to Porgy, and his temper was greatly tried, when he beheld his favourite dishes almost left untouched before the naturalist, who evidently gave decided preference to certain bits of fried eel, which formed a part of the dinner of that day.

"Eel is a good thing enough," he muttered *sotto voce,* "but to hang upon eel when you can get terrapin, and dressed in this manner, is a vice and an abomination."

Then louder—

"How do you get on, George?" to Dennison; "will you scoop up a little more of the soup, or shall we go to the pie?"

"Pie!" said Dennison. "Have you got a terrapin pie?"

"Ay, you have something to live for. Tom, make a clearance here, and let's have the pie."

Tom had returned from serving Singleton and his immediate companions. These were Humphries, John Davis, Lance Frampton, and perhaps some other favourite trooper. They had dipped largely into the soup. They were now to be permitted to try the terrapin pie upon which Porgy had tried his arts. They sat in a quiet group apart from the rest of the command, who were squatting in sundry messes all about the swamp hammocks. Let us mention, *par parenthese,* that John Davis had mustered the courage to make a full confession to his superior of his last night's adventure, of his projected duel with Hastings, and how the latter was murdered by the maniac Frampton. Of course, Singleton

heard the story with great gravity, and administered a wholesome rebuke to the offender. Under the circumstances he could do no more.
To punish was not his policy, where the criminal was so clever a trooper.
He had done wrong, true; but there was some apology for him in the
wrongs, performed and contemplated, of the British sergeant. Besides,
he had honestly acknowledged his error, and deplored it, and it was
not difficult to grant his pardon, particularly while they were all busy
over the soup of Porgy. If forgiveness had been reluctant before, it
became ready when the pie was set in sight. Porgy's triumph was complete. Singleton did not finish his grave rebuke of the offender, while
helping himself from the natural tureen which contained the favourite
dish. Nothing could be more acceptable to all the party. When the
pie, shorn largely of its fair proportions, was brought back to our epicure, his proceeding was exquisitely true to propriety. Loving the commodity as he did, and particularly anxious to begin the attack upon it,
he yet omitted none of his customary politeness—a forbearance scarcely
considered necessary in a dragoon camp.

"There, Tom, that will do. Set it down. It will stand alone. Did
the major help himself?"

"He tek' some, maussa."

"Some! Did he not help himself honestly, and like a man with
Christian appetite and bowels?"

"He no tek' 'nough, like Mass Homphry, and Mass Jack Dabis, but
he tek' some, and Mass Lance, he tek' some, jis' like the major."

"Humph! he took a little, you mean. A little! Did he look sick,
Tom—the major?"

"No, sah! He look and talk berry well."

"Ah! I see; he helped himself modestly, like a gentleman, at first;
we shall try him again. And now for ourselves. Gentlemen, you shall
now see what art can do with nature; how it can glorify the beast;
how it can give wings to creeping things. George Dennison, you need
not be taught this. Help yourself, my good fellow, and let this terrapin
pie inspire your muse to new flights. Mr. Wilkins, suffer me to lay a
few spoonsful of this pie in your calabash. Nay, don't hang back, man;
the supply is abundant."

The modest Mr. Wilkins, who was coquetting only with his happiness, was easily persuaded, and Porgy turned to Oakenburg, who was
still eeling it.

"Dr. Oakenburg!" with a voice of thunder.

"Sir—Lieutenant—ah!" very much startled.

"Doctor Oakenburg, let me entreat you to defile your lips no longer with that villanous fry. Don't think of eel, sir, when you can get terrapin; and such as this."

"I thank you, lieutenant, but—yes, I really thank you very much; but, as you see, I have not yet consumed entirely the soup which you were so good——"

"And why the d—l haven't you consumed it? It was cooked to be consumed. Why have you wasted time so imprudently? That soup is now not fit to be eaten. You have suffered it to get cold. There are certain delights, sir, which are always to be taken warm. To delay a pleasure, when the pleasure is ready to your hands, is to destroy a pleasure. And then, sir, the appetite grows vitiated, and the taste dreadfully impaired after eating fry. The finest delicacy in the world suffers from such contact. Send that soup away. Here, Tom, take the doctor's calabash. Throw that shrivelled fry to the dog, and wash the vessel clean. Be quick, you son of Beelzebub, if you would hope for soup and salvation."

The indignation of Porgy was making him irreverent. His anger increased as the tasteless doctor resisted his desires and clung to his eel.

"No! Tom, no. Excuse me, lieutenant, but I am pleased with this eel, which is considerably done to my liking. It is a dish I particularly affect."

Porgy gave him a savage glance, while spooning the pie into his own calabash. Tom, the negro, meanwhile, had possessed himself of the doctor's dishes, and the expectant dog was already in possession of the remnant of his eel.

"Maussa say I must tek' um, Mass Oakenbu'g," was the apologetic response of the negro to the remonstrances of the doctor.

"Clean the gourds, Tom, for the doctor as quickly as possible! That a free white man in a Christian country should prefer eel fry to terrapin stew! Doctor Oakenburg, where do you expect to go when you die? I ask the question from a belief—rather staggered, I must confess, by what I have seen—that you really have something of a soul left. You once had, doubtless."

The poor naturalist seemed quite wobegone and bewildered. His answer was quite as much to the point as it was possible for him to make it at any time.

"Really, lieutenant, I don't know; I can't conjecture, but I trust to some place of perfect security."

"Well, for your own sake, I hope so too; and the better to make you secure, could I have a hand in disposing of you, I should doom your soul to be thrust into an eelskin, and hung up to dry in the tropic from May to September every year. Of one thing you may rest assured—if there be anything like justice done to you hereafter, you will have scant fare, bad cooking, and fry for ever, wherever you go. Prefer eel to terrapin! Tom!"

"Sah!"

"Bring me a clean calabash of water, and hand the jug. A little Jamaica, my good fellow, to wash down our Grecians. Prefer eel to terrapin! George Dennison, have you done at last? How these poets eat! Mr. Wilkins, you have not finished? Come, sir, don't spare the pie. It is not every day that happiness walks into one's lodgings and begs one to help himself. It isn't every day that one captures such terrapins as these, and sits down to such cooking and compounding. Tom and myself are good against a world in arts. What! no more? Well, I can't complain. I too have done, a little morsel more excepted. Tom, hand me that tureen. I must have another of those eggs."

The epicure scooped them up and swallowed.

"What a flavour—how rich! Ah! George, this is a day to be marked with a white stone. Tom, take away the vessel. I have done enough."

"Ki, maussa, you no leff any eggs."

"No eggs!" cried the gourmand; why, what the deuce do you call that, and that, and that?" stirring them over with the spoon as he spoke. "Bless me, I did not think there were half so many Stop, Tom, I will take but a couple more, and then—there—that will do—you may take the rest."

The negro hurried away with his prize, dreading that Porgy would make new discoveries; while that worthy, seasoning his calabash of water with a moderate dash of Jamaica from the jug beside him, concluded the repast to which he had annexed so much importance.

"So much is secure of life!" he exclaimed, when he had done. "I am satisfied—I have lived to-day, and nothing can deprive me of the 22d June, in the year of our Lord one thousand seven hundred and eighty, enjoyed in the Cypress Swamp. The day is completed: it should always close with the dinner hour. It is then secure—we cannot be deprived of it: it is recorded in the history of hopes realized, and of feelings properly felt. And, hark! the major seems to think with me, since the bugle rumbles up for a start. Wilkins—old fellow—if you'll give me a helping hand in hoisting on this coat"—taking it from the bough of a tree (he had dined, we may add, in his shirt sleeves)—"you will save me from exertions which are always unwisely made after dinner. So! that will do. Thank you! It is a service to be remembered."

The camp was all astir by this time. Porgy looked around him coolly, and chafed at the hurry which he beheld in others.

"Ho! there, Corporal Millhouse, see to your squad, my good fellow. Dennison, my boy, you will ride along with me. I shall want to hear some of that new ballad as we go. Ah! boy, we shall have to put some of your ditties into print. They are quite as good as thousands of verses that are so honoured. They *are* good, George, and *I* know it, if nobody else. . . . So ho! There! Tom, you rascal, will you be at that stew all day? Hurry, you sable son of Ethiop, and don't forget to unsling and to pack up the hambone. Needn't mind the calabashes. We can get them every where along the road. . . . What! you're not about to carry that snake along with you, Doctor Oakenburg! Great Heavens! what a reptile taste that fellow has! . . . Ha! Lance, my boy, is that you? Well, you relished the pie, didn't you?"

" *'Twas* good, lieutenant."

"Good! It was *great!* But you are in a hurry. Mounted already! Well, I suppose I must follow suit. I see the major's ready to mount also. Do me a turn, Lance; help me on with my belt, which you see hanging from yonder tree. It takes in a world of territory. There! That will do."

Humphries now rode up.

"To horse, lieutenant, as soon as you can. The major's looking a little wolfish."

"Ay, ay! needs must when the devil drives. And yet this moving just after a hearty meal upon terrapin! Terrapin stew or pie seems to impart something of the sluggishness of the beast to him who feeds upon it. I must think of this; whether it is not the case with all animals to influence with their own nature, that of the person who feeds on them. It was certainly the notion of the ancients. A steak of the lion might reasonably be supposed to impart courage; wolf and tiger should make one thirst for blood; and"—seeing Oakenburg ride along at this moment—"who should wonder suddenly to behold that crane-bodied cormorant, after eating fried eel, suddenly twisting away from his nag, and, with squirm and wriggle, sliding off into the mud? If ever he disappears suddenly, I shall know how to account for his absence."

Thus it was that Lieutenant Porgy soliloquized himself out of the swamp. He was soon at the head of his squad, and Singleton's orders became urgent. Once with the duty before him, our epicure was as prompt as any of his neighbours. In an hour, and all were ready for the start—the partisans and their prisoners; and, conspicuous in the rear of his master's command, Tom, the cook, followed closely by his dog; a mean looking cur significantly called "Slink." Never was dog more appropriately named. All negro dogs are more or less mean of spirit, but surly, and cunning in the last degree; but Slink was the superb of meanness even among negro dogs. He was the most shame-faced, creeping, sneaking beast you ever saw; as poor of body as of spirit; eating voraciously always, yet always a mere skeleton, besmeared with the ashes and cinders in which he lay nightly—a habit borrowed, we suspect, from his owner; and such was the meanness of his spirit, that, having, from immemorial time, neglected the due elevation of his tail, he now seemed to have lost all sense, and indeed, all capability, for the achievement. There it hung for ever deplorably down, as far as it could go between his legs, and seemed every day to grow more and more despicably fond of earth. Such was "Slink" always in the white man's eye; but see "Slink" when it is his cue to throttle a fat shote in the swamp, and his character undergoes a change. You then see that phase of it, which, more than any thing besides, endears the dirty wretch to his negro master.

It was an evil hour for Slink, when, under the excitement of departure, he suffered himself to trot ahead of his owner, and pass for a moment from rear to front of the command. It was not often that he suffered himself to put his beauties of person too prominently forward. What evil mood of presumption possessed him on the present occasion, it is difficult to conceive; but Slink in proper keeping with Tom, his owner, in the swamp, might keep himself in perfect security, as well as Oakenburg. His danger was in passing out from his obscurity into the front ranks. Lieutenant Porgy beheld the beast as he trotted in advance, with a rare sentiment of disgust,—a feeling which underwent

great increase when he saw that the dog's spirit underwent no elevation with his advance, and that his caudal extremity was just as basely
drooping as before. Porgy summoned Tom to the front, and pointed to
the dog. Slink instantly saw that something was wrong, and tried to
slink out of sight under the legs of the horses. But it was too late. Eyes
had seen his momentary impertinence which seldom saw in vain.

"Tom," said Porgy, "that dog's tail must be cut off close to his
haunches."

"Cut off Slink's tail, maussa! You want for kill de dog for ebber?"

"It won't kill him, Tom. Cut it off close, and sear the stump with
a hot iron. It must be done to-night."

"But, maussa, he will spile de dog for ebber."

"Not so, Tom; it will *make* him, if any thing can. Don't you see
that he can't raise it up; that it's in the way of his legs; that it makes
him run badly. It is like a dragoon's sword when he's walking: always
getting between his legs and tripping him."

"Slink can't do widout he tail, maussa!" answered Tom with becoming doggedness.

"He *must*, Tom."

"He lub he tail 'twix he leg so; he no hu't (hurt) he running."

"All a mistake, Tom. It's in his way, and he feels it. That's the
true reason why he looks so mean, and always carries his head so sheep-
ishly. It must be a terrible mortification to any dog of sensibility when
he has a tail that he can never elevate. Cut off the tail, and you will
see how he will improve."

"*You* t'ink so, maussa! *I* nebber ken t'ink so. 'Twon't do for cut
off Slink tail."

"Either his tail or his head. He must lose one or t'other to-night,
Tom. See that it is done. If I see him to-morrow with more than one
inch of stump between his legs, I shoot him! By Jupiter Ammon, Tom,
I shoot him! and you know when I swear by a Greek god that I am
sure to keep my oath. In this way, Tom, I mortify Greek faith! You
understand, Tom, with more than one inch of tail he dies! Let it be
seen to this very night when we come to a halt."

"He 'mos (almost) as bad for cut he tail as he head, maussa."

"Be it the head then, Tom; I don't care which; and now fall back,
old fellow, and whistle back the beast. The sight of his miserable tail
distresses me."

And Porgy rode forward; and Tom, whistling back the unhappy
cur, muttered as he fell behind:

"Maussa berry sensible pusson, but sometimes he's a' mos' too d—n
foolish for talk wid. Whay de harm in Slink tail? Slink carry he tail
so low to de groun', people nebber sh'um (see 'em)—nobody gwine
sh'um but maussa, and he hab he eye jes whay nobody ebber want 'em
for look."

But the last bugles sound shrilly and mournfully as the cavalcade
speeds away in a long train through the swamp avenues, and Tom is
compelled to forego his soliloquies and hurry forward with the dog,
Slink, who, as if conscious of his error, has dropped just as far back in
the rear, as before he indiscreetly went ahead. The miserable beast little
anticipates the loss that awaits him. Fortunately Tom feels for him all
that is proper. He rides forward enveloped in his own and master's
luggage, and he too and Slink both finally disappear in the far shadows
of the wood. The cypress swamp of the Ashley rests in the profoundest
silence, as if it never had been inhabited.

*The military strategy planned called for the gathering of the partisans
under Marion in his hiding place in a swamp on the Santee. The
Swamp Fox's assignment was to retard the movements of Lord Cornwallis, who was then in Charleston, until General Gates, the victor of
Saratoga, could arrive from the north with his army of continentals or
regulars. Under Gates then the aggregated army was to confront Cornwallis. Of Marion, Simms declared that "His moral and military character, alike, form the most perfect models for the young, that can be
furnished by the history of any individual of any nation." (Simms's
praise of Marion may seem extravagant; but for a surprisingly similar
estimate from a modern historian, see Ward,* The War of the Revolution, *II, 661.)*

*The approach of Singleton's detachment to the central lair of the
Swamp Fox on an island in the Santee was revealed by the secret
whistle used by the partisans, which resembled the hooting of an owl.
With them, was Porgy, who was in good spirits.*

Porgy was absolutely overcome with anticipations. He could not re-
frain—such was the good-humour which the novelty of their progress
inspired—from addressing Doctor Oakenburg, who sat beside him in
the boat, on the subject of his musings.

"This, Doctor Oakenburg," said he, "this is a region—so Major Single-ton tells me—which, in the language of Scripture, may be said to flow with milk and honey."

The doctor, terrified before into silence, was now astounded into speech.

"Milk and honey!" he exclaimed, with wondering.

"Ay, doctor, milk and honey! that is to say, with fish and terrapin, which I take to mean the same thing, since nobody would desire any land in which there was no meat. The phrase, milk and honey, simply means to convey the idea of a land full of all things that men of taste can relish; or we may even go farther in this respect, and consider it a land teeming with all things for all tastes. Thus, yours, Doctor Oaken-burg—even *your* vile taste for snakes and eels—has been consulted here not less than mine for terrapin. Along the same tussock on which the bullet-head reposes, you will see the moccasin crawling confidently. In the same luxurious wallow with the sow, you will behold the sly alligator watching the growth daily of her interesting little family. The summer duck, with its glorious plumage, skims along the same muddy lake, on the edge of which the d—d bodiless crane screams and crouches; and there are no possible extremes in nature to which a swamp like this will not give shelter, and furnish something to arouse and satisfy the appetite. It is a world in itself, and, as I said before, with a figura-tive signification of course, it is indeed a land of milk and honey."

"Land indeed!" said one of the troopers; "I don't see much of that yet. Here's nothing but rotten trees and mud-holes, that I can make out when the lightwood blazes."

"Never mind, my lark," said one of the conductors in a chuckling reply; "wait a bit, and you'll see the blessedest land you ever laid eyes on. It's the very land, as the big-bellied gentleman says, that's full of milk and honey; for, you see, we've got a fine range, and the cattle's a plenty, and when the sun's warm you'll hear the bee trees at midday—and such a music as they'll give you! Don't be afeard now, and we'll soon come to it."

"I doubt not, my good friend," replied Porgy, with a singular gravity of tone and aspect—"I doubt not what you say, and I rejoice that your evidence so fully supports my opinion. Your modes of speech are scarce-ly respectful enough, however; for, though a man's teeth are prime agents and work resolutely enough for his belly, yet it is scarcely the part of good manners to throw one's belly continually into one's teeth."

"Oh, that's it," said the other; "well, now don't be skittish, mister, for though I am Roaring Dick, I never roars at any of our own boys, and I likes always to be civil to strangers. But it's always the way with us, when we don't know a man's name, to call him after that part that looks the best about him. There's Tom Hazard now, we calls him by no other name than Nosey; 'cause, you see, his nose is the most rumbunctious part that he's got, and it's a'most the only part you see when you first look on him. Then there's Bill Bronson—as stout a lark as you've seed for many a day—now, as he's blind of one eye and can hardly see out o' t'other, we calls him Blinky Bill, and he never gets his back up, though he's a main-quick hand if you poke fun at him. So, stranger, you must not mind when he happen to call you after the most respectable part."

"Respectable part! I forgive you, my friend—you're a man of sense. Dr. Oakenburg, your d—d hatchet hip is digging into my side; can't you move a jot further? There, that will do; I am not desirous of suffering martyrdom by hip and thigh."

"Now we're most home," said Master Roaring Dick to his little crew. "One more twirl in the creek, and you'll see the lights and the island; there, there it is. Look, now, stranger, look for yourself, where the Swamp Fox hides in the daylight, to travel abroad with old blear-eye— the owl that is—when the round moon gets out of her roost."

And very picturesque and imposing, indeed, was the scene that now opened upon Porgy and the rest, as they swept round the little bend in the waters of the creek, and the deeply embowered camp of the partisan lay before them. Twenty different fires, blazing in all quarters of the island, illuminated it with a splendour which no palace pomp could emulate. The thick forest walls that girdled them in were unpierced by their rays; the woods were too impenetrably dense even for their splendours; and, like so many huge and blazing pillars, the larger trees seemed to crowd forward into the light with a solitary stare that made solemn the entire and wonderful beauty of the scene. Group after group of persons, each busy to itself, gathered around the distinct fires; while horses neighed under convenient trees; saddles and bridles, sabres and blankets, hung from their branches, and the cheery song, from little parties more remote, made lively the deep seclusion of that warlike abiding-place.

The little boat floated fairly up to one of the fires; a dozen busy hands at once assisted the new comers to alight, and a merry greeting hailed the acquisition of countrymen and comrades. Boat after boat, in the same way, pressed up to the landing, and all in turn were assisted by friendly hands, and saluted with cheering words and encouragement. It was not long before the strangers, with the readiness which belongs to the life of the partisan, chose their companions in mess and adventure, and began to adapt themselves to one another. Lively chat, the hearty glee, the uncouth but pleasant jest, not forgetting the plentiful supper, enlivened the first three hours after the arrival of Singleton's recruits, and fitted them generally for those slumbers to which they now prepared to hasten.

"Well, Tom," said Porgy to his old retainer, as he hurried to his tree, from a log, around which his evening's meal had been eaten in company with Roaring Dick, Oakenburg, and one or two others—"well, Tom, considering how d—d badly those perch were fried, I must confess I enjoyed them. But I was too hungry to discriminate; and I should have tolerated much worse stuff than that. But we must take care of this, Tom, in future. It is not always that hunger helps us to sauce, and such spice is always a monstrous bad substitute for cayenne and thyme. How about the dog, Tom?"

"I cut he tail, maussa, as you bin tell me."

"Well, how did he like the operation?"

"He bleed bad. He no like 'em 'tall. I don't tink he can ebber run like he been run before."

"Poh! poh! I've no doubt he'll run a thousand times better for it, besides being able to carry his head more genteely. He'll be a little sore for a few days, but a sore tail is a cure for a sore head, Tom; as an ulcer is a relief to a troubled liver. Let me see the dog in the morning. You left him but an inch, Tom?"

"Jis' about, maussa."

"Well, only tie a pine-burr under the stump, and that inch will stand out with proper dignity. Did you sear the wound with a hot iron, boy?"

"Jis' as you tell me, maussa. A'terward, I put some pine-gum on de cut."

"No use, Tom; but no man is quite free from quackery of some sort, and where water is a good wash of itself, the fool fancies it still needs salting. Make yourself clean to-night in the Santee, Tom, before you sleep, and 'Slink' needs a dipping also. Take him with you. Here, —help me off with this coat."

With Tom's assistance, the man of girth proceeded to strip for the night. He was helped out of his coat, the dimensions of which seemed daily more and more to contract; and after certain examinations of his belt, which needed to have a few extra holes opened, to admit of freer use, Porgy prepared to lie down for the night; when the examination of the place assigned for his repose aroused his discontent anew.

"This will never do, Tom. The bed is as hard as a bed of racoon oysters. You must get me a good armfull or two of rushes and pine straw, though you rob some other man's sleeping quarters for it. Stay! What is that hanging from yonder beech? Isn't it—bless my soul, Tom, —isn't it a blanket?"

"Da blanket for true, maussa. 'Spec' (expect) he b'long to somebody."

"Very likely, Tom; but God knows I'm somebody—I have some body, at least, to take care of and provide for: so bring it hither. It shall help to smoothe the rough places among these roots."

The blanket was brought, Tom remarking, as he spread it according to the directions of his master—

"Ha! de man wha' claim dis blanket will sartin to be feel 'bout you to-night, maussa!"

"Will he, then? Well, you may let the whole swamp know that I sleep with sword and pistols, and, if waked too suddenly, that I am sure to use them. Do you hear? But you needn't roar about, you rascal, of what materials my bed is made?"

Tom chuckled, while the epicure rolled himself up in the borrowed blanket, and in such a way as to leave no ends free to meddling fingers. His saddle formed his pillow, and all things adjusted to his satisfaction, he bade the negro take himself off, and, take care of himself. Ten minutes had not elapsed when the proprietor of the blanket came to look after his property. Porgy had already become an old soldier. Never did nose insist more sonorously upon its owner's slumbers than his. The intruder looked upon the apparently sleeping man, and saw how comfortably he was enveloped. In the dim light of the camp-fires, he fancied the blanket bore a resemblance to his own; but our epicure lay in it, calm, assured, confident, as if he were the real proprietor. The man doubted—retired, plucked a brand from the fire, and waved it over the figure of the sleeper. Meanwhile, the hilt of our lieutenant's sabre, and the muzzles of his big horseman's pistols, had been made to protrude from the covering, convenient to his gripe. The stranger was duly cautioned. Still he looked and lingered. Porgy's nose, at this moment, sent forth an emphatic and prolonged snore. The man began to meditate. The night was tolerably warm and pleasant. He really did not know that he should need the blanket, to which he yet felt ready to make oath. No doubt the usurper of his goods had only made a slight mistake. There is something cruel in disturbing a man in a profound sleep after a long journey, only to correct a mistake; and so the good-natured proprietor of the stolen goods resolved to forego his claim, for the night at least; and retired quietly, to the great relief of our cunning epicure. Scarcely had he gone from sight, when Tom heaved himself up from the opposite side of the tree, and, with a chuckle, cried out—

"Hah! maussa, you snore de man out o' he blanket dis time."

"Ah! rascal, are you watching me?" answered Porgy, in good-humoured accents. "Well, remember to restore the blanket to the fellow in the morning, and give him, with my compliments, a sup of the Jamaica. He has the bowels of a Christian, and will relish it. Meanwhile, Tom, let this be a lesson for you. Always fall asleep when the lion's in your path. When your conscience don't feel easy, make your body easy. And now, begone, for I must do some real sleeping, if I can."

Next morning nearly everyone was awake before the fat lieutenant.

Porgy *had* slept, and still slept, with the profound wisdom of a soldier, who will always secure every opportunity for the performance of this duty. Porgy valued sleep too well to abridge its enjoyment unnecessarily. Whenever this necessity occurred in his case, it impaired the serenity of his temper. Now, his colleague, Lieutenant Humphries, had kindly dispatched a sergeant to awaken his brother officer. The sergeant was a rough, untutored forester, who usually adopted the most effectual processes for effecting his object. In the present case, he had seized forcibly upon the ends of the blanket in which our epicure was still comfortably wrapped, and had hauled away with the energies of a person whose muscles were perpetually claiming to be employed. Under his very decided action, one of Porgy's arms was nearly twisted from its socket, and one of his legs was dragged out from beneath the covering, tossed over its fellow, and let to fall with an emphasis which effectually tested the sensibilities of the other member. Porgy opened his eyes in the dim light of the morning star, with a soul full of indignation.

"It is scarcely civil, young man," he cried, endeavouring to unwrap himself from the thrice twisted folds of blanket in which he slept— his anger increasing with the increasing difficulties of the effort. Scarcely civil, young man, I repeat! What if the blanket is your property"— the idea of its adroit appropriation by himself, the night before, still running in his head—"suppose it true, I say, that the blanket is your property, is this the way to seek for it? I have never denied it, sirrah, and a polite demand for it would have at once obtained it. But to disturb, in this rude and insolent manner, the repose of a gentleman! It's a foul offence—an offence which shall have its punishment, by Hercules, or I'm not the man to thresh an impertinent. Let me but unwrap. I'm a pacific man. My temper is not harsh, not irritable. I'm slow to take offence. I'm of forgiving nature. But there are some things which mortal patience cannot bear, and which, by Jupiter, I will not bear. To disturb one's slumbers, which are so absolutely essential to the digestive functions of a large man, is an offence not to be forgiven."

By this time he had extricated himself from his wrappings, and stood erect. What would have been his next proceeding, it would be difficult to say. The sergeant, who aroused him, was evidently bewildered by his evident indignation. Porgy advanced upon him, and with sabre in hand, though scabbarded, he would, in all probability, have laid it heavily on the shoulders of the offender, but for the happy interposition of Humphries, who now showed himself.

"What's the trouble, lieutenant?" demanded this third party. "What vexes you?"

"This rascal—I but wrapt myself in a strange blanket, which, I suppose, belongs to the brute—I say this rascal has been pulling me to pieces, dislocating my legs and shoulders, and depriving me of a glorious morning nap, and a most delicious dream; and all because of his d—d blanket."

"Pshaw, that's a mistake; I sent the sergeant to wake you."

"You did! and why the devil did you take an improper liberty, I pray?"

"Why, man, don't you hear the bugles—don't you see all the camp in motion? Don't you know that the Swamp Fox is for an early start, before daylight? It was a kindness, lieutenant, to have you wakened in season."

"It was d—d unkindly done. Hark you, my good fellow,"—to the sergeant—"remember, hereafter, when you waken a gentleman, that it is scarcely necessary to pull him to pieces to effect your object. I forgive you this time, as you meant well; but see that you sin no more in the same manner. You were, no doubt, a blacksmith before you became a soldier. Forget your old vocation hereafter when you deal with me. If you seek to make a vice of your fingers, you will find something more than vicious at the end of mine!"

The sergeant moved off much wondering.

"Now, bestir yourself, lieutenant, and get yourself in harness," quoth Humphries.

"Take that fiery faggot from my eyes, Humphries, unless you wish to blind me eternally. What blasted folly is this of moving daily and loading the troops with such an infinity of broken slumbers! Are you dreaming, or I? Do you really mean that we are to leave the swamp?"

"Even so."

"Why, we have just got into it. I haven't seen it fairly, and know nothing of its qualities. Major Singleton assured me that it was boundless in its treasures of fish, flesh, and felicity. He spoke of its terrapin as superb. To leave it without tasting! This is shocking. I had hoped to have had a rest here of a few days to have compared its products with those of the cypress."

"You're to be disappointed, nevertheless. I'm sorry for your sake, old fellow, that it is so! But the major's orders are to breeze up as fast as possible. You mustn't delay now for trifles."

"What do you call trifles? Life, and that which feeds it, are no trifles. The tastes which enter into the dressing of food are among the best essentials of life. Who presumes to call them trifles? I trust, Lieutenant Humphries, that it is you who are the trifler now. There is surely no movement now on foot?"

"As sure as I'm a sinner, it's truth; and you must stir up. Let me help to brace you. The major's on horse a'ready. The Swamp Fox, as the people here call Marion, has been about and busy this hour. Look at him yonder—he that has his cap off—standing where those dragoons are in the saddle. He's talking to the men, and they say he talks seldom, but short and strong; and we ought to be there to hear him. Hurry yourself a bit now, or we shall lose it all."

"There's no policy so vicious. Never hurry, John Humphries. Keep cool, keep cool, keep cool! These are the three great precepts for happiness. Life is to be hoarded, not to be hurried. Happiness is found only in grains and fractions, and he who hurries finds none. It is with pleasure, as with money-making—according to that cunning old Pennsylvania printer—take care of the pence, and the pounds will take care of themselves. Take care of the moments, and you need never look after the hours. That's my doctrine for happiness—that is the grand secret. Hurry forbids all this. You skip moments—you skip happiness. Why do you sip rum punch? Why, indeed, do you sip all goodly stomachics?—simply to prolong the feeling of enjoyment. It is your beast only that gulps, and gapes, and swallows. It is only your beast that hurries. Happiness is not for such."

"But we must hurry now, Porgy, if we want to hear what he says."

"I never hurried for my father, though he looked for me hourly. I will not hurry for the best speech ever delivered. Do oblige me with that belt; and lay down your torch, my good fellow, and pass the strap through the buckle for me. There—not so tight, if you please; the next hole in the strap will answer now; an hour's riding will enable me to take in the other, and then I shall probably try your assistance. Eh! what's that?"

The pitiful howling of a negro, aroused from his slumbers prematurely by the application of an irreverent foot to his ribs, now called forcibly the attention of the party, and more particularly that of Porgy.

"That's Tom's voice—I'll swear to it among a thousand; and somebody's beating him! I'll not suffer that." And with the words he moved rather rapidly away towards the spot whence the noise proceeded.

"Don't be in a hurry now, Porgy; remember—keep cool, keep cool, keep cool," cried Humphries, as he followed slowly after the now hurrying philosopher.

"Do I not, Humphries? I am not only cool myself, but I go with the charitable purpose of cooling another."

"But what's the harm?—he's only kicking Woolly-head into his senses."

"Nobody shall kick Tom while I'm alive. The fellow's too valuable for blows;—boils the best rice in the southern country, and hasn't his match, with my counsel, at terrapin in all Dorchester. Holla! there, my friend, let the negro alone, or I'll astonish you."

The soldier and Tom, alike, became apparent the next moment, the former still administering a salutary kick and cuff to the growling and grumbling negro. Porgy soon grappled the assailant by the collar, and shook him violently. The latter, taken by surprise, and seemingly in great astonishment, demanded the cause of this assault. He was one of that class, some of whom are still to be found in the country, who, owning no slaves, are very apt to delight in the abuse of those of other people. Porgy had his answer in his usual fashion.

"That's the cause, my good fellow; that's the cause,"—pointing to the negro,—"an argument that runs upon two legs, and upon which no two legs in camp shall trample."

"Da's right, maussa," growled Tom, indignantly. "Wha' for he kick nigga, what's doing not'ing but sleep? Ax um dat, maussa."

The soldier grew ruffled, in spite of Porgy's uniform, and answered savagely—

"His dog stole my bacon, cappin, and when I chunked the varment, the nigga gin me sass. He's a sassy fellow."

"Ah! he's a saucy fellow, is he? That may be, but I'll let you know that I'm the only one to take the sauce out of him. As for the dog—so, Tom, your dog stole this man's bacon?"

"He say so, maussa, but I ain't sh'um (see um). De dog hab shin-bone, but how I know whey he git um? Slink never tief we bacon, maussa."

"Ah ha! Slink never steals our bacon, you say? That shows him to be a dog of discrimination—that knows where his bread is buttered —what we can't often say for wiser animals. But did he ever steal bacon before to your knowledge, Tom?"

"Nebber, maussa."

"Then, Tom, it's all owing to that cutting off his tail. You see he plucks up spirit, you rascal; for a certain amount of spirit is necessary to a thief. His enterprise grows the moment that you take off the miserable appendage that kept down his spirit. The only misfortune is, that in exercising his new quality, he has not been trained to distinguish between the *meum* and *tuum*. Now, that's your fault, Tom."

"Wha' you mean by *meum* and *tuum*, maussa?"

"Well, Tom, as far as concerns us, who have no goods to lose, the distinction is not of much moment; but the lesson is not the less valuable for Slink to learn, in a camp where other people possess ham bones, in which they claim special rights. See to it, hereafter. As for you, my good fellow, you must see that the dog had no felonious intentions. The *animus* makes the offence. He did not steal—he simply appropriated. Do not suffer yourself, my friend, to indulge again in the defamation of character. The rising spirit of the dog must not be kept down because you have a shinbone of ham. Do you hear that! And further, let me tell you, that any second attempt to kick that fellow— who is decidedly the best cook in the Southern army—will subject you to the chance of being kicked in turn. As it is, I let you off this time, with a simple shaking."

The soldier grew savage and insolent. He was tall and vigorous; did not seem to regard the epicure's epaulet with any great degree of veneration; and, as he replied with defiance, Porgy again took hold of his collar. The affair might have ended in the soldier's tumbling our fat friend upon his back, but for the timely approach of Singleton on horseback, at sight of whom the soldier stole away, pocketing his hurts of self-esteem for a more advantageous occasion.

"To saddle, Mr. Porgy, to saddle," was the command of Singleton. "Be ready, sir, for a movement in five minutes. The Colonel has already given orders for a start, and I would not that any of my command should occasion a moment's delay."

"Nor I, Major Singleton—nor I. Honourable emulation is the soldier's virtue, and though I would never hurry, sir, yet I would never be a laggard. The golden medium, major, between hurry and apathy, is still to be insisted upon. It is a principle, sir, which I approve. But haste, sir, hurry, is my horror. Slumbers once broken—visions rudely intruded upon—seldom return to us in their original felicity. Here have I had my sleep torn in twain, as I may say, just when the web of it had become precious to body and soul. Just as the one was at perfect repose, after a toilsome march, and just as the other had become refreshed with a dream of delights which almost compensated for an empty stomach."

"It is a hard case," was the reply of Singleton, who knew the humours of our friend, "but you must allow for circumstances. Perilous necessity is a despotism, Mr. Porgy, to which it is only wisdom to submit with as much resignation as we may. Necessity overrules all laws, as well of stomach as of soul."

"A manifest truism, Major Singleton; and in its recognition, I will even hasten to obey our present orders. But you err, major, in speaking of soul and stomach as independent organizations. Be assured, sir, the relation between them is much more near than is vulgarly supposed. For my part, I would not give a sixpence for any human soul without a stomach."

Singleton waited to hear no more, but putting spurs to his horse, repeated his request that Porgy should follow soon. The latter turned to Tom.

"So, Tom, that fellow has bloodied your nose. There is an ugly abrasion of your left nostril."

"He feel so, maussa. He feel berry much as ef he been breck (*break* —for broken)."

"Pon my soul, you're right. The bridge is broken. It was ugly enough before; it is scarcely *passable* now. You are disfigured for ever, boy. Fortunately, the nose, however essential to the lungs, is hardly of importance to the genius. You are no doubt as good a cook as ever. Were it likely to affect your skill in that department, I should deem it a duty to have that soldier up at the halyards. Well! I don't see what we can do for it. Wash it as often as you can. Meanwhile, tighten that girth, and bring up the horse. Lead him to that stump. One's own girth is greatly in the way of his steed's. By the way, Tom, you're sure that Slink has not made off with our ham as well as the soldier's. If he has, he's a dead dog from this moment. You have it in the buckskin safely? We shall need it to-morrow, old fellow, for our hard riding promises nothing better."

Tom's assurances in respect to the ham-bone and Slink's fidelity, were promptly given, and, talking to himself or others as he rode, Porgy soon joined himself to his command, where he found the several squads of the partisans already assembled, prepared to see and hear "The Swamp Fox," whom many of them were now to behold for the first time.

Marion addressed his men. He read a resolution passed by Congress declaring its determination to save all the provinces, and denying the rumor circulated by the tories that South Carolina and Georgia were to be sacrificed to the invader. He presented the plan for action; gave a frank picture of the great strength of the enemy; and offered to any who were unwilling to obey the orders of any officer on the staff of General Gates the chance to depart from the ranks. Cheering the Swamp Fox, the men shouted unanimously they would stay. The articulate Porgy put into words his explanation of Marion's effectiveness.

"A devilish good speech," said Porgy to Humphries, as the latter rode beside him, a little after leaving the island—"a devilish good speech, and spoken like a gentleman. No big words about liberty and death, but all plain and to the point. Then there was no tricking a fellow—persuading him to put his head into a rope without showing him first how d—d strong it was. I like that. I always desire to see the way before me. Give me the leader that shows me the game I'm to play, and the odds against me. In fighting, as in eating, I love to keep my eyes open. Let them take in all the danger, and all the dinner, that I may neither have too little appetite for the one, nor too much for the other."

"Ah, Porgy," said Humphries in reply, "you will have your joke though you die for it."

"To be sure, old fellow, and why not? God help me when I cease to laugh. When that day comes, Humphries, look for an aching shoulder. I'm no trifle to carry, and I take it for granted, Bill, for old acquaintance' sake, you'll lend a hand to lift a leg and thigh of one that was once our friend. See me well buried, my boy; and if you have time to write a line or raise a headboard, you may congratulate death upon making the acquaintance of one who was remarkably intimate with life."

General Gates, "the hero of Saratoga," arrived from Virginia. Simms's analysis of the errors and limitations of Gates's conduct of the campaign in the South, which culminated in his decisive defeat at Camden, seems convincing. Gates's two salient qualities were, first, his precipitous haste, inborn, but at the moment accentuated by his recent success at Saratoga—a success partly due, said Simms, to luck and to the ability of Benedict Arnold; and second, his total ignorance that the southern terrain, far more than the northern, necessitated the use of cavalry. Baron De Kalb, a professional soldier of German birth, tried in vain to make Gates realize that success could be achieved only by extensive use of mounted men.

On the third day of August, the "little partisan corps of the Swamp Fox," including Porgy, rode into the camp of Gates south of the Pedee.

Colonel Marion was at once introduced to the marquee of the general, but his troops remained exposed to the unmeasured jest and laughter of the continentals. One called them the crow-squad, from their sooty outsides; this name another denied them, alleging, with a sorry pun, that they had long since forgotten how to crow, although they were evidently just from the dunghills. A third, more classical, borrowed a passage from Falstaff, and swore he should at once leave the army, as he wouldn't march into Coventry with such scarecrows; but a fourth said that was the very reason that he should stick to it, as Coventry was the only place for them.

The fierce low-countrymen did not bear this banter long or with patient temper. As they sauntered about among the several groups which crowded curiously around them, sundry little squabbles, only restrained by the efforts of the officers, took place, and promised some difficulty between the parties. Our friend Porgy himself, though withal remarkably good-natured, was greatly aroused by the taunts and sarcasms uttered continually around him. He replied to many of those that reached his ears, and few were better able at retort than himself; but his patience at length was overcome entirely, as he heard among those engaged most earnestly in the merriment at his expense, the frequent and boisterous jokes of Colonel Armand, a foreign mercenary, who, in broken English, pressed rather rudely the assault upon our friend Porgy's equipment in particular. Armand himself was lean and attenuated naturally. His recent course of living had not materially contributed to his personal bulk. Porgy eyed him with wholesale contempt for a few moments, while the foreigner blundered out his bad English and worse wit. At length, tapping Armand upon the shoulder with the utmost coolness and familiarity, Porgy drew his belt a thought tighter around his waist, while he addressed the foreigner.

"Look you, my friend—with the body of a sapling, you have the voice of a puncheon, and I like nothing that's unnatural and artificial. I must reconcile these extremes in your case, and there are two modes of doing so. I must either increase your bulk or lessen your voice. Perhaps it would be quite as well to do both; the extremes meet always most readily: and by reducing your voice, and increasing your bulk at the same time, I shall be able to bring you to a natural and healthy condition."

"Vat you mean?" demanded Armand, with a look of mixed astonish-

ment and indignation, as he drew away from the familiar grasp which
Porgy had taken upon his shoulder.

"I'll tell you; you don't seem to have had a dinner for some time
back. Your jaws are thin, your complexion mealy, and your belly—
what there is of it—is gaunt as a greyhound's. I'll help to replenish it.
Tom, bring out the hoecake and that shoulder-bone, boy. You'll find it
in the tin box, where I left it. Now, my friend, wait for the negro;
he'll be here in short order, and I shall then assist you, as I said before,
to increase your body and diminish your voice: the contrast is too great
between them—it is unnatural, unbecoming, and must be remedied."

Armand, annoyed by the pertinacity, not less than by the manner
of Porgy, who, once aroused, now clung to him tenaciously all the while
he spoke, soon ceased to laugh as he had done previously; and, not
understanding one-half of Porgy's speech, and at a loss how to take
him, for the gourmand was eminently good-natured in his aspect, he
repeated the question—

"Vat you sall say, my friend?"

"Tom's coming with ham and hoecake—both good, I assure you,
for I have tried them within the hour; you shall try them also. I mean
first to feed you—and by that means increase your bulk—and then to
flog you, and so diminish your voice. You have too little of the one,
and quite too much of the other."

A crowd had now collected about the two, of whom not the least
ready and resolute were the men of Marion. As soon as Armand could
be made to understand what was wanted of him, he drew back in
unmeasured indignation and dismay.

"I shall fight wid de gentilmans and de officer, not wid you, sir," was
his reply, with some show of dignity, to the application of Porgy. A
hand was quietly laid upon his shoulder, as he uttered these words, and
his eye turned to encounter that of Singleton.

"I am both, sir, and at your service, Colonel Armand, in this very
quarrel; though, in justice, you owe the right to Mr. Porgy, who just
asserted it. You waived your own rank, sir, when you undertook to
make merry at the expense of the soldier and the simple ensign, and
thus put yourself out of the protection of your epaulet. But conceding
you all that you claim, I claim to be your equal, and beg to repeat, sir,
that I am at your service."

"But, sare, who sall be you—vat you sall be name?"

"I am a leader of the squad that has provoked your laughter. I am Major Singleton, of the Brigade of Marion. He will answer for my rank and honour."

"But sare,—*honneur*, I sall not laugh at de gentilmans and de officers."

"The officer and the gentleman protects the honour of his followers. Will you compel me to disgrace you, sir?" was the stern demand of Singleton, who had felt quite as keenly as Porgy the ridicule of the foreigner.

Colonel Armand's corps and Major Singleton's squad were on the verge of fighting each other. But the "loud voice of command from general officers was heard, the drum rolled to quarters, and Gates, with De Kalb and Marion" appeared; and the belligerent soldiers retired "like so many machines." Gates and his staff returned to their interrupted conference.

Porgy was quite soured that Armand had gone unwhipped. Somebody mentioned that this personage was, in fact, a Baron.

"Did you know that he is a foreign Lord, Lieutenant, a Baron de la Robbery or something; and would you whip a Lord?"

"As the Lord liveth," declared the unimpressed Porgy, "I should have whipped him out of his breeches!"

The partisans were the most American of the Americans; and Porgy here voiced their resentment at being undervalued by these foreigners. The slow-wittedness of the European as Porgy is bantering the (apparently French) Colonel anticipates the Rose Bud Gam in Moby-Dick, *wherein Stubb "diddles" an uncomprehending Frenchman. The compulsion to assert the superiority of Americans to Europeans, so common in the literature of the Age of Jackson, was here infused with humor by the recurrent Porgy gourmet motif, as the portly officer prescribed hearty American food for the disgustingly underfed Frenchman.*

"The reader will scarcely believe" that Gates actually refused Marion's proffered services, and the "famous Partisan of Carolina, the very stay of its hope for so long a season—he who, more than any other man, had done so much towards keeping alive the fires of liberty and courage there, until they grew into a bright, extending, unquenchable flame—was very civilly bowed out of the Continental army, and sent back to his swamps upon a service almost nominal." According to Simms, here was a chief cause of the defeat at Camden of Gates. Such

cavalry as he had was led in a charge by Armand only to be decisively repulsed.

We next meet Porgy back in the main partisan camp on the Santee, after Marion had carried out well the minor missions assigned him by Gates. The scene is important for its giving the real beginning of the friendship of Porgy and Lance Frampton, who was to become the most sympathetic of the stout lieutenant's retainers.

Lieutenant Porgy, on the present occasion, held the post of a sentinel. This duty, at such a juncture, was special and complimentary, and Marion employed his best officers upon it. A good watcher was Porgy, though the labour was irksome to him. Could he have talked all the while, or sung, with no ears but his own to appreciate his melodies, he would have been perfectly content; but silence and secrecy were principles in the partisan warfare, and tenaciously insisted upon by the commander. Porgy looked east and west, north and south, without relief. The banks lay beautiful before him, in a deep quiet, on both sides of the river. Near him ran a dozen little creeks, shooting into the swamp—dark and bowery defiles, whose mouths, imperceptibly mingling with the river, formed so many places of secure entry and egress for the canoes of the warriors. Stretched along the grass, he might be seen to survey one of these little bayous, with an increasing heedfulness which indicated some cause of disturbance. Then might you see him carefully rise from his luxurious posture, and take up his rifle, and look to the priming, and put himself in the attitude to take aim and fire; when, presently, a shrill whistle reached his ears; and quietly returned the signal, he crawled along the bank towards its edge, and looked down to the little creek, as it wound in, behind him, from the river. The signal which he had heard proceeded from that quarter; and from the recess, a few moments after, a little "dug-out" shot forth, propelled by the single paddle of Lance Frampton. Concealing the boat behind a clump of brush that hung over the mouth of the creek, the boy jumped out, and scrambling up the sides of the bluff, was soon after alongside of the pursy sentinel.

"Harkee, young man," said Porgy, as the youth approached him, "you will pay dearly for good counsel, unless you heed carefully what I now give you. Do you know that you had nearly felt my bullet just now, as I caught the sound of your paddle, before you condescended to give the signal? A moment more of delay on your part would have given us both no little pain, for truly I should have sorrowed to have shot you; and you, I think, would have been greatly annoyed by it."

"That I should, Mr. Porgy; and I ought to have whistled, but I did not think."

"You must learn to think, boy. That is the first lesson you should learn. Not to think, is to be vulgar. The first habit which a gentleman learns, is to think—to deliberate. He is never to be taken by surprise. The habit of thinking is to be lost, or acquired, at the pleasure of the individual; and not to think, is, not only to be no gentleman, but to be a criminal. You will suffer from the want of such a habit. It is the vulgar want always, and, permit me to add, the worst."

"I try, sir, to think, for I know the good of it; but it takes time to learn everything, sir."

"It does; but not so much time as people usually suppose. The knowledge of one thing brings with it the knowledge of another; as in morals, one error is the parent of a dozen—one crime, the predecessor of a thousand. Learn what you can, and the rest will come to you; as in fowling, you inveigle one duck, and the rest of the flock follow. Talking of ducks, now, boy, puts me in mind of dinner. Have the scouts brought in any provisions?"

"No, sir—not yet; and no sign of any."

Porgy looked, with a woe-begone expression, towards the sun, now on the decline, and sighed audibly.

"A monstrous long day, Lance—a monstrous long day. Here, boy, draw this belt, and take in another button-hole—nay, take in two; it will admit of it."

The boy did as he was directed—Porgy stretching himself along the grass for the purpose of facilitating the operation—the boy actually bestriding him; the slender form of the latter oddly opposed to the mountainous mass of matter that lay swelling and shrinking beneath him. While engaged in this friendly office, the boy started, and in a half-whisper, pointed to the opposite shore, exclaimed—

"Oh! Mr. Porgy, look! the deer! What a beautiful shot! I could kill him here, I'm sure, off-hand. I could lay the bullet betwixt his eyes, without damaging the sight!"

"You'll damage mine, if you show me such sights very often!" murmured Porgy, as he let the rifle drop heavily to the ground. He had started at Frampton's words, followed the guidance of his fingers, and seized the rifle, had taken aim without a word; but immediately after he remembered his special duties, and was compelled to forego his prey. Well might he be mortified. Before him, on the opposite bank, his whole figure standing out beautifully in the sunlight, in perfect relief, was a fine buck of the largest size. The young horns were jutting out like great spikes, giving promise of the glorious antlers which he would wear by Christmas. Now he tossed his head in air, now seemed to snuff the breeze; at length he bent his nose to the stream, prepared to drink, and anon suspiciously lifted his head to listen—in all these changes of attitude, the spirit and grace of the beautiful creature furnished a fine study for the painter not less than the gourmand.

"Master Lance Frampton," continued Porgy, "you will certainly be the death of me. You show me a deer, yet deny me a dinner. Why, boy, the beast is nearly half a mile away, and you talk of shooting him through the head! I could sooner pitch you on his back."

The boy laughed.

"Don't laugh, boy; it is too serious a matter, quite. It is too provoking. D—n the beauty! look at him—he seems to see us, and to know our mortification—mine, at least. Now could I be tempted to send him a shot, if it were only to scare him out of his breath. He looks most abominably impudent."

"He looks scared, sir," said the boy, as, starting to one side of the bank, and towards the thickening swamp on the right of it, the animal seemed to show alarm, and a desire for flight.

"Yes: something has frightened him, that's clear; and what troubles him, may be equally troublesome to us. Lie flat, boy—draw that brush a little more in front of you, and take off your cap. You can see through the leaves well enough."

At this moment, a whistle behind them announced a friend, and Humphries joined the two a little after.

"What do you see, Lieutenant?"

The gourmand pointed to the deer, which now, in evident alarm, bounded forward a few paces into the stream, then, swimming a few rods up the river, sought a cover in the swamp thicket to the right.

Humphries squatted down behind the brush, and the cause of the deer's alarm was soon discovered to be the approach of a tattered and tired man. Porgy spotted him as a whig, and probably a messenger. After resting, the newcomer constructed a make-shift raft by binding two rails together with a handkerchief. He threw the raft into the stream and plunged after it.

"The ridiculous booby, he will certainly drown; he can never resist the current in his present state!" said Porgy, half rising from his place. Humphries pulled him down and bade him be quiet.

"But we must not let the poor devil drown, Bill."

"We must do our duty—we must not expose ourselves if we can help it, Porgy. His life is nothing to our own; and we don't know who comes behind him."

"That's true: d—n the fellow—let him drown!—who cares?"

The poor fellow's efforts were becoming less effective, and he was soon being carried downstream.

"We must help him, Humphries, my dear fellow, or he will drown and be d—d," said Porgy.

"Oh, yes, sir—do let us help him!" exclaimed Lance, who had watched the scene with an anxiety that kept him starting anxiously, with every movement of the swimmer.

"If it must be done, Porgy," said Humphries, in reply, "there's only one of us that can do it. The 'dug-out' won't carry more, and I'm the best hand at [it] . . . Lie close, and if the chap can keep above water till I get to him, I'll save him."

The athletic Humphries was able to do so. The exhausted swimmer was carried into camp. He was indeed a fugitive patriot, bringing the gloomy news of the crushing defeat of Gates at Camden.

Gates had heedlessly rushed into attacking. Among his follies was his having the idea he had seven thousand troops, when actually he had been correctly told he had only three. He was, moreover, fighting against a skillful tactician, in Cornwallis, who launched a counter attack and so won the day.

Among a number of whigs captured by the British, was Colonel Walton, who, now firm in patriotism, refused the offer of a British commission. Cornwallis then decided to save the captive colonel for the moment so as to hang him dramatically in Dorchester to impress the people with British might.

With some difficulty Singleton secured permission from his superior, Marion, to have a chance to rescue Walton, on the way to, or, as a last effort, in Dorchester. Singleton was in love with Katharine, Walton's beautiful daughter; and felt responsible for having persuaded Walton to join the American cause.

Among the twenty volunteers Singleton took with him was Porgy, fortunately, as men must eat. Camp was made for a night on the way. "*Porgy was quite at home, and not the less pleased that the eel-loving Oakenburg had forborne to volunteer. He soon set the peculiar talents of black Tom in requisition; and a little foraging furnished the scouts with a sufficient supply for the evening feast."*

Among the volunteers was the brave youth Lance. The light of the camp fire lighted up a figure approaching in the surrounding dark. It was the maniac Frampton, who came to his son Lance and played for a moment with his hair, but then hurried to the supping-place.

"Poor fellow—he doesn't seem to have eaten for a month," said Porgy as the maniac voraciously devoured the meat set before him. "No wonder he's mad—I should be mad myself, I doubt not, were I to go without eating even a day. I felt something like it on the Santee, one day, when required to deliberate and not dine. An empty stomach justifies insanity."

Porgy in this, his last appearance in The Partisan, *showed his deep capacity for pity, and gave still another variation on his unifying gustatory theme.*

The final chapter gives Singleton's "thrilling" rescue of Colonel Walton from a "rebel's" degrading death by hanging, followed by Katharine's consenting to her engagement to the noble rescuer. The cost was heavy enough, as five of the twenty volunteering partisans were killed, and half of the beautiful village of Dorchester burned in a fire set to create confusion as a cover for the foray of the rescuers. The action was considered a minor American victory, and called the "Battle of Dorchester."

3. Porgy
in
Mellichampe

Simms describes Mellichampe, *in the prefatory "Advertisement"* *signed by him, as "an episode in the progress of the 'Partisan'" rather* *than a continuation. A sort of discursion, as he indicates in this "Ad-* *vertisement," it is less illuminative of the war than are the other Saga* *romances, excepting only* The Scout. *Yet in his dedicatory letter for* Katharine Walton, *he says that with* The Partisan *and* Mellichampe, *that* *work constitutes a trilogy to illustrate a period of the war "in our* *parish country."*

The main plot concerns the love of the young, intense patrician *Ernest Mellichampe and Janet Berkley, heiress of "Piney Grove," which* *is obstructed by the devices of Barsfield, a ruthless tory, who had killed* *Ernest's father and received his plantation "Kaddipah" as a reward from* *the British, and thus had risen from a low beginning to a redcoat* *captaincy.*

Mellichampe *is not without merits; it is well unified; the headlong,* *immature Mellichampe, compared by Davidson to a Sartoris, and not* *so perfect a compound of all the virtues as Singleton, may seem more* *lifelike; and Janet Berkley is surely the most interesting of Simms's* *young heroines, in her actions rather than in her rather stagey speeches.*

The melodramatic subplot, the blood feud of Humphries and Blonay, which had started in The Partisan, *is tied in quite adroitly with the main plot. A fine scene showing this knitting and also perhaps support- ing my case for the heroine, may be mentioned. Janet was forced, as are other ladies in the Saga, to play the unwilling hostess in her stately home to a tory detachment, here led by Barsfield, and guided by Blonay as scout. To Barsfield's amazement and discomfiture she insisted that the low-born "Goggle" Blonay, unprepossessing but competent as a scout, be seated with them at dinner. Thus she at once showed herself the true Southern Lady, and also was able to put Barsfield in his place when she said that others of dubious origins were being honored by her hos- pitality.*

The unforgettable climax of the subplot, in which Humphries stuffed the living Blonay up a hollow cypress, only to be driven later by a feeling of guilt for this cruel action to return and pull his victim out and so give him a fighting chance, has been admired; as also has the character- ization of the scout Thumbscrew Witherspoon.

He had been overseer of "Kaddipah" while the Mellichampes, the rightful owners, were in possession. Despite (to quote The Forayers, *p. 295) "the almost immeasurable space which in a society like that of South Carolina separates the overseer's family from that of his employer," the mature Thumbscrew served as mentor of the hot-blooded adolescent Ernest; not only in matters of scouting or "woodcraft," but also in the code of "fair play," particularly when he defended himself to the young aristocrat for not shooting Barsfield from ambush. Barsfield is a tory, and thus an enemy in war, and also an object of revenge, as "murderer" of Ernest's father. Still he must be killed in honorable and open combat, Thumbscrew tells the impetuous gallant. It is interesting, and surely to the credit of Simms, himself a patrician, for according such fine quali- ties to the supposedly low-caste overseer.*

Despite these merits, the romance is pervasively theatrical, especially in the dialogue of the aristocrats. It is not, I think, entirely fortuitous that in this, the most humorless, with the sole exception of The Scout, *of the books of the Saga, Captain Porgy comes on so briefly. Even he, seemingly in harmony with the somber tonality, is seen in an incident of pathos.*

Blonay came to spy on Marion's camp, hoping to get his revenge on Humphries, who was there, and to locate Mellichampe, who also was there. Barsfield had commissioned Blonay to trap or kill Mellichampe.

Porgy was in the camp too. Despite the smallness of Marion's band, the men were cheerful, and boyishly amusing themselves by athletics or cards.

Of all the groups and persons visible in the partisan camp, there was but a single individual who seemed in no way to participate in the moods and employments of the rest—whose thoughts were certainly foreign to all amusements. This melancholy exception was no other than our philosophic epicure, Lieutenant Porgy. You behold him, where he sits upon a fallen tree, his belt undone, his sword across his lap, his elbows on his knees, his great chin within his palms, his eyes looking out vacantly and sadly, without seeming to perceive the groups or the sports around him. He sits in silence, for a wonder; he has no soliloquies; and when he seems to be growing thoughtful, it is with such a disconsolate expression, that one apprehends some very serious misfortunes impending. Why should Porgy be sad? Perhaps he has gone without his supper. The new swamps have probably failed in the treasures of terrapin which endeared those of the Ashley to his affections.

But Tom appears—the cook *par excellence*—and we look to him for explanation. There is no falling off of flesh in the case of Tom, or his master; and there is an unctuous—shall we call it greasy—appearance, about the mouth and cheeks of the negro, that will not permit us to think that he, at least, has suffered any recent diminution of his creature comforts. Now, we can not suppose that, where Tom can find fuel for himself, his master will be permitted to sit without a fire. If Tom can procure hoe-cake and bacon for his own feeding, it is very sure that Porgy will not go without his supper. His cause of trouble lies in some other quarter than the stomach. But Tom is about to clear his voice for speech, as his master looks up, inquiringly, at his approach.

"He's berry bad, maussa!"

"Worse?"

"He's berry bad, sah."

"Worse, I say?"

"Hah! who kin say but he 'se'f? De hoss hab de wuss 'flictions dis time, I ebber see!"

"Will he die, Tom?"

"Ef he no git better, maussa, I 'spec' de buzzard hab fine chance for put up meat to-night."

"You are yourself a buzzard, you rascal; to speak in this way of the condition of the beast."

"Ki! maussa, whey's de ha'm? [harm] Hoss hab for dead jis like white man and nigger. You no bury hoss, like you bury man, and de buzzard *hab* for git 'em!"

"Tom, when you die, there shall be no weight of earth put upon you. You shall be laid out bare, just where the horse is laid—should you suffer him to die! and I shall have a trumpeter to sound a notice to all the buzzards, for fifty miles round, to attend your funeral."

"Come, come, maussa; 'twunt do for talk sich ting! Tom nebber for bury when he dead? None but buzzard for ax to he fun'rel? and jis 'kaise you hoss gwine for dead, and nobody for help 'em! wha' Tom kin do? He a'n't hoss-doctor. 'Speck, maussa, you better try Doctor Oakenburg. 'Speck he hab something to gee de hoss. He can't cure de *man,* when he sick; may-be, he kin cure de *hoss!* Better ax 'em, maussa."

"What! are you such an enemy of the poor beast, Tom, that you want to subject him to new miseries? What pleasure can you find in seeing such a beast as Oakenburg torturing such a beast as Nabob? and you have fed and groomed Nabob for five years! Have you no affection for an animal that you have been intimate with for so long a time? You have ridden him a thousand times. He has borne you as tenderly as your own mother. Have you no gratitude, you rascal, that you wish to thrust one of Oakenburg's decoctions into his stomach?"

"Oh! go 'long maussa; you too foolish! How I want for gee de hoss misery? I wants for care 'em! Da's it! I 'speck de physic, wha' de doctor mek', will mek' de hoss well—"

"What! though it kills the man! Tom, I sometimes think you are half a fool at best. No, Tom; Nabob must get well without help from Oakenburg, or he's a dead beast. His stomach has always been a good one till now. It shall never be defiled by any of Oakenburg's decoctions. But you, Tom, as a cook, and a good cook, ought to know what's good even for the stomach of a horse. Medicine, itself, is only the proper sort of food for a morbid condition. Is there nothing now that you can think of, Tom, that the poor beast can make out to eat. Think, old fellow; think."

"I see dem gib hoss-drench, mek' wid whiskey, and soot, and salt;

but whay you guine git salt here for hoss, and you no hab none for sodger?"

"Where, indeed? The prospect is a sad one enough:—and you say, Tom, that all the salt is gone that came up last week from Georgetown?"

"Ebbry scrap ob 'em, maussa—no hab 'nough to throw on bird tail ef you want to catch 'em. Dis a bad country, Mass Porgy—no like de old cypress, whay you can lap up 'nough salt from de swamp to cure you meat for de year round, and season you hom'ny by looking at 'em only tree minutes by the sun."

"And you know nothing, Tom, that will ease the animal?"

"No, maussa, I see de buckrah gib drench heap time, but I nebber ax how he been mek."

"Has Humphries come in yet, Tom?"

"Long time, sir: he gone ober to Wolf island wid de major bout two hours 'go, and muss be coming back directly; and, jist I speak, look at 'em, coming yonder, by de big gum!"

"I see! I see! I must consult Humphries. You may go now, Tom, and see after your own dinner. I feel hungry, myself, in anticipation of a march that I feel that we shall be called upon to make hurriedly. Yet how to march if Nabob dies, it is difficult to conceive. Tom, unless you have some peculiar delicacy, you need prepare no dinner for me. That beast's misery won't suffer me to eat. Go and see to him, Tom, and report to me how he gets on now."

Tom disappeared, and our fat friend rose from his sitting posture with the air of a man who had no longer any uses in the world. He was sufficiently sad to be thought melancholy, and half suspected it himself.

"D—n the poor beast," he muttered as he went; "I can't bear to look at him. I can't bear to look at the sufferings I can't help. If by a fierce wrestle now, a hand-to-hand fight with an enemy, or even a match-race on foot with an Indian runner, I could do the creature a service, I could go to work cheerfully. Any physical or mental exertion now—no matter of what sort—that would do him good, I would undertake with a sort of satisfaction. But only to look on, and do nothing, sickens me; it may be because I raised the rascally beast myself!"

Thus muttering to himself as he went, our epicurean moved slowly along by the several groups, taking the route toward Humphries, who was seen approaching on the edge of the island. The philosopher was too sad to enjoy the sports of others at this moment. But his boon companions, who knew his usual humors, and seldom witnessed his exceptional turns, were not disposed to permit his unnoticed progress. A dozen voices challenged his attention from all sides, all anxious to secure the company of a good companion.

"I say, Lieutenant—Lieutenant Porgy. This way."

"And this way," cried another and another.

In all these cries, Porgy fancied there was something of an official tone, and he answered one for all.

"How now, you unfeeling brutes? What are you howling about, at such a rate? Have you no sensibility? Must the dying agonies of the poor beast be disturbed by such horrible sounds as issue from such monstrous throats? or do you suppose me deaf? Say what you want. From whom come you? Speak out, and do not think me so deaf as indifferent. I would not hearken, but that you compel me to hear, and will hardly heed unless you speak in more subdued accents. You will crack the drum of my ear by such howlings!"

"Ho! ho! ho!—Ha! ha! ha!"

"What a damnable chorus!" muttered the philosopher. "And this disrespect is the fruit of my good nature. Familiarity breeds contempt. He who sleeps with a puppy is sure of fleas. Now, all because of my taking these rascals into my mess, and treating them like gentlemen, do they presume to howl, and shout, and yell in my ears, as if they were so many bedfellows? Well, Mr. Mason, what is it *you* would say? Speak out and have done with it. A short horse is soon curried."

Dick Mason growled sulkily at the reflection upon his dwarfish size. He was the monster in little of the camp, being but four feet eight.

"Why, lieutenant," said he, "you're mighty cross to-day."

"Cross!—And well I maybe, since here's Nabob, my nag, as fine an animal as man would wish to cross, racked with all the spasms of an infernal colic! Tell me what I can do for *him;* if not, hold your peace, and go to the devil without bothering me with your sense of what is due to your master."

"Your horse!—what, Nabob?" with interest.

"Yes! my horse! Nabob!" pertinently.

"Give him red pepper tea!" said one.

"Soot and salt!" cried another.

"Gunpowder and rum!" a third.

"Turpentine and castor oil!" a fourth.

"A feed of pine burrs is the very best remedy, lieutenant," said a fifth.

Other suggestions followed, half in jest, half in earnest, until the angry lieutenant, seizing one of the party by the hair of his head with one hand, and snatching up a cudgel with the other, was preparing to make a signal example of the one offender, for the benefit of the now dispersing group, when Humphries seized him from behind, and drew, for a brief moment, the fury of the epicure upon himself.

"Who dares?" he demanded, wheeling about.

"Why, you're as full of fight as a spring terrapin of eggs."

"The comparison saves you a cudgeling, Bill Humphries, though you half deserve it for saving these rascals. They've been jeering me, the heartless blackguards, about the condition of my horse, who's dying of colic!"

"Colic!—do you say? Is he bad off."

"He's no horse if he isn't. Bad as he can be! So bad, that even Tom prescribes Oakenburg."

"Oakenburg will kill him, if he undertakes the cure. But there's a Santee jockey here, that's famous as a horse doctor. So ho! Here! Tom Jennings," calling to a lanksided sandlapper, "be off quickly, and hunt up Zeke Turpin, and send him here. Tell him that Lieutenant Porgy's horse has colic from eating his master's dinner by mistake."

"Ah! villain, you take advantage of my grief," said Porgy, with an effort to smile.

"He'll cure it if anybody can! So give yourself no concern. Only, you must put yourself in readiness as soon as possible. That's the order now."

"What's to be done, Humphries?"

"Work! Fight's the word!"

"Fight! With whom now?"

"The tories!"

"The tories! Whereabouts do they gather?"

"At Sinkler's meadow, where there's to be a mighty gathering. They are promised arms and ammunition from the city. We are to have warm work, they tell us, for there's to be a smart chance of the rascals together; but devil take the odds. The job will pay for itself, Porgy, since they're to have a barbecue and plenty of rum."

"Ah, ha! That's encouraging as a prospect, Humphries; and now the question is, whether we shall let them feed before we fight them, or fight them before they feed."

"I don't see why that should be a question. We've got to fight them as soon as we can get a chance at them, and whether before or after the barbecue don't matter very much."

"An opinion that argues great simplicity on the part of Lieutenant Humphries," was the reply of Porgy. "The difference is vastly material to our interests, and ought to govern our policy. If we let them feed before we fight them, we shall find them easier customers, since every third man will be surely drunk, and no second man sober."

"Well, there's something in that, certainly," said Humphries.

"Ay, true; but look at the other side. If we fight them before we suffer them to feed, we shall have the greater spoil since barbecued beef and Jamaica, which have been already consumed by a hundred or two starving tories, is so much clear loss to our commissariat. Now, Bill, I'm for the tougher job of the two—the harder fighting and the greater saving. The wretches! only to think that they are to have a barbecue, while we are compelled to eat—Tom, what are we compelled to eat?— what have you got for dinner, to-day, old fellow?"

Tom reappeared in season to answer.

"Wha' for dinner! Huh! Hab some tripe, sah, and hom'ny, and bile acorns."

"Tripe, hommony, and boiled acorns! And they to have a barbecue! Roast beef—a whole ox—stall-fed, no doubt!—and a puncheon of Jamaica! Ah! Humphries, it is a problem which none of us can solve. There seems to be something unreasonable in this partial distribution of the gifts of Providence. Has a tory a better stomach than a patriot? Is his taste more refined and intellectual? Does he need more fuel for his furnace? Are his nervous energies more exhausting! Are his virtues higher? Has he the right of the political argument? In other words, ought we to prefer George the Third to the Continental Congress, for that is the question that naturally occurs to us when we find the tories better supplied with the creature comforts than ourselves."

"Well, Porgy, that's certainly a new view of the case."

"Truly; but I see how it's to be answered, without a sacrifice of principle. The rascals have the good things, Bill; but shall they be allowed to keep 'em? That's the question. On the contrary, they are but so many agents of Providence, in gathering and getting ready the feast for us. We shall spoil the Egyptians, Bill; we shall be able to come upon them—shall we not?—before they shall have touched the meat. I like vastly to take a first cut at a barbecue. The nice gravy is then delicious. After a dozen slashes have been made in it, it imbibes a smoky flavor which I do not relish. We must come upon them, Bill, when everything's ready, but before they have made the first cut."

"Right! but I'm afraid *you'll* not be in time for the cut, lieutenant," said Humphries gravely.

"And why not, pray?"

"Your horse!"

"Ah, that I should have forgotten the poor beast, thinking of the barbecue. Tom, how's Nabob now?"

Tom shook his head deplorably.

"Ah! well, I suppose I shall have to lose him. I must leave him with your Santee jockey, Bill, and see what he can do for him. But to that barbecue I'll go! Flat! I'll borrow the nag of that old German that's sick—old——"

"Feutbaer! Well, he'll carry you safe enough; it will be for the tories to say if he will bring you back. But what's this?—ha!"

Humphries started as the two approached the little hollow in which Tom carried on his preparations for the humble meal of the squad for which he provided. The trooper seized a rifle that stood against a tree beside him, and lifted it instantaneously to his eye. The muzzle of it rested upon the strange dog that burrowed amid the offal strewn about the place, unnoticed by the busy cook who purveyed for him. Porgy was about to declare his wonderment at the sudden ferocity of mood exhibited by his companion, when, motioning him to be silent, the trooper lowered the weapon, and called to John Davis, who was approaching at a little distance.

"Davis," said he, as the other came near, "do you know that dog?"

"I think I do; but where I've seen him I can't say. I'm sure I know him."

"Is it possible?" exclaimed Humphries, somewhat impatiently, "that you should any of you fail to remember the brute? What do you say, Tom? Don't you know the dog?"

This was addressed to the negro in tones that startled him.

"He face is berry familiar to me, Massa Bill," returned Tom after a pause, in which he seemed to study the matter with grave severity;

"he face is berry familiar to me, 'cept he a'n't bin wash 'em much. But I loss de recollection ob de name for ebber."

"But why the devil," quoth Porgy, "should that dirty-looking beast so much interest you? Positively, you are all in a stew and sweat."

Porgy's Tom then was able to recognize the lurking dog belonging to Blonay; and so Humphries was alerted to the nearness of his enemy and was able to ward him off.

Marion received a warning of the approach of redcoats, and decided to go into action to prevent the ruthless Tarleton's unit from joining forces with Barsfield's. He ordered his men to evacuate their camp quickly.

Our fat friend, Lieutenant Porgy, had a narrow chance of being left. Were we to consider his bulk simply, he might have been classed with those whom Marion spoke of as quite too "cumbrous" for movement. But his energy and impulse were more than a match for his bulk. Still, the best will and blood are not proof against the decrees of fate; and while Marion was yet giving his orders, Tom reported to his master the death of the horse Nabob. The epicure was for a moment overcome. He proceeded, however, with commendable promptness, to what was styled, *par courtesie,* the hospital, where Fentbaer, the German, lay sick. From him he proposed to borrow his horse. But, even while negotiating with the sick man, Tom entered with great outcry and much rejoicing, conducting a sergeant, who brought with him a fine horse, and a message from Singleton, begging Porgy to use him until a better steed could be captured from the enemy. The animal brought him was a noble bay, one of a pair, and Porgy was not the man to underrate a generosity so unusual as well as handsome. Of course, he accepted the gift, and was lavish of thanks. But he said to Humphries, with a sigh: "A handsome present, Bill; our major is the man to do handsome things. This is a very fine animal, and just suits me—perhaps even better than Nabob; but Nabob was a sort of half-brother to me, Bill. I raised the ridiculous beast myself."

Humphries thought the use of the word "ridiculous" rather an abuse of language, but it was employed for a purpose—was in fact designed to conceal a sentiment. When, half an hour after, Porgy beheld Tom stretching the skin of poor Nabob in the sun, he felt like cudgelling the negro, whom he called an inhuman beast.

"Why," he asked, furiously, "why did you skin the animal, you savage?"

"Oh! maussa, kaise I lub 'em so! Nabob and me guine to sleep togedder a'ter this, for ebber and for ebbermore."

Tom was even more "an old soldier" than his master. Porgy growled—

"Some day that will be the scoundrel's apology for skinning me!"

The romance continues in a sometimes exciting and usually gothic vein, which does not provide a milieu in which Porgy would flourish; and we do not see or hear of him again.

Janet Berkley was rewarded; for by her kindness to the primitive and vengeful Blonay, she had begun to win his devotion. He revealed not only gratitude but also a capacity for admiring her patrician qualities, and even developed sympathy for her love for Mellichampe. Blonay, therefore, double-crossed Barsfield, his employer in evil projects, and disclosed to Janet the whole of Barsfield's dastardly plot against Mellichampe's life. It was thus Blonay who finally guided Mellichampe on an escape—planned with Janet—from Barsfield, who had imprisoned our hero. Thus was started a complicated chain of incidents that led at last to the happy ending of the marriage of Ernest and Janet, after Barsfield—most appropriately in a romance of the Old South, had been killed by Janet's faithful slave, old Scipio. In the melee, however, Thumbscrew had been mortally wounded and died expressing satisfaction in having helped to save his "Airnest" and in anticipating the wedded happiness of the young couple.

4. Porgy

in

Katharine Walton

In his dedicatory letter for Katharine Walton *Simms states that while* The Partisan *and* Mellichampe *concerned the "interior" or rural areas, the present novel "brings us to the city" and the "social world of Charleston." It is, more than* Mellichampe, *a continuation of* The Partisan *in that while that novel continues a minor plot, this one continues the main plot, of the initial novel.*

The central story of this third novel features Katharine as carrying on her romance with her true love, her cousin, now promoted to Colonel, Robert Singleton, which had been commenced in The Partisan. *Love's course is violently roughened by the determination of Colonel Nesbitt Balfour, the British commandant of Charleston, to espouse the beauteous Katharine. Her father, Colonel Walton, rescued at the end of* The Partisan, *was soon recaptured; and the villainous Balfour sought to compel her to accept him by making her promise of marriage vows the price of her father's reprieve from projected hanging.*

It is a less well-built work of fiction than Mellichampe. *Its relative structural inferiority is reflected in the lesser appropriateness of its title. While Ernest Mellichampe is actually the central figure of the novel entitled for him, Katharine occupies too small a proportion of the pages*

*of the next novel to make it really well-named. Other matters detailed
at length include Robert's activities as a spy; his friendship for a young
British officer, Proctor, whom he induces to come to sympathize with
the American cause; a subordinate love affair, of Proctor and Ella Monk-
ton; elaborate depiction of the doings of society in Charleston; and
finally and fortunately, extensive passages featuring Captain Porgy.*

Despite its relative lack of unity, Katharine Walton *is a more valuable novel than* Mellichampe. *Its richer historical relevancy makes it
more interesting. Its much greater attention to Porgy is enough to give
it higher rank; indeed next to* Woodcraft *itself, this is the novel revealing
the largest number of facets of his personality. Characters dear in his
book to Porgy are here introduced first, or developed further; and many
of his discourses and actions seem actually designed as groundwork for
what he does in the book Simms made just for him. Finally there is,
I believe, a psychological connection between the very presence of Porgy,
though he is some twenty miles away at all times, with the fact that
some, though not all, of the Charleston drawing room incidents reveal
in Simms a real talent for social comedy. (My idea is based on a suggestion made by Davidson,* Letters, *I, xlix.)*

*Never once did Porgy come near the town houses and gardens of
Charleston in these war times. He was out at Marion's camp, not shirk-
ing his share of the fighting, and especially employed in feeding the men.
Young Lance had just distinguished himself by shooting a splendid deer
with his bow and arrow. While some of the men were busy making
more arrows, four persons "were busy in preparations of another sort."*

The carcass of a fine buck lay between them, and two of the party
were already preparing to cut him up. One of these persons with arms
bare to the elbows, flourished a monstrous *couteau de chasse,* with the
twofold air of a hero and a butcher. This was a portly person of the
most formidable dimensions, with an abdominal development that might
well become an alderman. He had evidently a taste for the work before
him. How he measured the brisket! how he felt for the fat! with what
an air of satisfaction he heaved up the huge haunches of the beast! and
how his little gray eyes twinkled through the voluminous and rosy
masses of his own great cheeks!

"I give it up!" he exclaimed to his companions. "There is no wound
except that of the arrow, and it has fairly passed through the body, and

was broken by the fall. I give it up! I will believe anything wonderful that you may tell me. You may all lie to me in safety. I have no more doubts on any subject. Everything's possible, probable, true hereafter, that happens. But that you, such a miserable sapling of a fellow as you Lance, should have sent this reed through such a beast—clean through —is enough to stagger any ordinary belief!"

The person addressed, a tall, slender lad, apparently not more than eighteen or nineteen, laughed good-naturedly, as, without other reply, he thrust forth his long, naked arm, and displayed, fold upon fold, the snaky ridges of his powerful muscles.

"Ay, I see you have the bone and sinew, and I suppose I must believe that you shot the deer, seeing that Barnett gives it up; but I suppose you were at butting distance. You had no occasion to draw bow at all. You used the arrow as a spear, and thrust it through the poor beast's vitals with the naked hand."

"Shot it, I swow, at full fifty-five yards distance! I stepped it off myself," was the reply of the person called Barnett.

"I give up! I will believe in any weapon that brings us such meat. Henceforth, boys, take your bows and arrows always. The Indian was a sensibler fellow than we gave him credit for. I never could have believed it till now; and when Singleton took it into his head to supply such weapons to our men, for the want of better, I thought him gone clean mad."

"Yet you heard his argument for it?" said Lance.

"No. I happen to hear nothing when I am hungry. I shouldn't hear you now, but for my astonishment, which got the better of my appetite for a few moments. I will hear nothing further. Use your knife, Lance; lay on, boy, and let's have a steak as soon as possible."

"Sha'n't we wait for the colonel?" said Lance.

"I wait for no colonels. I consider them when I consider the core *(corps)*. What a glorious creature!—fat an inch thick, and meat tender as a dove's bosom! Ah, I come back to the Cypress a new man! Here I am at home. The Santee did well enough; but there's a sweetness, a softness, a plumpness, a beauty about bird and beast along the Ashley, that you find in the same animals nowhere else. God bless my mother!"

"For what, in particular, lieutenant?"

"That she chose it for my birthplace. I shouldn't have been half the man I am born anywhere else; shouldn't have had such discriminating tastes, such a fine appetite, such a sense of the beautiful in nature."

And thus, talking and slashing, the corpulent speaker maintained the most unflagging industry, until the deer was fairly quartered, a portion transferred, in the shape of steaks, to the reeking coals, and the rest spread out upon a rude scaffolding to undergo the usual hunter-process of being cured, by smoking, for future use. The skin, meanwhile, was subjected to the careful cleansing and stretching of the successful hunter.

And then the whole party grouped themselves about the fire, each busy with his steak and hoe-cake. There was the redoubtable Lieutenant Porgy, and the youthful ensign, Lance Frampton, already known as the taker of the prey, and little Joey Barnett, and others, known briefly as Tom, Dick, and Harry; and others still, with their *noms de guerre,* such as Hard-Riding Dick, and Dusky Sam, and Clip-the-Can, and Black Fox, and Gray Squirrel: a merry crew, cool, careless, good-humored, looking, for all the world, like a gipsy encampment. Their costume, weapons, occupation; the wild and not ungraceful ease with which they threw their huge frames about the fire; the fire, with its great, drowsy smokes slowly ascending, and with the capricious jets of wind sweeping it to and fro amidst the circle; and the silent dogs, three in number, grouped at the feet of their masters, their great, bright eyes wistfully turned upward in momentary expectation of the fragment; all contributed to a picture as unique as any one might have seen once in merry old England, or, to this day, among the Zincali of Iberia.

"Ah, this is life!" said Lieutenant Porgy, as he supplied himself anew with a smoking morsel from the hissing coals. "I can live in almost any situation in which man can live at all, and do not object to the feminine luxuries of city life, in lieu of a better; but there is no meat like this, fresh from the coals, the owner of which hugged it to his living heart three hours ago. One feels free in the open air; and, at midnight, under the trees, a venison steak is something more than meat. It is food for thought. It provokes philosophy. My fancies rise. I could spread my wings for flight. I could sing—I feel like it now—and, so far as the will is concerned, I could make such music as would bring the very dead to life."

And the deep, sonorous voice of the speaker began to rise, and he would have launched out into some such music as the buffalo might be supposed to send forth, happening upon a fresh green flat of prairie, but that Lance Frampton interposed, in evident apprehension of the consequences.

"Don't, lieutenant; remember we're not more than a mile from the river road."

"Teach your grandmother to suck eggs! Am I a fool! Do I look like the person to give the alarm to the enemy? Shut up, lad, and be not presumptuous because you have shot a deer after the Indian fashion. Do you suppose that, even were we in safer quarters, I should attempt to sing with such a dry throat? I say, Hard-Riding Dick, is there any of that Jamaica in the jug?"

"It is a mere drop on a full stomach."

"Bring it forth. I like the savor of the jug."

And the jug was produced, and more than one calabash was seen elevated in the firelight; and the drop sufficed, in not unequal division, to improve the humor of the whole party.

"The supper without the song is more endurable," was the philosophy of Porgy, "than the song without the supper. With the one before the other, the two go happily together. Now it is the strangest thing in the world that, with such a desperate desire to be musical, I should not be able to turn a tune. But I can *act* a tune, my lads, as well as any of you; and, as we are not permitted to give breath to our desires and delights, let us play round as if we were singing. You shall observe me, and take up the chorus, each. Do you understand me?"

"Can't say I do," said Futtrell. "Let's hear."

"You were always a dull dog, Futtrell, though you are a singer. Now, look you, a good singer or a good talker, an orator or a musician of any kind, if he knows his business, articulates nothing, either in song or speech, that he does not *look,* even while he speaks or sings. Eloquence, in oratory or in music implies something more than ordinary speech. It implies passion, or such sentiments and feelings as stir up the passions. Now every fool knows that, if we feel the passion, so as to speak or sing it, we must *look* it too. Do you understand me now?"

"I think I do," was the slowly uttered response of Futtrell, looking dubiously.

"Very well. *I* take it that all the rest do, then, since you are about the dullest dog among us," was the complimentary rejoinder. "Now, then, I am going to sing. I will sing an original composition. I shall first begin by expressing anxiety, uneasiness, distress; these are incipient signs of hunger, a painful craving of the bowels, amounting to an absolute gnawing of the clamorous inhabitants within. This is the first part, continued till it almost becomes despair; the music then changes. I have seen the boys bringing in the deer. He lies beneath my knife. I am prepared to slaughter him. I feel that he is secure. I see that he will soon be boiling in choice bits upon the fire. I am no longer uneasy or apprehensive. The feeling of despair has passed. All is now hope, and exultation, and anticipation; and this is the sentiment which I shall express in the second part of the music. The third follows the feast. Nature is pacified; the young wolf-cubs within have retired to their kennels. They sleep without a dream, and a philosophical composure possesses the brain. I meditate themes of happiness. I speculate upon the immortality of the soul. I enter into an analysis of the several philosophies of poets, prophets, and others, in relation to the employments and enjoyments of the future; and my song subsides into a pleasant murmuring, a dreamy sort of ripple, such as is made by a mountain brooklet, when, after wearisome tumblings from crag to crag, it sinks at last into a quiet and barely lapsing watercourse, through a grove, the borders of which are crowded with flowers of the sweetest odor. Such, boys, shall be my song. You will note my action, and follow it, by way of chorus, as well as you can."

All professed to be at least willing to understand him, and our philosopher proceeded. Porgy was an actor. His social talent lay in the very sort of amusement which he now proposed to them. He has himself described the manner of his performance in the declared design. We shall not attempt to follow him; but may say that scarcely one of those wildly-clad foresters but became interested in his dumb show, which at length, became so animated that he leaped to his feet, in order the better to effect his action, and was only arrested in his performance by striding with his enormous bulk, set heavily down, upon the ribs of one of the unlucky dogs who lay by the fire. The yell that followed was as full of danger as the uttered song had been, and quite discomfited the performer. His indignation at the misplaced position of the dog might have resulted in the wilful application of his feet to the offending animal, but that, just then, the hootings of an owl were faintly heard rising in the distance, and answered by another voice more near.

"It is Moore," said Lance Frampton. "It is from above. We shall have the colonel here directly."

"Let him come," was the response of Porgy; but he is too late for the music. That confounded dog!"

The "owl" was actually a partisan scout, whose "hoots" indicated that Colonel Singleton was approaching through the trees. Porgy had saved some supper for his colonel, and urged him to try the venison steak. Singleton admitted he liked steak cooked out in the woods better than dishes from the "fashionable kitchen," but declined because he had already eaten his evening meal.

"You must certainly *taste* of the meat, colonel," was the response of Porgy, "if only because of the manner in which it was killed—with bow and arrow."

"Indeed! Who was the hunter?"

"Lance! You know I laughed when you spoke of bows and arrows for our men. I confess I thought it monstrous foolish to adopt such weapons. But I am beginning to respect the weapon. What put you in the notion of it, colonel?"

"We had neither shot nor powder, if you recollect."

Singleton continued with an informative defense of the bow and arrow, with which in the time of Henry VII the English could slay at four hundred yards. There were advantages even now, as with such weapons one never lacked ammunition in the woods; and the silent shots did not give away the bowsman's location. He wanted to prepare his men, as the time might come when the bow and arrow might be their only weapon.

Singleton then took Porgy aside to assign him a mission—to take a party of soldiers to keep watch at a point on the road leading inland from Dorchester.

"Is there anything more, Colonel Singleton, in the way of instructions?"

"Nothing."

"Then let me have a word, colonel; and you will excuse me if I speak quite as much as a friend as a subordinate."

"My dear Porgy——"

"Ah, colonel——"

"Let me say, once for all, that I regard you as a comrade always, and this implies as indulgent a friendship as comports with duty."

"Do I not know it? I thank you! I thank you from the bottom of my heart!—and I have a heart, Singleton—by Apollo, I have a heart, though the rascally dimensions of my stomach may sometimes interfere with it. And now to the matter. I am concerned about you. I am."

"How?"

"As a soldier, and a brave one, of course you know that you are liable to be killed at any moment. A wilful bullet, a sweeping sword-stroke, or the angry push of a rusty bayonet, in bad hands, may disturb as readily the functions of the bowels in a colonel as in a lieutenant. For either of these mischances, the professional soldier is supposed, at all times, to be prepared; and I believe that we both go to our duties without giving much heed to the contingencies that belong to them."

"I am sure that *you* do, lieutenant."

"Call me Porgy, colonel, if you please, while we speak of matters aside from business. If I am proud of anything, it is of the affections of those whom I esteem."

"Go on, Porgy."

"Now, my dear colonel, that you should die by bullet, broadsword, or bayonet, is nothing particularly objectionable, considering our vocation. It may be something of an inconvenience to you, physically; but it is nothing that your friends should have reason to be ashamed of. But to die by the halter, Colonel Singleton—to wear a knotted handkerchief of hemp—to carry the knot beneath the left ear—throwing the head awkwardly on the opposite side, instead of covering with it the Adam's apple—to be made the fruit of the tree against the nature of the tree—to be hitched into cross-grained timbers, against the grain—to die the death of a dog, after living the life of a man—this, sir, would be a subject of great humiliation to all your friends, and must, I take it, be a subject of painful consideration to yourself."

"Very decidedly, Porgy," was the reply of the other, with a good-natured laugh.

"Why will you incur the dangers of such a fate? This is what your friends have a right to ask. Why put yourself, bound, as it were, hand and foot, in the keeping of these redcoated Philistines, who would truss you up at any moment to a swinging limb with as little remorse as the male alligator exhibits when he swallows a hecatomb of his own kidney.

Why linger at Dorchester, or at 'The Oaks,' with this danger perpetually staring you in the face? There are few men at 'The Oaks,' and the place is badly guarded. The force at Dorchester itself is not so great but that, with Col. Walton's squadron, we might attempt it. Say the word, and, in forty-eight hours, we can harry both houses; and if swinging must be done by somebody, for the benefit of 'The Oaks' hereafter, why, in God's name, let it be a British or a Hessian carcass instead of one's own. I might be persuaded, in the case of one of these bloody heathens, to think the spectacle a comely one. But in your case, colonel, as I am living man, it would take away my appetite for ever."

"Nay, Porgy, you overrate the danger."

"Do I! Not a bit. I tell you these people are getting desperate. Their cruelties are beginning only; and for this reason, that they find the state unconquered. So long as there is a single squad like ours between the Pedee and the Savannah, so long is there a hope for us and a hate for them. Hear to me, colonel, and beware! There is deadly peril in the risks which you daily take."

"I know that there is risk, Porgy; but there are great gains depending upon these risks, and they must be undertaken by somebody. Our spies undertake such risks daily."

"A spy is a spy, colonel, and nothing but a spy. He was born to a spy's life and a spy's destiny. He knows his nature and the end of his creation, and he goes to his end as to a matter of obligation. He includes the price of the halter, and the inconvenience of strangulation, in the amount which he charges for the duty to be done. But we who get no pay at all, and fight for the fun and the freedom of the thing only—there's no obligation upon us to assume the duty of another, at the risk of making a bad picture, and feeling uncomfortable in our last moments. No law of duty can exact of me that I shall not only die, but die of rope, making an unhandsome corse, with my head awfully twisted from the centre of gravity, where only it could lie at ease! My dear colonel, think of this! Say the word! and fight, scout, or only scrimmage, we'll share all risks with you, whether the word be 'Oaks' or 'Dorchester!'"

"The peril will be soon over, Porgy. Three days will end it, in all probability; and, in that time, the same prudence which has kept me safe so long will probably prevail to secure me to the end. Have no fears—and do not forget that you can always strike in at the last moment.

Your scouts see all that goes on, and, in a moment of danger, you know the signal."

"Be it so! we're ready! Still I could wish it otherwise. But, by the way, talking of what we see, there's something that Bostwick has to tell you. He was stationed between 'The Oaks' and 'Dorchester' during the afternoon, and came in soon after dark. Here, Bostwick!"—and as the fellow came out of the front to the place where the two had been conversing, Porgy continued:—

"The colonel wants to hear of you what took place between the commandant of the post of Dorchester, Major Vaughan, and the chunky red faced fellow, whom you did not know."

Bostwick (one of the villains of Woodcraft) *told of catching Proctor's servant betraying his master to his personal enemy Vaughan.*

A day or so later a British wagon train under the command of Lieutenant Meadows came along the road from Dorchester headed for Camden. Singleton was with the British disguised as a loyalist officer named Furness, who was being held captive by the Americans. As the British approached the place where Singleton had ordered Porgy to take a station, Singleton galloped ahead and heard the owl signal. The onslaught of the partisans began as the confused British cried "Marion's men!" Meadows was surrounded as the partisans, in dark green or blue, under the command of Porgy, showed up among the trees. Meadows wheeled his steed and confronted a group which was just coming out of cover.

He clapped spurs to his steed and met the leader of the assailants, who, on foot, had reached the open road-space, and was entirely withdrawn from the shelter of the thicket. This person was no other than our epicurean friend, Lieutenant Porgy, who, with an audacity quite inconsistent with his extreme obesity, advanced with sword uplifted to the encounter with the British lieutenant. A single clash of swords, and the better-tempered steel of the Englishman cut sheer through the inferior metal of the American, sending one half of the shattered blade into the air and descending upon the cheek of Porgy, inflicting a slight gash, and taking off the tip of his ear. Another blow might have been fatal. Meadows had recovered from the first movement, and his blade was already whirled aloft for the renewal of the stroke, when Porgy, drawing a pistol from his belt, shot the horse of his enemy through the head. The animal fell suddenly upon his knees, and then rolled over perfectly dead. The sword of Meadows struck harmlessly upon the earth, he himself being pinioned to the ground by one of his legs, upon which the dead animal lay. In this predicament, vainly endeavoring to wield and to use his sword, he threatened Porgy at his approach. The latter, still grasping his own broken weapon, which was reduced to the hilt and some eight inches only of the blade, totally undeterred by the demonstration of the Briton, rushed incontinently upon him, and, in a totally unexpected form of attack, threw his gigantic bulk over the body of the prostrate Meadows, whom he completely covered. The other struggled fiercely beneath, and, getting his sword-arm free, made several desperate efforts to use his weapon; but Porgy so completely bestraddled him that he succeeded only in inflicting some feeble strokes upon the broad shoulders of the epicure, who requited them with a severe blow upon the mouth with the iron hilt of his broken sword.

"It's no use, my fine fellow; your faith may remove mountains, but your surrender only shall remove me. You are captive to my bow and spear. Halloo ' 'nough!' now, if you wish for mercy."

And, stretching himself out on every hand, with arms extended and legs somewhat raised on the body of the dead horse Porgy looked down into the very eyes of his prisoner; his great beard, meanwhile, well sprinkled with gray, lying in masses upon the mouth and filling the nostrils of the Englishman, who was thus in no small danger of suffocation.

"Will nobody relieve me from this elephant?" gasped the half-strangled Meadows.

"Elephant!" roared Porgy. "By the powers, but you shall feel my grinders!"

His good humor was changed to gall by the offensive expression, and he had already raised the fragment of his broken sword, meaning to pummell the foe into submission, when his arm was arrested by Singleton, now appearing in his appropriate character and costume. Meadows was extricated from horse and elephant at the same moment, and by the same friendly agency, and rose from the ground sore with bruises, and panting with heat and loss of breath.

"It is well for him, Colonel Singleton, that you made your appearance. I had otherwise beaten him to a mummy. Would you believe it? —he called me an elephant! Me! Me an elephant!"

"He had need to do so, lieutenant; and this was rather a compliment than otherwise to your mode of warfare. He felt yours to be a power comparable only to the mighty animal to which he had reference. It was the natural expression of his feelings, I am sure, and not by way of offence."

"I forgive him," was the response of Porgy, as he listened to this explanation.

"Colonel Singleton, I believe, sir?" said Meadows, tendering his sword. "The fortune of the day is yours, sir. Here is my sword. I am Lieutenant Meadows, late in command of this detachment."

Singleton restored the weapon graciously, and addressed a few courteous sentences to his prisoner; but, by this time, Porgy discovered that his ear had lost a thin but important slice from its pulpy extremity. His annoyance was extreme, and his anger rose as he discovered the full nature of his loss.

"Sir—Lieutenant Meadows," said he—"you shall give me personal satisfaction for this outrage the moment you are exchanged. You have done me an irreparable injury! You have marked me for life, sir—given me the brand of a horse-thief—taken off one of my ears! One of my ears!"

"Not so, my dear lieutenant," said Singleton. "Only the smallest possible tip from the extremity. Once healed it will never be seen. There is no sort of deformity. You were rather *full* in that quarter, and could spare something of the development."

"Were I sure of that!"

"It is so, believe me. The thing will never be observed."

"To have one's ears or nose slit, sir"—to the Briton—"is, I have always been taught, the greatest indignity that could be inflicted upon a gentleman."

"I am sorry, sir," said Meadows—"very sorry. But it was the fortune of war. Believe me, I had no idea of making such a wound."

"I can understand that, sir. You were intent only in taking off my head. I am satisfied that you did not succeed in that object, since, next to losing my ear, I should have been particularly uncomfortable at the loss of my head. But, if my ear had been maimed, sir, I should have had my revenge. And even now, should there really be a perceptible deficiency, there shall be more last blows between us."

The British lieutenant bowed, politely, as if to declare his readiness to afford any necessary satisfaction, but said nothing in reply. Singleton suffered the conversation to go no farther; but, drawing Porgy aside, rebuked him for the rude manner of his address to a man whose visage he himself had marked for life.

"You have laid his mouth open, broken his teeth, and injured his face for ever; and he a young fellow, too, probably unmarried, to whom unbroken features are of the last importance."

"But my dear colonel, think of my ear; fancy it smitten in two, as I did, and you will allow for all my violence. The mark of the pillory ought to suffice to make any white man desperate."

It is probable that Meadows, when he became aware of the true state of his mouth, and felt his own disfigurements, was even more unforgiving than Porgy.

Among the partisan casualties was Walter Griffin, a brave soldier whose daughter Ellen was loved by Lance. The mortally wounded Griffin, in his dying words, gave Lance his watch and two guineas (to which Singleton added eight), asking the young man to take them and a letter to his wife and daughter. While Lance grieved deeply, Griffin was buried. Most of the men then rested.

Two of the partisans, however, were drawn aside by Singleton for farther conference that night. These were Lieutenant Porgy and the young ensign, Lance Frampton. To these he assigned a double duty. With a small detachment, Porgy was to take charge of a wagon with stores, designed for Colonel Walton, whom he was to seek out between the Edisto and the Savannah. In order to effect his progress with safety, he was specially counselled to give a wide birth to Dorchester—to make a considerable circuit above, descending only when on the Edisto. Singleton was rightly apprehensive that the report of Meadows' disaster would set all the cavalry of Dorchester and Charleston in motion. The wagon was to be secured in the swamps of Edisto until Walton could be found; and, with the duty of delivering it into his keeping fairly executed, Porgy, with Frampton, was to seek out the dwelling of Griffin's wife and daughter, who dwelt in the neighborhood of the Edisto, conveying a letter from his colonel, and the little treasure of which the poor fellow died possessed—Singleton having added the eight guineas which he had promised to the dying man; a gift, by the way, which he could not have made but for the timely acquisition of the hundred and fifty found in the British money-chest.

The duty thus assigned to Porgy and Frampton was one of interest to both parties; though the corpulent lieutenant sighed at the prospect of hard riding over ground so recently compassed which lay before him. At first he would have shirked the responsibility; but a secret suggestion of his own thought rapidly caused a change in his opinions. To Lance Frampton, who stood in a very tender relation to Ellen Griffin, the daughter of the deceased, the task was one equally painful and grateful. To Porgy, the interest which he felt was due to considerations the development of which must be left to future chapters.

Two hundred pages, many depicting war time society doings in Charleston, follow, before we rejoin Porgy and Lance on their latest mission.

WIDOWS THE BEST MATERIAL FOR WIVES.

It was noon of the day which has thus been distinguished by the rescue of Williamson and the capture of Colonel Walton, when two horsemen might have been seen slowly riding in a southerly direction, on the route between the Edisto and the Combahee rivers. They were both well mounted and armed; the one who seemed the leader carrying sword by side, and pistols in his holsters; the other, in addition to pistols, having a neat, well-polished, and short rifle, lying across the pummel of his saddle. In the portly person and fresh, florid features of the former, we recognise Lieutenant Porgy, of Singleton's command: in the latter the young ensign, Lance Frampton.

If the reader has not forgotten some former passages in this true history, he will find it easy to account for the presence of these two personages in this neighborhood, at the present juncture. It has probably not been forgotten, that, soon after the defeat which Singleton had given to Lieutenant Meadows, and the capture of that officer and of his convoy, the former commissioned these two officers, Porgy and Frampton, to convey a baggage-wagon, with supplies, to the camp of Colonel Walton. As this camp was known to be erratic—as was usually the case among the partisans of any experience—the duty thus assigned them implied delay, difficulty, a tedious search, and the exercise of a constant caution. Lieutenant Porgy was instructed to take his wagon with as much despatch as was consistent with secresy, to the cover of the swamps of the Edisto, on the west side of that river; to leave it there in conceal-

ment, with a portion of his detachment, and then, himself, with Frampton, to proceed in search of the squadron of Walton. There was yet
another duty, if we recollect, which was assigned, at the same time,
to this officer and his young companion. This was to seek out the
widow of Walter Griffin, one of the soldiers of Singleton, who had fallen
in the engagement with the troop of Meadows, and to convey to her
and her daughter the tidings of his death and burial, together with his
effects, and a certain amount in English guineas, which Singleton was
fortunate enough to gather from the treasure-chest of Meadows, and
which he promptly shared among his followers.

This latter duty was properly confided in part to Frampton. He
might now be considered almost a member of Griffin's family; the tender
interest which he felt in Ellen, the fair daughter of the latter, having
received from Griffin, while he lived, every sanction, and being generally
supposed equally agreeable to the young damsel herself. The melancholy
part of his task, therefore, was not without its compensative considerations, and no one could better express the language of sympathy and
regret than one who was thus necessarily a sharer in the misfortune.
Nor, according to his own notions, was Lieutenant Porgy himself improperly assigned a portion of this duty. This excellent epicure had his
own secret. He had a selfish reason for his readiness to undertake a
search like the present, which, but for this reason, would have brought
him annoyance only. But we must leave it to himself and the sagacity
of the reader to unfold this secret motive as we proceed.

We need not very closely follow the footsteps of Porgy and his party,
from the moment when they left Ravenel's plantation on the Santee,
and proceeded to the Edisto. Porgy was a man nearly as full of prudence
as plethora. He was luxurious, but he was vigilant; fond of good things,
but neglectful of no duty in seeking them. He succeeded in conveying
his baggage-wagon in safety to the spot destined for its hiding-place, in
the swamp-thickets of the Edisto. Here he left it in charge of Lieutenant
Davis, a shrewd and practised ranger. This done, he set out, as we have
seen, with Ensign Frampton, with the twofold object of finding Colonel
Walton and the widow Griffin.

Of the former, the party had been able to hear nothing by which
to guide their progress. He was supposed to be ranging somewhere
between the Salkehatchie and the Savannah. In the route now pursued,
they had the widow Griffin in view, rather than the partisan. Frampton

knew where she dwelt, and it was hoped that, on reaching her abode, some intelligence might be obtained from her of Walton. The two had accordingly taken a bee line from the swamps of Edisto for the humble farmstead of the widow, and at noon of the day in question might probably be some ten miles from it. But they had ridden fast and far that morning, and when, after crossing a brooklet, or *branch,* which gushed, bright and limpid, across the high road, Frampton exclaimed— "It's only nine miles and a skip; we could make it easy in two hours, lieutenant;"—the other answered with a growl that singularly resembled an imprecation. "Only nine miles!" repeated Frampton, urgently.

"And if it were only three, master Lance, I would not budge a rod farther until I had seen our wallet emptied. No, no! young master, you must learn a better lesson. Never do you hurry, even if it be on the road to happiness. No man enjoys life who gallops through it. Take it slowly; stop frequently by the way, and look about you. He who goes ahead ever, passes a treasure on both sides which he never finds coming back. By pausing, resting, looking about you, and medi- tating, you secure the ground you have gained, and acquire strength to conquer more. Many a man, through sheer impatience, has swam for the shore, and sunk just when it rose in sight. Had the fool turned on his back and floated for an hour, the whole journey would have been safe and easy. If you please, master Lance, we'll turn upon our backs for an hour. I have an appetite just now. If I fail to satisfy it, I lose it till to-morrow, and the loss is irretrievable. There is some jerked beef in your wallet, I think, and a few biscuit. We will turn up this branch, the water of which is cool and clear, put ourselves in a close, quiet place in the woods, and pacify the domestic tiger."

The young ensign, eager, impatient, and not hungry, was compelled to subdue his desire to hurry forward. He knew that argument, at this hour, and under these circumstances, with his superior, was vain. He submitted accordingly without further expostulation, and with a proper grace; and, riding ahead, ascended a little elevation, which led him, still following the winding of the creek, to a cool, shady, and retired spot some two hundred yards from the roadside. He was closely followed by his more bulky companion; and, dismounting, stripping their horses, and suffering them to graze, they prepared to enjoy the frugal provision which was afforded by the leathern wallet which the young man carried. This was soon spread out upon the turf; and, letting himself down

with the deliberation of a buffalo about to retire for the night, Lieutenant Porgy prepared for the discussion of his dinner.

It was scarcely such as would satisfy either the tastes or appetites of
epicurism. Porgy growled as he ate. The beef was hard and black, sun-
dried and sapless. The biscuits were of corn-meal, coarse, stale, and not
palatable even to the hungry man. But the tiger was earnest, and the
food rapidly disappeared. Frampton ate but little. His heart was too
full of excited hopes to suffer his appetite to prevail. It would be doing
injustice to Porgy to suppose that he was glad to behold this abstinence.
Though fully equal, himself, to the consumption of the slender provision before them, he was sincerely urgent that the youth should feed.

"Why don't you fall to, boy! Do you suppose there's not enough
for both? Eat, I say! You've done nothing worth the name of eating
since last night. Eat! I know I'm a beast, seeking what I may devour,
but understand, that I regard you as one of my cubs, and will see you
feed, even before I do myself. Take that other biscuit, and there's the
beef. Cut, slash—it will need a sharp knife, and sharper teeth to get
at the merits of that bull's quarter."

Frampton complied, or seemed to comply with the command. Meanwhile, Porgy ate on, growling all the while.

"This is life, with a vengeance, and I *must* be a patriot if I stand
it much longer! Nothing seems to agree with me! Hand me the bottle,
Lance, and run down to the branch with the cup. I believe I should
perish utterly, but for the little seasoning of Jamaica which is left. Ah!"
looking at the small remains of the liquor in the bottle, "it is now only
what the poet calls the drop of sweetening in the draught of care."

"But if it be a draught of care, lieutenant," said Lance archly, taking
up the cup, and moving toward the branch, "why do you drink of it
so often?"

"So often! When, I pray you, have I drank of it before, to-day?"

"Only three miles back, at the Green Branch."

"Oh! I drank three miles back, at the Green Branch, did I? Well, it
was the cup of Lethe to me, since I certainly forgot all about it."

"There couldn't have been much bitterness in the draught lieutenant,
or the taste would still be in your mouth. But, have you forgotten the
other cupful at Swan's Meadows, about nine miles back?"

"Do you call that a draught, you ape of manhood, when you know
that the Jamaica was just employed to precipitate the cursed clayey sedi-

ment of that vile mill-pond water? Get you gone, and bring the water. This *is* good water, and I will have a draught now, a genuine cupful; since the others were only calculated to provoke the thirst and mortify the desire. Away!"

The boy soon returned with the water. The worthy epicure refreshed his inner man; threw himself back upon the green turf, under the pleasant shade-trees, and seemed deeply engaged in meditating the merit of his performances. Lance Frampton crouched quietly on the opposite side of the tree, and, for a little while, neither party spoke. At length Porgy, with whom taciturnity was never a cherished virtue, broke the silence.

"Lance, my boy, you are beginning life monstrous early."

"How so, lieutenant?"

"When do you propose to marry this little girl, Ellen Griffin?"

"Well, sir, I can't say. It's as she pleases."

"Pshaw, fool, it's as *you* please. When a girl consents to be married, she's ready to be married. Lay that down as a law. The consent to marry implies everything; and all then depends upon the man."

"Perhaps——"

"Perhaps! I tell you it *is* so, and more than that, I feel pretty sure that unless you are picked up by a British bayonet or bullet, you'll marry before the war is over."

"I should like it, I own, lieutenant."

"No doubt; no doubt; and you are right. I begin to think that marriage is a good thing. I have wasted many years unprofitably. How many women might I have made happy had my thoughts led me this way before. But I may yet do some good in this behalf before I die. I must marry soon, if ever."

"You, sir!" with something like surprise.

"Ay, to be sure! why not? am I too old, jackanapes?"

"Oh! not a bit, lieutenant!"

"Well! what then? what's to prevent? You don't suppose that I'm fool enough to think of marrying a slight, fanciful, inexperienced thing, such as you desire. The ripe, sir, not the green fruit, for me. I require a woman who has some knowledge of life; who is skilled in house-keeping; who can achieve successes in the culinary department; who knows the difference between hash and haggis, and can convert a terrapin into a turtle, by sheer dexterity in shaking the spice box. There is another quality which a woman of this description is likely to possess, and that is a due and reverent sense of her husband's authority. It is because of her deference for this authority that she acquires her art. She has learned duly to study his desires and his tastes, and she submits her judgment to his own. She waits to hear his opinion of the soup, and is always ready to promise that she will do better next time. I feel that I could be happy with such a woman."

"No doubt, sir."

"The difficulty is in finding such. There are precious few women who combine all the necessary qualities. They are not often native. They come from training. A wise father, or a wise husband, will make such a woman; she can not make herself. Were I, for example, the husband of a girl such as your Ellen—"

"My Ellen, sir!"

"Oh! don't be alarmed, boy; I have no idea of such a folly! But were I the husband even of such a young and inexperienced creature, and did we live together but ten years; were I then to die, she would be a prize for any man. She should be as absolutely perfect as it is possible with one of a sex, a part of whose best merits depend very much upon their imperfections. Now, this leads me to the reflection that, perhaps, widows are, after all, the best materials out of which to make good wives; always assuming that they have been fortunate in the possession of husbands like myself, who have been able to show them the proper paths to follow, and who have had the will to keep them always well in the traces. I am clearly of the opinion that widows afford the very best material out of which to manufacture wives."

"Indeed, sir."

"Yes indeed! my widow would be a treasure for any man; and if I could only find the widow of a man who in some respects resembled myself, I should commit matrimony."

"Commit!—when you said that, lieutenant, I thought murder was to be the next word, instead of matrimony."

"Did you! You are getting humorous in your old age, my son."

There was a pause, after this, of several minutes: but Porgy resumed, apparently taking up a new topic entirely.

"Poor Griffin! What a loss he must be to his wife! Poor woman! I do pity her! I liked Griffin, Lance. He was very much a person of my own tastes; not so refined, perhaps, not so copious or various, but with an evident tendency my way. Nobody in camp relished my terrapin soup half so well, and, for an ordinary stew, he was admirable himself. We once compared notes for our dressings, and it surprised us both to discover that our ingredients and the quantities were, almost to a fraction, the very same. I liked the poor fellow from that very hour, and he, I think, had quite a liking for me."

"That he had, lieutenant!"

"I am pleased to think so, Lance. Many of his other qualities resembled mine. He was generous, and spent his property in too great a hurry to see which way it went. He was a man of character, and detested all hypocrisy. He was a man of will, and when he put his foot down, there it stuck. It was law. I have not the slightest doubt that poor Mrs. Griffin is an admirably-trained woman."

There was a pause, in which Porgy himself rose, took his cup and bottle and went down to the brooklet, saying—"Thinking of poor Griffin, I will drink to his memory."

He soon returned and resumed the subject, somewhat, we should fancy, to the annoyance of his companion.

"I am of opinion, Lance, that Mrs. Griffin, when a girl, must have greatly resembled your Ellen. She has exactly the same eyes and hair, the same mouth and chin, and, allowing for the natural portliness of a woman of thirty-five, very much the same figure. She is a fine-looking woman now; and in her you will be gratified to see what her daughter will be twenty years hence. If she has trained her as she herself has been trained, you will have every reason to be satisfied. Did you ever observe, when Mrs. Griffin was in camp with us on the Santee, how frequently I dined in Griffin's mess? Well, it was in tribute to her excellent merit in preparing the dinner. Her husband shared the labor, it is true, and I sometimes contributed my counsel as an amateur. This, no doubt, helped her very much; but that should not be allowed to disparage her real merits, since, to be satisfied to submit to good counsellors, shows a degree of wisdom, such as ordinary women seldom arrive at. Poor woman! how I pity her! How such a woman, so meekly dependent upon her husband, can endure widowhood, is very problematical!"

There was another pause, Lance Frampton being heard to turn uneasily behind the tree, when Porgy resumed—

"Yes! the truth is not to be denied. I have been quite too selfish! I might have made many a woman happy—I might have carried consolation to the heart of many a suffering widow! I have lived thus long in vain. I must make amends. I must sink myself, in the sense of duty!—Come, Lance, saddle the horses, lad, and let us be riding."

GRIEF—BACON AND EGGS.

In less than two hours, our companions reached the humble farmstead which the widow Griffin occupied. The dwelling was a poor cabin of logs, with but two rooms, such as was common enough about the country. The tract of land, consisting of two hundred acres, was ample for so small a family. This property, with a few head of cattle, a score of hogs, several of which lay grunting in the road in front of the entrance, and other trifling assets, were the bequest of a brother, a cripple, who died but a few months before, and whom Mrs. Griffin, with her daughter, had gone from the camp of Marion to attend in his last illness. The place had a very cheerless aspect. The fences were dismantled, the open spots of field grown up in weeds, and some patches of corn, from which the fruit had been partially stripped already, stripped, indeed, as it ripened—added rather to the cold and discouraging appearance of the place.

Our companions did not, at once, and boldly, ride up to the habitation. They were too well practised as partisans for such an indiscretion. When within half a mile of the dwelling, they turned into the woods, made a partial *detour,* and while Porgy remained under cover, Lance Frampton stole forward, on foot, to reconnoitre. The horses, meanwhile, were both fastened in the thicket.

Lance was absent about a quarter of an hour only, but long enough to make his superior quite impatient. The youth, though eager to gain the cottage, was yet too well trained to move incautiously. He had carefully sheltered himself in his approach, as well as he could, by the cover of contiguous trees. These had been allowed to grow almost to the eaves of the building, in front and rear, affording an excellent protection from the sun, which, as the house was without a piazza, was absolutely necessary for comfort in such a climate.

The door was open in the rear of the building, and the first glimpses of it showed Lance the person of his pretty sweetheart, sitting just within it, busily engaged with the needle. The youth, his heart beating more than ever quickly, glided forward with increased stealthiness of tread, in the hope to surprise her. To creep beside the building, until he had nearly reached the doorway, and then, with his cheek against the wall, to murmur her name, was the simple art he used. She started, with a slight cry, at once of pleasure and astonishment, and exclaimed—

"Oh! Lance! Is it you? How you scared me!"

"I did not mean to scare you, Ellen."

"To surprise me so," continued the girl: "and I without stockings on;" and with a blush, she drew the delicately-formed white feet beneath her dress, but not before the eye of the youth had rested upon their whiteness.

"And how's father? where did you leave him?"

Lance was silent. The gravity of his face at her question did not escape her. She spoke eagerly—

"He's well, Lance, ain't he?"

"Where's your mother, Ellen?"

"In the room." She pointed to the chamber.

"Well, I must go and report to Lieutenant Porgy. *He's* here. He's got letters for your mother. There's been no British or tories about?"

"Yes: they've been about, I hear. Some passed up yesterday, by the other road. But all's safe hereabouts now, I reckon."

"I'll run, then, and bring the lieutenant. He'll be mighty tired of waiting."

"But you haven't told me about father, Lance."

"No!" said he, hesitatingly, "the lieutenant will tell you all."

"But he's well, Lance—he's well? You haven't had any fighting, have you!"

"Wait awhile, Ellen," he answered as he hastened away, and his evasion of the inquiry at once alarmed the quick instincts of the girl. She called immediately to her mother.

"Oh! mother, there's news from camp, and I'm afeard it's bad news."

"Bad news! Ellen," answered the mother, coming forth.

"I'm afeard; for Lance has just been here, and, when I asked him about father, he would tell me nothing, but has gone off to call Lieutenant Porgy, who is here too in the woods."

"Lance wouldn't bring bad news, Ellen."

"Not if he could help it, mother; but why didn't he answer me when I asked after father; and why did he say that Lieutenant Porgy would tell us all?"

"Lieutenant Porgy—he's here too?" said the mother, smoothing her cap and apron. "If it was bad news, Ellen, we'd hear it soon enough. It's never slow to travel when it's bad."

"I'm sure father's hurt; something's the matter. They've had a battle; and why didn't he write?"

"Well, I don't know; but maybe he did write."

"But, if he did, wouldn't Lance have brought the letter the first thing?"

"Maybe the lieutenant's got it! Don't be foolish, Ellen. I don't think Lance would be the one to come with bad news."

"Oh! I know he'd be sorry to do so; but, mother, he looked sorry enough when I asked about father, and he spoke so little."

"Come, child, you're always thinking of the cloud before it comes! That's not right. Go, now, and look up something for Lance and the Lieutenant to eat. I reckon they'll be precious hungry. Put on a pot of *hominy* at once, and kindle up the fire, and get down the gourd of eggs, while I slice off some of that bacon. I don't think there's any bad news. I don't feel like it! God knows we've had sorrow enough to last us now for a long time, and I ain't willing to believe that we're to suffer any more on a sudden. Come in, Ellen, and stir yourself; that's the way to lose the feel of trouble. Don't be looking out for *them*"— meaning the men—"it don't look quite proper for a young girl, Ellen."

"Oh! mother, how can you——"

The sentence remained unfinished. The girl obeyed, and was soon busied with the domestic preparations which the mother had suggested. The pot of hominy was soon upon the fire, the eggs laid out upon the table, and Mrs. Griffin herself, with a somewhat unsteady hand, prepared to cut from the shoulder of bacon the requisite number of slices. She was interrupted while thus employed, by the arrival of the expected guests. Her agitation, when she received them, was not less great, though less conspicuous than that of her daughter. The poor woman seemed to fancy that a certain degree of hardihood was essential to proper dignity. It is, indeed, a characteristic of humble life among the people of the forest country of the south and southwest, to assume an appearance of stoicism under grief, in which they resemble the Indian; appearing to consider it a weakness of which they have reason to be ashamed, when they give vent to their natural emotions under affliction. In like manner, it is their habit to suppress very much their show of impatience, particularly when they are conscious of an active and growing curiosity. Mrs. Griffin felt fully the anxieties of her daughter, but her training was superior to the nature which strove within her. She met her visitors with the air of one who had nothing to fear; and, that she really felt anxiety, was to be seen entirely in the measured and cold manner with which she welcomed them.

"I'm glad to see you, Lance. I'm sure you're welcome, lieutenant; sit down. You must be mighty tired with your long ride in this hot weather."

"Tired and hungry, and thirsty and sleepy, all together, Mrs. Griffin, I assure you. And how is Miss Ellen? has she no welcome for an old friend?" was the reply of Porgy.

The girl, who had hitherto hung back, now advanced and put her hand shyly within his grasp, but said nothing.

"Ah! you are still as bashful and still as pretty as ever, my little damsel. Don't be shy of me, my dear creature. I need not tell you that I am old enough to be your father; and I feel that I could love you like a father. You would hardly think, but I have a heart full of the milk of human kindness. It might have been better, perhaps, for me, in a mere worldly point of view, had I less. But I am content. The feelings which I possess are more precious to me than vaults of gold and wagons of silver." He released her hand as he spoke this, and, addressing Mrs. Griffin, proceeded as if the girl were no longer in hearing.

"Ah! madam, what a treasure to you to have such a child as that. She is all gentleness and sweetness, and all duty, I am sure."

"She is, indeed, a blessed child. There are few like her, Lieutenant Porgy."

Ellen stopped not to listen to her own praises thus began, but stole out, closely followed by Frampton. Porgy, obeying the repeated request of his hostess, proceeded to take a seat, while the good woman, having finished slicing her bacon, and thrown it into the frying-pan, laid the implement upon the table conveniently beside the eggs, and, having looked at the pot of hominy, giving it a stir, and pushing up the brands beneath it, drew a chair near the fireplace, and, folding her hands in her lap, assumed, unavoidably the look of a person in waiting and expectation.

The lieutenant surveyed her curiously as she sat thus, her eyes bent upon the ground, and only raised occasionally to look at the fire. Mrs.

Griffin was a comely woman, not much beyond the middle period of life, and, as thus she sat, plainly, but neatly dressed, with a face smooth yet, and fair, and with the bloom of health upon her cheeks, our lieutenant inwardly said—

"Verily, the woman is well to look upon."

His conviction took a somewhat different shape when put into words.

"Mrs. Griffin, you are very comfortable here; that is, you might be, with health and youth, and a pleasant abode—one that may be made so, certainly—but, don't you find it very lonesome?"

"I'm used to it, lieutenant."

"Yes, indeed; and that is fortunate. To be accustomed to lonesomeness is to be independent, in some degree, of the changes of life. Solitude, once familiar to the mind, ceases to be oppressive; and who is sure against solitude? We may have a large number of relatives and friends, but what is to secure us against the chance of losing them? We may have a full house to-day, and all shall be silent and cheerless to-morrow. Such are life's vicissitudes. It is fortunate, therefore, when one has been prepared already for such privations. Misfortune, then, can do us little evil, and should death steal into the household——"

"Death! Lieutenant Porgy?"

"Yes, Mrs. Griffin, death. We must all die, you know. One will be taken away, and another will be left, and the survivor will have need——"

"Lieutenant, a'n't you just from the camp?"

"Not very long, ma'am."

"And my husband—didn't he write—didn't he know that you were coming into these parts?"

"Why, no, ma'am, he didn't write—he didn't know—he—"

"Lieutenant, there's something you've got to tell!" interrupted the woman. "Speak to me, now that Ellen's not here. Let me know if there's anything the matter with my husband."

"Well, Mrs. Griffin, I'm sorry to say that something is the matter," replied Porgy, seriously—the earnest, sad, almost stern manner of the widow impressing him with solemnity, and compelling him, by a natural intuition of what was proper, to forego all the absurdities and affections of speech which a long indulgence had rendered, in great degree, habitual. He continued—

"You are a strong woman, Mrs. Griffin; you have seen much trouble and sorrow, and you must be prepared for more."

"Tell me!" she exclaimed, clasping her hands and bending toward him. "Tell me! Don't keep me in this misery."

"We have had a battle, Mrs. Griffin." Here he paused.

"And he was killed!—he was killed!" was her cry.

Porgy was silent. His eyes were cast upon the floor.

"Walter Griffin! Oh, my God! my poor, poor Walter! He is dead—he is dead! I shall never see him again!"

The head of the woman fairly dropped upon her knees, while strong, deep sobs broke from her breast, with occasional ejaculations.

"Walter, Walter, my poor, poor Walter!"

Porgy did not reason unwisely when he forbore all effort at consolation. He took the opportunity, now that she seemed to be in full possession of the fact, to relate the particulars.

"He died like a brave man, Mrs. Griffin, in battle against the enemies of his country!"

"Ah! I know'd he would. Walter was a true man. He had the heart of a lion in him!"

"That he had, indeed, Mrs. Griffin. I will bear witness to his courage and his manhood. He was a brave, generous, whole-souled fellow—a good companion and an excellent friend."

"Oh! yes! Poor, poor Walter! But you don't know half what he was to me, when there was nobody and nothing!—ah! how could you know? And what is to become of us now!—my child—my poor Ellen, fatherless here, in these cruel times, and in these lonesome woods."

"Ah! Mrs. Griffin, remember you are a Christian. Trust in God brings with it the best of promises. He tempers the wind to the shorn lamb. You will never want a protector, I am sure, and your sweet and gentle daughter will surely find a father and many friends."

"Oh! I don't see *where*, lieutenant; we are very poor, and very unbefriended. If the war was over, and the people would come back to the settlements!"

"The war will be over before very long; the people will surely come back to the settlements. You will have many and kind neighbors; and I can promise you, Mrs. Griffin, one among them, who will be as true a friend to you as he was to your husband. Let peace be restored to us, and if my life is spared me, I mean to live in this parish. I will be your friend. I will protect your daughter. I will be a father to her, out of the love I bore to her father."

"Oh! lieutenant, I thank you for your kindness, from the bottom of my heart. I reckon you will be as friendly as anybody in the world; but there's no such thing as replacing the husband and the father, and making us feel as if we had never known the loss. Oh! Walter Griffin, I was dubious always that you would be killed by the enemy! I know'd how venturesome he was, lieutenant. I told him he ought not to be rash, for the sake of his wife and daughter; and it's all turned out as I warned him. My God! what are we to do now, here in this lonesome wilderness! I don't see! I don't see! I feel as if I could lay right down and die."

"Don't give up, Mrs. Griffin. There's no help in despair. Death must come, at last, to all of us. It might be Griffin or it might be me. It might be on the field of battle, or it might be here in bed. We can't know the moment when the summons must be heard, and we must resign ourselves with philosophy, to a fate from which there is no escape. There's no use in sorrow."

"Oh! but who can help it, lieutenant! I know there's no bringing Walter back; but that don't make me feel easier because he's gone. If I didn't cry, my heart would be sure to burst."

Her speech throughout, was broken by continual sobs and wailing. The evidences of real feeling were quite too conspicuous to suffer Porgy to indulge in any follies, and what he said, by way of consolation, was respectfully and kindly said, though as usual in such cases, of no value. At length, he bethought him of Singleton's letter, and the money intrusted to his care.

"It ought to be a great satisfaction to you, Mrs. Griffin, that Walter had so completely won the love of everybody in camp. I've seen the colonel himself standing over him, with the big tears gathering on his cheek, as he listened to his last words. The colonel has written to you in this letter."

"God bless him! Colonel Singleton is a good man, and Walter loved him very much. Read the letter for me, lieutenant, for I'm too blind to see the writing."

The letter of consolation was read accordingly. It set the stream of tears flowing anew.

"Really," thought Porgy as he watched her, "a most exemplary woman.

It is pleasant to think that we shall be thus wept and remembered when
we are no more."

This reflection led to another. "What a profitless life is mine! Were
they to assign me my last tenement to-morrow, I doubt if a single eye
would give out water; unless, indeed, this youngster, Lance, and possibly,
Tom, the cook! Verily, this thing must be amended. This poor woman
is the very person to whom I must administer consolation, and from
whom I must receive it. But, not now! not now! We must give ourselves time. She feels her sorrow, that is clear, and does not merely
feign it; but the stream flows too freely to last over long; and the foun-
tain that exhausts itself quickly, will soon feel the need of new supplies."

Such was the unspoken philosophy of our epicure. He really persuaded himself that the sort of consolation, which he proposed ultimately
to offer to the widow, was the proof of a certain virtue in himself. He
congratulated himself with the conviction, that he was about to do a
charitable action. An interval in the grief of Mrs. Griffin allowed him
to place in her hand the ten guineas which had been sent her by Singleton, Griffin's watch, and some other trifles which he brought. She gave
them little heed, emptying the gold upon the table, and putting the
watch into her bosom. Then, as if Singleton's letter had yet to be read,
she turned it over, and appeared striving to possess herself of its contents. But she handed it, a moment after, to Porgy, saying—

"I can't see the letter!" What does the colonel say, lieutenant?"

He again commenced the perusal of the letter, but had scarcely compassed a sentence, when hasty feet were heard at the entrance without,
and, in the next moment, Ellen Griffin and Lance hurriedly entered
the apartment. Both seemed very much agitated. The eyes of the girl
were red with weeping, and the big drops yet stood upon her cheeks.
But there was little time allowed for observation.

"The red-coats, lieutenant—the British!"

"Where?"

"Not a quarter above, coming down at a walk, dragoons, more than
fifty that I see! We must cut for the bushes. We'll have time, if we
move at once, but we must run for it."

"The devil! run! as if I had not an infirmity in my heel, like that
of Achilles!"

"Shut the front door, Ellen," cried the prudent Mrs. Griffin.

"Better gather up these guineas, Mrs. Griffin," cried Porgy, "or the

British will swear to the stamp. Lance, my boy, can we find cover all the way back?"

"Pretty much! There's a bend in the road above, just here at the corner of the cornfield, where there is a piece of woods that screens us for awhile, and if we get beyond that, we're in the thicket. But we must put out at once."

"To be sure we must! Mrs. Griffin, with your permission we'll withdraw the temptation of this bacon and these eggs from the eyes of these rapacious red-coats. We must not feed, or give comfort in any way to the enemy. Lance, tumble these eggs into the frying-pan—it already contains the bacon, and take it on your shoulder. I will take possession of the pot of hominy."

"But I have my rifle, lieutenant."

"What of that! carry both, can't you? I have my sword, do you see; yet, I mean to take the pot also."

"We must be in a hurry, lieutenant," said Lance, swinging the frying-pan, laden with eggs and bacon, over his left shoulder, and grasping his rifle in his right hand.

"Oh! yes! better go!" cried Ellen, entreatingly, who divided her time between a watch through the cracks of the door and her lover. Wiping her eyes with her apron, Mrs. Griffin hurried their departure also.

Porgy had already seized upon the hangers of the hominy pot, and was unbuckling his sword, to carry in his hand, that it might not embarrass him in walking. The sounds of the approaching horse were beginning to be faintly heard, as the two partisans stepped out of the door in the rear of the building, each armed after the fashion described, and stealing away under the shelter of the trees.

It required no extraordinary haste, for the British came slowly down the road. This was fortunate, since Porgy was not the man to fatigue himself in flight. He would much prefer to encounter odds in conflict at any time. His portly figure presented quite a picture, such as Cruikshank would have painted *con amore,* rolling, rather than striding, away beneath the trees, his sword in one hand, thrown out at right angles with his body, the better to preserve that balance which was necessary to his carrying the hominy-pot at a proper distance from his breeches. Mrs. Griffin and her daughter watched the two from the back door for awhile; then, as the nearer approach of the British was heard, closing the entrance in the rear as well as the front, and they prepared within for the possible necessity of receiving unwelcome visitors. The money, just received, and watch, with certain other portable treasures, were dropped down within a secret hollow in the floor; and, with a hope that the enemy would pass by without pausing, the widow and the daughter both sat down, seemingly busied in knitting and needle-work.

But they were not thus destined to escape. The dragoons in advance stopped at the entrance of the dwelling, and, as the several divisions came up, they paused also. There was some delay, during which all was anxiety in the hearts of the widow and her daughter. A knock followed at the door, and a voice of authority demanded entrance. It was immediately thrown open by Mrs. Griffin herself, while her daughter sought shelter in the chamber. Let us leave the widow with her unwelcome guests while we follow the footsteps of our lieutenant and ensign into the forest.

PORGY PROVES POT-VALIANT ONLY.

The two partisans, laden as they were, the one with the pot of hominy, the other with the frying-pan, made their way to the woods with all despatch, and without detection. Fortunately, as we have said, the forest cover extended almost to the cottage. Our fugitives soon satisfied themselves that they were in a place of security, though but a few hundred yards from the dwelling. They were in a tolerably close covert, on the slope of a moderate hill, at the foot of which stole off a slender brooklet, the child of a great bay or wooded pond, that covered a hundred acres, more or less, a quarter of a mile distant. Here Porgy paused. He had found his pot of hominy, precious as it was, an incumbrance. He laid it upon the ground, cast down his sword beside it, drew a long breath, and wiped repeatedly the perspiration from his brows. Lance Frampton followed his example; and the youth, at the bidding of his superior, proceeded to strike fire in his tinder-box, which he brought from his horse furniture; the two steeds being fastened still farther in the woods, where, still bitted and saddled, they were allowed to nibble the grass, which was now tolerably rank. The fire kindled, and the pot set to boiling anew, Frampton proposed that he should take an observation—in other words, see how the land lay with the enemy.

"Ay, do so, lad. You are of no use here. You have no merits in the kitchen. I will do the cooking, for which I flatter myself I have a native faculty, and, if you do not stay too long, you will find your share of the dinner in waiting for you. And look ye, Lance, boy—don't forget your business, in your anxiety to have a chat with Ellen. Many a poor fellow's heart has been pampered at the cost of his head. Be on the lookout, for if caught, you will be trussed up to the first tree, hung against all odds, as no better than a spy; and I sha'n't be there to hear your last confession. Be off, at once, and show yourself back again as soon as possible."

The lad promptly acted on this permission. He sped away with the lightness of a deer, though with the cunning and caution of a much smaller animal. Porgy, meanwhile, went on cooking. In this province he was at home. His pot began to boil; with the aid of his *couteau de chasse* (vulgarly Jack-knife), which the partisans all wore as habitually as the sailors, he converted a bit of cypress clapboard, which he found convenient to his hand, into a *hominy-stick* (an article of which our northern friends know nothing, unless, perhaps, as a *baster* or *paddle,* as a substitute for school-birch, when an unruly urchin is to be admonished) with which he stirred the simmering grist, and occasionally drew it up for inspection. His eggs and bacon, meanwhile, lay ready in the frying-pan, to be clapped on the fire the moment that the hominy had reached the proper consistency. In these operations, our *cuisinier* was singularly deliberate. He knew what a good supper required, and he had no fear of the enemy. His calculations were that the British, on their way to Charleston, had made but a momentary pause; and as they had no suspicions, so far as he knew, of the proximity of any of the Americans, he saw no reason to suppose that they would penetrate the wood sufficiently far to disturb his operations. Besides, Lance was out upon the scout, and of his vigilance, Porgy had sufficient experience. During all these operations and calculations, the soliloquies of our lieutenant were frequent and prolonged. Had we leisure, it would be easy, from his own lips, to prove him equal epicure and philosopher. He mingled his philosophies with his occupations, and dignified the latter with all the charms of sentiment. He was indeed a rare compound of the sensual and the sentimental philosopher.

His hominy was about to assume the degree of consistency which rendered it fit for use, and he was engaged in hauling away the fire from beneath it, in order to set on the frying-pan, with its contents of eggs and bacon, when Lance Frampton reappeared. The youth was all consternation.

"Oh! Lieutenant, would you believe it? They've got Colonel Walton a prisoner!"

"The d—l they have!"

"Yes! I've seen him myself, sitting in a chair in the hall, under a guard of six dragoons with their pistols cocked and watching every movement. I counted more than seventy dragoons, and I reckon there's quite a hundred. How could it have happened? What's to be done? We ought to be doing something to get him clear!"

"Doing something, boy! What the d—l would you do with seventy dragoons or more? If we save our own bacon, it's as much as we can hope to do. Did the enemy look as if they were suspicious? Do they show any signs of stopping long?"

"Not that I see! They have only stopped to rest and refresh. They've been off to the spring and got some buckets of water for themselves, and most of them are leading their horses to the spring, and rubbing them down. I saw several of them out in the bushes, here and there, but they did not straggle far from the house. But what's to be done for Colonel Walton?"

"What can be done? He's a prisoner, and must wait for his exchange, I suppose, with what philosophy he may."

"Oh, Mr. Porgy, I'm afraid of something worse. I am afraid they'll not treat him as a common prisoner. You remember that they were going to hang him when our colonel rescued him before."

"That's very true," replied Porgy, with increasing gravity;—"that's very true. I had not thought of that. But, whatever may be their purpose with him, we have no power to serve or save him. We must only be on the lookout to see that we ourselves are not gobbled up by these scarlet-bodied dragoons—whether, indeed, they should not be called *dragons* rather than *dragoons?*"

"Lieutenant," said the youth quickly, as if with the resolution suddenly made, "I must hurry off to camp and let our colonel know all about it."

"Why, boy, Singleton's on the Santee by this time."

"Yes, sir, I reckon, but I'll find him."

"What good in that? Before you find him these dragoons will have their prisoner in the provost in Charleston. There would be some use in it, if there was time enough to enable Singleton to dash between and cut them off before they could get to the city, but that is impossible; and to know that Walton is in the provost, will be only annoying information, quite as pleasant to learn a month hence as now."

"I don't know, Mr. Porgy! Our colonel has a good many strings to his bow. I know he has working friends in the city, and has got some plans going on for getting up an insurrection there. Now, he ought to know of this capture, and if I set off at once, by hard-riding, I may give him the information much sooner than he would even hear of it from Charleston. I must go, lieutenant."

"You shan't go till you have eaten, boy."

"I don't want to eat, lieutenant; I'm not at all hungry."

"You are a fool! Not eat! defraud the docile animal that walks, rides, toils, fights, for you! send it supperless to bed, when its work is done! That won't do, boy. You shall eat before you ride. As for riding with you, helter-skelter to the Santee, and at this moment, I don't do it, for all the Waltons and Singletons between this and Huckleberry Heaven! You may go by yourself, if you choose; perhaps it's just as well that you should; for, as you say, Singleton has his plans, and conspiracies, and agents, everywhere, and he may do something to extricate his kinsman. But you sha'n't depart till you have eaten. Indeed, you can not expect to go till the enemy have disappeared."

"I can take the back track, lieutenant; steal off in that direction, going upward and westward, and then wheeling about and pushing for some of the upper fords on the Edisto."

"Yes, and defeat your own subject; lose half a day's time or more in this *roundabouting;* when, by waiting quietly and lying close, for an hour, you may be able to start off on the direct road, without an enemy in the way. Quiet, boy, and eat before you ride. I sha'n't go with you, mark that. I shall certainly stay to-night at the house of our friend. I have much to communicate—much to say, in the way of consolation, to this amiable and lovely widow. You may tell the colonel that I shall devote myself to the task, now that Colonel Walton is taken, of saving my little party, and our wagon of stores. My object will be to find Colonel Harden and furnish his command with all that is necessary, rather than risk everything by returning with such an incumbrance. Push up those brands, boy, and turn that bacon. Our mess will soon be ready. What a savory odor! Heaven send that it penetrates no worse nostrils than our own."

The boy did as he was directed, turned over the slices of bacon in the pan with an air of resignation, while Porgy gave the hominy a finishing stir, and drew the pot from the fire, to enable it to cool. He was thus busied when he heard Lance Frampton give a slight cry, and was astounded to see the youth leap away, at a couple of bounds, putting the brooklet and the bay between them. Just then, a harsh voice, just above him, in the direction of the house, cried out—

"Hoo noo! wha' would ye be after there, you overgrown divil that ye are!"

Porgy, the *pot-hooks,* with pot depending, still in one hand, and the hominy stick in the other, looked up only to discover a dragoon leisurely marching down upon him, and but a few steps off. He cast his eyes about him for his sword, but it lay where he had been sitting, to the windward of the fire, fully ten paces off. Here was a quandary. The dragoon was in the act of picking his teeth when he first saw him; he was now deliberately drawing out his sabre. Porgy's glance at his sword, and a slight step backward, moved the Scotchman to suspect him of flight; to prevent which, the latter rushed directly upon him, his weapon now flourishing in air.

The bulk of Porgy, the nearness of the enemy, and the distance at which his own sword lay, forbade the hope of his recovering it in season for his defence, and as the dragoon darted on him, obeying a first impulse, our epicure raised the pot by the hangers, with his left hand, caught one of its still burning feet in the right, and, with a desperate whirl, sent the entire contents of the vessel, scalding hot, directly into the face of his assailant.

The effect was equally awful and instantaneous. The dragoon dropped the uplifted sabre, and set up the wildest yell of agony, while he danced about as if under the direct spells of Saint Vitus. The hominy stuck to his face and neck like a plaster, and the effort to remove it with his hands, only tore away the skin with it. Porgy was disposed to follow up his success; and, knocking the fellow on the head with the empty vessel, was a performance which was totally unresisted. In the agony of the dragoon, his approach for his purpose was totally unseen. Down he rolled, under the wild shock of the iron kettle; and our hero, congratulating himself with his narrow escape, seized upon the frying-pan, not disposed to lose his bacon as well as his bread, and was wheeling to make off for the woods, when another dragoon made his appearance on the brow of the hill, making swift tracks in pursuit.

"D——n that fellow, Lance," muttered Porgy to himself, "he has left me to be butchered!"

He gathered up his sword, as a point of honor, but still held a fast grip upon the frying-pan. There was but one dragoon in chase, and if he could draw him yet further into the woods, the noise of the strife would probably alarm no other—that is, if the howlings of the first had not given the alarm already.

Our epicure, as we know, had little speed of foot, and with his impediments of sword and frying-pan in his hands, he made very awkward headway. The pursuing dragoon gained upon him; and Porgy was already preparing to wheel about for the purpose of defence, when his feet tripped in some roots that ran along the surface, and over he went, headlong, the contents of the frying-pan flying forward in all directions. In another moment, and when only half recovering—on his knees still, and painfully rising to his feet—the dragoon stood above him.

"Surrender, ye d——d ribbel, or I shorten you by the shoulders."

Furious at the loss of both meat and bread, Porgy roared out his defiance.

"Surrender be d——d! Do I look like the man to cry *peccavi* to such a sawney as you? Do your best, barelegs, and see what you'll make of it!"

With unexpected agility, unable to rise, he rolled over at these words, and now lay upon his back, his sword thrust upward, and prepared to parry that of the assailant, after a new fashion of defence. In this situation, no defence could well be made. The exhibition was, in fact, rather ridiculous than otherwise. The abdomen of Porgy rose up like a mountain, seeming to invite the attack. The dragoon, however, did not appear to see anything amusing in the spectacle. He showed himself in sober earnest. His brother soldier groaned hideously at this moment, and he had no reason to doubt that his hurts were mortal. He straddled the prostrate Porgy, and, in reply to his defiance, prepared to strike with his broad claymore at the head of the epicure. His sabre was thrown up, that of Porgy thrown out to receive it, when, suddenly the dragoon dropped lifeless upon our partisan, and the next instant the report of a rifle was heard from the neighboring wood.

"Ah!" cried Porgy, throwing off the incumbent body of his assailant, "that dog Lance; he has not abandoned me; and I should have known that he never would. The rascal—how I love him!"

The next moment Lance Frampton rushed in.

"Up, lieutenant, we have not a moment to lose. That shot will bring all the dragoons down upon us, and we don't know how nigh they are. The horses are ready, not thirty yards off. They've rested well and eaten, and we can soon leave these heavy English drags behind us."

"You're a lad among a thousand! I love you, Lance, by all that's affectionate!"

Then, as he bustled up, with Frampton's help, seeing the scattered eggs and bacon strewed upon the ground, he fairly groaned aloud in the tribulation of his spirit.

"I must lose my dinner after all! And that hominy was as good a pot as was ever boiled. It served a purpose, however; never, in fact, boy, did pot of hominy do such good service before."

But there was no time for trifling. This was said while our corpulent professor, hurrying off under the guidance of his ensign, was making such headway as, in later days, was quite new to his experience. They were both in the saddle, and in full retreat, when the British trumpets, sounding the alarm, faintly echoed through the forest. Pursuit was fruitless.

This is the last we hear of Porgy in Katharine Walton.

The concluding incidents occurred in Charleston, where the captive Colonel Walton was taken to be hanged. Balfour put pressure on Walton to try to get him to compel Katharine to marry him. When Balfour finally allowed Katharine to visit her father in prison, Walton, having been assured by his daughter that she and Robert Singleton truly loved each other, induced her to take an oath on the Bible that she would never marry anyone other than Robert.

But when Walton was tried and condemned for "treason," and the time of the execution was at hand, Katharine decided to yield to Balfour to save her father. To find Balfour, Katharine had to follow him to the home of Moll Harvey, whom he had spurned, but to whom he had now returned. Moll overheard Katharine giving in verbally to Balfour. Furious with jealousy at Balfour, and also truly sorry for Katharine, Moll determined to preserve the girl at any cost from espousing such a scoundrel. Moll, therefore, intercepted the order Balfour, to reward Katharine for finally consenting to marry him, had just sent—by a messenger—to stay the execution of Colonel Walton.

As Balfour was assuring Katharine her father was saved, the cannon announced the moment of his hanging. Katharine, of course, now rejected the villainous Balfour. Walton died "like a man." Katharine and Robert could finally be married.

5. Porgy
and
The Scout

Porgy does not appear in The Scout. *His absence is not the only reason for the inferiority of this work. More than any of the other six, it seems apart from the main Saga. Not only is Porgy absent, but also the characters who become definitely retainers of Porgy in* Woodcraft, *but have been coming in from time to time beginning with* The Partisan. *The historical time seems to be late 1780, but the action seems to be placed more vaguely chronologically than in the others. The Scout is very much the poorest of the novels of the Saga.*

The two Conway brothers, hurling at each other imprecations in high-flown aristocratic diction; the pursuit in disguise of the bad brother, Edward, of course a tory, by the humble girl he has seduced and spurned; her being unintentionally given a mortal head wound by her humble but worthy lover—all this is Simms at his worst. The dark brother-against-brother motif, grantedly faintly Faulknerian, only serves to make highly obvious the superiority of the twentieth-century master. Near the end Simms, as if wishing to brighten all this mournfulness, introduces a comic character, Dr. Hillhouse, who is a sort of caricatured Euphuist, amusing at moments, but utterly uncalled for by the main plot sequence, and often most unconvincing.

The Scout *is neither connected with the initial trilogy,* The Partisan, Mellichampe, *and* Katharine Walton, *nor with the final* Forayers-Eutaw *duology, indeed virtually one novel. Unlike* Woodcraft *it is not umbilically connected with both the trilogy and the duology; all six being entered at times by Porgy. It is not a matter of chance that in this, the most detached from the Saga, and actually the most humorless, the most gothic, or psuedo-gothic of the seven, our stout and jovial Captain Porgy could not live and breathe.*

6. Porgy
in
The Forayers

The Forayers *and* Eutaw, *the last written books of the Saga, are virtually one novel in two volumes. Indeed Simms originally planned them as one under the title* Eutaw. (Letters, *III, 333.*) *The second is an actual continuation of the first rather than a sequel. The* Forayers *covers June and early July, 1781. By late July, both armies were exhausted, partly by the heat of the "Dog-Days." The Americans planned to recuperate in a camp on the Santee Hills; the British were bottled up in Orangeburg and Charleston.* Eutaw *takes up the story in September after the August lull. It is indeed the same story prolonged.*

The Forayers-Eutaw *may well be the longest American novel of any importance. Distinctly separate from the initial trilogy, it introduces a completely new cast of characters, except in the short Porgy sections, featuring as hero Willie Sinclair and as villain Richard Inglehardt. The author, in* The Forayers, *gives the essence of the main plot in alluding to "the players at this game of war in our humble legend, Sinclair and Inglehardt." As rivals for the hand of Bertha Travis, they are also players at another game. Both games continue in* Eutaw, *only at the end of which both are won by the chivalric whig Sinclair not by the dastardly tory Inglehardt.*

Unresolved until the end of Eutaw *are the dilemmas of two middle-aged plantation owners, Willie's father and Bertha's father, who after vacillating through two volumes, finally come over to the American side. Also running through both is the duel of the two clever scouts, Jim Ballou for the whigs and "Hell-Fire" Dick Andrews for the tories.*

Although admittedly Major Willie Sinclair is an even more imposing compendium of virtues than Captain Robert Singleton; and that Captain Inglehardt is a more virulent compound of vices than Captain Barsfield; yet both hero and villain are more complexly, subtly, and convincingly adumbrated than their earlier prototypes; as can also be said of the two indecisive parents.

Indeed The Forayers-Eutaw *is a more mature and carefully wrought work than the first four books of the Saga. The first part of* The Forayers *is done with a narrative drive Simms had hardly matched even in* Woodcraft, *but later there is a slackening, connected probably with his growing inability to resolve the dilemmas without planning another six hundred pages of fine, fine print.*

Simms was very proud of The Forayers, *to judge from his letters, prouder than of any of his other novels. To Evert Duyckinck he wrote: "My friends here, Gen. Hammond, Paul Hayne, Jamison & others, pronounce it my best story, and (they say) the best of the American romances of anybody. You will smile at my repeating this, yet there is so much in the book that I find pleasure in, that I am only too happy to believe [it has pleased]. I wish you to find it a bold, brave, masculine story; frank, ardent, vigorous; faithful to humanity, yet faithful to the ideals which should crown humanity. . . . The book I hold to be fresh and original, and the characterizations as truthful as forcible [Letters, III, 411-12]." Hammond indeed called it a "grand Romance" (Letters, III, 425); and I think it may be ranked as next best to* Woodcraft.

Aside from supervising and preparing the feast for the "captains" almost at the end of the book, Porgy makes no appearances in The Forayers, *but he is at his best. Quite early in the book, however, there is a long discussion of Porgy at the dinner table at the Barony, the home of the Sinclairs, between Major Willie and his father the colonel. Willie was trying to gain his parent's approbation of his friend Captain Porgy. Although Colonel Sinclair did feel his profession of allegiance to the British was the best insurance his extensive property would be unmolested, he seemed sincere in his devotion to the crown. Willie's de-*

fense of his comrade Porgy was especially important as it was part of his prolonged endeavor to win his father over to the American cause. Actually the son was able to convince his father of Porgy's sterling worth quite easily, in fact more readily than of the justice of the American claims.

This dialogue, revealing Willie's enthusiasm for Porgy, serves as a preparation for the fat officer's grand entrance at the imposing collation he later provides at Marion's camp, and also gives evidence of Porgy's genius for winning friends. Also it highlights that aspect of Porgy which is the special province of The Forayers, his status as an aristocrat, and his ability to associate easily with the gentry, whether private citizens, generals, or the Governor of South Carolina himself. Bertha Travis, in telling her lover Willie she fears she is not from a good enough social background to be his wife, quotes her father, a vigorous social climber, as saying, "The Sinclairs are among our first families—rich, popular, distinguished." "Our" refers perhaps to Carolina, perhaps to the South. Among the characters in the Saga, the Sinclairs are clearly the "First Family of South Carolina" at least. Simms wants the reader to accept Willie as—to use Jefferson's famous phrase—a natural as well as an artificial aristocrat. As friend of Major Sinclair, Porgy is clearly patrician of the patricians.

At the Barony, dinner was late, and no wonder. Willie, aided by two faithful house Negroes and a few of the more dependable of the field hands—his father being too gouty to walk unaided—had been defending the mansion from an attack made by a gang of Florida rascals who had entered His Majesty's service just for the gold. Hell-Fire Dick was their leader. The presence of the fighting whig son gave them an excuse to storm the plantation, although their real motive was the prospect of rich plunder. They are "the Forayers" of the title, and are referred to once, interesting enough for Faulkner readers, as "horse-reivers." As Dick had been about to assault the old tory "Baron" in his own drawing room, Willie had entered the room, and with a correct lead "with right arm and shoulder," had knocked the tough Dick cold. Dick had been roped up and put in the basement, but had managed with amazing stoicism, in the most horrendously unforgettable scene in the Saga, to burn off his bonds and escape.

It was no wonder, then, that dinner was late. The "Baron" was "quite impatient at the prospect of having his roast lamb and boiled mutton . . . overdone."

"A cook that does her dishes to rags, Willie," quoth he, "is an emissary of the devil."

"An opinion," replied the other, "for which my friend Captain Porgy would embrace you, sir, across the table."

"Porgy—Captain Porgy, sir? Is it possible, Willie Sinclair, that your miserable service requires you to associate with persons having such detestable names? Why, sir, among gentlemen, even the fish of that name is only held fit for negroes."

"Sir, I believe, with Shakspere, that 'a rose by any other name would smell as sweet.' "

"And I don't believe in any such doctrine. Names are not only things, sir, but they are significant of virtues. Call a rose a radish and it bites the tongue. And that any respectable service should accord a commission to a man named Porgy is absolutely monstrous."

"Wait, sir, till you know my friend Porgy."

"God forbid, sir, that I ever should."

"When you do, sir—as I am now sworn that you shall know him—I will wager a wagon-load of continental money against a Jacobus, that you offer him not only a perpetual seat at your table, but the entire management of your cook. Captain Porgy, sir, is the only wit and buffoon, sir, that I ever met, or heard of, who never suffered you once to forget that he was all the while a gentleman."

Here is the only explanation Simms is ever known to have offered for Porgy's strange name. My own theory is that the name implies (1) that Porgy is such a gastronomical genius he can make a dish fit for a king, or even a South Carolina gentleman, out of the despised native fish; (2) that he is so talented and genteel he can rise above the handicap of a ridiculous name; and (3) that he stands on his real merits, not on formal dignity or inherited status. Willie's final sentence is the best summation of Porgy's qualities given in the Saga. Curiously enough, Porgy's first name is never disclosed.

And the party sat down to dinner.

"Now," said the *veteran*, "if these rascals will only hold off till we have swallowed dinner, I shall be in better mood for the conflict."

"Thoughts like an Englishman!" said the major of dragoons.

"And how should I think but as an Englishman, and where do you think the American or any other race, would think differently? Your rascally French allies are not to be quoted at all in such matters."

"And yet they are held to be perfect masters in such matters."

"Ay, sir, as cooks, to dress and prepare the food, sir, but not to eat it. Give them what credit you please, *as cooks,* but the grace, taste, and general ability, with which an Englishman eats, is unequalled, sir, by any people."

"The subject is one of endless ramifications, sir, and would require for its discussion more practical experience than I have yet had in such matters; but we may safely assume, I think, that a people who know so well how to prepare the dishes, is hardly wanting in the ability to do them proper justice."

"Well, sir, is that mutton to your liking?"

"Exactly, sir; and you see I am proving my ability after our poor American fashion. In respect, however, to the effect which a good dinner, not stinted, has upon the fighting man, you should hear my friend Porgy. He says, that an American should never be forced into battle with a full stomach. He admits the British to be differently constituted, but thinks that, even with them, the appetite should never be fully pacified before fighting. With all classes, he is of opinion, that the better course is to put the dinner before them—a good one—as good and tempting as possible—let them see it, till their eyes become fascinated—nay, let them taste it, but only taste—and then, let the drums beat and the bugles sound to quarters. Soldiers, thus tantalized, he asserts to be the most dangerous customers in the world—absolutely wolfish—who will then tear and rend their foes, having no fear; each man having, as it were, a personal feeling of revenge to gratify, as if robbed by his enemy of the choicest blessing of his life."

"He's no fool, that fish! There's sense in the notion."

"They tell a good story," continued the major, "of the mode which he employed to convert a timid fellow into a desperado. Just before the beginning of our Revolution—"

"Rebellion, sir."

"Well, sir, rebellion be it! I care very little *now,* for the distinction."

The father growled, and pushed the Madeira toward the son.

"Drink, sir, and imbibe more sensible notions at once of names and things."

"Long life and a good appetite for all good things, sir, to the end of the chapter! Carrie, my dear, wet your lips with us—"

"Well, sir, to your story."

"Porgy, sir, who, before the war, was a rice-planter on the Ashepoo, a *bon vivant,* and fast liver, though a great reader, and philosophical humorist, was employed by one of the Fenwickes to answer for him as a friend, in an interview with a gentleman who bore the challenge of one Major Pritchard. Porgy would have declined, as Fenwicke was supposed to be constitutionally timid; but the young fellow appealed to him with a good deal of pathos. He was, in fact, almost friendless on the occasion; had quarrelled with his family and associates, and was rather in Coventry, in consequence of some gaming transactions. Porgy's good nature made him yield; but he felt the awkwardness of going out with a person who might show the white feather. How was he to prevent such a discreditable exhibition? As I have said, Porgy is something of a philosopher, and entertains peculiar notions of the effect of food, and the various sorts of it, upon the moral as well as physical nature. Red pepper, for example, he avers to be an article, which, taken in quantity, will irritate the temper, but lessen the nerve. He has similar opinions of other condiments, spices, and even drinks, in lessening the courage. Whiskey, he holds to be decidedly hurtful to valor;—"

"Gad, there's something reasonable in the fellow's philosophy. I have that notion myself."

"He says that when our militia-men run—"

"As they are monstrous apt to do!"

"It is due to the fact that they drink whiskey, and not Jamaica, which he values much more as a good moral stimulus. But, like you, sir, he has a better faith in Madeira, than in any other known beverage."

"I fancy I shall like that fellow, Porgy."

"You will sir; but to my story. The arrangements made for the affair between Fenwicke and Pritchard, the time fixed, and all adjusted, Porgy took his principal home to his house the morning before the affair was to take place. This, he did, under the pretext of avoiding the sheriff's officers. He kept him locked up in an upper chamber, and left him to himself for twelve hours, on a slender supply of biscuit and Madeira. Before noon the supply was exhausted, and the housekeeper had no keys, and but three cold-boiled Irish potatoes—which Porgy esteems fine food for soldiers—were to be found in an open cupboard.

These Fenwicke devoured without salt or butter. At midnight Porgy made his appearance and made a thousand apologies. Fenwicke was compelled to look satisfied; but when he asked for supper, there was no satisfactory answer. Porgy pleaded some singular disappointments in his supplies. But he got out fresh biscuit and over a bottle of Madeira, he succeeded in putting Fenwicke into tolerable humor. They retired and both slept late; but descended finally to an admirable breakfast in which everything that could excite appetite was displayed. Fenwicke's eyes glistened. He rubbed his hands. He was as hungry, by this time, as a dragoon's horse on a long scout. He sat down, but was allowed to swallow only two or three mouthfuls, when Porgy pulled out his watch and started up in alarm. 'Good Heavens, Mr. Fenwicke,' said he, 'we shall be too late unless we go at a gallop. It is within forty minutes of the time, and we have three miles to get to the place of meeting.' Fenwicke looked at him like a hyena. 'Heavens, sir, I am famished!' 'Never mind,' quoth Porgy, 'we shall only have a better appetite after the affair is over. Everything shall be kept warm. See to it, Tom—on your life, see to it!' he cried to his cook—a famous fellow, by the way, sir, the best cook in the army—and thus speaking, he hurried Fenwicke off to the horses which had previously been got in readiness. They had scarcely mounted when Porgy called for a bottle of porter which he divided between himself and his companion. 'This will stay your stomach, sir,' he said, and this was all he allowed him, except a single biscuit, which Fenwicke snatched up from the table."

"But why the porter, sir?"

"To produce a more morbid condition of the stomach. To divert the impression as much as possible from the brain. Such was his theory at least. His philosophy is a curious one, and he insists greatly upon the important uses of porter in the case of nervous men, with an active imagination."

"Well, sir, what was the result?"

"Why, that Fenwicke was sufficiently angry, on the gallop, to quarrel with his second, goaded, it may be, by the provocative sort of conversation in which Porgy indulged by the way. He reached the ground in this humor, was impatient of all control, impatient for the fight—came up to the ring in handsome style, rushed desperately in upon his antagonist, got a flesh wound on breast and arm, but succeeded in running Pritchard through the body."

Carrie Sinclair shuddered as she said:—

"But he did not kill him, Willie?"

"On the spot! Yet, the moment the deed was done, he nearly fainted, and could scarcely mount his horse. He staggered off like one mortally hurt himself."

"The fellow was no coward," said the old man, "only tenderhearted."

"Porgy asserts that no man is absolutely a coward or absolutely brave; that all depends on training; that we are all, more or less, the creatures of circumstance; and that, in particular conditions of mind, or body, or situation, we are audacious or timid;—that every man, the most brave, has moments of fear,* and that the most timid, under particular training, or accidental influences, will show the most audacious valor; that the stomach has more to do with it than the brain or heart; and that the greatest secret in the training of the soldier, is proper food, of the proper kind, at the proper time, and properly cooked. He professes to believe that his cook Tom has done more toward teaching his men how to fight, than all the training of all the officers."

"I shall like that fellow Porgy, I fancy. You may bring him here, Willie, should a chance offer, as soon as your insurrection is over. But I do not believe in all Mr. Porgy's doctrines. For my part, I may safely say that I never knew the sentiment of fear in my life."

The major laughed—then suddenly exclaimed, as if in consternation:—

"Take care, Lottie, you are about to tread on papa's foot!"

The old man screamed—throwing up both hands:—

"For God's sake, my child!"

The child had never moved—was sitting quietly at the table—not near the gouty member! Such was the power of the imagination, that the old man had never exercised a single sense, before he screamed. The major of dragoons laughed merrily. The veteran was fairly caught. He stormed out at the commentary upon his confident self-applause, which was the natural result of the apprehensions which could so easily be awakened, and so completely revealed.

"Zounds, sir! Do you make *me* a subject of your merriment!"

But the laughter of the son, and even of the girls, could not be suppressed; and, in a moment after, the veteran himself joined in it.

* This was subsequently the opinion of Napoleon and Wellington.

"Ah! Willie, we are but poor devils, the best of us, with all our pretension! Pass the bottle, sir; the gout will make any man a coward!"

This incident, with its exposure of the fallacy in the only point in which old Colonel Sinclair dissented from Porgy's beliefs, certainly suggests that Simms is seconding the doctrines of the portly captain; as does also the praise from "our hero" Willie, who is set up by his creator as a paragon of intelligence and probity.

Dinner and conversation were now interrupted by the cook Congaree Polly, who came in to report that one of the forayers was approaching with a white flag. He brought an ultimatum that "Kurnel Sinekeler" must surrender Dick or be killed and have his house burned. Dick had not been able to rejoin his gang because of fear of being shot from the windows. Willie now reorganized the defenses of the mansion, and ordered Lottie not to show herself at the windows. Willie stationed himself and readied his arms in the room where his gouty father sat in an arm chair with his pistols pointed out a half-opened window.

"I am not sure, sir," said the major, "that I have had quite as much dinner as I desired."

"Not the worse for it, Willie, if your man Porgy be right in his philosophy. But the things are unremoved. Fall to, if you think proper."

"No! I find it not so easy to eat now. Still that mutton was very fine."

"Yes, but there is a proverb against *cold* mutton. Hack away at that tongue, which I can warrant. It is home cured."

"Ay, and of a quality to cure a man of absenteeism."

"Would it could cure you, Willie!"

"It will not just now, sir. By the way, sir, my friend Porgy insists that the English proverb against cold mutton is all a mistake of taste; that mutton is really more preferable cold than warm."

"Egad, I should have ventured the opinion long ago myself, but that I never take ground against a proverb. I shall certainly be pleased to know this Porgy. Can he fight as well as philosophize?"

"That is the most remarkable of his characteristics—somewhat in the teeth of a proverb also. He fights like a bull-dog, and in action almost seems to lap blood. But he always professes a reluctance to go into action, and insists that nothing but training has kept him all his life from showing a white feather. Come, sir, let me fill you a glass of this Madeira."

"Why not, Willie? I confess to relishing my wine more today, than I have done any day within the last six months."

"What! including the time of my Lord Rawdon's visit?"

"Ah!" with a deep sigh "—ah! no! That was an exception. I confess, Willie, that on that occasion I distinctly saw the 'Bottle Reel.' "

"That was a serious error, my dear father," said the son, with a grave shake of the head, "in the case of so *steady* a loyalist."

"Get out, you varlet. Ha!—we are to have it."

A wild scream from the woods, a shot, and the rattling of glass in the upper windows, silenced the conversation, and our major of dragoons was instantly upon the alert.

Windows were shattered by buckshot, and return shots fired from within the house; Willie and his men were able to hold the mansion for half an hour, when Captain Peyre St. Julien and his troopers arrived and rescued the Sinclair household. St. Julien was a Frenchman who had joined the Americans to fight under Willie. He was Willie's best friend, and the suitor of Willie's sister Carrie, to whom he is happily united at the end of Eutaw. *Colonel Sinclair's toryism was thus reduced to absurdity as he had to be saved from the tory marauders by the whigs.*

Among the numerous goings on in the many chapters between the discussion about Porgy and his actual appearance is the progress in the courtships of Carrie Sinclair by Peyre St. Julien and of Bertha Travis by Willie Sinclair. The malicious Inglehardt continued in his determination to marry Bertha by fair means or foul. When her father opposed the marriage, Inglehardt threatened to use documents in his possession to prove Travis had been a swindler. Travis had been trafficking with the British, but finally decided to reform and come over to the patriot side. Then Inglehardt, aided by his minion Hell-Fire Dick, captured Travis and his young son Henry, hoping to compel the father to induce his daughter to marry him. Travis resisted bravely, as he now wished Bertha to marry Willie.

Despite Inglehardt's achievement, there were growing signs that the Americans would probably at last win. In the British army there was growing discontent, especially among the native loyalists and the Irish. England was drawing on Ireland for soldiers now that the German supply had been used up. The British supply of horses was diminishing, a critical matter in terrain that required extensive use of cavalry. The well-mounted partisans, accustomed to the woods and swamps and heat were the most active part of either army.

A stalemate was developing. The British army was bottled up in Orangeburg and Charleston; while the American was not strong enough to risk a pitched battle. Both armies were exhausted, by months of hard fighting, by the weather, and by the extreme shortage of food. The Dog-Days of late summer had come in Carolina; and everybody was hungry in a land which had been raided for years for every chicken and pig.

And so we come to the camp near Orangeburg presided over by General Nathanael Greene, who had been sent down with his troops from the north. Marion's camp was nearby. His men were fatigued, starving, and hot. A "good supper on the Edisto" River was necessary. "What sort of supper was to be had, and where it was to come from, were questions that exercised the conjectural ingenuity of all parties to a far greater extent than did the future prospects . . . of the war." It was the evening of a torrid day, and most of the men were too weary to move.

To this general rest and languor of the army, there were, however, some striking exceptions. The command of Marion stretched toward the Caw-caw. In the woods of this region, an hour before sunset, there might be seen a squad of twenty troopers, dark, bronzed, half-naked young savages, following, with some interest, the speech and movements of a large, broad-shouldered, and great-bellied personage, wearing the uniform—somewhat doubtful, indeed, because of rents, stains, and deficiencies—of a captain of dragoons. He was on foot, and by no means active of movement, though taking his steps with the confidence of a war-horse, and the solid firmness of an elephant. He was a fine-looking fellow, in spite of the too great obtrusion upon the sight of his abdominal territory, a region which he, nevertheless, endeavored to circumscribe within reasonable bounds by a girthing of leather, only half covered with a crimson sash, which no doubt had the desired effect in some degree, though at some sacrifice of the wearer's comforts. His face was full almost as the moon at full, of a ruddy brown, his head massive, chin large and prominent eyes, bright but small, and mouth eager with animation. His nose was decidedly intellectual. At his elbow stood a negro, jacket off, and arms akimbo, who followed the motions of his superior with a mixed air of deference and assurance. Around these two the troopers were gathered. Before the group, slaughtered and skinned, hanging from a tree, was one of the lean beeves of the country—a poor skinny beast, weighing some two hundred pounds, gross, bone, meat, skin, offal! Near at hand stood a small, rickety, covered wagon, the contents of which we may conjecture. It was one of Marion's recent captures from the convoy of Stewart; and contained, no doubt, some resources, the value of which may be guessed from the mysterious looks which were, every now and then, cast upon it by passing groups of thirsty dragoons, the very glances of whom are apt to burst locks, and consume stores.

Our captain was busy with the commissariat of the brigade—not as the head of it, by no means, but as premier—head-counsellor, and legal and moral adviser.

"I tell you, Fickling, it will never do. Tell me there were no better beeves to be had! You have just taken what they please to give you. You are too modest. It is the infirmity of your family, whenever the interest is not absolutely and directly your own. We do this business of foraging for all the army, yet it seems that the meanest share is always to fall to us. Tell me nothing of Colonel Lee. He has an independent legion; let him pick up his own beeves. As for the field-officers, I do not see that their official position confers upon them any right to better tastes and appetites than a poor captain of partisan cavalry. I thank my stars that I have tastes which are as well cultivated as any brigadier or colonel in the army. And shall my tastes be defrauded, because these epauletted buffaloes are greedy, and you are mealy-mouthed? Why the devil don't you assert yourself, man, and assist us, as you should, when the distribution of the beef takes place? You are a fool, Fickling, for your submission! Colonel Lee's man steps before you, and says, 'Colonel Lee;' and Colonel Washington's man starts up, and says, 'Colonel Washington'—and these, and a score of others, even while they speak, clap hands on the best pieces, and choose the fattest flanks; and when all are served, you steal up, with finger in your mouth, and murmur, 'Is anything left for General Marion?' Is that the way to do business? I tell you, 'No, sir!' Your true way is to take the best that offers—lay bold hands on it—nay, thrust it through with your naked sabre, and say, 'Marion's brand!' Do the thing as you should, with the proper look and manner, and not a rapscallion in the army, representing no matter what division, dare lay hands on it after that! If they do, let me be at your elbow next time, with two or three fellows of my choosing!"

"But, Captain Porgy—"

"But me no buts, Mr. Fickling. I'll have you out of your office, if you do not but against this sort of distribution. You are to provide us; and, if you do not comprehend that our soldiers are just as deserving of good food as any continentals in the service, you are not fit for our service, and I'll have you out of it. General Marion himself submits quite too much to this sort of treatment. If there is a fine horse in the brigade, it is immediately wanted for some one of Lee's dragoons—some d——d henchman or bugleman—and off the colonel goes to Greene and tells him that his legion wants horses, and that Marion has enough and to spare, and we are called upon to dismount, and provide other people. Yet are we kept day and night on the trot—off to-day for the Pon-pon and Savannah, to-morrow for the Pedee—now running down tories, now cattle; seeking information, scouting, spying, called out at all hours; and how is this to be done, if we are to give up our horses. The brigade has covered all this low country, from the Pedee to the Savannah, for three years and more, and the best that is got in the forays that we alone make, are served out to these hungry feeders. I won't submit to it. They shall neither have my horses nor my cattle; and if you take any more such beef as this, Fickling, when better is to be had, we'll turn you, neck and heels, out of your department."

"But, Captain Porgy—"

"See to it!"

"But—"

"See to it! That's all! I say no more—to you!—Tom!"

"Sah!"

"Get our share of that carrion! See what you can do with it. We must have soup, I suppose. Make a pilaw. We have plenty of pepper now. You can hardly get a decent steak from the beast. But do what you can. I must see after something more. We are to have company to-night. I have asked the great men, the big-wigs, the governor, Generals Marion and Sumter, the colonels of the brigade, Maham, Singleton, and a few others. Have everything ready by ten o'clock. Did you succeed in getting any melons?"

"I empty one patch, maussa."

"Whose?"

"I dunn know quite 'zackly, but he's a fiel' jes' yer on de back ob de village. De melons is quite 'spectable."

"Ripe?"

"As de sunshine kin make 'em."

"Good! Do as much stealing in an honest way as you can! D—n the patriotism that can't eat stolen fruits!"

"Wha' else you guine hab, maussa."

"Who knows what I can get? I must look. There ought to be frogs here in abundance, and of good size. Not such as we can find in a rice reserve, Tom, but passable in war-time, and delicate enough for hot weather. I shall look out for a young alligator or two."

"Dat'll do! Gi' me two young alligator tail, and de frog, and I gi' you fus' rate tuttle soup and ball, and steak."

"Must have a ragout, Tom. Have you seen no pigs about. Tom!"

"Nebber yer de fus' squeak, maussa."

"Well"—with a grunt—"we must do as we can. Come, boys, are you ready?"

"Ay, ay, captain!" from a score of voices; and a dozen active young fellows presented themselves, armed with wooden spears and knives.

"Where's George Dennison?"

A voice answered from the foot of a tree.

"Come along, George; don't be lazy. What you shall see this evening will enable you to beat Homer in a new epic, in which cranes and frogs shall figure to posterity."

And, following the corpulent captain, the whole party pushed down to the swamp.

"There's a battalion for you, George Dennison. Not a rascal under six feet—half a dozen nearer seven. I chose them specially for the expedition. They are our cranes, and are all eager for the war."

"And the frogs are sounding for the conflict. Hear their tongues, already. The concert for the evening is begun. Hear the chirruping overture:—

> "Fry bacon—tea-table!
> Coyong! coyong! coyong!
> Supper on table—supper on table,
> Eat if you're able!
> Blood an' 'ounds—blood an' 'ounds."

"By the way, captain, a frog concert, would not be a bad speculation in the great cities of Europe. How a score or two of musical fellows, who had once or twice slept in our swamps, or lingered after sunset along our rice-fields, would make capital out of it! And such a sensation. What a hurly-burly, subdued to order, they could make of it."

"No doubt! The notes and tones occupy every note of the *gamut!* It is a rare original music. But the secret would lie in making the music tributary to satire. The frogs should furnish a running commentary on the follies and vices of society as in Aristophanes, only adapted to our times. It would task art admirably to work out of it an opera—the Loves of the Frogs! Little Squeaka, the dreaming sentimental damsel, just emerging into society—coming out; in her train some half a dozen Jockos—minnows of fashion, that sing in a love-lisp always—Therubina! ah! Therubina! Oh the rich fun of such a farcical! Of what a delightful variety would the affair admit! The lover, the villain, the priest, the mother—all the usual varieties, not forgetting Arlecchino. Of course, the frogs are not less fortunate than their betters. They have a Jack Pudding among them. The squirrels have I know."

"Don't forget the duenna! Hear her falsetto, squeaking through a score of crevices in her broken teeth:—

> " 'On your knees, O,
> Not a sneeze, O,
> Don't you hear your mother coming!'
> 'To be kissed, O,
> By the priest, O,
> Is the saintliest sort of mumming.'

> " 'O, alack, O,
> Such a smack, O,
> Makes the very echoes jealous;'
> 'But it proves, O,
> Holy loves, O,
> Most particularly zealous.'

> " 'Hark that drumming!'
> 'Mother coming!'
> 'And that pother!'
> ' 'Tis your father!'
> 'Awful sounds, O!'
> 'Blood and 'ounds, O!'—

"In full fresco swells the chorus,
From the motley group before us;
Sighing, swelling,
Barking, belling—

Such a moaning, such intoning,
So much groaning, honing, droning,
Calling, falling, bawling, drawling,
Speaking, shrieking, squeezing, squeaking,
　　"All subsiding to a quiver,
And a shiver,
Only to ascend, in thunder,
Rolling up and roaring under—
Blood and 'ounds, O! blood and 'ounds, O!
Awful sounds, breaking bounds,
Setting all the woods a-shaking,
Setting all the bog a-quaking,
All the swampy empire waking,
　　With the eternal blood and 'ounds, O!
　　"Rending, raging,
　　Battle waging,
　'Yond all musical assuaging—
O'er all mortal sounds uproarious,
O'er all mortal sense victorious,
Like the diapason glorious,—
That through pipes and stops,
Shrieks, and bounds, and hops,
Foams, and frisks, and frolics,
Rolls and rages, rocks and rollicks,
Feeding every mortal stopper, ah!
Of the grand Italian opera!"

Thus it was that the rustic poet of the partisans, gave forth extempore an embodiment of the music of the frogpondians.

"Hurrah!" cried Porgy, "hurrah, Geordie—why, man, you are native, to frog manor born, with all the pipes and bellows of the swamp in your own wind-bags; or to requite you in your own coin:—

　　"Worthy venison,
　　Geordie Dennison,
　You will soon require a stopper, O,
　　Scaring off with greater clamor,
　　Every leap-frog from his amour,
　Turning every mother's son of 'em
　Making fun of 'em,—
　To a hopper off, from a hopper, O!"

And thus doggrelizing as they went, the two led their laughing cohort down into the swamp.

The Caw-caw was in full concert. Bull and bell, squeak and shriek, moan and groan. All the artistes were in exercise, engaged, no doubt, in some rehearsal, preparatory to some great ceremonial—the bridal, possibly, of the young princess of the pondians.

Porgy and his corps, with their pointed spears of wood, wooden forks, baskets, and knives, stole down into the lagunes. What a picture for the stage! What an action for the burlesque drama! But the matter was a serious one enough for one of the parties. Long will the frogs of that ilk remember with wailing the raid of the cranes of that day. Could you have seen those long, gaunt backwoodsmen, each with shaft prong, or trident, striding hither and thither in the bog and lake, striding right and left, poised above their great-eyed enemies, and plunging forward to grapple the wounded and squalling victim before he should sheer off, or, as George Dennison said afterward, describing the affair in sonorous heroics:—

> "Could you have seen that theatre of frogs,
> As each in due delight and bog immersed,
> Sprawled out, at length, in slime and sandy bed;
> Great legs of green or brown outstretching wide;
> Great arms thrown out as if embracing heaven;
> With eyes dilating, big as Bullace grapes,
> Upturned, and gloating as with rapturous rage;
> Great flattened jaws, that, ever and anon,
> Distending with voluminous harmonies,
> Sent forth their correspondences of sound,
> In due obedience to the choragus,
> Who still, at proper intervals, pour'd out
> The grand refrain—sonorous, swelling still,
> Till, at the last, the apex diapason
> Was caught, was won, in glorious 'Blood and 'ounds!' "

It was a war of shallow waters. Habitual croakers are only justified when they perish. They have nothing to complain of. They always seem to anticipate their fate, and this seems to prove it only just execution after judgment—which, of course, is legal and becoming. Our partisans had grown expert in this sort of warfare. The Caw-caw swamp was a region in which the frogs held populous communities and cities, and— you know the proverb—"Thick grass is easier cut than thin." It was a massacre! Every spearman could count his score or two of slain, and, really, a very pretty spectacle they made when, emerging from the swamp, each carried his victims aloft, transfixed upon a sharp and slender rod, run through at the neck, eyes wider than ever, and legs and arms spread about in all directions. Nor was this all. No less than three young alligators and three times as many terrapins were surprised and captured, almost without a struggle, and borne off in triumph to the camp! The wailing in the Caw-caw that night was not greatly lessened by the loss of so many sonorous voices, since we may reasonably suppose that maternal suffering sent up such extra clamors for the absence of precious young ones, as more than atoned for the diminished forces of the community.

"On your lives, boys, not a word of what we have been doing," said Captain Porgy. They all swore to keep faith.

"There are thousands of clever people in the world," he added, "who require to be surprised into happiness. Some of my guests, to-night, are probably of this description. I shall teach them a new pleasure—nay, a new moral in a new pleasure—teach them how absurd it is to despise any of the gifts of Providence."

And, following out this policy, it was with great secrecy that the spoils of the frog campaign were conveyed to his quarters, and delivered over to the custody of Tom, his cook. Tom, we may add, like every sensible cook, made a sufficient mystery of his art to keep prying curiosity away from the kitchen whenever he was engaged in any of his culinary combinations. Let us leave these for other parties, and for proceedings of more imposing consequence if less attractive performance. We shall seek to be present when supper is on the table.

Porgy felt he had good reasons for his great exertions. During the lull in the fighting, General Greene had called a sort of "military conference for the interchange of opinions" to which were summoned all the leading officers on southern duty. John Rutledge, Governor of South Carolina, who had been given dictatorial powers, served as moderator.

After the conference a dinner, indeed a banquet if at all possible, was suitable, and so Captain Porgy had risen to the occasion and, taking the initiative, had invited all the high command, with the exception of Generals Greene and Lee to his own dinner party. Greene did not know of Porgy's intention and announced he had planned a big supper. There was an embarrassed silence, which the governor himself broke by saying that Greene was too late, as the gentlemen were engaged elsewhere.

*Rutledge admitted he himself was committed "with my own grateful
will, and gratified consent, to the supper of Captain Porgy's of Marion's."*

"And I."

"And I."

"And I,"—from all present, the general himself and Colonel Lee
excepted.

"Captain Porgy!" said Greene, "Captain Porgy! Where have I heard
of Captain Porgy."

"From me, sir, I suspect," said Lee rather sullenly. "I have dined
and supped with Captain Porgy. He is a rare companion—a strange
fellow, with a clever French faculty, of making a dish out of a June bug,
and a dinner out of—out of—."

"A mere matter of moonshine!" added Rutledge. "And a good dish
and dinner he makes of it too, let me tell you. He will contrive to sup
bountifully upon elements, upon which simpler folks would starve. If
Colonel Lee would finish now, he will tell you that he never supped
better in his life than when he supped with Captain Porgy."

"Never, sir; I admit it. I did not feed with the less pleasure that I
never once guessed what were the ingredients of the dish."

"Really, gentlemen," said Greene, "I had no idea that I had such a
competitor. And what am I to do? I have ordered supper for twenty,
and find myself without a guest."

And the general really appeared much mortified.

"Were it consistent with proper discipline and military practice, general," quoth Rutledge, "I shall counsel you to do as the rich man had
to do in scripture, who made a great feast, and, like yourself, was
disappointed in his fine company—so sent out with a dragnet and took in
the lame, halt, blind, and every way destitute. But this will hardly answer in our day and country. But, if you will suffer me, I will reconcile
all difficulties. If you will permit me to order your cook and butler to
send all your supplies to the quarters of the swamp-fox, with my respect
to the worthy Captain Porgy, apprizing him that you will honor his
table to-night, all will be right. I will take leave to include Colonel Lee
in the invitation."

"But this would be a great liberty, governor," said Greene.

"Not a whit, sir. Captain Porgy will feel himself honored, I assure
you;—nay, will be greatly pleased that we have dealt with him so frank-

ly. He is a gentleman, sir, of an old house and feather, and knows how to requite a courtesy whatever its aspect."

"But—we shall take him by surprise—so many."

"You forget that nearly all of us are already secured as his guests. Beside, you will send over your own supplies."

Marion *sotto voce*—"If Porgy will suffer them to be brought on table."

And he whispered to Rutledge:—

"Let the meats be sent over before the general's cook has touched them."

"Right! I comprehend," said Rutledge, in a whisper also. Then aloud—

"Trust to me, general; I know my man—I shall be careful not to commit you. I confess my anxiety that you should know Captain Porgy, and see what are the resources of our Low-Country partisans. He will be honored, I repeat, by our frank proceedings; and," in a whisper—"the effect will be good upon our people. They love to see a frank simplicity and open confidence in great men."

Greene smiled at the compliment, his blue eyes looking archly into those of Rutledge:—

"Ah! governor, you are more of a tactician than any military man I know."

"In the commissariat, perhaps," responded the other. "Well, you give me permission."

"If you say so."

"I do! and will give all the necessary orders, despatch a note to our host, and send over the provisions. But the latter must be done at once, and before your cook has handled them."

"Why so—why not let them be dressed?" said Greene.

"For the best of reasons. If dressed, they would be held in no condition for Captain Porgy's table. Do not be mortified, general, to be told, that your *cuisinier* would never receive his diploma from the hands of Captain Porgy. He is a martinet in the kitchen. He refines upon soups, is sublime in sauces, and altogether scorns and despises the cruel maceration of meat in hot waters, which is the vulgar usage of our cooks in camp. Understand, again, that Captain Porgy is no vulgar person; but a rare fellow for company, a man of soul and humor, and at his table you will be sure to find an appetite though you had already fed to surfeit. As Colonel Lee says, you must be wise enough to take your supper as you take your religion with a perfect faith, which is never guilty of the impertinence of Peter, of questioning the cleanness of the meats which Providence has furnished."

"But everything's wholesome!" said Greene, with a simplicity which argued his Rhode Island ignorance of such authorities as Ude, and Glass, and Savarin.

"Wholesome!" exclaimed Lee—"By Jupiter, General Greene, I do not know that I have tasted wholesome food since my last supper with Captain Porgy. I know not why he has not invited me, since I am very sure no man could have done more justice to his fare."

Lee was evidently piqued.

"An omission easily accounted for, Colonel Lee," answered Rutledge promptly, "since you had not come in from below, when the invitations were sent out; no one could say that you would be in to-night. I take upon myself to say that no one will be more welcome to his table than yourself."

"Well, if the taste to do justice to his table is sufficient commendation, I may safely assert that you are right," said Lee, his complacency always making belief easy, in respect to his own welcome. Marion looked grave, but said nothing. *He* knew that Porgy would not, of himself, invite Lee. He had too seriously displeased the partisans; but Marion was not displeased that Lee should invite himself, which, in his, as in the case of Greene, was substantially the fruit of Rutledge's diplomacy. The latter, as usual, had his own way. The despatch was sent to Porgy, and Greene's cook was seasonably arrested in the very act of doing murder upon his edibles. The party adjourned to meet at the sylvan camp of the swamp-fox.

DOINGS IN THE APOLLO CHAMBER.

Our partisan division of the army, with their horses, occupied no small extent of territory. Our Captain Porgy, himself, with his little personal equipage, demanded considerable space. He was the person always to secure that "ample room and verge enough," which, as he himself said, were essential to his individual girth. "My breadth of belt," he was wont to say, "implies a fair field; and, having that, I ask no favors." Besides being of social habits, his mess was always a large one. Among his immediate associates, retainers rather, he kept not only his cook, but his poet; the one almost as necessary as the other. Then, he

never was without a guest, and whenever his commissariat was particularly well supplied, he was sure to have a full table. Such an idea as a
good table, without an adequate number of guests to enjoy it, seemed to
him a thing vile, unreasonable, inhuman, and utterly unchristian. We
have seen that, particularly fortunate in his foray among the green-
jacketed denizens of the Caw-caw, he had made arrangements for a
larger circle than usual. His own tastes and purposes requiring it, Captain Porgy usually chose his own ground whenever tents were to be
pitched. He had a great eye to proper localities.

"The open woods, on the south and west," was his rule. "Let the
swamp and thicket cover my back on the east. That east wind has been
of evil tendency from the earliest periods of time. The Bible speaks of
it. A bad-tempered person, soured and surly, growling always, and in-
sufferable from bile and conceit, is said to fill his bowels with the east
wind. It has a bad effect on the best bowels. Give me just opening
enough on the east for the purposes of draught, but let your tent be
open to the full pressure of the winds from south and west. You need,
in our climate, an eastern opening at the dinner-hour, dining at three, or
thereabout; but beware of it after the sun has set. Don't sleep with the
east wind blowing upon you. If you do, face it—let your feet receive
it first. Every wind that blows has a specific quality. The east, northeast,
and southeast, are all more or less pernicious, muddy, insidious, hateful.
Our natural winds in midsummer are from the south and west. The
south persuades you to languor, pleasantly relaxes, discourages the exertion which would be too exhaustive for the season. The west is the
agitator, the thunder-storm wind, that purges and purifies; the northwest
is the cleaning wind, that sweeps up the sky, and brushes off all its
cobwebs. Each wind having thus a specific mission, it is wonderful that
men who build know so little of the means of ventilation. Now, you
see, I choose my ground with an open pine-forest in front, that is south
and west and northwest. I take care that the land slopes down from me
in all these directions. If there be hill, swamp, or dense thicket, I put
them, with the devil, behind me. I have here chosen the very pleasantest
spot in the whole encampment. There is not one of these continental
officers who knows anything of the subject. Yet, to the health of an
army, a difference of fifty yards in the location of a camp, is very frequently all the difference between life and death!"

And, in that broad, terrace-like spread of wood and thicket, he had chosen the most agreeable region. The pine-woods opened at his feet, and spread away almost interminably, giving the necessary degree of shade, yet leaving free passage for the wind.

"Free circulation, Geordie Dennison," said he, as with hands outspread he seemed to welcome the gentle play of the breezes reeking up from the southwest—"that is the secret of health—free circulation for the winds, the waters, and the blood. It is stagnation that is death. This is the reason why a pine-forest is more healthy than any other. It is the only forest that suffers free play to the winds. Hence you hear the music in a pine-forest which you hear in no other. The breezes pour through, and swell up, until all the tree-tops become so many organ-pipes. The vulgar notion is that there is some virtue in the odor of the pines to neutralize malaria. But this is all nonsense. Pine-woods that have a dense undergrowth, are not more healthy than any other. It is the shape of the tree, a tall column, without lateral branches, naked a hundred feet high, and arching above, umbrella fashion, into a grand ceiling, which shuts out the intense heat of the sun, and suffers free exercise to the breeze. Here it plays with delight and impunity. In the dense thickets it trickles only, and finally stagnates; and hence the fevers of uncleared lands. Bays, swamps, ponds, are unhealthy, not because of the water which they contain, but because of the dense thickets which they nurture. The hottest place in the world in midsummer, is a deep forest or thicket, with a close undergrowth. Fools talk of decaying vegetation as the secret of disease; yet when our fevers are raging most, vegetation has not begun to decay. Gardens, fields, forests, are never more fresh and beautiful, never more vigorous and verdant, than when death seems lurking under every flower, like some venomous reptile watching for and creeping to the ear of the unconscious sleeper. But, Geordie Dennison, boy, once suppose that the air is stagnant in any locality, and you need not suppose the necessity for its impregnation by any deleterious agent. A stagnant atmosphere is, *per se,* malaria. And that fact that we can assign a distinct locality for the disease—that we can say with confidence, to sleep here is death, while you may sleep with safety within half a mile—establishes the fact conclusively that the atmosphere is localized—no matter by what cause—though even that is a matter which I have considered also—and once let the atmosphere be fixed, and it is only in degree that it differs from that of an old sink or well. It is putrid, and to inhale it is a danger. You can not impregnate with miasma any region, where the winds are allowed to penetrate freely from three points of the compass, and where they do penetrate. When we are very sickly, you will always find a pressure of winds, daily from a single quarter, for a long-continued period of time. The atmosphere loses its equilibrium, as it were; the winds lack their *balance;* and running one course only, they run into a *cul de sac,* as water that can not escape, rises to a level with its source, becomes a pond, and stagnates. A thunder-storm purifies, not from its electricity, as some contend, but because it is a storm. All storms purify because they agitate. They disperse the local atmosphere over a thousand miles of space, and restore its equilibrium."

"But, Captain Porgy, were it not better that you should be thinking of your supper and company, instead of philosophizing here about the atmosphere?"

"It is because I am thinking of my company and supper, Master Geordie, that I do philosophize about the atmosphere. A wholesome atmosphere is half of a good supper. We can eschew the water. We need not drink that, if we can find any other liquor; but make what wry faces we will, the atmosphere we must drink, even though we know it to be impregnated with poison. Better drink the vilest ditch-water a thousand times. That may disorder the stomach, but the other must vitiate the lungs and so directly disease the blood and the heart. I am trying to teach you, sir, that in giving a good supper or dinner to your friends, you are to serve it up in properly-ventilated apartments."

"Well, we have it airy enough here."

"True; but had it been left to anybody else, ten to one you would have had our tents pitched in a villanous thicket where we never could have got a breath of air. Look, now, at the Legion encamped on the left; they are in a bottom, the breeze passing clean over their heads. Their camp-master had no idea of what was the duty to be done, beyond the simply getting room enough for the horses and wagons of some three hundred men. Sir, the partisan cavalry have never been so healthy as when I have been permitted to select the ground for their bivouac."

"That's true!"

"To be sure it's true; and you see the fruits of it in the pleasant sleeps that we enjoy, and the hardy elasticity with which we travel. There never was any people so exposed as ours have been, night and day, in all weathers, and the most wearisome marches, that have ever enjoyed

such admirable health. And they owe it to me, sir—to me, Geordie
Dennison—yet, d—n 'em, they are not half so grateful for this blessing
as for my soups and suppers. They would readily compound to drink
any quantity of malaria, if they could swallow a pint of my rum-punch
after it."

"Ah, they regard the rum-punch as the antidote, and there is nothing
unreasonable, therefore, in their practice. But, captain, the hour latens."

"*Latens!* By what right do you use that word?"

"It's a good word, captain."

"So it is; but I never heard it used before."

"Very likely; but would you permit that argument to be used against
any new dish that Tom should put on the table to-night!"

"No, sir; no, Geordie, you are right. You could not have answered
me better if you had argued a thousand years. And I will remember
the word;—so, as the hour *latens,* Geordie, get up and help me with these
tables. I must summon Frampton and Millhouse. We shall need their
knives and hatchets. I have invited thirty-one guests, Geordie, not counting you and Lance; we three will make the number thirty-four. There's
no such table to be spread in camp to-night. Think of it;—a simple
captain of militia giving a supper to thirty guests, and upon such short
commons as are allowed us. Half of the poor devils in camp think it
monstrous impudent of me to give a supper at all—and to thirty persons——"

"They can't guess how it's to be done."

"No! indeed! the blockheads! But their vexation increases when they
find my guests all outranking myself. The envious rascals! Beware of
envy, Geordie—it is the dirtiest, sneakingest, meanest little passion in the
world, the younger brother of vanity, furnishing all the venom to its
sleek-skinned and painted senior."

"And you are to have the governor, captain?"

"Ay, he accepts. John Rutledge is a great fellow, without affectation,
Geordie—no pretender—one of the few men who really do *think.* The
greater number, even when they greatly rank, only repeat each other—
they do not think. Thought, George Dennison, is really confined to a
very few. Men, as a race, are not thinking animals. They are gregarious
and imitative. They go in droves and follow a leader, whom they contrive after a while to mimic after a monkey fashion. Thought is always

an individual. But—where is that boy Frampton? Sound your whistle, George."

The whistle was sounded.

"Now help me with these poles. There are forty cut. We must have crotch-sticks—two, four, six, eight, ten, twelve—it will require twenty-four; we must make our tables solid."

Lance Frampton now appeared, followed by half a dozen stout young troopers, bearing slim green poles upon their shoulders, forked sticks, and all the appliances necessary to the construction of the rustic tables and seats of the company. Long practice had made all of them familiar with the rude sort of manufacture which was required. The crotch-sticks were soon driven upright into the ground, in frequent parallels; cross pieces were laid in the crotchets of these, and the poles were stretched along, forming a crossed table with four ends, for so many dignitaries, and capable to accommodate forty guests with ease. Of a similar, but stouter fashion, were the seats for the guests. It was surprising how soon the area was filled—how soon the mechanical preparations for the feast were fashioned. The amphitheatre beneath the pines was ample. Porgy, as he boasted, had the proper eye for a locality. When reared and steadied, stanchioned and strengthened, the tables were covered with great oak-leaves, green, looking very clean, nice, and fresh—a verdant tablecloth.

"Now, see that you have torches, Lance; for, though we have a glorious moon, we need torches for the dark corners. Many of the guests will bring their negroes to wait. But we shall need some waiters besides. Engage some of these young chaps. They shall sweep the platters clean. Forget nothing, boy. We are to have big wigs to supper, remember. Geordie, come with me to *our* wagon. I think we shall astonish these epauleted gentry to-night.

And the two turned off to another part of the wood where stood the little wagon already described—a sort of covered box—a thing which one man might have rolled, but to which a couple of stout hackneys were harnessed, when taken.

"Little," said Porgy, as he unlocked the cover of the vehicle, "little did stuttering Pete dream what he lost and we gained, when we cut off the four wagons of Stewart. His eyes opened only upon the big wagons. He never gave a look at the one little one upon which I fastened—as if the most precious commodities were not always packed in the smallest compass! Yet, look there, Geordie."

The poet looked in:—

"Lemons, captain."

"Ay, lemons and white sugar, and nutmegs, and cloves, and spices of all sorts, and an anchor of Geneva, and a box of cocoa, and a bag of coffee, and a good supply of old Jamaica, and, see you that keg?—tongues, beef-tongues, English beef-tongues. Now please you to read the name on the cover; ay! Lord Rawdon's own prog, by the pipers, specially selected for his table and palate. We shall astonish these wooden-headed continentals to-night, Geordie! won't we? You thought me mad, didn't you, when I invited so many? But I knew what I was about. They shall stare, they shall sup, though they lament for ever, after the acquisition of such a taste as their vulgar fortunes can never hereafter satisfy. But mum! Not a word in anticipation."

And Porgy closed the wagon with haste and locked it, as half a dozen troopers lounged carelessly by, looking, with some curiosity as they passed, to the proceedings of the two.

"Stay here, Geordie, and keep watch till I return. I must put Millhouse on duty over this wagon, or there will be a Flemish account of its contents when supper's called. The morals of the dragoon service, imply theft as a necessity. A good scout has all the capabilities of a good pickpocket."

And, moralizing as he went, Porgy hurried off for succor. Dennison was relieved by Millhouse, a one-armed trooper of iron aspect, and as stubborn of purpose as a mule. The wagon was safe in his keeping as long as his left arm could lift sabre or pistol—and he was duly armed with both.

The next visit of our host was to Tom, the cook, who had a precinct of his own, some twenty-five yards from the spot where the tables had been spread. The terrapin soup was discussed, the *ragout;* the stew; the boiled tongues; nothing escaped attention. Then, a survey was taken of the crockery; the bowls, plates, dishes; the knives and forks; the spoons of iron, the drinking vessels of delph, tin, or calabash. These commodities were too frail of character, not to need the greatest care and attention; and every feast given by our captain, mortified him with the slenderness of his resources. But there was no remedy. If half a dozen good bowls of delph, and platters of tin, could be provided for the more

distinguished guests, the rest might surely be satisfied with clean calabashes. We will suppose our captain satisfied in respect to these things.
He was in the midst of the examination, however, venting his annoyances at his limited resources, in uneasy exclamations, when a messenger
from Rutledge brought him the note from that personage apprizing
him that Greene and Lee would appear among his guests. The governor
wrote:—

"I shall take the liberty, my dear Captain Porgy, of bringing with me
a couple of additional guests, in General Greene and Colonel Lee, knowing that your provision will not only be ample, but that the taste which
usually presides over your banquets will give to our friends from Rhode
Island and Virginia such a notion of the tastes of Apicius and Lucullus,
as certainly never yet dawned upon them in their own half-civilized
regions. Your own courtesy will do the rest and will, I trust, sufficiently
justify the confidence with which I have insisted upon their coming.

"Yours,

"JOHN RUTLEDGE"

"Humph!" exclaimed Porgy, "I should not have ventured to ask General Greene, not that I stand in awe of his epaulettes, but it is so rare
to find a *parvenu* who would not hold such an invitation from a poor
captain of militia, to be a piece of impertinence and presumption. Our
own folks know me too well to exhibit any such *gaucherie*. As for Lee,
he is a popinjay! I should never ask him myself; but have no objection
that he should occasionally appear among gentlemen who can teach him,
by example, how gentlemen can be good fellows without any loss of
dignity.—Geordie—your pen and a scrap of paper. I hope I diminish
none of your verses by consuming your foolscap."

The pen and paper were had, and our captain wrote:—

"Governor Rutledge can take no liberty for the propriety of which
his name is not a sufficient guaranty. Captain Porgy will be most happy
to welcome any guests whom he may think proper to bring."

This written, he handed it to the messenger. It was then that Greene's
cook uncovered a small tumbril or box in a wheelbarrow, containing the
uncooked provisions which had been destined for his own table. Porgy
looked at the bloody and livid meats with unqualified disgust.

"But," said he *sotto voce,* "we can't reject them. Here, Tom."

The cook appeared, apron in front and knife in hand.

"Tom, take charge of these provisions. They are sent by the general

—General Greene, do you hear? Use them. Cook them. Turn them into soup, hash, steak, what you will!" then, as the messengers of Rutledge and Greene disappeared— "but d—m you, boy, don't let them show themselves upon my table. The meat is villanously butchered. That alone should condemn it. Make it up for some of these young fellows that have been working for us. And—Tom—"

"Well, maussa—talk quick."

"Don't forget the balls. Let there be a plenty in the soup."

"Psho, maussa, enty I know."

"Enough! Begone!"

The active mind of our corpulent captain began to grow restless. He had seen to everything that he could think of, and grew peevish from nothing to do. Suddenly he stuck his fingers into his hair.

"No! the vessels for the punch; Geordie. By heavens, I had almost forgotten. Let us after the punchbowls, and then for the manufacture. *You* are good at that; a poet should be. Curious problem, Geordie—the affinity between poetry and the bottle."

"Not at all. It only implies the ardency of the poet. It is so with the orator. You never saw poet or orator yet, that was not ardent and fond of the juices of the grape."

"Not the didactic orders, surely. But how is it, then, that Bacchus is not your deity instead of Apollo?"

"Because Apollo, with virtues of his own, includes those of Bacchus. He is a ripener of Bacchus, and loves not the wine less, nor is less the true god of it, because he employs a vintner. I see no difficulty in the matter."

"And, perhaps, there is none. Yet what would Apollo say, or Bacchus even, to such a punchbowl as ours."

And he pointed to an enormous calabash, holding a couple of gallons at the least, that, duly valued and taken care of, had survived all the vicissitudes of the campaign.

"They would, either of them, feel that there was wholesome propriety in the vessel. It is one which Ceres has presented for the occasion, to a kindred deity. Boon nature has provided where vulgar art has failed. It would be much more staggering to either of the ancient gods to try them with the Jamaica, instead of the blood of Tuscany."

"Ah! they never got such liquor on Olympus. Their nectar was a poor wishy-washy sort of stuff, of not more body than some of those thin vaporing French and German liquors, of which we have had a taste occasionally. Their wine of Tuscany, nay, the Falernian of Horace, would not take rank now-a-days with the juices of the common corn, prepared according to our process. Drinking whiskey or Jamaica, Nero might have been a fool, a wretch, a murderer—might fire his city or butcher his mother—might have committed any crime, but cowardice! Whiskey or Jamaica might have saved Rome from Gaul and Vandal. The barbarians, be sure, drank the most potent beverages."

"A notion deserving of study. We drink deep now-a-days. Will our descendants beat us? Will they laugh at our potations, which rarely leave a gentleman on his legs after midnight?"

"Ah! say nothing of our progeny. Do not build upon the degenerates. It may be that the milksops will fancy it bad taste, nay, even immoral, on the part of their ancestors, to have swallowed Jamaica or whiskey at all. In proportion as their heads are weak, will they pronounce ours vicious; and just because we have a certain amount of strength in our virtue—a certain quality of brawn and blood and muscle, to keep our sentiment from etherealizing—growing into mere thin air—will they presume to stroke their beards in self-complaisant satisfaction, thanking God that such poor *publicans,* have given way to a more saintly race of sinners. I am half inclined to thank my stars that, when I disappear, the race of Porgy will not be continued in the person of one who prides himself upon having no head—for a bottle!"

"Yes! save us from all degenerate children. But, captain, will this *one* calabash of punch suffice for forty? Impossible. Two gallons among forty! Never in the world! Why, sir, there are three generals, and one governor, a score of colonels, and others of inferior rank, who are emulous of great men's virtues. Two gallons to forty such persons."

"Oh! don't stop to calculate. Luckily there are two calabashes."

And the little wagon yielded up the desired article.

"Make it rich, Geordie."

"Captain Porgy, when they drink of this liquor, each man will feel that his will has been made. He will feel that he has no more care in life—will fold his robes about him for flight."

"Or fall! Well, give us a taste. I profess to be a very competent judge of what a good Jamaica punch should be."

Smacks his lips.

"The proportions are good: the acid has yielded to the embrace of the sugar with the recognition of a perfect faith, and both succumb to the spirit, as with the recognition of a perfect deity. Next to poetry, Geordie, you are an adept at punch."

Geordie somewhat proudly:—

"Yes, captain, on this score I feel safe. I am not always certain of my verses. I sometimes feel that they lack the sweet and the ardent—but I am never doubtful of the perfect harmony that prevails among all the elements when I manufacture punch."

Porgy quaffs off the contents of the *dipper*.

"Geordie, you are a benefactor. When this war ceases, you shall partake my fortunes. You shall live with me; and, between punch and poetry, we will make the latter end of life a felicitous *finale* to a very exciting drama. By the way, Geordie, talking of poetry and punch reminds me. You must be prepared with something good to-night. I shall have you out. You shall give us some heroic ballad. I know you have not been drowsing in that thicket for nothing. Have you got anything ready?"

"I *have* been doing a trifle, but—"

"None of your buts. Get aside, and memorize it. These two vessels of punch, meanwhile, we will put under lock and key, and yield to the guardianship of Sergeant Millhouse."

HOW PORGY FEASTED THE CAPTAINS.

With vulgar people, a dinner party is the occasion of much fuss and fidgeting. The vulgar egotism is always on the *qui vive* lest something should go wrong—lest something should be wanting to the proper effect —lest, in brief, some luckless excess or deficiency should certainly convey to the guest the secret of those deficiencies, in taste, manners, experiences, and resources, which would, if known, be fatal to the claims of good breeding and high tone which the host is most anxious to establish. Those, on the contrary, who feel assured on such points are apt to take the events of a dinner-table coolly and with comparative indifference. A blunder or a deficiency of steward or servant, occasions little or no concern; is never allowed to disturb the equilibrium of the master, who takes for granted that such small matters will be ascribed, by every sensible guest, to the right cause; and for the opinion of all other persons he cares not a button.

The result of this equanimity is to enable him to keep *his mind "in hand"* for the entertainment of his company. He is able to observe and to minister with promptness and full resource, as his wits are not disordered by any feverish workings of his *amour propre*. He sees what is wanting at a glance; supplies the deficiency with a nod; his servants are duly taught in the value of his nod and glance; and the skill of the host, by which the guests are diverted, enables Jack and Gill to wipe up the water which they have spilt so awkwardly, in their uphill progress, without attracting any notice—without filling the scene with most admired disorder.

Our host *knows* his company, and conjures up the special topic which appeals directly to the tastes or the fancies of each. He is vigilant even while he seems most at ease; when his indifference is most apparent, it is made to cover a becoming solicitude for the comfort of the humblest person present. He provides himself with the proper cue to all your prejudices and affections, as by a divine instinct, so that he steers clear of the one, and shapes his course directly for the other; and when the waters are unluckily ruffled, by some bull-headed companion, who treads on his neighbor's toes without even suspecting that he has corns, our host is at hand to pour oil upon the troubled waters, and soothe to calm the temper which is ruffled. He contrives, at the same time, that the offender shall be taught the nature of his offence, without being brought up to the halberds and set in pillory,

"Pour les encourager les autres."

There was nothing doubtful about the *aplomb* of Captain Porgy. Having prepared his feast according to the full extent of his resources; drilled his awkward squad to the utmost of his capacity and their susceptibilities; seen that they were in sufficient numbers for proper attendance; and made, in brief, all his preparations, he gave himself no further concern, but prepared to receive his guests, with the easy good nature, the frank politeness, the smiling grace, of an old-school gentleman. And it is quite an error to talk, as we are apt to do, of the formality of the old-school gentleman. The gentleman of two hundred or one hundred years ago, differed very slightly in his bearing from the same class at the present day. In due degree as his ceremonials ran into formalities, did he lose the character of the gentleman. In no period was mere form and buckram ever confounded, by sensible people, with politeness and refinement.

Never was gentleman more perfectly at ease in crowded assembly, yet more solicitous of the claims of all about him, than our corpulent captain. His shrewd good sense, nice tastes, playful humors, and frank spirit, all harmonizing happily, enabled him to play the host generally to the equal satisfaction of all his company. He had the proper welcome for each as he drew nigh; the proper word, which set each person at his ease, and prepared him for the development of all his conversational resources.

Among the first of his guests to appear were Governor Rutledge and General Greene. "The really great," said Porgy to Lance Frampton who stood behind him, "never keep the table waiting."

The approach to the scene was through a great natural avenue of lofty green pines, through which the moon was peeping curiously with a bright smile, a disinterested spectator of the proceedings. Music timed the approaches of the guests, the army band having been secured for the evening. Porgy welcomed his guests at the entrance of the area in which his tables had been spread.

"General Greene, Captain Porgy," said Rutledge. Greene took the outstretched hand of the host, saying:—

"What I have heard of you, Captain Porgy, makes me trespass without fear of the consequences."

"And what I know of General Greene enables me to welcome him with every hope of the consequences. I am very grateful to Governor Rutledge for doing that which, as a poor captain of militia, I should scarcely have ventured to do myself."

"I knew my customers both, my dear captain," said Rutledge, "and knew how little was necessary to render the regular and volunteer service grateful to each other."

"Be seated, gentlemen," said Porgy, "while I put myself on duty for a while;" and he resumed his place at the opening of the avenue, while Sumter, Marion, and the rest severally presented themselves, were welcomed and conducted to the interior by young Frampton, who did the duties of an aid. Colonel Lee was among the latest to appear.

"My dear Porgy," said he condescendingly—"I am late; but the cavalry of the legion is on vigilant duty to-night, and a good officer you know— eh!"

And he left it to our host to conceive the rest.

"Col. Lee may be forgiven, if late among his friends, when we know that his enemies rarely reproach him for a like remissness."

The grace of Porgy's manner happily blended with the grave dignity of his address. Lee smiled at the compliment:—

"Always ready, Porgy—never to be outdone in the play of compliment, or the retort courteous;" and while speaking he was ushered in with other visiters.

The company was at length assembled. The music ceased. A single bugle sounded from the amphitheatre, and the guests disposed themselves without confusion under the whispered suggestions of Lieutenant Frampton. Porgy took his place at the head of the table, standing, till all were seated.

"Gentlemen," said he, "be pleased to find places at the board. Colonel Singleton, you are my *vis-a-vis*. Governor Rutledge will you honor me by sitting at my right. General Greene, I have presumed to assign you the seat at my left."

Right and left of Singleton, Marion and Sumter were placed. At one end of the table crossing the centre of the board, Colonel Lee was seated, Colonel Maham occupied the other. Carrington, Horry, Mellichampe, St. Julien, and others found places between these several termini. Scarcely had they been seated when four great calabash tureens were placed severally at the extremities, the odorous vapors from which appealed gratefully to every nostril in company.

"Turtle soup!" was the delighted murmur.

"And lemons!"

And as the smoking vessels were set before the governor and General Greene, the former exclaimed:—

"Faith, Captain Porgy, your last voyage to the West Indies seems to have been a highly prosperous adventure."

"In truth," said Greene, "I am half inclined to think that there must have been some such enterprise, of which General Marion has forgotten to apprize me."

"I begin seriously to suspect him," said Rutledge. "The fact is that General Marion is so fond of secret enterprises, and audacious ones—does things with so much despatch, and thinks it so easy to do the impossible, that I half believe he has made a three nights' run for the Havana, or sent off a favorite squad on a sortie in that direction. Say, general, is it not so? Let us know the truth of it. You found, among your captures at Georgetown, some ready-rigged sloop or schooner, and sent her out on a cruise in anticipation of this very occasion."

"Nay, governor, the merits of the enterprise, such as it was and the fruits thereof, are due entirely to our host. It was his adventure wholly, though we share the spoils."

"But, where—where—where—" began Peter Horry, stuttering, "where the devil did he—did he—get 'em—turtles and lemons! I don't—don't—understand it—at all."

"Better not press the inquiry, Horry," said Singleton with a sly smile upon the company—"the discovery will hardly add to your own laurels."

"How—my laurels! What—what—I want to—to know—have my laurels—to do—to do—with the matter?"

"Let's have it, Colonel Singleton," said Rutledge eagerly. "Out with the story. Colonel Horry is so seldom to be caught napping that I shall rejoice to have one story at his expense."

"Ay, ay, the story, Singleton," from a dozen voices around the board.

"Tell—tell—tell, if you will," stuttered Horry—"only be sure, and tell —the—the truth, and shame—you know—who."

"The adventure illustrates the military character of the two gentlemen most admirably," said Singleton. "Colonel Horry is a gentleman of large eyes and grapples with objects of magnitude always. It is Captain Porgy's pleasure to be discriminating and select. The lemons and a variety of other edibles are furnished, unwillingly, I grant you, by Lord Rawdon himself. They form a part of the supplies brought up by Colonel Stewart. In dashing at Stewart's convoy, Horry passed a mean little wagon in the rear, as quite unworthy his regards. He swept off as you know three or four others of considerable value to the army. But the very littleness of this wagon which Horry had despised, fixed the regards of our host. He quietly possessed himself of it, and was rewarded with the private stores designed for Lord Rawdon himself." The story produced a laugh at the expense of Horry.

"Who—who—who—the devil," said he, "would have thought—of—of —anything good in—that rickety concern? I'd like to know, Captain Porgy, what you got besides the lemons?"

"White sugars, coffee, tea, spices, Spanish sweetmeats, preserved ginger, three kegs of Jamaica, and a goodly variety besides!"

"The d—l!—and—and—I to miss 'em all."

"But you got loads of bacon and flour, Horry."

"Several bales of blankets."

"Ay, and a bathing-tub and complete set of chamber crockery!"

"What," said Rutledge, "was there a bathing-tub and chamber crockery?"

"Yes, indeed."

"Who could have wanted that, I wonder?"

"Some young ensign of the buffs or blues," said Porgy, "whose mother was duly considerate of the young man's skin in a warm climate. You should have discovered Colonel Horry's visage when that wagon was burst open and the contents revealed. The bathing-tub and furniture filled the wagon."

"What did he say, Porgy? Tell us that!"

"Say! Ah! What was it, colonel? Deliver it yourself: nobody can repeat it half so well."

"Re—re—repeat it yourself, if you can!" said Horry stuttering and dipping up his soup with increased rapidity.

"Out with it, Captain Porgy. Horry's speech."

Porgy nodded to Singleton, who answered:—

"I heard it, and as Horry permits will deliver it. He said, stamping his feet in a rage: 'Throw out the d——d basins, and break up the blasted tub. Who would have thought of any fellow being such a bloody booby as to bring a bathing-tub and chamber crockery into a pond and bush country?'"

And slightly imitating the stammer of Horry so as to give a lively idea of his manner, Singleton set the table in a roar. When the laugh had subsided:—

"But did he break up the crockery, Porgy?"

"Every bowl and basin. He was merciless. You never saw such havoc. His broadsword played elephant in the crockery shop to perfection, and the dragoons, delighted with the humors of their colonel, went into the work of demolition with a rush."

"I had—no—no—no use for the d——d — d——d — d——d things," said Horry; "and I was—de—de—de—termined to give the d——d puppy that owned them a lesson."

"Ha! ha! ha!"

"But where did the turtles come from?"

"From the genius of my cook, Tom," said Porgy. "The turtle are terrapin from the Caw-caw."

"Not the alligator terrapin, captain, I hope," said Sumter. "I could never bring myself to eat any of that order."

"You have done it on this occasion," said Porgy.

"And very effectually too, general," said Singleton, "since I have helped you to a second supply, and you seem in a fair way to need a third."

Sumter looked a little blank.

"Do not be discomfited, general," said Porgy, "since I took the precaution to have all their tails cut off before they were hashed up for the soup."

"But what did you do with the tails?"

"Ah! they were made into balls, with a due proportion of beef and bacon."

"You have caught me beyond escape, captain, since I confess to have done as much execution on the balls as on the soup."

"And you are surprised into a wisdom, general, that has cured you of the prejudices of twenty years! What we call the alligator terrapin is the best of the tribe—the fattest, richest, best flavored. It requires only that skill in the dressing which my man Tom supplies."

The bugle sounded. Sergeant Millhouse marshalled the waiters to their stations, and the emptied vessels were removed. With another blast of the bugle, new dishes were set on the table.

"A noble-looking fish," said Greene. "What fish is this, Captain Porgy?"

"The greatest delicacy of a fresh-water river, this is the Edisto blue cat—for very nice people a most discouraging name.—Gentlemen, look to yourselves. Here is boiled fish, such as George the Third can not procure; dressed in a style which would not discredit the table of our great ally, the king of France. Men of *goût* will of course prefer the boiled—for the undeveloped taste, the fry is abundant. There are perch and trout in those several dishes. They are all fresh from the Edisto within five hours."

"Your troopers have been busy, captain."

"Ay, sir, and my cook. He was fortunate in his search along the river this morning, to come upon three or four fish-traps, which he emptied without leave. Governor, the melted butter is beside you. By-the-way, those naval biscuit are also from the stores of my Lord Rawdon. —General, do not dream of defiling that fish with vinegar. It is an abomination in this case. The fish only entreats the butter, and the dressing is complete."

The eye of Porgy swept the table. The guests discussed the fish with the relish of starving men. There was a cessation. The finger of Porgy was lifted. Millhouse's bugle gave tongue, and the fish was superseded with a variety of dishes.

"General Greene—Governor Rutledge—suffer me to persuade you both to the ragout which is before me."

"What is it, captain?"

"Try it, general. It is the alerta—the green alerta—a sort of chicken you will find it, but far superior. The stew is of the *lagarta,* according to the Spaniards, and a dish quite as rare as exquisite on table. Gentlemen, interspersed with these dishes you will find more familiar, but inferior ones. There are hams and tongues, both from the stores of Lord Rawdon, and, in fact, most of this course will be found of foreign character. You will please ask me for no more revelations touching my mode of procuring supplies, as I have no wish to expose the breaking of any more crockery. It is not every one of our partisans who can bear, with so much equanimity as Colonel Horry, the story of his own acquisitions, and how made."

"This—what do you call it?" said Greene.

"Alerta!"

"Is delicious!"

"And nothing could be more savory than this stew, Captain Porgy."

"Yes, indeed, governor—the Spaniards have the merit of the discovery. But gentlemen, with this course, it is time to spiritualize the feast."

The speaker's finger was uplifted, and two enormous bowls of punch were set down at the two ends of the table.

"Gentlemen, we owe a great deal to the providence of Lord Rawdon."

"And the improvidence of Horry," whispered Rutledge, "for, of a verity, had he captured these spoils, he would never have made the same use of them as our host has done."

"Sir," said Porgy with solemnity, "he would have wasted them— naked, upon his dragoons.—Gentlemen, you will please fill for a sentiment. Colonel Singleton see that your end of the table charges duly."

"We are ready, captain."

Porgy rising:—

"Gentlemen, our first regular sentiment: 'The cause of Liberty—the cause of the American continent—the cause of all continents wherever man has a living soul!' "

"Music." And the bands struck up.

"Captain Porgy," said Lee, "send me, if you please, a second supply of that dish which you call the alerta. I don't know what sort of bird it is, but the savor is that of young pigeons. It is wonderfully nice."

"I agree with you, Lee," said Colonel Williams, "though I have no more idea what the bird is than of the mansions of the moon. Let me trouble you also, Captain Porgy."

"I must also trespass, captain," said Carrington. "Ordinarily, I seldom suffer myself to eat of dishes of which I know nothing; but these foreign meats come to us under good guaranties, though half the time without a name at all."

"Unless French, which is so much Greek to me," said Maham. "Captain, that *lagarta* stew is princely."

"No crowned head in Europe enjoys the like. Shall I help you, Colonel Maham?"

"Thank you, yes. But I thought you called it foreign."

"So it is—in one sense; but this is not imported. It is wholly domestic."

"Well, foreign or domestic, it is first rate," said Greene. "I will try a little more of it, Captain Porgy."

"Ah! general,"—with a smile—"suffer me to say that it is only in the militia service, after all, that the taste properly refines. Governor, shall I serve you?"

"Thank you, I will mince a little of your *lagarta,* captain," and a sly glance of Rutledge apprized the captain of his suspicions. But the face of Porgy made no revelations.

"Gentlemen," said Singleton, at the other end of the table, "fill your glasses."

"Ready, all," said Porgy.

Singleton rose, and gave:—

"South Carolina—almost freed from the footstep of the foreign tyrant, and rising to the full assertion of her own sovereignty!"

A brilliant burst from John Rutledge, brief, but like a fiery tongue speaking to the soul, followed this sentiment; and the music rose into a triumphant peal as his voice died away upon the echoes. Other sentiments succeeded other speeches; Rutledge, Greene, Marion, Sumter, Lee, were all duly honored with toasts, and all responded, each after his own fashion, all unaffectedly, simply, and with the proper earnestness of soldiers. And the punch flowed anew into fresh goblets, and the merriment grew high, and some of the grave barons began to sing in snatches, and the volunteer toasts filled up the pauses in the conversation. Meanwhile, a score of melons were placed upon the board, and the preserved fruits from the West Indies, guava and ginger, were crowded upon the board, and provoked new merriment at the expense of Rawdon, who lost, and Horry who refused to find the prize.

And while they gashed deeply the purple centres of the melons, Rutledge suddenly said to Porgy:—

"And now, captain, that you have had your triumph, that all present have borne testimony in the least equivocal manner to the merits of your feast, I would fain know of what those foreign dishes were compounded, of which, knowing nothing, all have partaken so freely. Hams and tongues, fresh from Britain, designed for my Lord Rawdon's own table, have been sent away from yours uncut—proof of homage, the most profound, to yet preferable meats. Pray tell us, then, what were the elements of your *lagarta* and your *alerta*—your *ragouts* and stews."

"Ay, ay," seconded the company, "let us know. What were the birds?"

"I should really be pleased to know, Captain Porgy," said General Greene, bowing, "touching those birds."

"There need be no mystery in it now, general, since, as Governor Rutledge says, the feast has triumphed. But I am afraid I shall too greatly confound you, when I state that the dishes contained no birds at all. The stew of *alerta* was compounded chiefly of the race which helped Homer in the construction of an epic—a race which Milton describes as the—

" 'Small infantry
Warred on by cranes.' "

"You surely do not mean *frogs,* Captain Porgy?" cried Lee, with affected horror in his accents.

"Your guess is a sagacious one, and worthy of the legion, Colonel Lee."

"Good heavens! and is it come to this, that the soldiers of liberty should be reduced to the necessity of frog-eating?"

"Necessity, Colonel Lee!" exclaimed Rutledge. "By heavens, sir, it should be matter of taste and preference, sir, if only in due deference to our great Gallic ally; but, of a truth, sir, after to-day's feast, it should be a new argument in behalf of liberty, that she has brought us to such rare fine feeding and such improved tastes."

"And the other dish, Captain Porgy," demanded Sumter, "the stew with the Spanish name?"

"The name speaks for itself—*lagarta*. It is of the great lizard family —the cayman—in vulgar speech, the alligator. But the specimens employed, gentlemen, were mere juveniles; young vagabonds, whose affectionate parents had hardly suffered them out of sight before. They had probably never fed on larger prey than their neighbors of the alerta family."

"One question, Captain Porgy," said Carrington; "be so good as to inform me, if, among your several unfamiliar dishes, I have had the happiness to eat of the rattlesnake, the viper, the moccasin, or the boa-constrictor?"

"Alas! colonel, I grieve to say that you have not. I should have been pleased to have got a couple of young chicken-snakes, but I was not fortunate in the search. We got glimpse of a few runners [black-snakes], but they were quite too swift of foot for the hunters. The chicken-snake is of unexceptionable tenderness; the runner is a little too muscular, if not previously well sodden; but, unless near a hencoop, or a corncrib, it is not easy to find the chicken-snake. I repeat my regrets that I could not secure this delicacy for my table. But another time, Colonel Carrington, should you sup with me, I will make a special effort in your behalf."

"I thank you, sir; do not suffer your regrets to disturb you. For that matter, I am half doubtful whether your *alerta* and *lagarta,* of which I have, in my ignorance, partaken somewhat too freely, will continue to lie lightly on my soul or stomach."

"Have no fears, sir; and the better to secure their repose, do me the honor, sir, of a bowl of punch with me. Gentlemen, I entreat the whole table to our companionship."

And the vessels were filled and emptied.

"And now, gentlemen," continued the host, I give you—"The poets, who minister at once to Apollo, to Bacchus, and to Mars, and beg to introduce you to the only representative of the faculty in our squadron, Mr. George Dennison, my ensign. If I mistake not, he has been this day as busy with the muse, as I with my cook; and, if we will suffer him, he will bring us gifts from Parnassus not unworthy of those which we have enjoyed from the provision-wagon of Lord Rawdon."

"In which Horry, going from Dan to Beersheba, could see nothing."

"Having a taste for baths, warming-pans, and chamber-furniture."

" 'Nough of that—that—Singleton! I—I—I'm a sinner be—be—beyond salvation, if I ever pass a little mean-looking wagon again, without seeing what's in it."

"But—Mr. Dennison," said Rutledge.

"George! Geordie!" said Porgy, good-humoredly. The poet, hitherto the only silent person at table, now rose—a tall, slender person, of bright, lively eye, mouth full of expression, Grecian nose, and great forehead rising up like a tower. His cheeks were flushed, his frame trembled, and there was an evident quivering of the lip which was discernible to every eye about him. Dennison sang the verses, which he wrote, in a clear, military voice, shrill like a clarion. There was, perhaps, no great deal of music in his composition, but enough for the present purpose, and of the kind best suited, perhaps, for a military gathering—bold, free, eager and full of animation. His ballad had been the work of that very afternoon.

He had no prefaces. But, waiting till the music hushed, and the voices, he then began:—

THE BATTLE FEAST.

To the dark and bloody feast,
   Haste ye battle vultures, haste;
There is banquet, man and beast,
   For your savage taste:
Never on such costly wassail
   Did ye flesh your beaks before;
Come, ye slaves of Hesse Cassel,*
   To be sold no more!

Small your cost to George of Britain,
   One and sixpence sterling down:†

* The Hessians, hired at so much per head to the crown of Britain, for the war in America, formed no small portion of the British army.

† We are not sure that Master George Dennison is altogether right in this statement of the hire of the Hessians per head, but the difference is immaterial, whether in poetry or history.

Yet for this, ye sorry chapmen,
    Each will lose his crown;
Freedom knows no price for valor,
    Yours is measured by the groat,
Britain pays in gold and silver,
    We in steel and shot.

Recreants, ye from Scottish Highlands,‡
    Lately rebels to the throne
Of that brutal foreign despot,
    Now, whose sway ye own;
Ye are welcome to the banquet,
    Which is spread for all who come,
Where the eater is the eaten,
    And the deathsman goes to doom.

And ye braggart sons of Erin,
    Loathing still the sway ye bear,
Groaning in the very fetters,
    Ye would make us wear;
Ever writhing, ever raging,
    'Neath the bonds ye can not break—
Here the bloody banquet woos ye,
    Gather and partake!

Stoop, ye vultures, to the issue,
    It will be ere set of sun!
Mark whose valor bides the longest,
    Blood of price or blood of none.
Comes the Tartan of Glenorchy,
    Comes the sullen Saxon boor,
Comes the light-heeled German yager
    Crowding to the shore!

Who shall meet them by the water
    On the mountain, in the vale,
Meet them with the stroke of slaughter
    Till the right arm fail?
Wherefore ask? Yon pealing summons,
    Finds fit answer, sharp and soon,
Answer fit for peers and commons,
    Yager and dragoon.

‡ The exiled rebels of '45, when settled in America, almost wholly proved adherents of that monarch whom, as followers of the Stuarts, they opposed to the knife. The disasters of '45 cured them of all propensity to rebellion. Even the Macdonalds, the famous Hector —Flora who saved the Pretender—all became loyal to George the Third in America, and fought against the patriots.

Lo! the soul that makes a nation,
  Which, from out the ranks of toil,
Upward springs in day of peril,
  Soul to save the soil!
Comes a high and mighty aspect,
  From the shores of Powhatan;—
Lo! in him the nation's hero,
  Glorious perfect man!*

Follows, rugged as his mountains,
  Daring man from Bennington;†
Blacksmith stout from Narraganset,‡
  Good where deeds are done:
Comes the keen-eyed Santee rifle,
  Sleepless still and swift as flame,
Rowel rashing,§ bullet winging¶
  Man of deadly aim.

Stoop, ye vultures, to the issue,
  Stoop, and scour the bloody plain
Flesh your beaks where fat the carnage,
  Mountains up the slain:
Whose the skull your talon rendeth;
  Eye, within your dripping beak,
Speechless tongue that loosely lolleth
  On divided cheek?

In the tartan of Glenorchy,
  Scarlet of the Saxon boor,
Gray frock of the Hessian yager
  Strewn from mount to shore,
Read the fate of hireling valor,
  Read the doom of foreign foe,
Know that he who smites for freedom,
  Ever strikes the deadly blow!

It was in the midst of the compliments of the party to the poet, that Willie Sinclair stole in to the table, and plucked the sleeve of Marion, who rose quickly and quietly, and went out with him in silence. The company sat at the table some time longer.

"Why your poet seems a genuine Birserker, Captain Porgy. This chant was worthy to be sung in the hall of Odin. Does he fight as bravely as he sings."

* Washington.   † Stark.   ‡ Greene.   § Sumter.   ¶ Marion.

"Every bit, sir, and he goes into battle with the same convulsive sort of tremor with which he begins to sing or to recite. But that passes off in a few moments, and then he fairly rages. In fact, sir, it is not easy for him to arrest himself, and he sometimes shows himself rather too savage in strife—with rather too great an appetite for blood."

"You are as fortunate, Captain Porgy, in your poet as your cook; I would I could persuade them from you!—Who?—Do you say?"

These last words were spoken to Lieutenant Frampton, who had whispered something into Rutledge's ear.

"Colonel Sinclair, your excellency. He waits you without, along with General Marion."

"Instantly"—and, watching his opportunity, while beakers were filling, Rutledge stole away. Greene followed his example, so did Sumter and the elder officers; the young ones remained, and soon Captain Porgy, his veneration no longer active, was in full flight, keeping the table in a roar, with merry jest, jibe, and story, till the hours grew something smaller than the stars, and the moon had a hooded, downcast looking visage, as if she had seen or heard something to shock her modesty. Let us leave the revellers while they make a final onslaught upon the punchbowls.

Ward said, in The War of the Revolution *(p. 825), "The Americans as well as the British had suffered much from the extreme heat, the incessant marching, and the lack of food," in the summer of 1781. He quoted from Henry Lee's* Memoirs of the War in the Southern Department *(1769): "Rice furnished our substitute for bread . . . of meat we had literally none. . . . Frogs abounded . . . and on them chiefly did the light troups [partisans] subsist. Even alligator was used by a few."*

Against a background of meager meals or actual hunger, thus is projected the image of the glowing epicurean festival. Yet Porgy can scarcely be accused of depriving any one of the common soldiers of food, for he was using, first, what Greene would have used less skillfully; second, what limited supplies Porgy himself had, which did not amount to much; third, the captured British wagon; and fourth, the materials gleaned from river and swamp, the possibilities of which were largely ignored by the British, and even by the Americans, especially the continentals.

After the feast scene, the novel is done except for a short chapter to tell the readers who are curious about the fate of the characters that they must find it in another volume; but that scene is considerable compensation for any disappointment at finding the story thus terminated as in midstream.

By his triumph as host Porgy proves the equality or superiority of the partisans to the other branches of the American army. He is also showing the famous pre-eminence of the South in hospitality. Finally, by his ability to achieve his great success without the background of his beautiful plantation mansion, and with what native and seemingly so unpromising materials he has at hand, he exemplifies the self-reliance of the American.

7. Porgy
in
Eutaw

Less spontaneous than The Forayers *is its continuation* Eutaw. *Perhaps the author—as well as the reader—sometimes felt fatigue, especially in the latter part of the second work. Still the narrative is often carried on with considerable verve, and vivid characterizations abound.*

Eutaw *introduces and features Captain Porgy in an entirely new guise in the Saga, as a keen and rather acrimonious critic of military tactics. Each time he appears, he discusses errors he believes have been made by his own side in battles. Although in this new role he may be less entertaining, a cubit is added to his intellectual stature; and the implication is that he has not been given as important a command as he is qualified for. He does say as much, but emphasizes mainly that more authority should have been given to General Marion, his own superior.*

The opening chapters seem unrelated to the action of The Forayers. *They concern the violent doings of a band of Florida refugees who had come north for plunder, and caring little which side they were on, found they could grab more if they were nominally for the crown. Later the two books begin to be tied together as the refugee gang captured Bertha*

Travis and her mother, who had been forced by the tories to flee from their plantation in their coach.

Meanwhile our same villain Inglehardt, still plotting to marry Bertha, has her brother Henry and her father captive in "Bram's castle", a hovel in a swamp. The jailor was Hell-Fire Dick. (One of the most effective passages in Simms tells how the conscience of this bloody and illiterate rapscallion was aroused by his affection for the boy and by the boy's reading to him from Pilgrim's Progress. *Dick slipped food to Henry, unknown to Inglehardt, and so kept the boy from being reduced to virtual madness by starvation, as was the fate of his father.)*

On Porgy's first appearance, he was assigned a mission of some importance. The tory Colonel Sinclair had been most unwisely persuaded by Lord Rawdon to attempt to go in his coach from his Barony to Charleston. Sinclair had not gone far when he fell in with the retreating British army and moved along with them toward the city. The Americans attacked from the rear and caught up with the coach. An American officer rode up and ordered the Negro coachman to turn his vehicle aside into the woods. Colonel Sinclair raised a pistol and shot at the officer, only to discover that he had missed his own son Willie by an inch. The father was naturally much distressed. Willie strongly urged his father to return to the Barony; and pointed out an American officer riding toward them.

"Where? who?"

"Here, sir, on the right."

"What! that big fellow? Why, he's a mountain on horseback!"

"But his horse seems big enough for the mountain."

"Yes, indeed! It is the largest horse, I think, I ever saw. But what a huge man to be a dragoon! and what a belly for an officer to carry!—and yet, see what a monstrous girth he wears! And, what a uniform!"

"Hush, sir! he approaches."

The officer rode up, and, bowing politely, said, in musical tones—

"Colonel Sinclair, I believe."

"At your service. And who the devil are you, sir?"

This rude speech was prompted—we must say apologetically—by a sudden and sharp twinge of the gout at this moment. But the stranger was prompt to reply in the same spirit.

"The devil himself, sir, at your service: but—you will please remember, my dear young lady," addressing himself to Carrie—"that, whatever his other demerits, the devil has the reputation of being a gentleman."

"An assurance," answered Carrie, with a smile, "which should surely reconcile us to his representative."

"You are a woman of sense, madam—a rarity among your sex. You may rest assured that I shall do nothing to forfeit the social reputation of my principal."

"Well, sir," said our baron, whom the gout was troubling at this moment especially, and who, as an old aristocrat, was exceedingly impatient of the familiar tone which the stranger employed when speaking with his daughter—angry, indeed, with Carrie herself for the civil speech with which she had simply designed to do away with any ill effects that might have arisen from the rude apostrophe of her father—"well, sir, to what do I owe the honor of this interruption to my peaceful progress?"

"Peaceful progress," quoth the stranger coolly. "My venerable friend," he continued, "I do not come hither to retard or prevent your very peaceful progress, but if possible to render it more so. I promised your son to see you safe beyond our lines."

"Pardon me, sir; you are the gentleman that he promised to send me. I thank you, sir—I thank you very much. Forgive me, if I have seemed to you peevish and uncivil, but I am a victim to the gout, sir, and am besides in a devilish bad humor."

"No apologies, my dear sir, further. Both of these are gentlemanly privileges. I respect them. I am glad to believe, my dear young lady, that you are not troubled with the gout also."

"And why should you suppose her free from it?" growled the baron.

"Simply, because, as a lady, she ought to enjoy neither of these gentlemanly privileges. I can answer for it, sir, that she gladly yields the monopoly to you of the other gentlemanly privilege."

The baron growled good-humoredly—"Do not dwell, sir, upon my rudeness. You are a wit, I see, and must suffer yourself to be opposed by other weapons than your own. Few persons practice well at the foils with this class of person. It is fortunate for his majesty's cause, I fancy, that you are not allowed to lead in this attack."

"Your sagacity, Colonel Sinclair, or your instincts, it matters not which, has conducted you to a truth which revelation would hardly suffer the American Congress to receive. It *is* fortunate for his majesty's cause that I was not the leader in this expedition, or that I was not permitted to select the leader. The results, I promise you, would have been very different. We should not have allowed the British army to slip through our fingers."

This was said with a sort of savage gravity, as if the speaker solemnly felt it all, and felt, besides, that not only a great wrong had been done to himself, but that a serious mischief had resulted also to the country.

"Well, sir, I'm not sure but that you might have done as well, or better, than those who do lead your troops; but you will permit me to hint that it is hardly possible that any leader could have secured you success against the troops of Britain. I infer, you perceive, from your words, that you are in a difficult situation—what the vulgar call 'a tight place'—that, in short, you are about to receive a drubbing."

The corpulent captain lifted his eyebrows. Then he laughed merrily.

"My venerable friend, you never, I fancy, heard of Ike Massey's bull-dog?"

"You are right in your fancy."

"Well, sir, Ike had a bulldog—a famous bulldog—that whipped all other dogs, and whipped all bulls, and Ike honestly believed that he could whip all beasts that ever roared in the valley of Bashan. On one occasion, he pitted him against a young bull, whom he expected to see him pull down at the first jerk, muzzle and throttle in a jiffey. But it so happened that Towser—the name of his dog—had, in process of time, lost some of his teeth. He did take the bull by the nose, but the young animal shook the old one off, and with one stamp of his hoof he crushed all the life out of Towser. But Ike, to the day of his death, still believed in Towser, and swore that the dog had no fair play; that the bull had improperly used his hoofs on the occasion; and that, in fact, having honestly taken his enemy by the nose, according to bulldog science, the victory must still be conceded to him. Now, your faith in British science is not unlike that of Ike Massey in his dogs; but the bull may safely concede the science, so long as he can stamp his enemy to pieces. We are working just in this fashion in our fighting with the British. They have the science, but they are losing the teeth; while we are young and vigor-ous, lack the science, and have the strength. Scientifically, the British whip us in all our contests; but we do an immense deal of very interest-ing bull-stamping all the while; and it is surprising how much dog-life we are crushing out of the British carcass. As for the present affair, you are quite out if you suppose that we are in any tight place. Our difficulty is that the place is rather a loose one. You err equally in supposing that we are about to be lathered. Our difficulty is that the British are running, and we can't get at them, on account of a paltry creek with a paltry bridge over it that is not passable. It is all owing, I am afraid, to a poor apish trick of emulating British science, that we haven't stamped the dog to pieces this very day. We have done a little, however, toward taking the life out of the animal. We have captured the rear-guard of a hundred men, and taken all the baggage and the money-chest."

"Captured, without a fight! Captured a pack of cowards!"

"No, no! my venerable friend. The fellows are no cowards, not a man of 'em; but they had no such love for British rule that you entertain, and gave themselves up to better society."

"You should be grateful for their civility, I think."

"I am. Do you remember how the fat knight of Eastcheap conquered Sir Coleville of the Dale. We felt on taking our raw Irishman as Falstaff did in that conquest, and said to them—almost in his language—'Like kind fellows ye gave yourselves away, and I thank ye for yourselves." We did not have to sweat for them any more than Sir John, for *his* prisoner. But your driver will please to quicken his pace. The woods are open enough here for trotting. I must hurry you discourteously, for my company has these liberal Irishmen in charge, and all the baggage; and the treasure is too precious to neglect. There are some casks of rum, too, among our stores; and such is the mortal antipathy of the Irish to this American liquor, that they would waste it even on themselves, sooner than not get rid of it."

"One question, sir. Are you not Captain Porpoise?"

The eye of our captain was sternly fastened for an instant, upon the face of the speaker, but there was no sinister expression in the baron's countenance leading him to suppose that any offense was meant. Before he could speak, however, Carrie Sinclair corrected him.

"Oh, father, it is Captain Porgy!"

"Bless my soul, so it is! What have I said! Pray forgive me, Captain Porgy, it was in pain and some bewilderment, that I committed the mistake. I asked the name, sir, only through most grateful motives, and as, from my son's very favorable account of you, at his last visit to the barony, I was anxious to know you."

"His description seems to have been a close one, Colonel Sinclair,"

answered Porgy, with a grim smile. "Colonel Sinclair, your son, is a
friend whom I very much honor."

"And he honors you too, Captain Porgy," interposed Carrie, eagerly,
anxious to do away with any annoyance that her father's blunder may
have occasioned. She continued—"And my father, sir, and we all, will
be pleased to welcome you, should you ever do us the kindness to visit
the barony."

"To be sure, Captain Porgy, to be sure. Come and see us. Though
you are a rebel, sir, like my son, you are a gentleman, I believe, and a
man of honor; and all that I have ever heard of you is grateful. Nothing,
I assure you, will give me more pleasure, in a social way, than to have
you at my board; and I promise you, if you will come, to put some old
Madeira before you, of the vintage of 1758, such as is seldom broached
now-a-days in Carolina. I pray you, sir, to believe that I am sincere, and
forgive that stupid blunder of mine in taking your name in vain."

All this was said very heartily, and in just the tone and strain to make
its way to Porgy's heart.

"To be sure, you are sincere, Colonel Sinclair. A man with the taste
to keep Madeira twenty years in his house must be an honest man;
and to broach it freely to his guest, proves him a gentleman. You may
look to see me, should occasion ever offer. As for your mistake in my
name, sir, let it never trouble you. I never take offence where I am
assured it is unmeant; and, when we look at the facts, you really conveyed a compliment. In respect to relative dignity, the porpoise must
take precedence of the porgy. Let the matter never trouble you, my dear
young lady. I can see that you felt your father's mistake much more
than I did. You are a true woman, which means, that you possess the
exquisite sensibility, which fears to inflict pain, much more than it fears
suffering. I would I were a young fellow, for your sake. But we are
friends, are we not?" He offered her his hand. She gave hers readily.

"Oh! yes, sir, my brother's friends are all mine."

"Would they were friends only," muttered the baron, *sotto voce,*
remembering Peyre St. Julien.

"Yes, yes," said Porgy, "but we must be friends on our own account,
not on your brother's."

"Well, as you please. I am sure that you will do me honor."

"I'll try. And now, my dear old gentleman," said Porgy, "we have
reached the end of our tether. You are here on the edge of the road.

Yonder is the king's highway—where the king dare not wag a finger, or cut a pigeon-wing. You can find your way home without trouble, and I hope without interruption. We can do no more for you just now. Hurry home as fast as you can, for the woods will be in a blaze for some time to come. We are smoking out the 'varmints.' God bless you now, and good-by. It is time for me to see if I can't find a chance to stick a finger in this business. Good-by!"

And, thus separating, our baron pushed into the main road, while Captain Porgy dashed off to join his command at full speed, as if neither himself nor his gigantic steed had any weight to carry.

"How he rides for so large a man," was Carrie's remark.

"His face is positively handsome," said the father.

"But his figure, father."

"Ah! no more of that, or I shall be sure to call him porpoise again when next I meet him. But what do you stop for, Sam?"

"Whay for go now, maussa?"

"Home, rascal! didn't Willie Sinclair tell you? Ah, Willie! Willie! That I should have lifted pistol at my son's head. Oh, Carrie! if it were possible, I should like to kneel, here where I am, and give thanks to God for his mercies, that interposed and saved me from my son's murder."

"The heart may kneel, father, as well as the limbs. The soul that feels, and the mind that thinks, its obligations to God, are always busy in prayer."

The carriage was soon out of reach of bullet from the scene of war, and Porgy was equally soon at the head of his company, condemned to the dreary task, while battle was impending, of keeping watch over captured men and wagons. Let us leave both parties, and resume our progress with the active combatants.

The maneuver during which the Sinclair coach had been sent home was called by Simms the "ill-managed attempt upon the British at Quinby bridge." Before retiring that night Porgy was to explain more fully his own bases for censuring this "attempt."

We have seen what were Sumter's opinions; and we may say, *par parenthese,* that Captain Porgy is no mean authority in such matters. We have heard his opinions also. But we must not dwell upon this sore subject; and would not, for a moment, but that we share in Porgy's vexation, who was wont to say that half of the battles he had ever seen lost, were lost by a petty *finessing*, when plain, honest, direct, up and down fighting, was all that was essential.

Very bitter was the talk in Marion's camp that night. Marion said nothing, but he paced the rounds himself, as if dreading to seek repose. In one part of the *bivouac* there is a group, all of whom we know, discoursing of the events of the day.

"God has been too bountiful to us!" said Captain Porgy, in his peculiar manner. "He has been too profligate of great men. This seems to have been our curse always. Our great men have been too numerous for our occasions always. They are in each other's way. They rob one another of the sunshine. They behold in each other only so many offensive shadows that pass between them and glory. I think it would not be difficult to prove that this has been one of the chief causes of all our disasters. I can enumerate them from the time of Bob Howe, who was half-witted; Charley Lee, who was only fit to head a charge of cavalry, no more; and who, properly to be prepared even for this performance, should have been invariably horsewhipped before going into action. And there was old Lincoln, who might have been a good army nurse, or chaplain, but should never have been suffered to enter the camp in any other capacity. Then came Gates—but the chronicle is too sickening; and it is such blockheads as these that decry the militia. I tell you, that the instincts of the militia nose out an imbecile in a week's duty, and they naturally contemn and despise the authority in which they have no confidence. I don't wish to excuse the faults of the militia. They are improvident. That word covers all. They waste time—take no precautions—have no forethought; and are only worth painstaking, when you are allowed to have 'em long enough for discipline. But, whatever *their* faults, they are precisely such as most of these blundering captains have shared along with them; with this difference, perhaps, and in favor of the common soldiers, that they are not troubled with that vainglorious pretension which curses too many of their captains, and which has but too frequently been made to cover not only incompetence, but cowardice."

"Enough, Porgy, my dear fellow," said Singleton—"the subject is one of great delicacy. You hit right and left. Remember, we are not now under the command of our own brigadier."

"Would we had been! I don't blame Sumter; since he never pretended to any strategy; and what he did claim to do, and that was fighting, he always did well. Would he, think you, have let those brave fellows, Armstrong and Carrington, and Maham and Macaulay, risk themselves *alone,* to-day, in that *melée* at the bridge? Never! He'd have been first across, I tell you. He committed some mistakes. He mistook Coates's covering party for an attack; then suffered Coates to protract his shows of action, without forcing it upon him. To suffer one's self to be amused for *three* hours with such mere overtures was a great mistake."

"Another time, Porgy," said Sinclair.

"Yes, we shall have time enough, and provocation enough for such discussion hereafter; but I could eat my sword with vexation! Then, here comes the field-piece, of which such large expectations are formed; and not an ounce of powder!"

"Plenty of bullets," quoth the lieutenant. "Help yourselves, gentlemen!"

"And yet," continued Porgy, "here are hundreds of pounds of powder taken in Dorchester, by Colonel Lee, and sent—where? Up to General Greene, in his camp of rest, as if he had any use for it! As if it were not wanted *here!* By heavens! gentlemen, say what you will, and try to make excuses as you may, but the blunders of this expedition are so atrocious, that I can not but think them wilful, and designed for sinister purposes. We can only suppose them otherwise, by assuming for the actors such a degree of stupidity as would henceforth assign them only to asinine associations."

Sinclair defended Sumter.

"Oh! hush, Willie Sinclair, you know I don't mean Sumter! D—n the fellow, I admire him! I prefer our own brigadier, it is true; but, next to him, I hold to Sumter. But he has suffered Lee too much independent exercise; and he himself feels it; and if he is sore about any one thing especially to-night, it is in not giving precedence to Maham's cavalry and his own. And Lee would have done better had he not been spoiled by Greene—much better in this foray, had he not had his head turned by his unexpected success with the rear-guard, and his capture of these d——d baggage-wagons. It was the fear of losing these spoils that made him turn back, on the report that Campbell was stirring up his raw recruits for mutiny; turn back, when he was within six hundred yards of the bridge and the enemy, leaving those brave fellows, Armstrong and Carrington, to their fate, when everything depended upon following up the rush of the first two sections, by others, in prompt succession, his legion cavalry, by ours, and all together overwhelming all opposition. The British never could have rallied. They must have been crushed under the first rush of the horses. There was no room for display, for a single evolution, and any efforts would only have ended in their being cut to pieces and trampled under foot! And this chance was lost—on what pretence? This rear-guard was beginning to mutter and resume their arms. And if they were, was not Marion and Sumter with an overwhelming force, coming down upon them at a trot? And might they not have been left to our tender mercies, Lee knowing exactly where we were, how nigh, and never doubting, I fancy, that we were perfectly competent to the management of these raw Irishmen? No! no! It was the baggage that he feared to lose. He is famous for securing the baggage. I have no doubt, when he hurried back, that he took a peep into the wagons to see if the fingers of plunder had not been busy in his ten or twenty minutes absence."

"Porgy, Porgy, you are unjust. Lee is a good soldier—fights well and bravely."

"But that's not enough for a good soldier."

"Keeps his legion in admirable discipline."

"I grant you; but is disposed to sacrifice everything for his legion. It is that which causes our mischiefs. He would strip every other command in the army, of its rights, resources, securities, to keep his legion in handsome order."

"Allow the fact as a fault, still, my dear fellow, it should not be permitted to decry his other merits. He has done good service, has fought bravely, has been always active and vigilant; is never to be caught napping, and is rarely to be found wanting. I grant you that he has committed some serious faults, especially in this campaign; but these, I suspect, really arise from a jealousy of his reputation. He is greedy after glory, and loves not to see any one preferred to himself."

"In other words, in his greed of glory, he would sooner see his superior officer defeated or embarrassed, than successful in any achievement beyond his own."

"Shocking, Porgy, shocking. Do not speak in this manner. Do not think thus," said Singleton.

"It is the thought of the whole army, let me tell you. He has got Greene by the ear. He is an earwig. He whispers him to the disparagement of Sumter, Marion, and in fact everybody; and Greene, unfortunately listens to him. This is what even the common soldiers see and say. His legion is petted and patted on all occasions, and to the neglect and disparagement of other commands. All others must be sacrificed, while the legion is to be economized and kept in bandbox condition for state occasions—great shows and solemnities. And here, taking large bodies of stores at Dorchester, powder included, he packs it all off direct to Greene, as if to say 'see what I have done,' and to keep us from all share in the things which our ragged, half-starved people need. Who has a better right to these stores than we? To whom should he have despatched them but Sumter, under whose immediate command he was serving? and why send off to an army in camp that has no present need of these things, the very munitions of war which are absolutely necessary to our present purposes?"

"No more of it, my dear Porgy; we have causes enough of vexation without diving after them."

"But if by diving after them we can bring up the truth—by the locks—rescue it from drowning—we may have some reasonable prospect hereafter of curing these causes of vexation."

"Ah! my fat friend," quoth Singleton—"the naked, barefaced truth would be indecently exposed just now, and would only afford new causes of vexation. Think no more of this matter—at all events, speak no more of it. Your language, such as you now use, can only do mischief, if put in circulation."

"In circulation! Bless you, it's the talk of all the camp; and if Lee does not himself hear of it, it's only because of a continued deafness, such as he caught when he encountered one of the Spanns, at the time the legion served with us against Georgetown."

"What happened then?"

"Why Lee, whose insolent haughtiness of manner was always employed to humble the common soldiers, sitting on a log with his coat off, and sleeves rolled up, and seeing our Lieutenant Spann, dipping up a bucket of water from a branch, cried to him, 'Hark ye, my man, bring me a bucket of that water.' Spann was in homespun, and Lee did not notice the epaulette on his shoulder. The answer of Spann was as quick as a pistol bullet. 'You be d——d! Wait on yourself, as your betters have to do!' Lee became deaf on the instant, and fortunately, for he might have heard a thousand such speeches, but for this profitable infirmity. He will probably be compelled to hear of them after this affair, unless his deafness is absolutely incorrigible."

"Now, hark ye, Porgy," said Singleton, "I see what your humor is; but for the sake of the service, and of our own general, do not you make any such speeches in Lee's hearing or in that of anybody else."

"And do you think, Colonel Bob Singleton, that I care a straw whether he hears me or not?"

"No! I know you too well to suppose that you do care! I take for granted that nothing would give you more satisfaction, in your present temper, than to make him hear."

"You are right, by Jupiter! I feel it in my soul, to ring it in his ears with a trumpet summons."

"Precisely! And that is the very thing that you must not do. You are not to suffer your private moods to stir up strife in the army, upon a subject that is already sufficiently troublesome, and to the defeat of the cause that we have in hand. This, by way of warning, my dear Porgy, for I have reason to know that the 'Fox' himself has heard of some of your angry speeches, and means to speak to you about the matter."

"Let him speak! Nay, my dear boy, don't suppose that I shall so, consult my own humors as to do any public mischief. It is because I am thus restrained that I feel like boiling over. But, between us, the 'Fox' knows, as well as you and I, that what I say is true—true, every syllable!"

"Be it so! Although, I repeat, your prejudices against Lee prevent you from doing justice to his real merits. But let us change the subject somewhat. You have seen this afternoon's work. Have you any idea of Coates's force in the house and grounds?"

"Four or five hundred."

"Six hundred regular infantry, at least. Nearly twice the number with which we made the attack."

"How do you arrive at the fact?"

"We found, in the captured baggage, the commissary's return of the issues of the army for the day—nine hundred rations, and forage for two hundred and fifty horses."

"And that we should lose all this prey, when it only needed that we should lay bold hands upon it!" said Porgy.

"Nay, no more growling, my dear Porgy," said Sinclair. "Instead of dwelling upon what we have failed to do, let us try and console our-selves by looking to what we have done. We have killed and wounded two hundred of the enemy at least; we have safe in hand, bagged, more than one hundred and fifty prisoners, not including nine commissioned officers. We have captured a large convoy of baggage, with nearly a thousand guineas in the army-chest—"

"Ah! these d——d baggage-wagons! It is to them we owe it, that we haven't done everything that we should have done. At first I thought Coates a blockhead, to put his baggage-wagons in the rear, under a feeble guard, when he was in full retreat from a pursuing enemy. I now suspect him of a profound policy. I suspect he reads his bible on Sunday. He has learned his military lessons from Scripture. He put the temptation *behind* him, and *before* us. He knew how greedy we were. He felt sure that we could not withstand the bait, any more than a hungry maw-mouth perch in midsummer. He was right, and baiting us, he got off from the hook himself."

"Well, well!" continued Sinclair. "To proceed:—We *have* the bait nevertheless, the baggage and plunder. Besides, we rescued from the flames, at Biggin, a large body of stores, captured and destroyed four schooners at the landing, and beat back the British bayonet at Shubrick's house. The charge was beautifully repelled."

"You say that the British lost two hundred men at the house to-day —killed and wounded—how do you know the fact?" demanded Porgy.

"We do not *know* it. But we have some facts which render this a reasonable estimate. The crack riflemen of the brigade have not been peppering away at their enemies, sometimes on the open plain in column, sometimes at doors and windows, for three mortal hours, without inflicting, as well as breaking *pains!* Pardon the pun, my dear Porgy; its demerits are due to the annoyance of our *lee* shore experience, and the rough wind, which make even a dragoon's humor costive. I have no doubt that Coates does not get off to-day with less than two hundred *hors de combat*. At the bridge he lost one commissioned officer and five privates killed, and four wounded."

"And what to-morrow?"

"Sufficient for the day!—But we must go the rounds. If Coates be at all enterprising, he may beat up some of our drowsy sections with a warm bayonet to-night."

"Not he! But he has that dashing young Irishman, Fitzgerald, with him, who has spirit enough for the attempt. By the way, St. Julien, you had a pass or two with him to-day, at close quarters—that is to say, across the fence."

"But a pass!" said the taciturn St. Julien. "It is the second time that we have crossed blades unprofitably."

"You have both reason to beware of the third passage," said Porgy, "I believe in the *fate in threes!* And so let us sip a little of this punch, which unites the sweet, the sour, and the strong! It would be almost justification for a man to get drunk to-night, particularly on such liquor, after so many mortifying disappointments to-day."

Porgy makes no appearance during the next hundred and fifty pages, but the author offers two interesting remarks about him.

Also that same night, Colonel Sinclair found lodgings in a little inn on his way home. He was suffering from his gout, and even more from having nearly killed his own son. In bed at the inn, he was visited and wakened by Lord Rawdon. Sinclair groaned. "He had been aroused from sleep just as he had fallen comfortably into it; an offense—according to Captain Porgy—which merits death in the offender." It will be recalled that Porgy was almost as much of a believer in the importance of sound sleep as of first-class food.

Inglehardt is not only the black-hearted villain of The Forayers-Eutaw, *but he lacked Porgy's competence in feeding armies. Inglehardt did have a tremendous problem: "to supply food and forage to two thousand hungry soldiers—no easy matter—particularly as few of the bull family can easily be persuaded to find the chicken snake a delicacy, the alligator a* bon bouche, *or the frog nutritious. Captain Porgy would have been a rare commissary at such a juncture. If Arnold was worth ten thousand guineas, for his nonprofitable treason, our partisan epicure should command thrice the amount for his services in art. His ingenious capacity for the* cuisine *would equally improve the resources in the department, and the tastes which the soldiers fed. He would have raised the standards of the British morale, by inculcating a higher order of kitchen sentiment."*

Needless to say, our Porgy was no traitor, and no imaginable number of guineas would have induced him to devote his great talents in procuring and preparing food to the service of his country's enemy.

We do not meet Porgy again until after the Battle of Eutaw, quite near the end of the novel. It was an important battle; for, as Simms says,

"The British power in Carolina was broken at Eutaw." Although the author does not take time to present his approval of what Porgy is to say about this battle as fully as in the case of the Quinby Skrimmage, he does make clear his agreement with some aspects of Porgy's censure of the later engagement. Like Porgy, Simms contends that the American victory at Eutaw was by no means as complete as it might have been if the Americans had not blundered in what he calls the latter part of the drama. He says that, after the British line gave way, if it "had been pressed without reserve by the legion cavalry," that commanded by Lee, the British "disaster must have been irretrievable." "But this seems not to have been done. Why, can not now be well explained, nor is it exactly within our province to undertake this explanation." It will be seen that Porgy does offer an explanation, based upon a point Simms does here make, that Lee was with his infantry, rather than with his cavalry. Apparently Simms then lets his Porgy offer reasons which he considers plausible but does not feel he is in quite the position to present as absolutely demonstrable. Let us see what were Porgy's judgments.

In the camp of the partisans the night after the Battle of Eutaw, Porgy was discussing the events of the day with St. Julien, Sinclair, and others. He "was in the hands of the surgeon at this very juncture."

He was hurt in the thigh, not seriously, but he had suffered considerable loss of blood, which had served, in some degree, to modify his usual elasticity. Still, he was less subdued than the rest; and his words flowed almost as freely as ever. He was in an irascible mood, and showed no small impatience at the deliberation, and searching examination, of the surgeon while attending to his hurt.

"There," said he, "that will do! The thing is nothing. I knew, all the while, that it was a flesh wound only—nothing to make a fuss about. It will take a long-winded bullet to make its way fairly into my citadel."

"You bled like a stuck pig, nevertheless," said Mellichampe.

"Had you said *'stuffed'* instead of *'stuck,'* I had never forgiven you, Ernest. The comparison is irreverent, anyhow!"

"Don't risk another, my dear boy, lest you make me angry. I am in the humor to resent any impertinence to-night. I have been in the humor to fight any, the best friend, half-a-dozen times to-day. Wounds of the body, I feel none. I got this in the beginning of the action. It was smart not pain. But pain there is! Great God! to think of our useless loss to-day: of the profligate and blundering waste of life; of those poor fellows of Washington's legion, most ridiculously sacrificed; of a complete victory suffered to slip out of our hands, when we had only to close upon them, and make it secure?"

"Nay, Porgy, no more! What good will it do to canvass the affair so close? We have got the advantage, if not the victory. We shall be wiser of our mistakes hereafter. We shall know better next time."

"Pardon me, my dear Sinclair, but it is you that mistake. We shall never repair this sort of blundering if we never expose it. We are altogether too mealy-mouthed when we come to the discussion of the faults and blunders of the great. As for improving hereafter, I do not believe it, so long as we serve under the same leaders. And, there is a particular reason why we poor militiamen, rangers, riflemen, and partisans, as we are called, should lay bare, whenever we can, the vices and the worthlessnesses of these martinets, and regulars, who invariably excuse their own defeats by charging their disasters upon the militia. Gates had it, that the militia ran at Camden. And, no doubt, they did. And very right too. But he, himself, was among the first to run. I do not so much blame him for that. He had a particularly large carcass to take off, and a world of genius and ability to economize and preserve for other more auspicious occasions. But how can a militia be expected to stand fight, when their general conducts them into a false position, and finds himself in the thick of battle without dreaming of the approach of an enemy? Now, one of the very first necessities of a general is, to inspire his men with confidence. But when the general's own incompetence is so glaring that the meanest camp follower is able to detect it, how should you expect to inspire this confidence? The militiamen, who had no weapons but our mean, long-handled, bird guns, without bayonets, are pushed forward, in the first rank, to encounter British regulars, all of whom are armed with the best Tower muskets of large bore, and bristling with bayonets. They seem to be put forward, as David put forward Uriah, to be slain certainly. Why are they thus put forward; forming a regular line of battle, when they have no means of resistance when it comes to the push of steel? To be slain? Well, no; not exactly: *but really to draw the enemy's fire, in order to lessen the dangers to the regulars when the bayonet is required to be used!* In other words, they are food for powder. Their lives are nothing. We can waste them—expose them—and, just in proportion as they are shot down, will you lessen the same danger to those who follow them. Well, a militiaman understands all that. He sees that there is no scruple shown when *he* is to be sacrificed—that his general has no sympathy with *him*—that he exhibits no such economical regard for *his* life, that he shows for his regulars; and that he should be expected to stand the charge of a weapon which he himself does not use, is quite enough to make him distrustful of a generalship, which requires him to take the worst risks of the battle, merely to lessen the danger to his favorites. No wonder that he runs."

"But our fellows did *not* run to-day, Porgy, until the bayonets were almost into them."

"True; and why? Because they are mostly *old* soldiers, and because their own favorite generals were immediately in command. And let me say, that no militia in the world, and few regulars, ever behaved better than our boys to-day. Had you swopped guns with the regulars, and put *them* forward, to do the same business, and endure the first brunt of the battle, as our fellows did, you would have had them all scampering at the first volley. But the case is not altered because our fellows stood fire manfully. I repeat, that this whole plan of battle is false, and immoral, which thus makes a first regular column of attack, of a badly-armed militia."

"It is the usual plan, nevertheless."

"And it is the secret of so many of our disasters! It is a vicious plan, and might reasonably be expected to work us defeat in every action. For, do you not see that, once taught to understand that he is expected to run, if not shot, the instincts of the militiaman are always ready;—well, he runs, and, though it is expected that he will run, the effect of such an example is necessarily bad upon the regular; he has not only an example, but a plea for running also. But, if the militia, *en masse,* and in their panic, fling themselves back upon an advancing column of regulars, it is scarcely possible to escape that degree of confusion, which is next in effect to panic; and the whole army is thus demoralized. No. You must employ militiamen—call them what you will, sharpshooters or rangers, on the flanks, and as skirmishers, or, when they are old soldiers, you must intermingle them with the regulars, either in alternate bodies, or, as a second line, when the army is displayed for battle. Any plan but the present. Disparaged if not despised, denounced as only made to run; without the proper weapons for close combat; they are yet required to exhibit all the moral forces which are needed for the *first* encounter; why, every school-boy's experience might correct this folly. There is not an urchin, knee-high to a cock-sparrow, but will tell you that the first blow is always half the battle."

"Well, but, Porgy, it is admitted that the army to-day suffered nothing, from the first line being made up wholly of militiamen."

"But *they* suffered! But that is nothing to the argument. Answer me! Suppose the same endurance, hardihood, and audacity, which our boys showed to-day, in the case of men who, after disorganizing the entire British line by their sharp-shooting, were prepared, with proper weapons, to start forward at the *pas de charge,* and do you suppose that a single company of the enemy could have escaped annihilation? That is the true question. The army lost nothing in the affair to-day, perhaps, because of their first line being militia. Marion and Pickens have the art, always, of keeping their men firm so long as they are disposed to keep the field themselves. But how many such leaders as Marion and Pickens are you to find in the armies of the world? Suppose, however, that their troops had been employed in the woods and on the flanks as skirmishers, while the regulars had played their game from the first, and all the while, as manfully with their bayonets as the militia did with their shot-guns and rifles—what, then, must have been the result? The annihilation of the British army! When the British line pressed upon the militia, and they melted away out of the path of the continentals, the British column was already dreadfully disorganized—in fact, hardly a line at all, but undulating, in ridges of advances; here a billow, and there a gulf—here a swell, and there a hollow—and comparatively easy game for a uniform charge of bayonets brought squarely up to the business. And I am free to allow that the continentals did their part handsomely. They came up to the scratch in beautiful style; and here, if anywhere in America, the British regulars were met, hand to hand, and beaten at their own weapon, the bayonet—driven from the field before the bayonet! But, would they have been thus driven, but for the previous havoc made by our shot-guns, and their subsequent demoralization at the hands of our militia?"

"That, surely, is an argument, Porgy, in support of the present practice."

"Not so. It would be an argument, perhaps—though I deny even that—were you always sure of your militia as you might be always in the case of the brigades of Marion and Pickens; but if sure of them, why not give them the bayonets also, and let them rank with the regulars? The fact is, we are perpetually making a distinction in this matter, where there is no substantial difference. Look to the real meaning of your phrase, and all *veterans* are regulars, and all *raw* troops suffer from the inherent difficulties of an inexperienced militia. They are *ranked* as *militia* only because they are *raw;* and no matter what the weapons you put into their hands, an inexperienced body will be apt to make very doubtful use of them, even if they make any use at all, while the old soldier will work vigorously with any sort of tool. It is, in fact, because of the *rawness* of the *British* troops of late, that we have got most of our advantages over them. Their new Irish recruits know nothing of drill, do not appreciate the moral strength derived from the touch of a comrade's elbow, have no knowledge of the gun, whether rifle or musket, and are only beginning the necessary training for battle when the battle is upon them. Here lies much of the secret of our late successes, and particularly that of to-day, when the two lines came to the push of the bayonet.

"But, dismissing this point, let us look to other matters which more certainly cut us off from the victory of which we were secure.

"The battle was clearly won when the British line was broken, and their masses scattered and driven from the field. How was it lost, then? By the dispersion of our regulars among the tents; by the mad fury with which they fastened upon rum and brandy. But where were their officers, that they were suffered to do this?"

"Pendleton says," was the remark of Singleton, "that when Greene sent to Lee to charge Coffin, Lee was not with his cavalry at all. Subsequently, he was found riding about the field with a few dragoons, giving orders to everybody—in fact, usurping the entire command."

"Well, where was Greene, when his favorite was thus employed? What was he doing? Should he not have been present? Why did he not, instead of sending an army surgeon to tell Williams to sweep the field with the bayonets of his divisions—why did he not gallop to their head, and lead them into action himself? That was the moment when a general should peril himself greatly, if necessary, in order to achieve great results. It was the crisis of the action. The British were shaking everywhere. If, then, the general had dashed to the front, and, with all the thunders of his voice, had cried out to his men, 'Follow ME, boys, and let us sweep these red-coats from the field!' they would have gone forward with a maddening cheer; would have stormed the gates of h—l; would have never paused nor faltered, never stopped for tents, or drink, or gaudy equipage and plunder; and we should have had the brick-house in our possession before Sheridan could have won the entrance with a single man. Then, there could have been no Lee to usurp the field, and assume the grand direction of affairs. Where was your general all this time, that the subordinates were playing fool and monkey? In the rear, and despatching slow orders through unofficial agents, whom nobody was bound to recognise."

"Greene was very angry with Lee, according to Pendleton."

"Angry! He should have ordered him under arrest—ordered him to the rear—nay, cut him down—cut him out of the path; anything, rather than suffer such an impertinent and ridiculous proceeding. And had Greene been present—there—in the very place, where he should have been—he probably would have done nothing less! But, even this was really a small matter compared with some other proceedings of this day. We owe our worst mischief to other causes. When the British were driven into the house, they held, in that, and one other position only—the thick wood on the edge of Eutaw creek, where Marjoribanks was posted with his flank brigade. Everywhere besides, they were routed; flying in absolute, irretrievable defeat and retreat, in all other quarters. What remained to us? Why, we had them in our grasp completely. We had only to bring our fieldpieces into action. Well. The fieldpieces were brought up, and instead of taking position a hundred and fifty or two hundred yards from the house, and battering it down at leisure, what do the blockheads do, but rush both pieces up to within fifty yards of the building, while the sharpshooters swept away the artillerists as fast as they approached the guns. Where were the commanding officers here? Where the sense, or generalship? What next? Why we are to dislodge Marjoribanks from his cover along the creek. And how is this to be done? Marjoribanks, with three hundred picked infantry, well armed with muskets and bayonets, and covered besides with a dense forest of black-jack, is to be dislodged by *horse*. By horse! Was ever such an absurdity conceived before? Washington's cavalry is required to hurl itself upon this wall of black-jacks, this forest of bayonets—a dense wall; a bristling barrier of steel blades—and the fortress to be won by unsupported cavalry. Why, had the object been the utter annihilation of the

corps, the device could not have been better chosen. Even were there
no bayonets, no muskets, no Marjoribanks, the black-jacks would have
proved impervious to all the cavalry in the world; and so these poor
fellows were really sent to be slaughtered; and when half their saddles
were emptied, you might see the survivors, still wilfully obedient, fail-
ing to urge their horses forward, wheeling about and trying to *back*
them into the thicket, while smiting behind them with their broad-
swords. Of course, a moment's reflection shows us that when they were
ordered on such a duty, the wits of the general were in the moon!
Such folly is without example. And when we reflect that the whole
necessity was reduced to a simple use of the two pieces of artillery!
With one of these pieces battering down the house at two hundred
yards, with the other, stuffed to the muzzle with grape and raking the
copse where Marjoribanks was covered, twenty minutes would have
sufficed for dislodging both parties; when, with Washington and Lee's
cavalry, both on hand, and our mounted men of Maham and Horry, we
had every man of them doomed as food for the sabre, and nothing but
prompt surrender could have saved the lives of a single mother's son of
them! I'll engage that if Marion had been the master of the army
to-day, we had done these very things, and no less. Regulars, indeed!
I tell you that, all old soldiers are regulars, even though you arm them
with pitchforks only. Had our militia shown the white feather to-day,
in the first of the action, they would have been burdened with the whole
discredit of its failure. Had they been the troops to break into the
British camp, and to grow insubordinate, while wallowing in strong
drink, we should never have heard the end of it! Luckily, they fought
this day to make these continentals stare; and we owe it to them, and
their weapons, that all of these fine regulars were not slaughtered in
these tents. But for our covering rifles, Coffin and Marjoribanks would
have swept every scamp of them into eternity."

"Supper, maussa!" quoth Tom, the cook, entering at this moment,
and making a spread upon the turf.

"But you will eat nothing, Porgy," said the surgeon.

"Will I not!" roared the other, looking round with great eyes of
indignation. "Shall a hole in my thigh insist upon a corresponding hole
in my stomach? Because I am hurt shall I have no appetite? Because
you would heal, have you a right to starve me? This is a ridiculous
feature, my dear doctor, in your medical philosophy. Let me tell you

that one great secret of the art of healing is to strengthen the defence of Nature, so that she herself may carry on the war against disease. And let me tell you further, that one of Tom's suppers will hurt no man who sleeps with an easy conscience. Starve your sinners as much as you please, my dear fellow; they deserve it on moral grounds, and it may help them in physical matters; but for a virtuous soldiery, like ours, feed them well and they need no physic. But, where would you go, Sinclair, now, just as supper's coming in?"

"I wish none, Porgy. I have no appetite."

"No appetite! Go after him, St. Julien. Something's wrong. A Christian without an appetite is as strange an anomaly as a soul without a wing!"

But St. Julien did not stir.

"Let him alone," said he, "and do not observe him, Porgy. He has need to be sad just now. He has much to trouble him."

"Well, there's a need of sadness, at times, if only to make the sunshine agreeable. Let him go. We shall keep something for him when he gits back. All ready, Tom?"

"You kaint be too quick wid de supper, maussa. He jist warm enough for de swallow."

"Draw nigh, and fall to, boys. What if there be blockheads in camp, shall we go to bed supperless for that? Because there are ambitious dunderheads, shall good soldiers feed on bullets only? I dream of a time, when every man will, perforce, fall into his right place! In other words, I think a millenium possible. Meanwhile, let us eat, drink, and be satisfied, though tomorrow we sup on steel!"

With this scene, wherein after all his serious arguments about the battle, Porgy ends on the familiar lighter gustatory note, Simms bids farewell to him in his guise as a soldier. The author needed, however, forty-six more pages to end the plot he had commenced in The Forayers.

Inglehardt, in a final desperate attempt to force Bertha Travis, incarcerated nearby, to marry him, ordered that Henry Travis be cruelly tortured. The boy's imprisoned father was so maddened by having to witness this that he found strength enough to knock over a table and beat to a pulp the villain's head; but in the fracas Inglehardt killed Travis with his sword. Meanwhile Willie Sinclair was coming to the rescue. He killed Hell-Fire Dick at the prison door and rescued Henry and Bertha. The two couples, Willie Sinclair and Bertha Travis, and Peyre St. Julien and Carrie Sinclair, were happily married at the end of the war.

Throughout the war novels of the Saga there has been constant and growing emphasis on the importance of the South Carolina partisans. In The Forayers *Porgy had exemplified their equality or superiority socially to the rest of the American army; and now in* Eutaw *he became their direct and articulate advocate, calling attention to what they had actually done in battles, and contending that they were capable of having done much more if better strategy had been used. The partisans were southerners, and Porgy was, in a larger sense, stressing what the South did actually contribute and might have contributed. Porgy is a veritable image of the South itself; but if this image is to be complete, he must be seen not only as soldier but as civilian. Simms had four years earlier than* Eutaw *written about Porgy rebuilding his life after peace had come, in* Woodcraft.

8. Porgy
in
Woodcraft

The various reasons Woodcraft *is Simms at his best all evolve from the permeation of its texture by Captain Porgy.* Woodcraft *tells of his friends and of the amusing or touching forms their loyalty takes. It tells of his enemies, and the foiling of their adroit plots against him, and of their motivation, which is more believable than that of villains elsewhere in the Saga. It tells of Porgy and women. It sets up Porgy as evidence of the unjustness of Yankee censure of the South. Hence it has unity.*

Woodcraft *commences thus: "The provisional articles of peace between the King of Great Britain, and the revolted colonies of America, were signed at Paris, on the 13th November, 1782." The opening scene is on December 11 of that year, three days before the evacuation of Charleston by the British, when one of them, Colonel Moncrieff, was surprised in his office by an unexpected visitor, Mrs. Eveleigh "—a fair and comely dame, scarcely forty, with a fresh healthy expression, a bright . . . blue eye, a sweet, intelligent mouth, as indicative of character as of beauty, and a frank, buoyant expression of countenance. Her figure was tall, yet somewhat inclined to* embonpoint, *though her carriage was equally dignified and graceful."*

The owner of a fine plantation on the Ashepoo River, she had been well occupied during a stay in Charleston. She had learned that Moncrieff had made huge profits by seizing Carolina-owned Negroes and shipping them to the West Indies, and has made plans to dispose thus of two hundred more, including seven of her own and seven of Captain Porgy's. Aided by her competent overseer, Fordham, she had discovered her Negroes and those of her neighbor and friend Porgy had been impounded in an old hulk lying in the harbor. She had managed to get an order from the British General Leslie to deliver those Negroes to her. The chagrined Moncrieff hedged, saying he would be glad to do so if he could find these Negroes. The clever widow then revealed that she had already located them, and had even seen the "hulk book" in which these Negroes were entered in Moncrieff's name. Thus caught, Moncrieff retired to an inner office with a cool, shrewd tory, the Scotchman M'Kewn, in his secret employ, to try to devise a way of disobeying the order.

The British officer and his minion thus unwisely had left the office to the alert Mrs. Eveleigh, who discovered on the table a paper containing a long list of the names of slaves, bracketed opposite the names of their respective owners, including herself and Porgy. Also against each column was a memorandum containing a reference to the agent who had been instrumental in procuring the Negroes. "She read the name of M'Kewn as the person who had put her Negroes in the possession of Moncrieff." There was, furthermore, Moncrieff's acknowledgment and signature—besides other incriminating items. She thus had indisputable evidence that Moncrieff, aided by M'Kewn, had seized all these Negroes to sell them. Saying she was dealing with "enemies," she put the paper in her pocket. (This is the paper—*sometimes denoted* papers—*which is such an important property in the plot.)*

She also saw skulking across the room, hoping she would not see him, Bostwick, a neighboring squatter, whose poverty-stricken family she had charitably fed for years. She correctly surmised that "Bostwick has been the creature of M'Kewn, as M'Kewn is the creature of Moncrieff."

Overriding M'Kewn's protests, Moncrieff told him they must give the widow the Negroes, or the whole racket would be aired and they would lose the rest of the two hundred Negroes; and he yielded to her and gave her an order releasing both her slaves and Porgy's. After her departure, Moncrieff discovered and revealed to M'Kewn that the papers *had disappeared. M'Kewn maintained the widow had pocketed them; but Moncrieff contended that she was too much a lady to do such a thing, and that Bostwick had them.*

The loss of the incriminating papers *was much more serious for M'Kewn, who had invested all his funds in American real estate, than for Moncrieff, who was leaving the country for good.*

With brilliance and relish, Simms depicts the evacuation scene, with the redcoats retreating to the ships, and the bluecoats marching proudly in, to the merry sound of trumpets and drums. Cavaliers from other colonies were also present.

At a celebration party that evening at the home of her Charleston hostess, Mrs. Merchant, Mrs. Eveleigh, to her surprise, met M'Kewn, who had been able to pose as a patriot. Despite her great poise, she was not quite able to keep something in her manner from reinforcing M'Kewn's conviction that she had the papers. *She confided her discoveries to a "celebrated Carolina lawyer" (Charles Coatsworth Pinckney), who advised her to use them only to protect good whigs, as most of the debtors were tories who would not dare to oppose Moncrieff. The lawyer did agree that they must save Porgy's Negroes.*

Excluded from the gay festivities marking the evacuation were the gallant partisans, ostensibly because the American high command—entirely unjustly, insists Simms—suspected them of counterrebellion plans. General Marion, in a scene revealing the warm affection between him and his men, dispersed in his woodland camp the four hundred he had left; and they all started for home.

We will accompany one of these parties, a group consisting of four persons, all well mounted, and, comparatively speaking, all well armed and caparisoned. Two of them in fact are officers. One of these is a stout, and somewhat plethoric gentleman; full, and smooth, and florid of face, with indubitable signs of a passion for the good things of this life. His features are marked and decisive, with a large capacious nose, a mouth rather feminine and soft, and a chin well defined and masculine. But for the excessive development of the abdominal region, his figure would have been quite worthy of his face. He rode a noble gray, of great size and strength, good blood and bottom, and with his fires but little subdued by hard service.

Beside this man (Captain Porgy) rode a youth of nineteen (Lieuten-ant or "Ensign" Lance Frampton). "He was slender and tall, but wiry and agile; with features rather pleasing and soft, than expressive; and which might have been somewhat lacking in manliness but for the dark bronzing" by the sun. He was "well mounted" and "tolerably well dressed."

The third person was a "man of altogether inferior appearance, tall, rawboned, and awkward, with features harsh and irregular, redeemed only by a certain frankness and honesty of expression" and "a large and gentle eye of hazel, and a broad good-natured mouth [Sergeant Mill-house]. He carried an enormous beard almost of lemon color, and his hair streamed down his shoulders in waving masses [like] a mountain torrent. A stout chunk of a horse . . . bore his weight. He wore no other uniform than the common blue . . . hunting shirt of the rangers [or partisans], a cap of coon skin, an immense broadsword, and a pair of pistols."

These weapons, we may add, he could use with the left hand only—the right being wanting. He was one of the few who, in the miserable deficiency of the militia service, had survived a hurt which had com-pletely shattered the limb. His safety was due to his own stout heart, and the unflinching promptness of the friend and superior whom he fol-lowed. His right arm, torn into strips by a brace of bullets from a musket held within a few paces, was stricken off at his entreaty, by his captain [Porgy], and the bleeding stump was thrust instantly into hot, seething tar. The wounds healed, Heaven knows how, and he recovered. But for this proceeding he must have perished. At that time there was not a surgeon in Marion's brigade, and every hurt which affected the limbs of the victim was certain to end in death. Sergeant Millhouse, the man in question, became the devoted adherent of a superior, who had the firmness to comply with the stern requisition of the patient, and him-self perform the cruel operation, which the sufferer bore without a groan.

The fourth person was "a negro—a native African—the slave of the captain; a fellow of flat head and tried fidelity; of enormous mouth, but famous as a cook; of a nose that scarcely pretended to elevate itself on the otherwise plain surface of an acre of face": but having "an amazing genius for stews." "Tom had a reputation . . . for his terrapin soups, which made him the admiration of the whole brigade. He well

*knew his own merits, and was always careful to be in a condition to
establish them. The horse which he rode was covered, accordingly, with
a variety of kitchen equipage. Pots and kettles were curiously pendant
from the saddle, strapped over the negro's thighs, or hanging from his
skirts. A sack, which exhibited numerous angles, carried other utensils,
to say nothing of pewter plates, iron spoons, knives and forks, and sundry
odds and ends of bread and bacon." Tom was "really buried in his
kitchen baggage." But all this did not slow his riding, and he kept
"close to the heels of his master" listening, and occasionally commenting, "the camp-life having done much toward perfecting the republicanism of all the parties." (Today we should surely write here "democracy"
—the change in meaning of the word "republicanism" is interesting.)*

*There had, however, been little conversation during the couple of
hours they had journeyed. "Our Captain, who bore the name of Porgy,
was almost the only speaker. He was one, in fact, who possessed a liberal
endowment of the gift of language, and greatly delighted, on ordinary
occasions, in his own eloquence." But he was rather at the time re-
pressed by thinking of his own future, and by the sterility of the country
through which they were passing "—reaped by the greedy sickles of the
enemy, and sending up no cheerful smokes from the homesteads of welcoming friends." The day was chilly, if not cold. The party was depressed by the "ruins of ancient farms and decaying fences."*

At length, however, Captain Porgy broke the silence, as he alone
had hitherto done, by something that sounded monstrously like an oath,
but which we may render into more innocent language.

"By St. Bacchus, Lance, I must drink—I must eat—I must be guilty
of some fleshly indulgence! Let us get down here. There is a branch
before us, the water of which I have tried before. We have still a bottle
of Jamaica. Tom must knock us up a fry, and we must eat and drink,
that we may not grow stupid from excessive thinking. If one must
think, its most agreeable exercise, to my experience, is over toast and
tankard. Tom, 'light, old fellow, and get out your cookables. Lance,
you carry that Jamaica; I would see if it loses any of its color in these
dark and drowsy times."

*Tom began to obey the order instantly, although it took care and time
for him to extricate himself from the straps holding the kitchen equipment, and he had to have assistance from Sergeant Millhouse. Soon, by*

*means of tinder, flint, and steel he had kindled a blaze near running
water. To this Porgy and Lance advanced, and Porgy, in a pewter mug
"had brightened the clear, but rather unmeaning complexion of the
water with the bright, red liquid of Jamaica; . . . and having first, with
his nostrils, inhaled the fragrance of the rum, our captain held it to his
eye for a moment, surveying it with a glance of decided complacency,
before he carried it to his lips." He drank, and offered the cup and bottle
to Frampton, who "declined the liquor respectfully, and drank directly
from the running stream." "Millhouse . . . was more easily persuaded,
and Captain Porgy, as he beheld him pour with liberal hand into the
cup," might have wondered if it was wise to let "a man with but one
hand to adjust his own measures, particularly when the source of supply
was so distressingly small." "But he allowed the soldier to help himself
. . . and sat down"—no easy matter—at the foot of a pine. "Hither,
when the horses were fastened, came the ensign, Frampton," while Millhouse helped the cook.*

A hoarse sigh, that, issuing from plethoric chest, might have been held
a groan, betrayed, in Captain Porgy, a more than usually serious sense
of his situation. The ensign, who had thrown himself down on the
opposite side of the tree, modestly remarked—

"I think, Captain Porgy, you are more sorrowful than I ever saw you
before. Indeed, I can't say that I ever saw you sorrowful till now."

"Well: quite likely, Lance;—I have reason for it. Othello's occupation's gone."

"Othello, captain? Was the gentleman a soldier?"

"Ay, indeed, a Moorish soldier!—a blackamoor—a sort of negro—of
whom, it is quite likely, you have never heard—of whom you will, probably, hear no more than I shall tell you. He was a famous fighter in his
day; but there came a day when his wars were ended—like ours—and
then!—"

"And then?"

"He swallowed his sword through an artificial mouth!"

"What? How? Swallowed his sword?"

"In other words, cut his throat!"

"What! because he could no longer cut the throats of other people?"

"Partly that—and reason enough, too! Throat-cutting was his business. Nobody ought to survive his business. Now, if I were quite sure
that my wars were wholly ended—that I should never be permitted to

cut throats again, according to law—I should certainly request of you the favor, Lance, as an act of friendship, to pass the edge of your sabre across my jugular."

"I should do no such thing, Captain Porgy."

"Oh, yes! you would—that is, if I particularly requested it; and I don't know but I shall have to do so yet. You will certainly oblige me, Lance, when the necessity shall arrive, and when I make the entreaty."

"I don't think, captain. No! I could never do it."

"Oh, yes, you will; but the necessity is not apparent *yet,* since my nose tells me that Tom has still some material left, by which my throat shall find agreeable employment. I suppose, so long as one may tickle his throat with fish, flesh, and fowl, and soothe it with Jamaica, he may still endure a life relieved of its usual occupations. But, this is the doubt, Lance. How long shall there be fish, and flesh, and fowl, and Jamaica? I am a ruined man! I go back to the ancient homestead of my fathers, to find it desolate. Negroes gone, lands under mortgage, and not a rooster remaining in the poultry-yard, to crow me a welcome to dinner. Such a prospect does not terrify *you.* You have not been reared and trained to position, and artificial wants. You are young, just at the entrance of life, my dear boy, and can turn your hand to a thousand occupations, each of which shall supply your wants. Such is not the case with me. At forty-five, neither heart nor head, nor hand, possesses any such flexibility. A seven years' apprenticeship to war has left no resources in peace. Othello's occupation's gone!—gone! There is little or nothing now that I should live for;—family, wife, friends, fortune—I have none;—loneliness, poverty, desolation—these are the only prospects before me!"

This was spoken with so much real mournfulness, that it compelled the warmest sympathies of the youthful hearer, who, in spite of many eccentricities on the part of the speaker, which he failed to understand, and a strong and active selfishness, which he comprehended well enough, had yet a real affection for his superior. He crept near to Porgy, and said—

"Oh! it can't be as bad as all that, captain. You have many friends. There's General Marion, and there's our colonel, and many besides; and you've got a fine plantation, and I reckon some of your negroes are left——"

"Tom only! The last accounts reported that every hair of a negro was gone—all carried off by the tories, I suppose, or the British. As for the plantation, it's under mortgage to a d——d shark of a Scotchman; and, even if it were not, it would be worth nothing without the slaves. I tell you, boy, I see no remedy but to get my throat cut like a gentleman, and die in my epaulettes and boots."

"Oh! something will be sure to turn up, captain. Remember what old Ben Brewer used to say when anything misfortunate had happened —'Look up, I say,—God's over all!' God's your friend, captain."

"Well, in truth, Lance, I've so seldom called upon him, among my other friends, that, perhaps, he might do something for me now."

The irreverence was rebuked by his young companion in the following terms—

"Oh, captain! don't talk so! He's been doing for you all along! Who has taken care of you till now, when you're forty-five years old? Who saved you so often in fight?—and that's another reason, captain, why you should have faith in his mercies. I reckon God always puts in, at the right time, to save people, if so be they only let him! It's we that *won't* be saved, and that's continually fighting against his mercies."

"You talk like an oracle, Lance! One thing's certain, that at times, when a fellow discovers that he can do nothing to save himself, the best philosophy is to confide in powers superior to his own. Of one thing, rest assured, my lad—I shall never hurry my own case to judgment. I should fear the judge's charge would be against me, let me plead as I might, and be his mercies as great as I could hope for. It will be always time enough to end one's own history; and since I've escaped the British bullet and bayonet, during a seven years' service, I shall certainly not use either to my own disquiet. The smell of Tom's fry, makes my philosophy more cheerful. It is, indeed, surprising how a man's griefs dwindle away toward dinner time. Ho! Tom! are you ready?"

"Jes' ready, maussa," was the prompt reply of the cook.

"Let us eat, Lance. I see that Millhouse has his cleaver out already. Help me with an arm, boy, while I rise to a sitting posture. I am no small person to heave up into perpendicularity."

On Wednesday, Mrs. Eveleigh in her great family carriage started from Charleston to her plantation. With her were her son Arthur, sixteen, a fat Negro maidservant, and much luggage. Following not far behind was the plantation wagon. Some of her seven slaves and some of Porgy's seven rode in the wagon, some rode mules, some walked.

Part of the time Arthur rode on his little pony, along with the overseer Fordham on a big horse, frequently in advance of the vehicles.

About noon they were ambuscaded by several masked riders. One of these outlaws (Bostwick, as we discover later) seized a "richly in-laid mahogany case" from beneath the seat, after he forced the women out of the carriage. Two of the outlaws rode ahead, and shots were heard. The mother then saw her son riding back toward the carriage. A bandit shot Arthur's little horse; and two ruffians bound Arthur, re-porting that the boy had shot Bill Sykes ("He's ate his last bacon"). The bandits had bound Fordham, and tied Mrs. Eveleigh's hands behind her and fastened her to a tree. They had gagged Jenny, the Negro maid, to quiet her screams, but in the confusion had not bound her hands; she was therefore able to free her mistress and Arthur after the bandits rode on. Then Arthur could free Fordham. Meanwhile the Negroes and wagon caught up. Some of the slaves recognized Bostwick's coal-black horse, which he had left tethered when he disappeared into the woods with the precious box. They recalled it was Bostwick who had caught them to take them to be shipped away. A couple of the brigands now rushed out of the forest and captured six Negroes, but two, Mrs. Eveleigh's John Sylvester and Porgy's Pomp, carrying his fiddle, escaped.

Arthur fired from hiding and gave an outlaw a minor wound. The bandits roped the Negroes. Fordham insisted that they leave Mrs. Eve-leigh to take care of herself, as the bandits "won't do anything to her but rob her," but ". . . we ain't got the protection of a petticoat"; and that they leave the horses, and crawl, indeed, snake away. The outlaws came back, gagged Mrs. Eveleigh and her maid and tied both to her carriage. Mrs. Eveleigh saw her son in the bushes, and cried out a warning. One outlaw threatened to cut out the widow's tongue, and Arthur, firing recklessly, buried a bullet in his brain. Bostwick decided to leave with what they had, including seven Negroes. They set Norris to rifling the wagon. Fordham lay low and kept still.

Meanwhile—

Captain Porgy, and his little suite of three persons, having been making easy progress since we left them—have advanced considerably on their way homeward, and are now almost within striking distance of the Ashepoo. A few miles beyond it, and the captain will once more be able to contemplate his ancient homestead—the paternal house and hearth, the well-known fields and woods—a once valuable property which

had been transmitted to him through three or more careful generations
—he, alas! being the only careless one of the race—in whose hands their
continued accumulations had constantly undergone diminution, until
now, when, what with his own profligacy and the misfortunes naturally
following the sort of war through which the colony had just gone, his
homestead was almost wholly desolate, stripped of negroes, and covered
with debt as with a winter garment.

Porgy had been a *fast youth*. He had never been taught the pains
of acquisition. Left to himself—his own dangerous keeping—when a
mere boy, he had too soon and fatally learned the pleasures of dissipation. The war found him pursued by debt and embarrassments, as un-
relaxing as the furies that hunted the steps of Orestes.—He had found
temporary relief from the hands of usury, and may thus be described
as falling from the grasp of the Furies, into the worse keeping of the
Fates. He held himself very nearly a ruined man, when the war began;
and the loss of numerous negroes, carried off by the enemy, gave him
no reason to doubt upon the subject. His lands were mortgaged, the
negroes gone, his debts cried aloud against him for judgment, and he
had reason to know that his chief creditor was on the watch for his
return. The cessation of war, which stripped him of his occupation, was
an event which necessarily restored the common law to its fearful activity.
The camp was now doomed to pale in the shadow of the court; arms
must give way to gown; and the laurels of war soon wither, in sight
and from remembrance, when the tongue only is allowed to carry on
the contests of human antagonism.

*As never before in his life, Porgy, now "passed middle age" (he was
forty-five), felt compelled to assess his resources for facing his problems
and asking what he could do.*

Porgy was the man to feel, thoroughly, the discouraging and sad, in
this survey; for he was a man really of good sense and many sensibilities;—but he had moral resources which kept him from basely cowering
and whining beneath the cloud. He was only not so blind as not to see
it with oppressive distinctness—to feel its pressure, to acknowledge the
doubts and embarrassments which crowd upon his path;—not to shudder
at them basely, or to yield to any weaknesses of mood, in consequence.
Besides, he had a taste for pleasure, was not a little of an epicure—there
may have been, indeed, some affectation in this characteristic—and he

prided himself upon the fact that he could extract his morals always from his appetites. He took philosophy with him to his table, and grew wise over his wine. So, at least, he claimed to do.

We have seen him, in a previous chapter, resorting to this sort of remedy against the cares which he was yet compelled to contemplate— appealing to his appetites against his griefs, and seeking consolations against thought, in his last bottle of Jamaica. It so happens that in resuming our acquaintance with his party, we find him again similarly engaged. It is noonday and past. Our partisans feel the necessity of stopping for refreshment, on the route.

Porgy and his band came to a pleasant spot where a "rill of sweet water" [trickled] "across the sandy highway. . . ." There were "still a few bright drops in the corpulent bottle of Jamaica—one of a size and shape that we do not often see . . . in these degenerate days. It was . . . an oblong square . . . holding, perhaps, a trifle under a gallon." They had drinks, and Tom prepared hoecake and bacon.
Millhouse praised Tom's skill at broiling ham.

"I ought for know, Mass Millhouse! Maussa show me how for cook 'em hese'f. Mass Porgy fus'-rate cook! He 'tan' [stand] ober me when I fus' begin for l'arn. May-be he no cuss when I sp'ile 'em! Sometime I do 'em too much, sometime I do 'em too little; he cuss bote times, and sway [swear] he'll make me see h—l ef I do 'em so nex' time. Wha' den? I no want for see h—l, and I min' [mind]. I l'arn! Once I l'arn, I nebber forgit. Maussa hole me to 'em. He quick for cuss—like the debbil!—Sometimes he lick! But, wha' den? I always hab good share of wha' I cook. Ef Maussa only hab skin ob de pig, he sure for gib me de yays [ears] and tail."

"He's a d——d good fellow, Tom—Cappin Porgy. I'd 'a been a dead dog ef 'twa'n't for him. But he seems mighty dull, these times, Tom;— droopy, I may say; like a young turkey in wet weather."

Tom looked with interest toward his master, who was sitting some steps off—reclining, rather than sitting—beneath a tree, with young Lance Frampton, the ensign, in attendance. In the low tones of voice employed by the sergeant and the negro, in this conference, they were quite un- heard by the subject of their dialogue.

"I sh' um [see 'em]," responded the negro. "De trute is, Mass Millh'us —de bakin is most gone; de bottle, I 'spec' [expect] hab room 'nough for fill agen;—I most 'fear'd der's no quite 'nough lef' in 'em, to gib you and me anoder dram; and de army's broke up, de British and torys, day say, all gone; and nobody lef' for we ravage 'pon, and git new supplies. Da's it! Wha' we for do now, is de t'ing. It's dat wha', make Mass Porgy look like young tukkey in rainy wedder."

"Tom, old boy, we'll have to work for the cappin."

"You work, Mass Millh'us?—wha' you kin do when you only got one han'?"

"But I'm got a h—l of a big heart for my friend, Tom, by thunder; and when there's heart enough in a man's buzzum, Tom, he kin always find arms enough to sarve his friend, even if so be both hands are chopped off."

"Der's trute in dat, Mass Millh'us," answered the negro gravely with an assured shake of the head.

"Truth! By thunder, Tom, it's all truth! It's the body and soul of truth, and I'm the man to prove it! I'll work! The cappin shan't want! He can't do much, Tom, for himself, seeing that there's to be no more fighting, which is the only work that a gentleman kin do, without s'iling his fingers."

"Mass Porgy is gempleman for true."

"Let anybody stand up and say he ain't, and I'll gallop through him, by thunder!"

"I trot t'rough arter you, Mass Millh'us."

"But he don't need that. He's the man to do all his own fighting, and mighty glad of the chance."

"Fight like de debbil, Mass Millh'us! You take some more of dis br'ile?"

"No, Tome, no more;—and yet, you do br'ile it so bloody fine that —yes! You may fork over that bit. The small bit, Tom, keep t'other piece for yourself."

"I done! Ef der' was only de smalles' drop o' dat Jimaica in de bottle!"

The fellow looked wistfully toward his master. The eye of Sergeant Millhouse took the same direction; but neither of them would have dreamed of doing, or saying, anything, which might declare their wants to their superior. But it was in proof of Captain Porgy's claim to the character they had both been pleased to assign him, that of the gentleman, that he always duly considered the claims of the inferior, and anticipated their reasonable desire. As if divining their wishes, he seemed to waken up at this moment, and cried out from his tree, to Millhouse:—

"Sergeant, there's still a drop of the Jamaica for you in the bottle. Give what you leave to Tom. There's, perhaps, a tolerable sup for you both; but it's the last. I suppose, whenever we deserve it, the good Fortune will send us more."

Millhouse did not wait for a second invitation. Tom smacked his lips as the sergeant approached him with the bottle.

"Wha' I bin say, Mass Millh'us? Ef Mass Cappin had only de skin ob de pig, he will gib we de tail and yays."

"He's a born gentleman, by thunder; and we'll work for him, Tom, more hard than any nigger he ever had."

"I 'tan [stand] up wid you for dat, Mass Millh'us. I cook myse'f 'fore I guine le' Maussa want for dinner. So long as dere's 'coon and 'possum, squerril and rabbit in de wood, pattridge and dub [dove]—duck in de ribber, and fish in de pond—so long, I tell you, Tom will always hab 'nough somet'ing to cook! As for de corn, we kin make dat too. Ef you no got two han' for hoe, Mass Sergeant, you kin drop de seed."

"But I kin hoe like h—l, with one hand jest as well as two. . . ."

The sergeant did agree to help Tom pack up his pots and pans now, and declared that he loved Porgy and would be his "nigger" when there was no "company." But if big shots, such as the "old Fox" or General Greene, came, he would insist on standing in uniform behind his captain. Porgy and Lance had also dined.

Crouched at ease, under the shadows of an enormous oak, they have feasted upon the simple fare provided by the hands of their excellent cook, and have done the amplest justice to the thin slices of broiled ham, "done to a turn," and the brown hoe-cake, in the proper composition of which, Tom had established in camp the most enviable reputation. These constituted the sum total of their commissariat. The sufficient potations of oily old Jamaica had followed; and with a sense of physical satisfaction which greatly brightened the prospect, Captain Porgy leaned back against the shaft of the tree, and closed his eyes in order justly to enjoy it.

That complacent sort of revery which usually occupies every mind, after the noon-day appetite has been subdued and satisfied, had already seized upon our corpulent captain. Under its present influences, the state of his affairs began to look less gloomy. The circumstances which more particularly pressed upon his thoughts at this juncture—the loss of his late employment, the involvement of his estates, the supposed abduction of all his negroes, the danger which threatened at the hands of certain creditors—sharks, in shoals, lying in wait, like tigers of the land, seeking what they may devour—these crowding and dismal figures upon his landscape which, before he dined, had rendered his thoughts a very jungle, worse than Indian, of lions, tigers, and snakes of mammoth dimensions—with the consummation of the noon-day meal, retreated from before his path, disarmed of most of their [t]errors, and, though still lurking and still hostile, looking so little capable of doing mischief, that our captain began to wonder at his own feebleness of soul which had, but a little while before, so greatly alarmed him on their account. A mild and soothing languor of mood, as if by magic, changed and modified all the figures in his landscape: and Nature, having gained time—which is the best capital, after all, as well in morals as in war—it was surprising how grateful and agreeable became the philosophy which she had taught our captain. He actually—to the amusement of Lance Frampton, who had tried in vain to soothe his melancholy mood as they rode together before dinner—began to chuckle aloud, yet unconsciously, during his revery, and finally afforded to his young lieutenant an opportunity to twit him, good humoredly, upon his sudden change of humor, by snapping his fingers in the air, as if at the flight of some enemy, whom he had successfully combated.

"Well, I say, captain, you don't seem quite so sick of life as you said you were before dinner. I reckon you won't be shooting yourself, as you threatened, only a little while ago."

"Well, boy, what then? Is life less loathsome because one learns to laugh at it as well as hate it?"

"But you don't hate it, captain—not now."

"No, and for a good reason—because I no longer fear it. I see the worst of it. I see all that it can do, and all that it can deny, and I feel, let it do its worst, that I'm the man for it."

"And what's made you so much stronger now to bear, captain, than you were only an hour agone?" asked the youth, with an insinuating chuckle.

"Dinner, you dog, I suppose—dinner and drink. Is that what you mean? Well—I grant you. We are creatures of two lives, two principles, neither of which have perfect play at any time in the case of a man not absolutely a fanatic or a brute. The animal restrains the moral man, the moral man checks the animal. There are moments when one obtains the ascendency over the other, and our moods acknowledge this ascendency. Before dinner, my animal man was vexed and wolfish. It rendered me savage and sour. I could not think justly. I could not properly weigh and determine upon the value of the facts in my own condition. I exaggerated all the ills of fortune, all the evils before me, my poverty, my incapacity, and the ferocious greed of my creditors. My soul was at the mercy of my stomach. But, the wolf pacified, my mind acquired freedom. The wild beast sank back into his jungle, and the man once more walked erect, having no fear. Philosophy, my boy, appears once more to comfort me, and the landscape grows bright and beautiful before my evening sun."

"Well, all's right then, captain, until you get hungry again."

"Poh, poh! boy—sufficient for the day is the evil thereof. God will provide. Vex me not with what to-morrow may bring forth, or refuse to bring forth. To-day is secure. That is enough; and the philosophy which to-day has brought, will, no doubt, reconcile me to-morrow. Hear you, Lance? It is the first policy in a time of difficulty or danger, always to know the worst—never to hide the truth from yourself—never to persuade yourself that the evil is unreal, and that things are better than they really are. When you know the worst, you know exactly what is to be done, and what is to be endured. In time of war, with the enemy before you and around you, you are required to see his whole strength, give him full credit for what he can do, and ought to do, and determine, accordingly, whether it be your policy to fight, or fly, or submit—whether you can fly—what will be your treatment if you yield, and what is the reasonable chance of safety or victory, if you resolve to fight. In time of peace the necessity is the same. Peace is only a name for civil war. Life itself is civil war; and our enemies are more or less strong and numerous, according to circumstances. One of the greatest misfortunes of men, and it has been mine until this hour, consists in the great reluctance of the mind to contemplate and review, calmly, the difficulties which surround us—to look our dangers in the face, see how they lie, where they threaten, and how we may contend against them. We are all quite too apt to refuse to look at our troubles, and prefer that they should leap on us at a bound, rather than disquiet ourselves, in advance of the conflict, by contemplating the dangers with which we think it impossible to contend.

I have just succeeded in overcoming this reluctance. I have arrayed before my mind's eye all my annoyances, and the consequence is that I snap my fingers at them. As old Jerry Sanford used to cry out when he was in a fight, 'Hurra for nothing!' Jerry was a true philosopher. His motto shall be mine. Hurra for nothing seems to me to embody the full amount of most men's matter for rejoicing."

"Well now, captain, it's a fine philosophy, I reckon, that'll bring a man to such a sort of feeling. But, if I may take the liberty, I'd just like to know, how such a philosophy can put a stop to the trouble, make the enemy quit the field, drive the creditors off the plantation, and fill the corn-crib when it's empty? I ask these questions with your permission, captain, seeing as how you've been good enough to talk to me upon your affairs, and your debts, and the troubles from the sheriff that you're so much afraid of."

"Afraid of the sheriff, boy! Who dares to say that of me? Never was I afraid of a sheriff in my life. D—n him! Let him come. I have the heart, or I'm no white man, to take the whole *posse comitatus* by the snout."

"*Posse comitatus!* Oh, I reckon you mean the deputies?"

"Ay, ay—the host of deputies—a legion of deputies if you will, from the Pedee to the Savannah. But you haven't caught my ideas, Lance. I must try and be more intelligible."

"I thank you, captain."

"You know, Lance, as well as anybody else, that I've been a d——d fool in my time."

"Yes, captain, to be sure."

Porgy's self-esteem was not pleased with so ready a concession.

"Well, boy, I don't mean exactly that. How the devil do you know anything of my folly?"

"Oh, I can guess, sir."

"Can you, indeed?" with a sardonic grin. "You are too knowing by half, sir—presuming to know, for one so young as yourself. I mean, boy, that I've done a d——d sight too many foolish things. This don't make a man utterly a fool."

"No, captain."

"Unless he continues to do foolish things, mark you."

"Yes, captain, I see."

"Most men, the wisest, do foolish things. I don't know, indeed, but that wisdom itself requires to go through a certain probation of folly, in order to acquire the degree of knowledge, which shall teach what folly is—what shape it takes, and how it will affect us. I suppose that it was in obedience to this law of nature, that my follies were performed. But my error was that I continued my probation quite too long. I was ambitious, you see, of the highest sort of wisdom. I made too many experiments in folly, and found them too pleasant to abandon them in season. The consequence was, that I began to grow wise only as I forfeited the means for further experiment. My wisdom had its birth in my poverty, and as it was through my follies that I became poor, I suppose, logically, I am bound to say that I was wise because I had been so great a fool. Do you comprehend me?"

"A little, captain; I think I see."

"You will understand me better as I go on. I wasted money—a great deal—ran into debt—sold negroes—mortgaged others—and when I joined the brigade, my plantation was mortgaged also—I can't tell you for how much. But, even if the British and tories had not stolen all the rest of my negroes, the sale of the whole of them would scarcely have paid the debt then, and there's some six years' interest since. A very interesting condition of affairs, you will admit, for my contemplation now."

"Very, sir."

"Now, to look fully these affairs in the face requires no small degree of courage. I confess, until I had finished dinner to-day, I was scarcely the man for it. But that last draught of that blessed and blessing old Jamaica—did Millhouse and Tom get a good sup of it?"

"Pretty good, captain."

"They require good measure, both! Well Lance, boy, that last sup of the Jamaica seemed to warm up my courage, and I resolutely called up the whole case, didn't suppress any of the facts, looked at all the debts, difficulties, duns, and dangers, and said to myself, 'A fig for 'em all.' Let the lands go, and the negroes go, and still—I'm a man!—a man!"

"That's the way, captain," responded the youth, with enthusiasm, seizing the extended hand of his superior, and pressing it with a real affection.

"It was just when I had come to this conclusion, Lance, that I snapt my fingers. I couldn't help it. It was the spontaneous sign of my exultation; and as I did so, I thought I saw the d——d mealy face, blear eyes, hook nose, and utterly rascally whole, of my creditor M'Kewn, back out from before me, and take to the woods at a full run. Along with him went the sheriff and the whole swarm of deputies, all of whom have been dodging about me the whole morning, shaking their d——d writs, ca. sa's, fi. fa's, and a thousand other offensive sheets of penal parchment in my face. I discomfited the wretches by that same snap of the fingers; and the adoption of old Jerry Sanford's cry of battle —'Hurrah for nothing!' has made me able to back poverty and the sheriff into the woods!"

"I'm so glad, captain!"—after a pause, was the response of Lance Frampton; but, with some hesitation, and perhaps not well knowing how to shape the question which he only desired to intimate—"but, captain, is that all? Will it end so?"

"End how?"

"Won't the sheriff come again?"

"What then! Give him another snap of the fingers, and the war-cry."

"But won't he take—"

"The property? Yes! I suppose after a while I shall have to surrender; but we'll make a d——d long fight of it, Lance; and we'll get terms, good conditions, when we give in—go off with our sidearms, flag flying, and music playing the grand march 'Hurrah for nothing!'"

"But, captain," continued the youth, "I don't altogether know. You're a man of learning, and can tell much better than me; but I'm rather dubious. When I was a boy, old Humphries of Dorchester, father of our Bill, you know, he sent the sheriff after my father, and took him, and took all the property besides, even to the very beds and bedding. Now, won't they take you, captain, if you can't pay?"

"Take me, boy! Do I look like a man in danger from the claws of a sheriff? No, no! There will be blows in that business. They know better, Lance. In fact they are content, dealing with a gentleman and a soldier, to take his baggage-wagons, his *impedimenta,* and that purely out of kindness, as they desire to free him from all incumbrances. They will hardly attempt more. That d——d harpy, M'Kewn, will be quite content, I suspect, to take the plantation. There are no negroes left, I fear."

"But Tom?"

"Tom! oh, ay! And you think Tom liable?"

"Ain't he, then?"

"Well, I suppose so. Tom is certainly a negro. Tom is certainly mine. As mine, Tom is liable for my debts, and it *may* be that some d——d fool of a creditor or sheriff may fancy that he can take Tom. But he shall have a hint in season of the danger of any such experiments upon my philosophy. I love Tom. Tom is virtually a free man. It's true, being a debtor, I can not confer freedom upon him. But let a sheriff touch him, and I'll put a bullet through his diaphragm. I will, by Jupiter! If I don't do that, Lance—if there's no escape for Tom—for they may seize him when I'm napping—after dinner, perhaps—then, I shall kill Tom, Lance; I'll shoot *him*—him, Tom—in order to save him. The poor fellow has faithfully served a gentleman. He shall never fall into the hands of a scamp. I'll sacrifice him as a burnt-offering for my sins and his own. Tom, I'm thinking, would rather die my slave, than live a thousand years under another owner."

"He *does* love you, captain."

"And I love him. The old rascal, I do love him. He makes the finest stew of any cook in Carolina. He shall cook for me as long as I'm able to eat; and when I'm not, we shall both be willing to die together."

"Well, but captain, you was saying—"

"Ah! yes. We are supposing that all's gone, lands, negroes, baggage —all the *impedimenta*. Everything but Tom—and what then? That is the point which I have reached, and to which my philosophy reconciles me. It is still possible for me to live."

"Oh, yes, sir!"

"How the devil should you know? To be sure, I could live precisely as you and a thousand others would live; but you see, Lance, life is a very different thing to different persons. One man lives like a dog, a hog, a skunk, a 'coon, or even a cabbage. With such a person, you can despoil him of nothing by any process. You can not rob him. Thieves can not break into his premises and steal. Take all he has, and he loses nothing. He can still find grubbage—water lies conveniently before him in every puddle—and he may swallow air without even vexing the fears of a chameleon. He acknowledges only the principle of distension, not of taste or even appetite, and there is no stint of grass and weeds for a starving heifer. 'Root pig or die,' is with him the whole body of law; and his snout has long since been practised in finding its way into the potato-hills after the crop has been withdrawn. But to reconcile a man, with my training, to such a life, requires a rare philosophy indeed. How, with such tastes as mine, am I to live?—how dig?- -where find potatoes, and with what substitutes for tea, and coffee, and Jamaica, refresh the inner man? That I should be able to cry 'Hurrah for nothing!' with perfect good-humor, after such a survey of my case, is the glorious triumph that I have this day achieved. Would you believe it, Lance, that I go out of the war with a paltry eleven guineas in my pocket? And this is all I really own in the world; but—"

"Captain!"

"Well!"

"I've got a *lettle* more than that. Here's twenty guineas that Colonel Singleton gave me more than a month ago. If you're willing, we'll put yours and mine in the same bag, and you shall have the keeping of it."

"You're a good boy, Lance, and I love you; but d——n your guineas. What should make you think that I want 'em? What should make you think so meanly of me as to suppose that I would rob you of your little stock in trade?"

"But it's no robbery, captain—I'm glad to—"

"Pooh, pooh! Put up your guineas, Lance. You'll want 'em all. Don't I know you? Are you not going to marry that pretty little witch, Ellen Griffin?"

"Well, sir—I reckon. Yes, sir, Ellen and me—"

"Give her the bag to keep! Don't trust yourself with it, or, in some fit of folly, you'll be for giving it to some other person, who will take you at your word. You will want all that, and even more, to begin your career in this world. As for me, I see exactly what I am to do, and will tell you."

"I'll thank you, sir."

"There was, many years ago, an old Frenchman, that came into our neighborhood. He was the most dwarfish and dried-up little fellow in the world. He was as poor as Job's turkey—"

"Why was Job's turkey so poor, captain?"

"I suppose that, being a favorite with Job himself, his wife never fed it. But don't interrupt me by asking such a d——d unnecessary question, Lance! As I was saying of this Frenchman, he was wretchedly poor, in purse as in body, owned no goods that I could see except the clothes on his back, and a miserable little single-barrel bird-gun, small in bore, but something taller than its owner. The only luxury that the old fellow indulged in was snuff; and with this, his upper lip, his shirt-bosom, coat-sleeve, and vest pocket, were all dyed deeply with a never-fading saffron brown. His snuff, gun, a supply of powder and shot, and an old box with some mean cooking apparatus, were his only possessions. I doubt if he had an extra pair of breeches. He alighted suddenly in the neighborhood, and presented himself before me, with a polite bow, and a most persuasive grin."

" 'Monsieur Porgy, I yer of you! You s'all let me live on your plantation! Dere is one house ob log by de *leetle* swamp! Dere s'all be nobody live in him! 'Spose you s'all soffre me, I s'all live in him! I have no money to pay! I live by my leetle gon! I s'all shoot your little—de dove, de—what you call him, patridge, de squirrel, de rabit, all de leetle beast. I no trobble de deer, and de big bird—de torkey! You s'all soffre me dat leetle house, and to hill, for my leetle dener, dese leetle bird, and de leetle beasts, I s'all be votre tres homble sarvant two t'ousand times, and s'all t'ank, t'ree, seven, eight, five times ovair!' "

"I consented to the very moderate entreaty; but offered that he should live with me—offered him money—but he refused everything but the simple privileges which he applied for, 'to liv' in de leetle pole house, by de leetle swamp, and kill de leetle birds and beasts.' There, accordingly, this poor fellow lived, for seven years, literally on nothing. He would accept no gifts, and even strove to put me under obligations. If, for example, he shot a pair of fine English ducks, which was sometimes the case, he would bring them to me with a grateful grin—

'Monsieur Porgy, you s'll do me de ver' great honneur.'

"At first I accepted, but when he steadily refused my help, I refused his game, except as a purchase. His wants were few and easily provided. His powder and shot, his snuff and coffee, salt and sugar, oil and vinegar, —these he procured from a peddlar who went the rounds of the parish at stated periods. To procure these articles, he sold at the cross-roads, or to neighboring families, his surplus game. He planted a couple of acres of corn and peas, just about his habitation, which, under his cultivation, yielded twice or thrice as much as any two of my best acres. His food, besides, was wholly procured by his gun, yet he was not a surprising shot. But he was indiscriminate in his slaughter of 'de *leetle* birds.' He showed few preferences. If the dove and partridge did not come immediately in his way, he shot down woodpecker and blue-jay. The hawk was not rejected from his cook-pot. He luxuriated in 'coon and 'possum when he could get them, and with this object, he frequently went on the night-hunts with the negroes. His taste required that his birds and beasts should be utterly stale before he ate them. His larder was hung with birds, of all sorts, almost dropping to pieces, before he thought them well flavored enough for his palate. Then, with a little salt, oil, and red pepper, he made his meal with the relish of one who has eaten of a princely feast. He was always cheerful as a lark. He sang and even danced alone beneath his trees. He had been on the place for about a year, when he went off suddenly, on foot, to Charleston. When he returned, he brought back with him an old violin, the vilest looking thing in the world, but stuffed to the core with the sweetest music, which the old fellow brought out with singular skill. The instrument was a genuine Cremona—a famous fine one—which, as I found out afterward, he had left in pawn in the city. His happiness was quite complete when he had redeemed it. I often strolled out to hear him play. He had no apparent griefs. He never complained—never even fretted—was always ready with a grin of good humor—smile he could not, on account of the peculiarly ill-formed mouth which he owned;—and so, for seven years, he lived, entirely companionless. Yet he had visiters, and of his own countrymen. At Christmas, he sometimes had no less than three or four guests, who came again at the close of spring. Without bedding or covering, except the scantiest for himself, they remained with him more than a week on each occasion. I was curious to see how he would entertain them, and always paid him a visit when I heard of their arrival. He received them with open arms. They were welcome to all he had. True, he had nothing; but what then? He made room for them, gave place by the fireside, spread a third of his room with pine straw, ground an extra quantity of corn and coffee; then, as they had finished their morning meal, he would say—'*Allons!* my friends— we s'all go shoot de leetle birds!' Each had brought his gun, and they knew that each was expected to find his own dinner; and he did so. I have encountered them on their return from a morning's excursion, and their bags were full—and such an assortment! They killed everything that crossed their paths, taking care, however, to spare the 'big birds and beasts.'

"Now, Lance, what I have told you is a history. Poor old Louis Du Bourg is dead: but he has left me his example! I see exactly how I may live, as happily and as independently as he—that is, when all's over, and I have seen the worst. I shall then turn to killing 'de leetle bird and de leetle beast,' squatting on some great man's property. I can surely get this privilege from some of my old associates; and with two acres of tolerable land, I shall hoe and hill my own corn; sow and dig my own potatoes; cook my own hominy; sell my ducks and birds when I want powder and shot, and be able, possibly, as I was once something of a hunter, to carry enough venison to market to procure me an occasional demijohn of good Jamaica. Perhaps, in process of time—but I need look no farther. Enough, Lance, my boy, that, like my old Frenchman, I shall be able, once or twice a year, to entertain my old friends. You shall come and see me, Lance, you and our friend here, Sargeant Millhouse; he shall help me set my snares, and you will help me kill my 'leetle birds and beasts,' and with a 'coon and 'possum hunt, by night, we shall lay in sufficient store of venison for a week's entertainment of any friends. . . .

Horrified at the prospect of Porgy's being reduced to doing actual field work, Lance began to insist that when he and his Ellen were married, Porgy must make his home with them. Thanking Lance for the kind invitation, Porgy began to insist vehemently that he maintain his own independent establishment even if to do so he must do manual labor.

A great outcry from Tom interrupted Porgy. "By dint of great exertions on his part, and with the strenuous help of his lieutenant, the huge bulk of Captain Porgy was lifted into the perpendicular," and both were ready to do battle. It was only Tom and Millhouse, bringing up with them two of the escaped Negroes, the widow's John Sylvester and Porgy's Pompey, junior.

Tom, "thrusting his hand familiarly into the wool of Pompey, and pulling him forward, said 'dis da' our own little Pomp, you know.'"

Porgy replied, "Little! The fellow's as tall as you are. Why, Pomp! is that you boy? Where have you been? What are you doing here? They told me you were carried off by the British."

Pomp answered "I git way, maussa! Dey tief [steal] me, but I git 'way! How you bin, Mass Cappin? God A'mighty! I so glad for see you;" and he "ran forward and shook his master's hand with the eagerness with which one welcomes the best friend in the world—'Oh! maussa, it's de blessed t'ing you is come. You hab sword and gun. You mus' mek' haste now.'" Pomp then told how the tories had captured the Negroes as well as Mrs. Eveleigh and her son and overseer, and that only John and Pomp had escaped. Millhouse vouched for the truth of Pomp's tale; and Pomp described his glad recognition of Tom.

Porgy at last snapped into action (the only time he seems a bit sluggish in reaction), and rapidly gave brisk orders.

"Boot and saddle, Lance! Millhouse, to horse! Tom, gather up and follow as fast as you can. John Sylvester—up behind Lieutenant Frampton. You, Pomp, jump up behind Sergeant Millhouse, and show the way between you. Ride apart, Lance, you and Millhouse, and see to your priming. Let these fellows tell when we are within three hundred yards from the spot where the affair took place. Give the whistle then, and haul up and move with caution. Don't dismount—we may have to dash in upon the rascals headlong. I'll take the woods between you— let there be some twenty yards between us each. And now, at a smart gallop, as soon as you can!"

It required but a few minutes to prepare the party in order for the march, as required. John jumped up behind Frampton, Pomp took his place in the rear of Millhouse, and Captain Porgy, setting these two horsemen in the proper direction, dashed forward through the piney woods with a spirit and celerity that seemed scarcely consistent with his great bulk, and the languor which he had exhibited but a little while before.

The group led by Porgy came up to the wagon. The captured Negroes were marching off, roped, in charge of the two ruffians. One of the outlaws, Dick Norris, had been left behind to take things out of the wagon. Porgy surmised that he in the wagon was working so "composedly" that the outlaws did not suspect anyone would pursue them. Porgy declared that "we must pursue these fellows who are marching away, cut them off, and rescue the Negroes," and so "compel the ambush to show itself." He ordered Lance, with Pomp and John to "capture the fellow in the wagon." Porgy and Millhouse dashed ahead to pursue the "robbers who had charge of the fugitive Negroes." Norris jumped out of the wagon, only to be captured and roped by Lance, John, and Pomp. Bostwick was hidden near enough to observe it all. He was tempted to sneak away; but was restrained by the thought that Norris might incriminate him by confessing. Bostwick was human enough not to want to leave the country and so never see his three children. Porgy and Millhouse caught up with the Negroes, "who cheered them with hearty shouts as they drew nigh." Porgy's own "almost with one voice cried" 'Da maussa! Hurrah, maussa! Gorra Mighty bress you! How do you do?" Porgy replied. "Young, boys, young and lively! God bless you! . . ." He found that only two tories had run ahead. Porgy left Lance to supervise putting the things back into the wagon, and with Millhouse rode ahead after the fleeing bandits. "Porgy applied his persuaders anew to the flanks of his own high-spirited horse. It was wonderful to see how well the animal sped with such a bulk upon his back! But the steed was a powerful one, chosen heedfully with reference to the severe duty which he was required to perform." As Porgy gained on an outlaw, the latter saw him and began to ready his pistols. Porgy knew there was danger—"but as he was apt to phrase it himself—"

"Danger is a part of the contract! It is to be counted on, but not considered! He who stops to consider the danger never goes into battle! No wise man, embarking in such an amusement as war, ever considers its mischances as likely to occur in his own case. He knows the fatal sisters have singled out certain favorites for Valhalla, but he always takes for granted that they have overlooked *himself!* He relies, always, on his peculiar personal star, and goes into battle—not to be killed, but to kill!"

With such reflections, our Captain Porgy, corpulent as he is, was very apt to behave in battle, as we are told the Berserkirs, or wild warriors of the Scandinavians, were wont to behave. To dash, with a sort of frenzy, into the worst of dangers, totally heedless of them all, as if bearing a charmed life—and only seeking to destroy! And such a practice, by the way, is very apt to carry with it its own securities. A rage that blinds the champion to all dangers, and makes him totally unconscious of all fears, is very apt to inspire fear in the enemy who beholds his approach. The onset of Porgy was well calculated to prompt such feelings. A mountain in a passion, and in progress—a human avalanche descending upon the plain—crashing, rending, overwhelming, as it goes—such, in some small degree, was the image presented to the mind of the trembling enemy, seeing the headlong rush of our plethoric captain!

The outlaw took a shot and hit Porgy's horse.

The steed of Porgy swayed round at the flash, threw out his fore-feet wildly, then settled heavily down upon the earth, in the immediate

agonies of death! Porgy, however, had sufficient warning that the animal was hit, and, releasing his feet from the stirrups as the beast was
falling, he escaped from being crushed beneath his weight. He recovered
his legs with some effort, but without injury.

Porgy was greatly distressed by the death of his fine horse:

"The scoundrel! Had he been Christian enough to have suffered
himself to have been cut down five minutes ago, and before that last
pistol-shot, I could have been sorry for him! But he has done for my
noble gray, the best of friends; a horse that has borne his own flesh and
mine so long to the satisfaction of both! I feel, sergeant, as if I could
blubber like a boy over his first colt!"

*Porgy let Millhouse have what he could find of value on the dead
outlaw, except his pistols. He said,*

"These and the horse shall be mine, Millhouse; and then I lose by
the exchange. My brave old gray! He was worth a score of such nags as
this!"

"Yet he must do! He has bone and strength enough, perhaps, for
a season in camp—peace and no active service! He will do to ride about
the plantation, and for a Saturday hunt. He *must* do. The devil take the
unchristian dog who should kill a man's horse in sheer wantonness, and
when it couldn't profit him at all!"

"He worn't to know that, cappin," was the suggestion of Millhouse.

"He's wiser by this time! He *should* have known it. Did he expect to
escape us both? Did he think I'd leave such an animal as mine un-
revenged? If you hadn't cut him down, sergeant, and I had laid hands
on him, I'd have scalped him! As it is, considering his condition, I
forgive him. God forbid that I should harbor malice against the dead.
But, were he living!—were he living!"

*Porgy and Millhouse returned to the wagon, where they encountered
the Negroes who had been cut free from their ropes by Lieutenant
Frampton. Norris now lay roped in the wagon. Porgy was too busy
at the moment to give much attention to greeting his Negroes after
these years of absence. Yet—"He had recognized the voice of his own
slaves, even in the hurry of his pursuit of the fugitives; but he had not
then scanned their faces. Their familiar features and affectionate assurances of love touched the soul of the sensual and the selfish soldier, who*

was not wholly made of clay." (This is not the only time Simms uses the word sensual *when he probably means* sensuous. *Also, is it really fair to call Porgy selfish? He will do and has done many very unselfish things.)*

Porgy thus greeted his Negroes:

"Thank you, boys—thank you, my good fellows. God bless you! I'm really glad to see you again, all of you; and to see that the tories haven't quite eaten you all; but, as for shaking hands just now, that's impossible. We must do our work first. Keep at yours, like good fellows; shovel in the kegs; and you shall all be rewarded. But now to business; and first, Lance, about the carriage, the widow and her party, and the rest of these robbers. What is your report? What have you seen? What heard? Speak—we have no time to lose!"

Lance replied that he believed there was a lady sitting in the carriage which was up front. Porgy agreed with Lance that they must approach the carriage with caution, as the enemies might be lurking near. Porgy asked Norris his name and how many there were in his company, but the outlaw did not answer.

"There's no use to waste words upon this scoundrel. We must put him to the hempen question! A rope, with a swinging limb at one end and a rogue at the other, will probably find an answer quick enough, and sometimes even rises into eloquence. The short way, now, is the best. Mount you, Lance, and we'll all three make a rush for the carriage. We can't be mousing all day with fruitless conjectures. Here comes Tom, too, just in season. We can trust him to keep watch over this rascal. Here, Tom, 'light, and take these pistols—keep them within six inches of this fellow's head; and give him his physic, a full dose from both bottles, if he offers to give you trouble, or if anybody comes to help him. 'Light, I say, you lazy rascal, and be quick!"

"Ki! Mass Porgy!—you talk as ef I hadn't a hundred poun' of pot and kettle on dis nigger t'ighs [thighs]! Gib 'em time, I tell you!"

"Sullen, eh? Well, we will find a way to make you speak!"

Mounted "upon the horse of the outlaw by whom his own had been shot," Captain Porgy led the charge toward the carriage: Fordham "sprang up from the bushes in which he had so long been crouching," and cried out a welcome, and after reminding Porgy of his name, was

*cordially greeted by the Captain. Fordham thanked God for Porgy's
coming.*

*Young Arthur Eveleigh now came up, and was introduced to Porgy
by Fordham, along with a word of praise for his bravery:* "He'll be a
man, I tell you, if ever there was one."

"Good!" answered Porgy, alighting and grasping the hand of the
blushing youth, with an encouraging frankness, "You've begun early, and
well, Master Arthur; and a good beginning is always half the battle!
I'm glad of it for your sake, and that of your parents! But, talking of
your parents, reminds me of your excellent and amiable mother, whom
I claim as an old friend. Let us go to her assistance. I trust that she's
not hurt."

As Arthur ran ahead to his mother, "The eyes of Porgy followed him."

"A fine, vigorous lad; well made; looks like his father in form, his
mother in face; bating the eyes, which are not blue, and which look far
less amiable. I should say the lad was a bold, rash, high-spirited fellow."

*Porgy reckoned that of the six—or possibly more—outlaws, two were
still at large, and that his men must keep alert.*

Meanwhile, Capt. Porgy proceeded toward the carriage, having con-
siderately delayed his own and the movements of Fordham, in that direction, by saying:—

"A moment or two, Mr. Fordham! Let the young man release his
mother himself!"

The youth, meanwhile, had sprung with proper alacrity to this grateful duty. The mother and son embraced with mutual tears and thank-
fulness. The glad widow held the happy boy apart from her, gazed
fondly in his face, and then, even where she stood, in the box of the
coachman, sank down upon her knees in silent prayers to Heaven. The
boy instinctively sank down beside her, and both yielded themselves, in
the sight of Heaven, to frank and fervent but silent prayer.

The good sense, and good taste, of Captain Porgy, sufficed to prevent
him from interrupting such a scene. He stood apart, conferring with
Fordham, seeming to see nothing at the carriage; but his eye took in
all the sweet picture of maternal love; of all the forms of love, perhaps,
the most pure, the least selfish, the longest lived! At length, the voice
of the widow was heard calling our partisan.

"Captain Porgy—will you not suffer me to thank you?"

Our captain, as we know, was not one of the most sprightly of living cavaliers. Agility, as he himself freely admitted, formed no part of his physical virtues; but he certainly made the most astonishing efforts, at this summons, to appear agile; and did succeed, we allow, in reaching the carriage in a tolerable short space of time, and without appearing too greatly breathed from the exertion. As he drew nigh, the widow, supported by her son, alighted from the box, and extended her hand to the grasp of her deliverer. Conspicuous on each of her wrists was a dark ring, the mark of the cords with which she had been tied by the ruffians.

"How much ought I to thank you, Captain Porgy—how much do I owe you, sir! See from what indignities you have rescued me?"

"Would I had been with you some hours sooner, my dear madam," cried the captain, seizing her hand and carrying it, in courtly fashion, to his lips. Those were days, be it remembered, of more lavish ceremonial than ours; and the act was held one of mere grace, rather than of gallantry. At all events, it seemed to occasion no emotion in the bosom of Mrs. Eveleigh, and lessened, in no degree the warmth of her acknowledgments.

"That you have come in season for our safety—to relieve my dear son, and this brave man to whom I owe so much, is quite enough to make me thankful to God, and for ever grateful to you! Ah! sir, I have passed a terrible hour and more! . . ."

Porgy rejoined that what

". . . has taken place has had its good along with its evil. It has brought out the manhood in your brave son, and shown the admirable stuff which he has in him for future work. Mr. Fordham has given me a glowing account of his conduct. I am really sorry, for his sake, that our wars are ended. I should like to take him into my keep as my ensign."

The mother was pleased, but Arthur blushed, saying that if "the Captain knew all he had done," he "wouldn't be so ready to praise me." Porgy "rejoined good naturedly and sensibly"—

"Ah! my dear fellow, you are conscious of some mistakes, perhaps; but that is only another proof in your favor. A fool is never aware that he has made any blunder—never! To be conscious that you have done so, is the first proof of wisdom—the necessary process by which to avoid them in future. You were too quick and rash; too hasty; and fancied you understood the whole game, when you were only taking the first lessons in it. An error, doubtless; but one, my dear boy, that seems natural to our climate; where one usually dates his manhood from the moment when he instructs his father in what way properly to break his eggs. You will soon get over all your mortifications of this description—too soon, perhaps."

Captain Porgy, himself, not regardless of duty, soon brought the merely amiable in their conversation to a close; though it was, evidently, very grateful to him. It seemed to restore him at once to the social sphere from which he had so long been an exile. He thus changed the topic—

"But we must reserve these matters, Mrs. Eveleigh, for a moment of greater leisure. We must not forget our duties now. The sun wanes, and you have yet to find your way home. We have accounted for all these outlaws, but two; and to do our work thoroughly, we should give an account of *them*. Two have been slain outright, one by your party, and another by mine; one is even now our prisoner; and the fourth man we have seen making his escape into the swamp, below, where we can not now hope to hunt him up. There are still two others, somewhere, lurking in the neighborhood, of whom we must ascertain all that we can within the next two hours, or before dark."

Mrs. Eveleigh recalled that two of the outlaws had hovered near her carriage, and that she had not seen one of them leave his position. Lance then found a dead outlaw, who had been killed by Arthur, but the boy himself said, "a chance *bullet."*

"Ah!" said Porgy, "you know not how wonderfully the hand seconds the eye, and both the will, when there is no time left for preparation. The best shots are frequently those which are taken when we are so conscious of a *purpose,* that we are wholly unconscious of an *aim*. If the will is right, the hand and eye obey, as implicitly as the slave of an Eastern despot!"

Porgy now set up a plan of action. Since there was only one outlaw now unaccounted for, who would hardly be hanging around anyway, he felt that Mrs. Eveleigh could and should at once proceed homeward, and that her son and Fordham, now alerted, would be "sufficient escort." Porgy would stay behind to guard the wagon. Moreover, Porgy would provide some of her "most courageous negroes," with pistols to aid in defending her. (Porgy's complete confidence in the Negroes here is notable.) He recalled her "active agency" in "recovering for him" his Negroes.

"I, too, have my thanks, my dear Mrs. Eveleigh, since, as I learn, but for your keen eye, and fearless spirit, my negroes would now be on their way to the British West Indies. But I must take a less hurried moment for making my acknowledgments."

"Don't speak of it, my dear captain; I did only as a neighbor should have done. But, of course, you will accompany my people to my house. Your own will scarcely give you a proper shelter just now."

"No, thank you a thousand times, but I have some of my old and young soldiers with me——"

"I have room for all," said the hospitable widow.

"I thank you again; but I must see to these negroes; and—"

The captain paused. The widow fancied there was some little embarrassment in his manner. She fancied there was a slight flushing through all the bronze on his cheeks. Mrs. Eveleigh was a woman of good sense and good feeling. Such a person always receives an apology —for what it is worth; at least she never disputes it, driving the apologist to the wall, and exposing to himself the poverty of his excuses. She behaved, accordingly, in the right manner. She forebore annoying him, the moment she discovered him resolved to excuse himself. She took for granted that he had his reasons, proper enough for himself, which it might not be proper for him to unfold. This was enough.

"As you please, captain. Remember, from this moment, I take for granted that you will feel yourself always welcome, and at home, at *my* house. Your old and young soldiers will share this welcome—all whom you command. Pray believe, in addition, that I shall desire to see you at an early moment. I have much to hear from you, and something to communicate. Why not ride over and dine with me to-morrow, or the day after, and bring your friends with you?"

"And very much delighted, indeed, to do so, Mrs. Eveleigh, if it be possible. At all events, I shall let you know in due season, if I shall not be able to come to-morrow. Believe me, I have not been living so long in camp as to have quite lost my relish for a good dinner."

"Visit her now," quoth Porgy, turning away to see after the coach and wagon, "with such a beard—mixed grey and brown, salt and pepper —and in this travelling gear—a break under the arm, a rent in——"

And he paused as if at some unmentionable difficulty—then proceeded—

"No! no! One puts on his best favors and front, when he goes to court, even in a republic. This grizzly beard!"—

Here he stroked his chin reproachfully—literally took himself by the beard—and added—

"Who the devil could have anticipated such an adventure!—That I should have put away my best things in my valise!"

While they were riding along, Mrs. Eveleigh received from Fordham a report of his recent visit to Porgy's place. Her overseer told her of the complete lack of provisions there; and she gave him orders to drop off from the wagon food, candles, blankets—and a jug of Jamaica. "The plethoric old soldier little dreamed, at that moment, what the charities of the amiable widow had decreed for his creature comfort."

Porgy had another reason for not escorting the widow—aside from the condition of his clothes. He felt that his duty compelled him to set up an extempore court of justice to try the surviving outlaw Dick Norris. There was no longer an army; but, on the other hand, civilian courts had not yet been re-established so soon after the termination of the war. As a captain of militia, he felt that ad interim he must act as a justice. He appointed Sergeant Millhouse to serve as sheriff to bring up the accused, to give the outlaw a chance to try to establish his own innocence. He did decide however, to relax, and "unbuttoned coat, vest, and smallclothes as far as he possibly could without actually discarding them." Such "looseness of habit . . . we are pleased to say, did not by any means represent his usual moral character." The unbuttoning, however, "was studiously forborne until . . . the fair widow was quite out of sight. Captain Porgy was one of that good old school, which . . . was always tender of the proprieties. The school is somewhat out of fashion now, and is supposed to need its apologies. . . ."

The prisoner gave a whistle, was silenced by a blow from Millhouse, and retaliated by butting the Sergeant "with bull-like ferocity." Meanwhile the Negroes were thoroughly enjoying the whole procedure. Pomp waved his fiddle aloft and executed a sort of coltish dance, and was ordered to settle down by Porgy. The accused was raised to his feet, and addressed by the acting magistrate (in a vein of rather unfeeling humor, it must be granted). Instead of following the custom of magistrates in dealing with old offenders of finding the offender "ill-looking," Porgy used a more original approach: "But that you have spoiled his nose for a time," quoth Porgy, "the offender would be a good-looking fellow—even handsome, stripped of his brush and with a clean shirt on. Is it not curious that these rogues should be so commonly handsome. . . . [Porgy proceeded to give several examples of good-looking criminals.] You see, my friend, that beauty is a snare. It makes many a poor fellow a rogue. I suppose, because it first makes him a fool. . . ." The whole affair had been witnessed, though imperfectly, at the distance of two or three hundred yards, "by the squatter Bostwick." The squatter did feel some compulsion to rescue Norris, some faithfulness to a "bond of brotherhood"; but his dominant concern was the fear lest Norris, under pressure, would squeal and thus incriminate Bostwick himself. He could not hear what was going on, but was sure he was in rifle range of the "provoking abdomen of the captain of partisans, now rendered doubly offensive to the eye by the removal of the usual restraints of button, belt and buckle." Or he could hit the raw-boned sergeant. He crept closer, and watched while his comrade "was undergoing 'The Question.'"— that is the inquisition.

Norris refused to give his name or to answer any inquiries made by Porgy, and insisted stubbornly that he was not in a court and Porgy was no judge.

"I'm sorry you think so, my good fellow," said Porgy, mildly: "for your own sake, you'd better come to the conclusion that we *are* a court, having the power of life and death; and prepare your defence accordingly. We give you a fair chance for your life. Tell the truth, the whole truth, and nothing but the truth, and you don't know what good it will do you —if not in this world, at all events in the next. Confess who set you on this expedition—who were your associates—where do they harbor—what are the names of those who survive? Turn state's evidence as fast as you can, if you would be treated with indulgence."

To Norris' reiteration that he was in no court, Porgy rejoined:

"You grieve me, my interesting fellow, by your imperfect knowledge of the law! I am, at this moment, both judge and jury; and my excellent friend, on the right, is my sheriff, and the executioner of my decrees! These sons of Ethiopia are all good men and true, having an abiding sense of authority and justice. You will find them fully capable of understanding all the facts in your case; and I feel myself equally able to expound to them the law upon it. As for the army, my friend, that is never broken up, so long as there are criminals, like yourself, to be broken in. The good citizens of a country must always constitute a standing army for the purposes of public justice and public security. Answer, therefore, as civilly and fully as possible, the questions I shall put to you, if you would secure for yourself the least indulgence. What may be your name?"

"I sha'n't tell you!" was the insolent reply.

"Well, perhaps that is not necessary. It is not necessary that we should know a man's name in order to hang him. In reporting our proceedings we shall, doubtless, find a name for you. For the present, we will consider you one John, or Tom, or Peter Nemo. Remember, Sergeant Millhouse, and you Pomp, and you, boys, generally, that the prisoner is called Peter Nemo, *alias* John Nemo, *alias* Nebuchadnessar Fish, *alias*——"

"I don't answer to any such name!"

"Silence gives consent! You don't answer to any name, nor, it would seem, to any thing! Don't deceive yourself, my pleasing prisoner. I don't care a straw whether you answer or not. That's just as you please. But we must go through certain forms, for your own sake; and, for the same reason—simply to give you every chance—I must put some other questions to you. I don't want you to answer, if you don't think proper to do so. Who were your confederates, your allies, your associates, in this highway robbery?"

"There's no highway robbery."

With slightly different phrasing Porgy continued to try to extract the information he desired, only to encounter Norris' repeated refusals to reveal anything. When Norris called him "old Porpoise," he began to be "chafed at the outlaw's insolence," but he "restrained every ebullition of temper, however, in recognition of what he held to be the solemn unimpassioned character of his present duty. . . ."

Turning to Millhouse, Porgy declared that the prisoner had rejected "every opportunity of mercy," and quoted the beginning of a proverb,

*"The bird that can sing, and won't sing"—which the acting "Mr. Sheriff"
completed "must be made to swing." Porgy ordered that preparations
be made to hang Norris; the noose was slipped about his neck; "the
negroes took the rope with alacrity," waiting for further orders from
the captain. Porgy began to count and declared that "if by the time I
have said* twelve, *you do not confess, you ride a nag that blacksmith
never yet tried to shoe."*

*Meanwhile Bostwick was watching from his hiding place in the brush,
trying to convince himself that Norris was tough enough to refuse to
confess, had hesitated to shoot at his captors, as he would probably be
able to kill only one of them.*

Now "the culprit was drawn up slowly into the air," with tied hands.

Porgy watched the effect with painful feeling. Practice had not in-
durated him, and, though satisfied of the outlaw's deserts, and fully sensible of the importance of procuring his confession, and not prepared to
quarrel with a process which the practice of the army had fully justified
—he was yet not insensible to the claims of humanity; and was disposed
to spare the victim as much as possible. It is indeed highly probable,
that, as was the conjecture of the prisoner himself, and of his ally the
squatter, our captain of partisans did not really meditate anything beyond the wholesome fright which would compel the outlaw to disgorge
his secrets. But the fellow remained obstinately silent, and his judges
were disappointed.

"Ease him down, sergeant," was the order of the captain.

*Another attempt by Porgy to get the outlaw to talk elicited only pro-
fane defiance. ("We suppress the oaths with which 'the culprit' garnished
every sentence.") The prisoner was raised again and again lowered.
Porgy was "unwilling to urge the torture beyond the degree necessary"
for the object; but the tough Millhouse wanted greater severity to get a
quicker confession.*

*From a keg he had found in the wagon, Lance gave Norris a drink
of Jamaica. Porgy teased the young man for concealing his knowledge
of the Jamaica from his captain; Lance showed a spark of humor in
replying, "Yes sir, but if you had seen the bottle, the sergeant and Tom,
sir, would have seen it too, and—"*

*The watching Bostwick could see by now that what Porgy wanted
was a confession, not an execution. Swung aloft the third time, Norris*

*broke down and began to confess. Bostwick, reasoning he could kill
only one of the captors by shooting, and thereby not helping Norris,
saw no alternative to shooting his comrade. Before the prisoner had said
enough to give anything away, a bullet from Bostwick's rifle was in his
brain. Tragedy was succeeded by comedy, as judge, jury, and all were
startled by this shot.*

"Scatter yourselves, boys! scatter if you would search and be safe!"
was the cry of Porgy. He, too, was in motion, with an agility really
astonishing in his case. He caught up sword and pistols in the twinkling
of an eye, and started off at a moderate trot to gain the tree where his
horse—that which he had taken from one of the slain outlaws—was
fastened to a swinging limb. But he was not destined to reach it so
easily, or in so short a space of time as he had allotted himself. He had
forgotten certain embarrassments in his own case—forgotten that he had,
in order to the more easy administration of justice, ungirthed and unbuttoned himself, when taking his seat under the royal oak. He was
suddenly restored to recollection on this subject, and brought to an abrupt
stand, by feeling himself fettered, with his nether garments clinging
about his legs. The circumstances in which he found himself were utterly indescribable, but it will not be difficult to conjecture them. He was
only brought to a full consciousness of his embarrassment by nearly
measuring his full length upon the ground.

"What a devil of a fix!" quoth he, soliloquizing. "Were I now to hear
the cry which aroused the Hebrew wrestler—'The Philistines are upon
thee, Samson!' what should I do? I should be shot, and sabred, and
scalped, before I could steady my legs for decently falling to the ground!
I should go over in a heap like a bushel of terrapins! And what a figure
I should make upon the earth! How dreadfully exposed! A most shame-
ful condition for 'man and soldier!' "

And thus speaking, he deliberately laid down sword and pistols, and,
looking about him cautiously, proceeded to draw up his inexpressibles,
and to button, and belt up—a performance less easy than necessary.

"It's well the war is over," quoth he, as he labored to contract his
waistbands over his enormous waste of waist, and to bring the strap and
buckle of his belt to bear. "I am no longer fit for war. It's wonderful
that I've escaped so long and so well! With such a territory to take
care of, it's perfectly surprising there have been so few trespassers! I

could not always have kept them off! They would have overcome me
at last! They might have caught me at some such awkward moment, in
some such awkward fix, as the present! Ah! There! It is done at last!
The wilderness is under fence at last!"

All pursued Bostwick, who had lost his rifle in his haste, but suc-
ceeded in concealing in a cypress tree in the nearby swamp the widow's
box "containing the fifty guineas, and the papers which M'Kewn so
much desired!" Night was coming on and Bostwick escaped. The pur-
suers found his rifle, on the stock of which were cut the initials, evidently
of a former owner. Lance read them aloud.

"M.T.C."

"Marcus Tullius Cicero!" quoth Porgy, very gravely.

"Who, captain? I never heard the name! Do you know him?" was
the simple inquiry of the lieutenant.

"I ought to; for I received many a flogging, when a boy, that I
might become intimate with him, and the old fellows he kept company
with. And you may be sure the flogging did not make me love him or
them any better! But I doubt if either Marcus or his companions owned
this rifle. If they did, then the historians have suppressed many an interesting fact in science. But, let us push out of this wilderness, Lance, and
get into the open road. Corporal, see to the negroes, and send them
on ahead.—Let them get wood and have fire for us at least, when we
reach home. It is getting monstrous chilly! Yes—we shall need a fire,
even more than supper!"

Supper, indeed! thought Porgy. It was his philosophy only which
preferred the fire.

Porgy and his retainers now advanced toward "his ruined home-
stead." He seemed in no hurry; of his men only Lance had told the
reason for his captain's reluctance, the cause of the somber mood "such
as his buoyant temper had never suffered him to betray."

In the ingenious subplot, Bostwick, who had begun as a cat's-paw
for the nefarious M'Kewn, proved unexpectedly shrewd. To prevent his
gaining the ascendancy, the wily Scotchman had his rebellious underling
lured onto a ship which sailed for Barbados. The papers which incrimi-
nated M'Kewn, however, remained hidden in the mahogany box, which

Bostwick had stolen from Mrs. Eveleigh and hidden in a "hollow cypress" in a swamp near his own hovel.

Though but a captain in the brigade of Marion, Porgy had been honored by a fair share of British hostility. His home, he knew, had escaped the torch of the incendiary, but his negroes had been stolen, and the plantation utterly laid waste. We have already seen what special additional causes of anxiety were at work to make him moody. Debt hung upon his fortunes like an incubus; and he possessed no conscious resources, within himself, by which to restore his property, or even to acquire the means of life. He rode forward, gloomy and comfortless, in spite of all his philosophy, scarcely exchanging a word with his companions.

Meanwhile, his negroes, under Tom's guidance, eager once more to regain their old homes, sped on, at a smart canter, which soon left their superiors behind. It was after ten o'clock at night, when the lights from a score of wild, gleaming torches, wavering in air, announced the approach to the avenue of "Glen-Eberly," which was the name of Porgy's ancient homestead—so named after a goodly grandmother by whom it had been entailed on her brother's children. Our captain of partisans was aroused to a consciousness of external things, by the loud shouts of the negroes who had preceded him, and who now hailed his approach after a fashion such as Moultrie describes . . . .

"T'ank de Lord, here's maussa g*i*t to he own home at last!—B*r*ess de Lord, Maussa, you come! We all *b*erry glad *for* see you, maussa—glad *too* much!"

And the same negroes who had been with him for several hours before, without so much as taking his hand, now rushed up and seized it, with loud cries, as if they were hosts, and welcoming a favorite guest. The tears stood in the eyes of our captain, though he suffered none of his companions to behold them; and he shook hands with, and spoke to them each in turn—few words, indeed, but they were uttered tremulously, and in low tones.

Fordham, the overseer of Mrs. Eveleigh, now made his appearance from the house. The wagon had departed, having left the supplies as the good widow had ordered. Porgy entered his house expecting to find it empty and cheerless. He was gratefully confounded to see the goods, blankets, drink, provisions, all around the hall, and shown to the best advantage under the ruddy gleams of a rousing fire in the chimney.

"Ah!" said he, "Fordham, Mrs. Eveleigh is a very noble lady. Make her my best respects and thanks. I shall soon ride over and make them in person."

"Well, my friends," said he to Frampton and Millhouse, when Fordham had departed, "I felt doubtful how to provide you your supper to-night; though, knowing this excellent lady as I did, I should not have doubted that she would contribute largely to it. See what she has done! Here are sugar and coffee; here are meal and bacon; here is a cheese; here—but look about you, and say what we shall have for supper. Supper we must have! I am famishing. Tom! Tom! where the d—l is that fellow! Does he think that he's free of *me,* because he's free of the army?—Tom! Tom!"

"Sah! yer, maussa! Wha' de debbil mek' [makes] you *holler* so loud, maussa when I's jis' [just] at your elbow? You t'ink I hard o' hearing, 'cause I got hard maussa, I 'spose!"

"Hard maussa, you inpertinent scamp! Another master would have roasted you alive long before this. See, and let us have something, in the twinkling of an eye. Look among these provisions, that Mrs. Eveleigh has sent us, and take out enough to give us all a good feed—*niggers* and all!"

"Miss Ebleigh! *He's* a bressed [blessed] woman, for sartin, for sen' we all sich good t'ings; de berry t'ings we bin want; and jis' when we want 'em. He's a mos' 'spectable pusson, is dat Miss Ebleigh. Ki! He's a'mos' [almost] ebbry t'ing for ge*m*pleman supper! . . ."

The kitchen had been destroyed, and the supper was cooked in the ample fireplace of the "salle a manger." *The meal was an adequate one, with hominy, "ho" and "johnny" cakes cooked on sections of a barrel head facing the blazing fire, "tender slices of ham," bacon, and coffee.*

Tom loquaciously lauded the quality of the provisions "Miss Ebleigh" had sent as far better than anything he had seen during the war years, praised the Lord, and damned the tories who had skinned the plantation.

For a table cloth, Tom ordered Pomp to use one of Mrs. Eveleigh's blankets, but Pomp replied—

"I no see table, uncle Tom!"

"Don't uncle me, you chucklehead! [Surely Simms was here thinking of Mrs. Stowe's novel.] Lay de table on de floor! Who could b'lieb dat a pusson could lib so long and grow so big, and nebber l'arn

nutting." (Such sharp language makes Simms's Tom very unlike Mrs.
Stowe's.) Tom was even independent enough to ask the gentlemen to
stand aside so he could spread the cloth, although, he averred, gentle-
men should have sense enough themselves to move without being asked.

"Hear that impudent rascal!" quoth Porgy, moving goodnaturedly, his
example followed by Frampton and Millhouse.

"Was ever fellow so completely spoiled?"

"I nebber *spile* supper, maussa!" responded Tom, with a toss of the
head, as if to say—"nobody knows my qualities better than yourself."

"No, indeed, Tom, and you presume on your merits, somewhat to
their injury; but you will be taken down, you scamp, when you are
required to find and hunt up the supper, as well as cook it."

"Ha! but you see, maussa, my business is cook—I knows um! It's
maussa business to fin' de *bittle* [victuals]. Put de meat and bread yer,
whay I kin put out my han' and git 'em, leff it to me to hab 'em ready
for eat; but da's all I hab a right for do."

"Ah! indeed, my buck; but I'll persuade you, at the end of a hickory,
that you have other rights."

"Wha' maussa; hick'ry for Tom! Nebber! Anybody else bin tell
me sich a t'ing, I say, widout guine to be sassy—'he's a d—n fool for he
trouble.'"

"Hear the fellow! Sergeant, do you want a negro—a cook?"

"I'll thank you, cappin, very much. Tom and myself agree very well
together. I like his fries monstrous."

"You shall have him—when I'm done with him."

"You nebber guine done wid Tom, maussa! I 'tick to you ebbry-
where; you comp'ny good 'nough for Tom in any country, no matter
whay you go."

"Thank you, Tom; but Tom, if you don't clap a hot iron to Pomp's
haunches, he'll never have supper on table to-night."

"De boy will be de deat' ob me!" cried Tom, starting up, and administering a sudden whack to the ear of Pomp, with the flat of an
amazingly rough hand. The lad reeled under the salutation. Pompey
was more dexterous at the violin, than in the capacity of a house-servant.
He had no idea of the novel duties he was required to perform; and,
jerking him by the collar to the fireplace, Tom clapped the several dishes
into his hand, . . .

To get Pomp, an inexperienced house-servant, moving, thus, Tom boxed his ear. Pomp speeded up, and soon at Tom's order, announced that supper was ready. The gentlemen seated themselves on the corners of the blanket on the floor. As Porgy's crockery closet was empty, the hominy and meat and gravy and coffee were served in the sooty vessels in which they had been cooked. Our hungry partisans ate vigorously, and "in the enjoyment of things of the flesh, Porgy began to forget the anxieties of the spirit. He smacked his lips over the luscious ham, exclaiming—"

"This may be called good, Tom—very good: in fact, I never tasted better. You have certainly lost none of your talent in consequence of your leaving the army."

"I bin good cook 'fore I ebber see de army."

"So you were, Tom; but your taste was matured in the army; particularly on the Pedee. But you were better at a broil, I think, before the war."

"Tom's jest as good, I'm a-thinking, at a fry as at a brile, cappin," quoth Millhouse, licking his chaps, while elevating a huge slice of his bacon into sight, upon the prongs of his fork.

"An' why you no say *bile,* too, Mass Millh'us'?" demanded Tom, apparently not satisfied that there should be any implied demerits in his case.

"En [and] so I mout [might]," answered the sergeant. "This here hominy now, to my thinking, is *biled* to a monstrous softness."

"An' de bake—de bread—wha' you say for him?" was the next exaction of Tom's vanity; and he handed up, as he queried, a fresh supply, from the fire, of a crisp, well-browned "Johnny-cake"—an article, by the way, which is too often served up, of most villanous manufacture, particularly at a *modern* barbecue; but which, in those days, might usually be commended, and which, in Tom's hands, was an achievement—a *chef-d'œuvre* of kitchen art.

"Well, Tom, I kin say with a mighty cl'ar conscience, that this is raal, gennywine bread. I only wish Miss Ebeleigh was here now, herself, jest to try a taste of it."

"Ha!" quoth Tom, heaving up—"I 'speck [expect] ef he bin yer, he would nebber le' maussa res', tell he beg me from em. He would want you to gib me to um, I tell you, maussa!"

"Give you, Tom! Give you to anybody? No! no! old fellow! I will neither give you, nor sell you, nor suffer you to be taken from me in any way, by Saint Shadrach! who was your blessed father in the flesh, and from whom you inherit your peculiar genius for the kitchen! Nothing but death shall ever part us, and even death shall not if I can help it. When I die, you shall be buried with me. We have fought and fed too long together, Tom, and I trust we love each other quite too well, to submit to separation. When *your* kitchen fire grows cold, Tom, I shall cease to eat; and you, Tom, will not have breath enough to blow up the fire when mine is out! I shall fight for you to the last, Tom, and you, I know, would fight to the last for me, as I am very sure that neither of us can long outlast the other."

"Fight for you, maussa! Ha! Jes' le' dem tory try we, maussa!" responded Tom, quite excited, and shaking his head with a dire significance. But Tom did not exactly conceive the tenor of his master's speech, or the direction of his thoughts. He did not conjecture that the earnestness with which the latter spoke, had its origin in his recent meditations; and these had regard to civil rather than military dangers—to the claws of the sheriff, rather than tory weapons! Once on this track, Porgy found relief in continuing, and in making himself better understood.

"They shall take *none* of you negroes, if I can help it! But they shall take *all* before they touch a hair of your head, Tom!"

"Da's it, maussa! I know you nebber guine part wid Tom!"

"Before they shall tear you from me, Tom——"

"Day [they] can't begin to come it, maussa! I 'tick to you, maussa, so long as fire bu'n!"

"But, it might be, Tom; the time might come; circumstances might arise; events might happen; I might be absent, or unable, and then, you might fall into the clutches of some of these d——d harpies, who take a malignant pleasure in making people uncomfortable. You have heard, Tom, of such an animal as a sheriff, or sheriff's deputy?"

"Enty I know? He's a sort of warmint! I knows 'em well! He come into de hen-house, cut chicken t'roat, drink de blood, and suck all de eggs! I know 'em, for sartain! Da him?"

"Yes, they are blood-suckers, and egg-suckers, and throat-cutters— that's true, Tom; vermin of the worst sort: but they still come in the shape of human beings. They are men after a fashion; men-weasels, verily, and they do the work of beasts! You will know them by their

sly looks; their skulkings, peepings, watchings, and the snares they lay;
by the great papers, with great seals, that they carry; and by their calling themselves sheriffs or constables, and speaking big about justice and
the law. If any of you negroes happen to see any such lurking about
the plantation, or within five miles, let me know. Don't let them lay
hands on you, but make for the swamp, the moment they tell you
'stop.' You, Tom, in particular, beware of all such! Should they succeed in taking you, Tom—should I not be able to help you—should you
find them carrying you off, to the city or elsewhere, to sell you to some
other master——"

"Gor-a-mighty! maussa, wha' for you scare me so, t'inking ob sich
t'ings?"

"Tom! sooner than have you taken off by these vermin, I will shoot
you!"

"Me! shoot me! me, Tom! Shoot me, maussa!"

"Yes, Tom! you shall never leave me. I will put a brace of bullets
through your abdomen, Tom, sooner than lose you! But, it may be,
that I shall not have the opportunity. They may take advantage of my
absence—they may *steal* you away—coming on you by surprise. If they
should do so, Tom, I rely upon you to put *yourself* to death, sooner than
abandon me and become the slave of another. Kill yourself, Tom, rather
than let them carry you off. Put your knife into your ribs, anywhere,
three inches deep, and you will effectually baffle the blood-hounds!"

"Wha', me, maussa! kill mese'f! Me, Tom! 'Tick knife t'ree inch in
me rib, and dead! Nebber, in dis worl' [world] maussa! I no want
for dead! I always good for cook! I good for fight—good for heap o'
t'ing in dis life! No good 'nough for dead, maussa! No want for dead
so long as der's plenty ob bile, and brile, and bake, and fry, for go
sleep 'pon. Don't talk ob sich t'ing, maussa, jis' now, when de time is
'mos' [almost] come for me eat supper!"

"Tom!" exclaimed the captain of partisans, laying down his knife
and fork, and looking solemnly and sternly at the negro—"I thought
you were more of a man—that you had more affection for me. Is it
possible that you could wish to live, if separated from me? Impossible,
Tom! I will never believe it. No, boy, you shall never leave me. We
shall never part. You shall be my cook, after death, in future worlds,
even as you are here. Should you suffer yourself to survive me, Tom—
should you be so hard-hearted—I will haunt you at meal-time always.

Breakfast, dinner, supper—at every meal—you shall hear my voice. I will sit before you as soon as the broil is ready, and you shall always help me first!"

The negro looked aghast. Porgy nodded his head solemnly.

"Remember! It shall be as I have said. If you are not prepared to bury yourself in the same grave with me when I die, I shall be with you in spirit, if not in flesh; and I shall make you cook for me as now. At breakfast you will hear me call out for ham and eggs, or a steak; at dinner, perhaps, for a terrapin stew; at supper, Tom—when all is dark and dreary, and there is nobody but yourself beside the fire—I shall cry out, at your elbow, 'My coffee, Tom!' in a voice that shall shake the very house!"

"Oh, maussa! nebber say sich t'ing! Ef you promise sich t'ing, you hab for come!"

"To be sure;—so you see what you have to expect if you dare to survive me!"

Tom turned gloomily to the fire, not a little bewildered. The bravest negro is the slave of superstitious fancies, and Tom was a devout believer in ghosts, and quite famous in the kitchen for his own ghost experience.

"But to your own supper now, with what appetite you may, and see that you feed the other negroes. I see that *we* have all supped."

"Lor'-a-mighty, maussa, you tek' 'way all me appetite for supper."

"You will soon enough find it, I fancy," quoth Porgy, coolly, as he lighted his pipe. Millhouse followed the example, and, accompanied by Lieutenant Frampton, the two adjourned to the piazza, leaving the field to the negroes, who, at a given signal, rushed eagerly in to the feast.

Since there were no chairs to sit on, and the piazza floor was decayed, our partisans went out to sit around a big campfire the Negroes had kindled near the house. Lance felt the hours long which kept him from his beloved "rustic beauty." Still—"his was a spirit of generous sympathies, and, spite of all Porgy's selfishness of character, the young man, through an intercourse of three years, had learned to love and honor him for the really good points in his nature in spite of his egotism. He mused quite as much upon the fortunes of his superior as upon his own."

Porgy and Millhouse were enjoying their pipes. Porgy, believing that common humanity required sepulture of enemies, gave instructions that

spades and shovels be borrowed from Mrs. Eveleigh to be used in bury-
ing the outlaws they had slain. He said that, after it was done, Lance
would want to ride over to visit the widow Griffin. "Of course you
know, my boy, that as long as I have house-room and enough for supper,
you shall share it. When you are married, you shall do as you please.
You may bring your wife here, if it suits you, and her mother too. At
all events, here is your home, so long as it is mine."

"That is, if she herself does not marry."

"Oh! I don't think she's going to do that. She was mighty fond of
her husband."

"Y-e-s!" quoth Porgy, taking out his pipe, and emptying the ashes.
"Y-e-s! it may be so—and yet the widow is tolerably young, fresh, and
good-looking. A dead husband is of no sort of use in this world, and
that is the present question. When I have smoked out my pipe, and
emptied the ashes, I am apt, after a little pause, to fill it with fresh
tobacco. He who has smoked one pipe, will be apt to try another, and
another, as long as he can smoke. That is, if the first has not sickened
him. That the widow has found one husband grateful, is good reason
why she should try another. Mrs. Griffin is a woman of sense, and has
too many good qualities to remain single. She is a good housekeeper—
everything is in trim about her. She takes care of everything, and herself neat. Besides, she makes a first-rate terrapin stew, quite as good as
Tom; and her broil and fry will pass muster in any camp. I remember
the blue cat, which she gave us on the Edisto, with a relish even now;
and that reminds me, by the way, that we must get hooks and lines ready
for the Ashepoo pretty soon. We shall have the spring upon us before
we get our tackle ready."

This aroused Millhouse to insist that Porgy would soon have to be
thinking about something besides going fishing, that the "niggers" must
go to work, "if he is to manage them." Porgy replies, "You, Millhouse!
Do you mean to volunteer as overseer?"
Such, indeed, was Millhouse's intention; and after Porgy admitted
he had been unsuccessful in planting, Millhouse began to lecture him
for hurrying nature—for not planting at the right time and for not
being patient enough and rushing into replantings. He ordered Porgy
not to meddle with the farming—not to do such things as let the water
off the rice lands when his cronies wanted to fish. Millhouse would be

his "sense-keeper" as well as overseer. Porgy must not come between him and the "niggers." The sergeant would do his work and would make the Negroes do theirs. "Ef there's any licking to be done, I'll lay it on. You may look on but you musn't meddle." Porgy asked, "I have your permission to hunt, and fish, and dine abroad, if I think proper. These, then, are my duties?"

Exactly, said Millhouse, but Porgy was not to take hands and horses "out of the crop" for his amusements. He was to choose one horse for his own riding and stick to that. Millhouse was even unsympathetic with Porgy's idea that in hunting birds he must have a dog to point and flush so he could do it like a gentleman and sportsman. Millhouse reminded Porgy he must do things the practicable way when he was "under bonds to a sheriff." "D—n the sheriff! Don't mention such an animal to me," exclaimed Porgy. Millhouse replied he agrees to "d—n the sheriff," but an educated white man must gather "substance"—that is property—about him.

According to Millhouse, there was a better sort of game than birds Porgy might hunt. Porgy was only a little over middle age; he was upright; his face hadn't a wrinkle. He ought to get married. He should find a clever woman who had "outlived all girlishness"—indeed, a widow, with "a smart chance of property." Such a woman would consider "that a man's a man in spite of his gairth"; would prefer a soldier; would "pass over the sprinkle of gray in his head, in consideration of his sound teeth and good wind"; would not object to his small legs. Indeed considering what a "mortal weight of flesh" Porgy had, it was just wonderful how much he could stand. Millhouse reckoned there was "more than a hundred such women here, in Carolina," who when they considered how many of the "handsome young fellows" were cut off in the war would be mighty glad to have Porgy. If he could get a woman who would "pay off that mortgage and . . . have something left over," he needn't fear that d——d warmint of a sheriff."

Porgy was somewhat surprised and overcome by this analysis of his problems. He turned uneasily and ordered Lance to have the Negroes clear a space for him in the house, as rain was beginning. "And so, Millhouse, you think I am still able to undergo the fatigues of matrimony?"

It was the very thing for the captain, and furthermore Millhouse had seen the very woman, the widow Eveleigh. She was liberal in giving; a *"beauty for a man at your time"; and had "looked on" him "amazing sweet."*

"It is something to be thought of, Millhouse, but as the widow isn't here just now, suppose we try the rum? What do you say to a toddy?" Millhouse agreed this was sensible, and together they returned to the house.

Porgy decided to sleep in his old bedroom, and ordered Tom to sweep it out and make a fire. He also told Tom to give a blanket to each Negro, and put the rest of the blankets in his own room. Lance reported that he had fastened the horses under the piazza and given them both corn and fodder.

The ruined room, all its window glass gone, showed signs of former elegance. There were fragments of the ancient mahogany bedstead on which Porgy had been born. The portrait of his mother had been torn from its frame and taken away.

Shedding a few tears at these desecrated mementoes of his mother, he contemplated gloomily his situation. "His lands were mortgaged to an amount five times their present value. A foreclosure of mortgage at the present juncture would not only take them away, but take his negroes also, and still leave him a debtor beyond all means of payment. . . ."

"He almost reproached the merciful fate which had saved him from the bullet or bayonet of the enemy." He felt willing to die now. "He would have rejoiced to find a full finish to his cares, in a desperate onslaught, at the head of his corps of partisans. 'But the wars were all over. . . .'" All he had was "his little force of half-a-dozen negroes in the rice fields under the doubtful management of Sergeant Millhouse."

There was Millhouse's suggestion: the widow Eveleigh. She was attractive; he "had perilled his life in her defense." He reassessed his own figure, disturbed by the sergeant's disparagement of his legs. Ah, it was only "in contrast with the mountainous abdomen" that the legs appeared inferior. That abdomen! "Certainly it is a monstrous necessity that I should be thus compelled to carry with me such a bag of bran. But what is to be done? It is an inheritance which one may not mortgage; a store house of which no sheriff can deprive the possessor."

Yet, at least it was not "insignificant." "It is not calculated to admit of the exhibition of grace; but what gentleman is ambitious of the renown of a dancing master. Still it is something on parade. Nobody finds fault with such an abdomen in a general. It embarrasses no man whose position requires that he should move with dignity. It guarantees the courage of the proprietor, since one is scarcely apt to run in battle, with such extensive stores to carry with him." His person was presentable enough. As he became sleepier he thought again of the advantages of marrying the widow. He recalled her dinner invitation, and almost in the same instant, all the articles he had to buy in town to run his plantation.

"A woman is never more flattered by a man than when he solicits her advice. She usually gives him more than he bargains for, but she not unfrequently gives herself into the bargain!" Just as he was about to drop off, his "nostrils furnished audible echo to" the sounds from "the proboscis of the sergeant" in the neighboring room. "Deep thus continued for a season to call unto deep. . . ." But "a more than ordinary explosion from the sergeant's nose" partially aroused Porgy.

"Zounds!" quoth he, drowsing again. "How Millhouse does snore! What an infirmity!—peculiar, I believe, only to the lower orders. Gentlemen never snore! How is it with ladies? Wonder if the widow Evel——" The conjecture remained unconcluded as "the mutual nostrils of captain and sergeant continued to respond to one another without causing any annoyance to either. . . ."

Toward morning these two snorers were awakened by a rushing sound, followed by a pistol shot. The Negroes, however, slept soundly on. Lance, "covered with mud, soaking with water, with a pistol in each hand, sprang up the steps," and reported that he had been aroused by a trampling among the horses, and had gone down to discover that a single steed was being ridden off down the avenue.

Millhouse was able to rouse the sleepy Tom fully only by telling him a wild tale about an attack from the tories, who had "scalped Lance, and shot the cappin in three places, his head, his belly, and his witals." Thoroughly aroused by this story, which he soon began to disbelieve, Tom hurried out to discover the horse missing was the "raw bone black" belonging to Bostwick.

Millhouse voiced his shame at not wakening sooner; but Porgy was kind, saying the war was over and "we had no reason to expect attack." Yet he could not forebear saying "he might have taken all, but for Lance. Millhouse, you sleep like a tomb-stone, and snore like the seven sleepers." He reminded Lance to see to the borrowing of the tools for the sepulture of the slain outlaws. Then—"Sergeant, will you take a little rum now, or wait for the coffee?"

"Well, cappin, jest to be a-doing, I'll do both." But Millhouse drank alone, as, while day dawned, Porgy contented himself with his pipe.

Later in the morning, Millhouse looked out at the fields and said they were "sure to bring fine corn." He asked Porgy when they were planted last. Porgy's answer was an apparently rather naïve but really ingenious admission of his own great limitations as a planter in the past. He said: "I can now see that they have been planted, and I suppose in my time; but really, my good sergeant, to say that I saw them in a crop, or ever saw the crop, of any kind, when I was professedly a planter, would be something of a rashness on my part. Pray believe that I was a very foolish, profligate person, who, in ceasing to be young, did not cease to be foolish, and continued his absurd vanities and excesses to the last." He went on to say that "the curse of my generation was that our fathers lived too well, were too rapidly prosperous, and though they did not neglect the exercise of proper industry in themselves, they either did not know how to teach it to their children, or presumed on the absence of any necessity that they should learn. . . . I will assist you when I can—"

"But don't meddle, cappin," replied Millhouse.

Porgy was willing enough to agree to let the sergeant "have full swing for a season, at least. . . ." Yet his account of his former inefficiency (possibly, indeed, something of an overstatement) was made with clever calculation, as "Millhouse was not quite satisfied to have his mouth shut so summarily by the frank confession of the faults and follies on the part of his superior. He was not content that a general confession, however sweeping, should anticipate the details, one by one, of Porgy's shortcomings . . . his deliberate purpose had been to take the captain over his territories, field by field, and extort from him at each some admission of fault or ignorance. It was with a growl that he yielded to the very decided manner of his superior which at once closed the door against further 'question.'"

Fordham had cantered over with the Negro who had gone for the implements to be used in the burial of the outlaws; he agreed that it was probably Bostwick who had been the leader in the assault on Mrs. Eveleigh. He gave a picture of Bostwick's humble and unhappy family, cruelly mistreated by a husband and father they could not get rid of; he said that Mrs. Eveleigh knew "what Bostwick is, but she has pity on the poor wife and children." She had given them work to do, and fed and clothed them. People were afraid to hire Mrs. Bostwick at their places for fear it would cause Bostwick to hang around.

Porgy insisted on going himself to assist with—or at least supervise —the burial of the outlaws, despite the continuing rain. The criminals would not have been buried if it had not been for Porgy's compulsion to have it done. A search for Mrs. Eveleigh's lost box proved fruitless.

Meanwhile Bostwick went back to where he had hidden the box and found it, but had no key. He had no intention of giving any of the fifty guineas in it to his family. He gloated over the power the papers *would give him over M'Kewn. He went home, primarily to get an implement to pry the box open. A scene in his miserable hovel, revealed the beauty, intelligence, and goodness of his twelve-year old daughter Dory or Dorothy, the one human being Bostwick loved. He had no love for his pitiful, cowering wife; and of his wife and two daughters and son, Dory was the only one he kissed. Dory was disturbed that he did not have his horse, and hoped he had not sold "Black Ball." Bostwick secured a knife, returned to the box, and pried it open. In the box he found a bag of fifty guineas, and many papers. Unable to read or write, he could only assume that the* papers *were among the others. He considered giving one lone guinea to Dory, but decided not to, and put everything back in the box, which he placed again in the hollow cypress.*

He then went home to get some supper; was disgusted to find Dory reading a Bible given her by Mrs. Eveleigh; and left saying good-by to Dory only.

Porgy, along with his men and Fordham, came over to Bostwick's shack. When Bostwick's wife said humbly she was not sure she recognized the captain, Porgy replied that he was "one of the few men of the army, madam, who fattened on starvation."

In a moving scene, Porgy shook hands with little Dorothy. She sensed intuitively his great gentility. "The child felt at ease as she surveyed his face. A single glance sufficed for this. He was no ruffian, that she felt sure; that he was a gentleman by birth and education, her instincts at once assured her. The fact was sufficiently proved by the ease with which he inspired confidence in both mother and daughter." On his part, Porgy was greatly taken with Dorothy's unusual beauty and obvious sweetness, and was sure she could not look like her outlaw father, whom Porgy had, apparently, never actually seen.

None of the men believed the poor woman had any share in her husband's recent villainies. Porgy asked Dory to knit him a great supply of stockings. He gave her a guinea as advance payment. She and her mother very gladly agreed to this arrangement. Porgy insisted that Fordham should desist from trying to get the child to testify against her father. He thought that this most "exquisite flower" should be removed from her degrading environment and "reared in a garden to herself."

But Porgy, on the way home, had to endure a reprimand from Millhouse for his extravagance in ordering "stockings enough for a regiment." Porgy replied he "did not give the guinea for the stockings," but for the child to buy "her own stockings . . . or whatever else she needs. I gave it from my heart, Millhouse, and not from my pocket." And Porgy admitted it was a "sort of charity." Not in the least mollified, Millhouse lectured Porgy on the shortness of his supply of guineas, and illustrated his argument by a tiresome fable about one "poor 'Lisha Dayton." He said Porgy would "want every guinea" he wasted. (Porgy's generosity was really considerable, as in terms of today's money a guinea of that time might be equated with thirty dollars. Porgy had, it may be recalled, told Lance that his entire capital at the end of the war consisted of eleven guineas.)

"Don't mistake, Millhouse. I waste no guineas. When I give money, it is only that I may get a good interest for it. The true man, Millhouse, does not live by money, nor by that which money will always buy—bread and meat. There is still better food than that for which I more hunger; and yet I know not the man living who has a better appetite for good living than myself."

Squatter Bostwick, on the way to an appointed meeting with M'Kewn, happened to stop at a hovel where Tony Hines, the only surviving member of his gang, lay sick with a fever. When he got to the place assigned for the meeting with the Scotchman, he met two agents of the latter, Barton and Drummond. Drummond led the way to a tent shadowed by enormous oaks in a swamp, known as "The Castle." When Barton came in, the three started to gamble, employing a game called "old sludge." As soon as M'Kewn entered, Bostwick began, with cool insolence, to demand money from him to gamble with. M'Kewn, sensing that Bostwick must have gained some advantage in the bitter game—of villainy, not cards, the two were playing—did give him three guineas, and then five.

Bostwick was skillful and won all the gold the others had. Impudently he asked M'Kewn to play the cards, but the Scotchman refused, as he refused to do more than pretend to drink of the Jamaica. M'Kewn became angrier and angrier, as Bostwick showed more and more such a consistent intention of being insolent as he had never evinced before. M'Kewn revealed that a schooner was coming to a nearby anchorage— indeed the very vessel in which M'Kewn had intended to send away the Negroes Bostwick had tried to capture.

After the two other men were sent out to see to the schooner, Bostwick, alone with his employer M'Kewn, became even more bold and even threatened to kill the Scotchman with a knife. Usually so cool, M'Kewn was almost paralyzed by such unanticipated rebellious behavior from his minion. Bostwick blamed M'Kewn directly for the death of the four men of the gang which had occurred during the ambuscade. It was indeed M'Kewn's business that four fine men were "a-laying stark in the cold night, and looking up and never once seeing the stars"; and that the only survivor, aside from himself, was sick with a fever. Bostwick gave a long account of the ambuscade, admitting the escape of the Negroes. M'Kewn was agog with trembling eagerness to find out whether he had the papers; but Bostwick demanded one hundred guineas paid before he delivered them. (Simms here displays even more than his usual verve and gusto in depicting scenes in which criminals match wits in seeking to undo each other.)

M'Kewn decided he must get rid of Bostwick. Before taking drastic action, he went to poor Hines pretending to be a physician. From Hines's report that Bostwick would let no one help him search the carriage, M'Kewn deduced that the squatter did indeed have the box containing the papers.

In another grimly amusing scene, Barton and Drummond in "The Castle" engaged Bostwick in gambling and drinking, acting on orders from M'Kewn. Bostwick shrewdly refused to go onto the vessel to gamble with the captain, who, they said, had a lot of money. At first Bostwick won all the gold, but lost all after he became drunk. Furiously he demanded to see M'Kewn to get more money. They told him he was on the vessel, and Bostwick was thus lured to the anchorage. But he still refused to go aboard, demanding they bring M'Kewn to him.

After they had left him supposedly to do this, three sailors came and carried the squatter aboard by force. He sank into a drunken sleep in the hold, and awakened seasick and out at sea.

While Millhouse and Porgy were at supper with Fordham as guest at Porgy's homestead Glen-Eberley, Millhouse took Porgy's giving the guinea to Dory as the start for lecturing Porgy about his incurable penchant for bestowing charity. For example, "If there was a poor camp woman that had lost her man in a scrimmage, the cappin was the first to empty his pockets in her lap. I've seed him do it a dozen times. Now, that was all great foolishness." He went on to censure Porgy for his befriending the useless Oakenburg. He got Tom to recall how he secured the clothes of a British officer Porgy had killed, only to have Porgy give them to Oakenburg. Tom was to be paid for this, and Millhouse averred Tom would indeed sooner or later be paid.

Then Millhouse (becoming, indeed, more and more disagreeable) attacked Porgy for having the poet Dennison around eating the allowance of other men. All Dennison could do was joke and make "foolish po'tries." Porgy's reply was an eloquent one:

"Come! come! Millhouse! you must not be running down my poet. Dennison is a great fellow and has frequently saved me from suicide. More than once, when we were starving in the swamps, I should have cut my throat, or yours, Millhouse, but for the consolation which Dennison brought me in his verses and songs; and Oakenburg, though as you say, a great fool, was yet a fool with a relish. He had the virtue of making himself laughed at, and that afforded relief to sensible people. He had his uses, and you must think better of him. I shouldn't be at all surprised to see both Dennison and Oakenburg here before long. I asked them both to come and see me."

Millhouse disapproved, saying that such people stick like plaster; and Porgy replied that was fine with him, and besides they had no place else to go. "Oakenburg and Dennison . . . still both work for me though not in the fields."

"I'd jest like to onderstand how, cappin."

"How!" quoth Porgy, emptying his pipe,—then looking up and around him, with a somewhat vacant gaze, silent the while, as if listening—after a few moments of pause he said—

"Do I not hear a bird? a mock-bird, singing? Hark! do you not hear it now?"

All parties appeared to listen; at length, says Millhouse—

"It's the singing of the fire, I reckon, cappin. I don't hear nothing. It's too soon in the season for mocking birds to sing."

"No! not when the weather is good. I have heard them, years ago, in all the trees around the house, singing through the winter, and frequently at night, and all night. They attach themselves to old and well settled habitations, and will rear their generations for a thousand years in the same trees, if left undisturbed. They belong to man. I am disposed to think they were created for him, and to do this particular duty. You like their music, Mr. Fordham, do you not?"

"Well, cappin, I can't say that I ever hears 'em much, onless when somebody tells me to listen. As for liking their music, I confess, cappin, I'd much rather hear a good fiddle."

"And so would I," quoth Millhouse, "though I don't count fiddle music as much either. A good horn is my music, and I count a boat horn on the river as the sweetest of all kinds of music. I kin listen to that hafe a night, that is, when I ain't too much tired and hungry."

"I like that too, Millhouse, and I can relish a good fiddle in a crowd. But what would you think of a person who should tell you that he didn't relish the boat horn, Millhouse."

"Why, I'd say he might as well be stone deaf and blind too."

"At least, you wouldn't suppose he was any the better man for not having an ear for the music of the horn."

"No! I'd be thinking he was rather the worse for it."

"Precisely! well, you'll permit me to feel the music of a bird's song and not think me very foolish or wicked perhaps, if I say I like to hear it very much."

"Well, I s'pose not! Every man to his own liking. I reckon there's a sort of natur in every man's liking."

"Exactly! That's the very word. There is a nature in it; and it was to feed this nature, and to work upon it in a mysterious way, that God appointed the birds to build their nests in the trees that surround a man's dwelling. Now, you must know, that it is a fact, however curious, that singing birds never harbor in uninhabited countries. In our great forests, you never hear birds. The smaller birds would become the prey of the larger ones, and they shelter themselves in places which are inhabited in order to be safe. And they reward man for his protection, by their songs, and by the destruction of insects. Now, Millhouse, Dennison is one of my song birds. He sings for me when I am sad. He makes music for me which I love. It is soul music which I owe to him, which finds its way to the ear of the heart, and seems to fill it with sunshine. Now, I call that being very useful to me."

"I could see how 'twas useful ef he was to eat up the grubs and insects, jest like the birds, but—"

"And so he does, Millhouse. The grubs and insects of the heart are its cares, its anxieties, its sorrows, its bad feelings, and vexatious passions. He drives them away—he destroys them. He is appointed for this very purpose, and if men were wise, they would rejoice when they could have such a bird of the soul under their roof trees. It would prove that they *had* souls, if they could show that they have an ear for his music. Now, you are not any *better,* sergeant, because you want an ear for soul-music. It is your misfortune, Millhouse, and you ought to be sorry for yourself, not angry with the musician, whose songs you can't understand. You should pray for the proper understanding, and work for it, too; for you must know that an ear for music of all sorts is to be acquired; and the ear opens so as to correspond with the growing wishes of the heart, and the growing wisdom of the mind. You hear a great deal said, perhaps, of education. Everybody seems to wish for education. I have heard you deploring, very frequently, the fact that you had no schooling. Now, schooling and education are meant for this very purpose, to give us an ear for music—the music of birds as well as men, the music of the soul, as well as of the throat—music which fills the heart as well as the ear—music which is not only sweet, but wise—which not only pleases but makes good; for, after all, the great secret of education is to open all the ears—which we call *senses*—of a man, so that he can drink in all the harmonies of that world of music, which we commonly call life!—Do not, my dear sergeant, suppose you are any better because you do not comprehend such music as George Dennison makes; and do not suppose that George is any worse man because he is too apt to give away, and perhaps waste, the things which he needs himself, quite as much as the person to whom he gives them. George finds it profitable to give away—to waste! If you knew the satisfaction which he feels at making other people happy, you might be even more extravagant. He may be wrong, sometimes, in his giving; but you are not altogether right in judging him so harshly. He values certain things too little; you, perhaps, value the same things too much. You both may be forgiven your offences, which are due to a want of proper education, provided you are modest enough never to censure the music which you do not understand."

Millhouse said that all that might be sensible, although he couldn't understand it, but he wanted to know what "sort of music" he got out of Doctor Oakenburg.

Porgy reminded Millhouse of a reel in a bottle, belonging to a little Frenchman, which amused the soldiers, including Millhouse, as they could not figure out how to get the reel out. There was nothing useful about the reel, "yet you were curious about it. You tried many a time to find out the secret . . . it interested you—it interested most of the soldiers; yet in itself it was perfectly worthless."

"Doctor Oakenburg is my reel in a bottle. His soul is my puzzle; how it got into his carcass—where it does nothing useful—where it does not even grow—is the problem which amuses me. Now, Millhouse, whatever interests a man is valuable, though it neither works nor sings. Whatever may amuse a man is an important agent in his education. Whatever exercises the ingenuity of man, though it be a fool's brains, or a reel in a bottle, is worthy of his care and consideration. I assure you that should George Dennison, or Doctor Oakenberg, pay me a visit, they shall both be welcome. I shall find use in both of them."

And Porgy added that, anyway, "God is good security for the debts of the poor."

Millhouse accompanied Fordham down the steps to his horse, continuing his wordy criticism of Porgy, which led up to the conclusion that what he needed was a woman to guide him aright. "Fordham shook himself free with difficulty."

Millhouse returned to the hall to continue his long-winded efforts to reform Porgy. He declared he loved the captain, and therefore wanted to teach him where to put his foot down on life's journey. Porgy replied that Millhouse's tenderness was of a most rough sort indeed; but Millhouse even went so far as to advise Porgy to shut up when in the company of "men of business like Fordham and me." He recommended that Porgy might have his say in front of inexperienced young people and—women, women especially, who were interested in such stuff as poetry and music. Porgy, he said, knew only what was "pleasant and amusing, and ridikilous, and what belongs to music, and poetry, and the soul," but would "always get the worst of it at a horse-swap." He continued that only those occupations were respectable which brought in "bread and meat and drink."

"Well, but, sergeant, when a man has earned all the bread and meat, and drink, and clothing, that he needs, is he to be satisfied?"

"Satisfied! no! He's to work on, and on, and what he's got over and above his wants, he's to send to market and sell, and git all the money for it he kin."

"Ah! well,—what is he to do with that money?"

"Why, increase his force, and his land, to be sure."

"Why, that will only increase his money!"

The sergeant responded that was what a man should aim at, and to strive to "make himself a sort of king, in the way of comforts," and cause the people to feel he has the money "to buy and sell them" all "ef he pleases."

"Well, that must be a very delightful sensation. But would you not use some of this money for charity—would you not give Oakenberg his living, if only to catch snakes and make a collection? Would you not help Dennison to his dinner?"

"Not a copper on your singing birds and idlers. They should starve for me. Not a fellow that wouldn't work would I feed."

"But, Millhouse, you would do something for religion, wouldn't you?"

The sergeant said yes, as it would hurt his business if he didn't put something in the charity box and "be decent and regular." Porgy averred that, at least "you have answered as correctly and fully as the most profound utilitarian philosophers would have done," and proposed a drink of Jamaica. Porgy offered a toast "to the man who is wise enough to open his mouth only in the proper company"; and Millhouse to the Lord's getting Porgy "into a strong position agin the approaches of the sheriff."

The colloquy was interrupted by Lance coming in with a fine coon dog given him by Mrs. Griffin, and inviting Pomp to join him on a coon and possum hunt. Tom announced he was going too, as he was hungry for coon. Millhouse (always the kill-joy) regarded the hunt sourly, declaring he hoped the "niggers would get back soon enough to git their sleep and be ready for a good day's work." Porgy asked what tools they would use; and Millhouse was glad to say he had borrowed them from Mrs. Eveleigh, and so was off again on a windy exhortation to Porgy to get at the project of bringing the widow to Porgy's "roost." Millhouse said he believed in speed in life, especially in wooing. He declared that experienced women (widows) were to be taken by storm, as a fort that has been stormed once can be stormed again; he admitted that a young girl was to be won by indirect methods. He was sure the widow would surrender.

"Certainly, you hold forth a very encouraging prospect. But, sergeant, marriage is a very serious business. To a man who has been free all his life, has had nobody to restrain his conduct, outgoings and incomings, there is something positively frightful in the kind of bondage which it makes. It sometimes happens that instead of the woman getting a master, the man gets a mistress. There's a great part of this in most marriages. To reconcile one to the danger, I suppose, the passion of love was invented——"

Millhouse regarded love as something for children; but Porgy declared that if he married, he wanted to consult his tastes in the matter. "I confess that I believe myself not a bit too old to have an affection . . . I am for having a certain feeling satisfied—call it taste, or affection, love or what you will, sergeant, if I'm to marry and lose my liberty, I must know that my jailer is a lovely one."

Needless to say, Millhouse regarded such notions as foolish. Porgy succeeded in startling the mercenary sergeant by saying—

"Suppose, to speak more to the point, there should happen to be another woman whom I happen to like better than Mrs. Eveleigh?"

"Ha! is it that? Well, the only thing to ax—is the other woman in the same sarcumstances as Mrs. Eb'leigh,—ready and able to help you out of the halter of the sheriff?"

"Don't name the animal quite so often, sergeant, if you please."

"Well, I wont; but I ax agin—is the other woman as well off as the widow Eb'leigh? Has she as many goulden guineas, as many niggers?—"

"Not a stiver that I know of—not the hair of a negro."

"Can't be, cappin, you're thinking of the widow Griffin?" exclaimed the sergeant, rising to his feet and confronting Porgy with a look of blank antonishment—"

"Griffin is a prettier woman than Mrs. Eveleigh."

"Diccance! cappin! what hev' you got to do with purty women. What's a purty woman to a man in your sarcumstances?"

"Why, Millhouse, do you suppose, because a man wants money, he must also want good taste."

"Taste!—that's another of them foolish idees! I thought I had given you a right notion of all sich things. A man what's poor and in danger of the sheriff has no right to hev' a taste."

"But suppose he can't help it, sergeant—suppose he *has* the taste whether he wills or no?"

Millhouse plugged tiresomely enough away at the financial advantages of the widow Eveleigh, though he did admit that an honest taste would indeed prefer her. They prepared to drink again, of the Jamaica mixed with water. Porgy filled his cup and when about to drink said,

"You are a philosopher, sergeant, such as the world everywhere respects. But though your philosophy succeeds pretty generally, in the world, *you* never would."

"*En'* why not, cappin?"

"Because the chief secret of the success of such a philosophy as yours is that it never vaunteth itself. Its professors never publish their virtues as you do. They are content to practise in secret what you mistakenly praise. They *do* what you *preach,* and *preach* against what they themselves *do.* Pride thus discourseth of humility with moist lips; selfishness thus becomes eloquent in its exhortations to self-sacrifice; and the good preacher will possess himself of the fattest ewe lamb of the flock while insisting on the beauties of a perpetual lent. But what say you to bed? It will be some hours, I fancy, before the lieutenant and the boys get back from their coon hunt, and we may enjoy a good sleep meanwhile. We must also rise soon in the morning, that we may see what we are to wear to-morrow. There must be some patching of my garments, before I shall be able perfectly to appear at the widow's table; and you too, in all probability, will need some adhesive plasters, front and rear."

After Porgy had retired, the sergeant lay down before the fire in the hall to sleep, mulling over the advantages for the captain of Mrs. Eveleigh, and giving a thought or so to Mrs. Griffin for himself. When half-asleep, he heard a step on the piazza, and suddenly a tall Negro female figure entered. He thought it might be a ghost. Calling him "my chile," she embraced him with surprising firmness for one who was so old. The sergeant, swathed in his blankets, was half suffocated, but finally threw her off. She then realized she had mistaken her man.

Porgy, hearing the commotion, entered. Now she was sure "Dis dah my own chile!" Porgy did not at once recognize her, indeed not until she told him she was his old nurse, or "mauma." She had embraced him, her "chile," to the amusement of the sergeant, who exclaimed, "And a pretty sizeable sarcumstance of a child he is!" Porgy was in his night clothes. The sergeant brought lightwood, and she could be seen more clearly.

She was about seventy-five, tall, thin, wrinkled, toothless. Her eyes were bright, and she was certainly not tongueless. She thanked heaven she was seeing Porgy again.

"But you no know me, my chile. You bin fo'git old Sappho! Enty I know. You kaint tell me. Hah! das de way wid de world. You back tu'n, you gone, you in de ground, de berry chile you bin carry in you' arms, he fo'git all 'bout you!"

"But I didn't forget you, mauma! As soon as I saw you fairly, I knew you; and I only wonder I didn't know you by your voice."

"It's de teet', my chile! De teet' gone! De old snag drop out,—de berry las' ob 'em drop out de beginning ob dis winter. *Nary* one [never a one] leff for me chaw 'pon. Ah! de ole woman is a-gwine fas', my chile. It's de preticklar blessing ob de Lawd dat I leff for see you git back to you' own home and people. De Lawd be praised for all he mussies!"

"Well, mauma, I'm truly happy to see you once more alive. It reminds me so much of everything—of my mother—of the old wagon—of the little bay ponies, and the rides we had together down to uncle Dick's. Why, how could you think, Sappho, that I should ever forget *you?*"

"It's de way ob de worl', my chile! an I was afear'd dat when you git out in de worl' fair, an' see de people, an' git mix up wid de sodgers, you would shame for 'tink 'bout poor ole woman, da's a nigger, too."

"Never, Sappho! I have thought of you a thousand times, and I'm more glad to see you now, still living, and still able to see and to speak, than I should be at meeting with the best white friend I have. But, Sappho, you must tell me about everything. I want to know how you escaped in the general sack and confusion. When I sent Tom out here once to see how things went on, he could find nothing of you, and hear nothing. He only gathered that the British and tories had been here, had gutted the plantation and carried off all the people. You were believed to be dead, Sappho, and though not much given to weeping, I shed some tears for you, mauma. You may believe me, old woman, for I remembered you not only for yourself, but for others who were very precious to me."

"Enty I blieb's you, my chile. It do de ole woman heart good to blieb you. I knows you got a good heart, yourse'f, my chile, and dough, I knows, you lub much better to laugh dan to cry, I knows too you kin cry when dar's c'asion for it.

She proceeded with a "long and somewhat tedious, but clear and intelligible account" of what had been happening. When she had heard the redcoats were coming, she had gathered together her three daughters, their husbands and children, "her ginerations," and gone off into the swamp, along with some other "niggers," to make a total of eighteen. They had managed to survive there until now. Millhouse at once was beginning to ask how many of them were fit for field work, but Porgy silenced the sergeant with "there are other more necessary questions— Sappho, have these people any clothing? Your own garments, mauma, are thin enough." They were mostly in rags, she said, but she was kept warm by the fire, and she praised the Lord that her "chile is come home to git his people clo'es and blankets."

Porgy was somewhat annoyed at Millhouse's interruptions to further reporting by Sappho, and announced it was time to go to bed. He proposed, first, they have a sup of Jamaica with his old nurse, and even Millhouse thought the "sensible" old woman deserving of a drink.

Tom, coming in from the coon hunt, was surprised to find Sappho in his room, which was where Porgy had conducted her. But Tom was too tired to listen long to her and was soon asleep.

Millhouse was up early, and at once called to Sappho to come out. He entered Tom's chamber, only to find only Tom there. Porgy had been up even earlier than the sergeant, and had spoken to Sappho at the window before she went off to report to her "ginerations" in the swamp. Millhouse encountered Porgy on the piazza, and expressed surprise that the old "skelleton" of a woman was off already.

"What woman do you mean, Millhouse?"

"What woman! Why old Sapphy, to be sure, that I tuk for a ghost— that come in upon me last night, and gin me such a huggin' and a-kissin', and all on your account."

"I really don't know what you're talking about, sergeant."

"Don't know what I'm a-talking about!" quoth Millhouse, in amazement—"Don't know, cappin! Why, Lord love you, the old woman, your nuss, that calls you her child, that hugged and kissed both of us till we was a-most choked and smothered—the one that's got the niggers in the swamp, seven ginerations and more, making in all eighteen good hoe hands. Lord save us, how kin you forgit sich a matter!"

"Forget! How should I remember a matter which I never heard of before. You're certainly dreaming, sergeant."

"Dreaming, cappin!"

Millhouse went on to narrate the coming of the old woman and her tale.

"You must 'member all that matter, cappin."

"Not a syllable! It's all news to me, sergeant!" And Porgy gazed on him with a well-affected amazement of stare that provoked the most natural consternation in the world in the features of the other.

"The d—l you say! But, Lord, cappin, you kaint be forgitting your own ole nuss, Sapphy."

"I never to my knowledge, Millhouse, had a nurse with such a name, which seems to be that of a heathen goddess."

"Heathen h–ll! cappin; she set thar, I tell you."

"Impossible, sergeant."

"And she warnt in your room last night?"

"Not that I know of."

"Lord help me, ef I shan't go crazy! And I warnt in your room last night?"

"It may be that you were. You know best. If you were, it was while I slept."

"Slept! By the powers, cappin, you was wide-awake as a black fish; and when the talk was over, we all kim out, and swallowed a little Jamaiky by way of medicine. And we gin the old nigger a cup for the good news she brought, and then you gin her a blanket, and you showed her yourself whar to sleep in Tom's room, and thar we left her."

"This is a strange delusion of yours, sergeant. But why not go to the room and find her there, if you say you saw her go there to sleep?"

"Lord save me, but you put her thar yourself."

"There you are mistaken! But, if such is your notion, go and seek her there."

"I've been thar, and she's not thar!" cried the sergeant, in a state of approaching perspiration.

"I thought so!" muttered the captain of partisans, in subdued tones, but sufficiently loud to be heard, and he touched his head significantly—

"Millhouse, your suppers are too heavy. I would counsel you against much meat at night. A single bit of that broiled ham—the slices thin— is quite enough for any decent white man. And in eating your hoe-cake, take my counsel to reject the softer parts; confine yourself entirely to the crisp portions, the crust. Besides, coffee is a wonderful stimulant of the brain. Don't go over a pint hereafter at night; and, perhaps, it will be well to deny yourself the freedom of the Jamaica after a certain hour. Say, a single glass after smoking your last pipe, and then to sleep. Believe me, my good fellow, by observing these simple forbearances, you will escape the visitation of the nightmare. She has evidently given you a fearful hug last night."

" 'Twas the old skillyton nigger, I tell you—'twas Sapphy, your nuss, and not any nightmar'. Lord, cappin, ef you wouldn't drive me 'stracted, don't you go on so. . . ."

"I can tell you nothing more, sergeant. You've certainly had a very lively dream last night, which I should greatly like to see realized."

"A dream! Lord! Lord! I shall go crazy and outright *re*stracted! And you hadn't a nuss named Sapphy?"

"Never!"

"Oh! Lord, what shall I be thinking!"

"Don't eat so much at night again, sergeant."

"It *kaint* be a dream!—"

"Leave off the coffee in particular!"

"I swow! it warnt no dream!"

"One drink only of Jamaica, after your last pipe."

"Ef 'twas a dream it was as much like the raal and living life as I ever seed it."

"That's always the case with pleasant dreams, sergeant; but they always lead to disappointment. What a glorious crop you could make if your dream of those eighteen negroes were true?"

"Lord, yes! and I had jest set my heart on beating Fordham out of sight. But O! sta*i*rs, cappin, it ought to be true and it must be true."

Just then Tom was heard below, calling to Pomp.

"Thar's Tom! He must ha' seed her ef she was thar. I'll ax him."

"Do so," says Porgy, "and satisfy yourself. It will do you some good and make you less certain of your dreams hereafter."

Millhouse sallied out, and Porgy darting to the window, caught the eye of Tom, ascending the stairs to the piazza, and motioned with his hands to him. At that moment Millhouse from the hall cried out to him—

"Look you, Tom, where's the old nigger-woman what slept in your room last night?"

Porgy shook his head negatively to the cook. Tom was quick to conceive, and knew thoroughly the habits of the captain of partisans, as a practical joker. He immediately conjectured what was required of him, and his answer was as prompt as if dictated by the very mother of the truth.

"Wha' womans you talk 'bout, mass Millh'us? I aint see *nary* old nor young woman 'pon dis place!"

"The h–ll you aint! The Lord be merciful to my poor senses."

"Somet'ing seem for trouble you, mass Millh'us; may be you is berry much hungry for you breakus."

"D—n the breakfast! Oh! thar's Pomp! I recken he must ha' seed the old woman."

Pomp was beginning to ascend the steps leading to the back piazza, at the head of which Tom stood. Tom replied for Pomp, in tones loud enough for the other to hear.

"Wha', Pomp! How kin he see ole woman in my room, ef me, Tom, no bin see 'em? Heh! Pomp? Speak, boy,—you *no* bin see no ole woman in de room whay we sleeps las' night?"

Tom's tone, and the fierce scowl which he put on while speaking to the boy, effectually taught the latter what sort of answer was required from him, and he responded without hesitation—

"Nebber see ole woman in de room, uncle Tom."

"Da's wha' I say, mass Millh'us. You muss ha' bin dream 'bout dat old woman."

"Dream! Lord! Lord! and here am I a loser of eighteen niggers, fus' rate fiel' hands, and nobody seems to care about it."

Millhouse went on lamenting the loss of the eighteen useful Negroes. A "strange voice was heard without." Porgy saw Millhouse "dart forward with a shriek of delight. The captain of partisans looked out of the window upon the piazza, and the spectacle of the night was reversed. It was old Sappho who was, this time, nearly suffocated in the embrace of the sergeant."

Millhouse now, as usual, loud and prolix, professed he actually loved the old "nigger," as he gave her another hug. Sappho thanked him, and "without struggling to extricate herself" said she thought he "wasn't so glad to hug de ole woman las' night!"

"Are you still dreaming, sergeant?" cried Porgy, emerging from his chamber, and coming out into the piazza.

"You're jest about the fattest sinner living, cappin, and can jest now lie as easy as ef a conscience warn't no sort of trouble to you at all. En, how did you put up that black faced satan, Tom, there, and Pomp, to back your lying for you? Lord! how nateral they did it. As sure as a gun you'll all go to the devil together, and not one soul of you miss the road."

"When that time comes, sergeant, you will be found leading the forlorn hope!—Well, Sappho, my good old woman, you are as sprightly as a girl of sixteen. You've done more work than all of us together. And these are my poor people. Charlotte, and Betty, and Cinda, I remember; and Ben—"

"An' Eli, maussa; you 'member Eli, enty?"

was the interruption of Betty's husband who now ascended the steps, leading the way for the group, and grappled the captain by the hand. His example was followed by all the rest; and numberless and sufficiently various were the exclamations of rejoicing on every hand.

"De Lord be praise, maussa, you come home at las'!" "Tanks be to de Fader!" "Oh! I so happy, aunty!" and—"Maumy, maussa come! Enty you glad?" "Glad for cry, my chile."

But we need not multiply the phrases. The character of the catalogue may be sufficiently conjectured from these samples. But he who knows what a Carolina plantation is—one of the old school—one of an ancient settlement—where father and son, for successive generations, have grown up, indissolubly mingled with the proprietor and his children for a hundred years, may follow out the progress, and repaint the picture for himself. Porgy had few words, but his sympathies were more clearly expressed, to the eyes of all the slaves, than if he had spoken them in the best chosen language. As the several groups passed up the steps, and gave way for each other, the men with their wives and their children, the calculating sergeant could not contain his joy. Now he strode up and down the piazza, counting with the fingers of his solitary hand. Anon, he paused to take with an affectionate grasp, some one girl or boy by the shoulder, according as the development showed a desirable strength.

The general tenor of the above passage, and particularly his use of the present tense is, certainly suggests Simms is here thinking of the present as much as, or even more than, the past.

Porgy then promised the Negroes to bring them clothes and blankets from the city, and to secure for them provisions. He went in to breakfast with Millhouse, after which Sappho was called to "take her portion from the table."

Now came the "embarrassing" project of examining the wardrobes of our partisans so they could make a proper appearance "at the dinner party of the widow Eveleigh," which occupies the rest of the chapter, entitled "Near Approaches to Sans-culottism." Naturally the outfitting of the captain came first, and because of the appalling limitations of his meager supply of clothes, the difficulty of getting him even presentably attired for the big social event was truly tremendous. As for coats, he had only two, a dress coat for parade, once red but now ineffectively dyed blue, and a "hunting shirt"—or coat—of blue homespun.

Naturally, the first and most urgent problem, was the matter of breeches. All he possessed, besides the faded ones he had on, in the way of small-clothes, were two pair, one more or less blue, the other buff. "The blue small-clothes were first examined." They seemed like "an enormous sack," large enough "to take in a bale of long cottons." Yet

*the captain had found that "they were by no means sufficiently ample
to afford him the degree of freedom which he required when dining
out." Although they had no rents or patches, and "no places so much
worn as to keep the wearer in constant apprehension of an explosion,"
Porgy, after subjecting them to "a severe scrutiny," with the "help of
Tom and Pomp," rejected them because they were too tight. They would
be the best, "if they were not so atrociously contracted about the hips
and waist. I'm always in dread lest I should burst them."*

"Day strong, maussa."

"Yes, Tom! But not strong enough for everything, and the widow
will, no doubt, give us a first-rate dinner, and I am in honor bound to
do justice to it. There will be wines, too, and I must drink,—I *will* drink,
and try every variety that's offered. By Bacchus! the very idea of wine
inspires me. It's long since I've smacked my lips upon the tears of the
vineyard. Lift up the buffs, Pomp."

The garment thus described dangled in the air from the extending
finger of Pompey.

"They would do well, in respect to size; but these d—d patches, Tom."

"Day mighty broad in de face, maussa."

"As the full moon, Tom, though less bright of complexion."

*Tom insisted that if his "maussa" put these on, he would have to
wear the hunting shirt, as the pigeon-tail (the dress coat) would not
cover up the patches.*

*The buffs it would have to be. Yet in the rear they had been patched
extensively with buckskin, a material chosen for two reasons. It was
thought nothing else "could possibly endure the constant strain and pressure in the ailing region"; and the buff cloth was not available in camp.
The art of sewing as practiced in camp was so crude as to leave prominent ridges where cloth and leather were joined, which were now
threatening to give way, requiring the "craft of the tailor."*

*Tom exclaimed, "Lor, a mighty, massa, you's too hard 'pon you
breeches. 'Taint decent and like gemplemans, de way you wear you
cloes."*

"Get out, you rascal, and get ready to sew them up at once. Get your
needle and thread; or see Sappho, and see if some of these grand-daugh-
ters of hers can't do the work less clumsily. I reckon she's taught some

*of them to sew." The girl was found, and was soon "busy on the
garment."*

Tom and his master agreed he would have to wear the hunting shirt,
although both preferred the dress-coat, as the shirt-coat was better at
covering the "wornout acres," as Porgy called them. There were certainly
acres, growled Tom, or big as the skirt of a saddle. The hunting shirt,
also, required some mending, but had to do.

Stockings were found, and Porgy's sole remaining shirt of "best Irish
linen," the "last of six dozen. Six dozen! heavens! was I indeed the
owner of six dozen shirts at one time!" A white vest, and yellow buckskin gloves were located, and so Porgy's entire habit was ready; and "he
proceeded, with the help of Tom and Pomp, to put himself in harness."*

Talk of the iron garments of ancient chivalry! Never did the closing
of rivets on the part of the knights of the English Harrys and Edwards,
on the eve of battle, require more time and painstaking, or cause more
anxiety to pages and squires, and armour-bearers and armorers, than did
the costuming of their master, that day, occasion to his two sable attendants. Such gingerly handling of coat, and vest, and shirt, and small-
clothes, was, perhaps, scarcely ever beheld before.

*As the central part of the white linen shirt was missing, they had to
put the garment on Porgy and have the Negro girl draw the sundered
sides together by stitches while Porgy sat motionless. Pomp told "Uncle
Tom" he could see no shoe-brush, and Tom told him he could clean
his master's boots with a piece of cloth.*

*As Tom was helping "maussa" on with his coat, he lectured him on
moving very carefully, lest he "breck" the worn coat. ". . . de breeches
will be for busting out too; and dat won't do no how, when you da
stan' [stand] 'fore the ladies." He must be very particular when he was
getting off the horse, must not raise his hand to heaven as if calling "de
sun and de moon" to be witness; he must sit down easy, for Tom did
not depend " 'pon dese breeches 't all." Porgy completed his entourage
with sword and coonskin cap, and just avoided having Millhouse take
in another hole in his belt, the sergeant claiming it would "better his
figure a little."*

*The captain's subordinates had similar embarrassments and difficul-
ties with their garments; but all three cantered off at last toward the
widow Eveleigh's. Porgy had to endure an exhortation from Millhouse*

to prepare to "scale and storm," for "A widow's jest like a fort that's used to surrendering."

"The plantation of Mrs. Eveleigh was one of the finest and best kept along the Ashepoo. She had been fortunate in the circumstances which secured her equally against the hostility of both parties during the late war." She had friends on both sides; her husband had been an officer in the British army. Her escape had not been harassed. She had an efficient overseer, and wisely lived during most of the year on her estate. Her presence promoted not only the success but the beauty of her plantation. On three sides, long avenues of trees led to her mansion. With her son Arthur she was awaiting her guests on the piazza.

Hearing Millhouse urging Porgy to marry the "widow," Lance, Porgy having gone ahead, unexpectedly reprimanded the sergeant, for "talking to the captain as if he was a boy, and you was his teacher." He asked "what can you teach him about fine people, and high life, and the sort of behavior he's to behave when he's in company with rich ladies in their own houses. He knows more of such people than you and I ever saw, and don't want any education how to do when he gets among them. You'd better shut up now in all these matters. I see he don't like it, and you'll some day go one step too far, and you'll rouse him."

Millhouse was surprised and indignant, insisting she was eager to have Porgy. Lance replied: "I don't believe she'll have him." He declared she had invited Millhouse and himself "because we helped to save her son's life and her own. It's because she's grateful . . . and if you're right-minded, you'll just be quiet all to-day while in her house, and be respectful, and listen only, and answer when you're spoken to; for we ain't asked to be heard."

Millhouse could only come back with the charge that Lance was "only a brat of a boy." In low tones Lance concluded by warning him he "would burn his fingers."

Arthur descended the steps to greet them heartily, while Mrs. Eveleigh, with accomplished grace, received them on the piazza. She began with an allusion to "that fearful day, from the perils of which you rescued us."

"Too happy you will believe, my dear Mrs. Eveleigh, in being of the slightest service to you," was the gallant answer of the captain.

Evidently heedless of Lance's warning, Millhouse broke in with the beginning of a long series of tasteless and tactless interruptions. The captain was born to be the protector of women, he insisted. Porgy glared at him.

Mrs. Eveleigh answered him kindly, but averred "we owe equally our gratitude" to the sergeant and Lance.

Irrepressible Millhouse went on about the captain's fury in battle and tenderness with "wimmin."

"Porgy could stand it no longer. He broke out—'Why, Millhouse, Mrs. Eveleigh will suppose that I have employed you especially as my trumpeter, and not as my overseer. Shut up! my good fellow, or speak of your own valor and your own tenderness, if you please. As I have no apprehensions that I shall be suspected of any deficiency when either is needed, it is no policy to insist upon them now, lest both of them becomes suspected [This is the only grammatical solecism in all of Porgy's dialogue.]' "

Mrs. Eveleigh's error in calling the sergeant "Miller," elicited tiresome remarks from him about a sergeant really named Miller.

"Yet it seems to have been proverbial that the most brave-hearted are also the most tender-hearted, always, captain," she said.

"The effect has commonly shown itself in the number of wars which have been occasioned by the sex, Mrs. Eveleigh. It is proverbial, also, that when all other arguments fail to inspire the man with the proper courage, you have only to goad him in the presence of the lady whom he most admires."

Porgy's courtly reply stimulated the sergeant into a vulgar disquisition on women as a stimulus to men's fighting, beginning with a cock and hen analogy, and including allusion to his blood boiling at the freedom of the redcoats with young farm women. All this, however, should not deter a personable man from taking a wife.

Beginning to sense the sergeant's drift, Mrs. Eveleigh pointedly shifted to a topic "which was . . . addressed wholly to the captain." She disclosed that she had ordered brought such of his furniture and cutlery as had not been destroyed by a first tory foray. Porgy told her the plate she could not find "was all melted down in camp" for living expenses. (His own overseer had helped despoil him.) He concluded, "My debt to you increases every hour, Mrs. Eveleigh."

"By no means, captain. I shall owe you a debt which my whole life could not repay." Misconstruing this, Millhouse cried, "that's it!"

Porgy gave him a single stern look—then turning to the widow, said—
"Do not talk of any debt to me, my dear Mrs. Eveleigh; you owe
me none. What was done for your rescue, by myself and my companions,
would have been done in behalf of the poorest creature of the country—"

"Let me interrupt you, captain, by saying that, in like manner, what
I have done for the saving of your chattels, in your absence, would have
been done for any other neighbor. But, the better course would be to
say nothing of these mutual services, however much we feel them."

"Edzactly—but the feeling!—" and the sergeant closed.

*Millhouse revealed he was to be the captain's overseer, and told of
the potentialities of Porgy's rich lands, but said that he was handicapped
by having only "twenty-five niggers." Mrs. Eveleigh was surprised that
Porgy had that many. Porgy told her about the coming of Sappho's
family.*

*Porgy quickly quashed Millhouse's claim there might be a hundred
more of his Negroes in the swamp, to be greeted with the gauche sergeant's assertion that the captain was wasteful and profligate, and having
only a hundred guineas, gave one to a beggar child.*

*"A hundred guineas, sergeant? Why what are you talking about?"
said Porgy indignantly, and drew forth and showed the eight or ten
which he said was all he possessed. Millhouse showed facially his great
indignation at this exposure, and Porgy sensed that his hostess was beginning to detect his game. Arthur and Lance, who had gone out to
look at the horses, reappeared, and she now invited her guests inside to
take refreshment. She offered a choice of old Madeira or Jamaica, and
motioned her chief guest into an adjoining room.*

*It seemed that neither of the young men drank; Arthur, because of a
vow made to his dying soldier father; and Lance, because he didn't like
the stuff. Millhouse, at his most tactless, showed some slight sympathy
with Arthur's attitude, but declared Lance's as showing a lack of taste
and sense. Arthur's growing distaste for the sergeant was increased by
his leering insinuation his "ma" and the "cappin" were out together for
a reason, and his hinting Arthur should be happy to have him "for a
father."*

*Arthur's sole commentary: "Is he drunk?" revealed intense disdain.
Lance said, "No!"—it was only his strange way of talking foolishly.*

The colloquy between the widow and the captain, utterly unlike

what the sergeant had wishfully imagined, was first devoted exclusively
to Porgy's financial problems, and then to the sergeant's own faults.

Mrs. Eveleigh, apologizing for taking a liberty, said she knew about
his fiscal difficulties. He asked her not to remind him "how greatly I
have been the profligate." She replied she knew he had allowed "hos-
pitality and good fellowship to fling prudence out of the window," and
that he had "got but little pay at the close of the war." "Not a copper,
Ma'am."

She offered to lend him equipment, ploughs, shovels, wagons, and to
extend him credit for provisions. If he made a good crop, he was to
return what he had borrowed if he could; if not, he was to pay her when
able. But he would also need cash.

She knew the worst, that his plantation was mortgaged to M'Kewn
for far more that it would sell for, but that he had no lien upon Porgy's
Negroes. She proposed that he give her a mortgage on enough of the
Negroes to come to five hundred guineas, and thus save the slaves from
M'Kewn. She had ready two letters, one a sort of draft on her banker
for the five hundred guineas; and another to Charles Cotesworth Pinck-
ney. Porgy must take his legal difficulties to this eminent lawyer, who
might be able to save him from M'Kewn. She had reason to suspect
M'Kewn of great frauds; and if she could recover the stolen box, she
could show Porgy a paper by which they could compel M'Kewn to
"come to reasonable terms." (Tom, however, was not mortgaged.)

"You have saved me, Mrs. Eveleigh. What woman would have done
for me what you have done?"

"Many, I trust; knowing the circumstances, and in the same condition to serve you."

The captain shook his head, and, taking her hand, said—

"You are a wonder of a widow! You have the soul of a man!"

She smiled.

"I suppose I must take such a speech as a compliment, coming from
one of the masculine gender."

"Ah!" said he, "you know what I mean! You are not a girl—not a
child—not frivolous or feeble. You *have* a soul! You have earnestness
and simplicity, and these make sincerity of character. You have faith,
too, and—"

"Which, by the way, captain, is not often a manly virtue.—There, I fancy, is where our sex has the advantage of yours. You, perhaps, are an exception. Here, for example, you are willing to trust me and my boy, with all your property, without any security."

"Ah, madam, I could cheerfully give it to you both, did you need it. The pleasurable feeling of sweet faith and confidence, and generous unreserve, and liberal sympathy, which you have this day shown me, is more grateful to me than any amount of wealth or money. I now know where I can confide. I feel, too, that there is one, at least, who can confide in me. We do not watch each other as victims, or as birds of prey; seeking to devour, fearing to be devoured. Madam, if you will permit me, I will be your friend—your friend."

She gave him her hand.

"No more now, captain; let us go to the hall. I hear the dinner signal."

They rose; she led the way out, but paused at the door.

"By the way, captain, your one-armed soldier seems a very queer creature."

The captain seemed annoyed, and peered into the eyes of the widow, as if to fathom the extent of her discoveries or her suspicions.

"Yes," said he, "a very queer creature. He will say many things to surprise you. Army life sometimes spoils a good fellow, who, if he remained humble, might be a favorite. Don't heed him, I pray you. He is good enough in his way—devoted to me—imprudently devoted, I may say; and sometimes officious enough to save me against my will."

"Surely, you should not complain of such officiousness."

"I don't know! One would have a vote in these matters. The sergeant's friendship is not sufficiently indulgent. Still, he is devoted to me—would die for me, without a murmur, and fight for me to the last; but the scoundrel wants to *think* for me, also; and that is an offence—if the thing were not so ridiculous—that I should not much tolerate. His misfortune is not to know how much a simpleton he is."

"Simpleton! I should suppose him rather shrewd than simple," said the widow, with a smile.

"Yes; he is shrewd after a fashion—shrewd in all those respects which belong to his mode of life, and the narrow range of his intellect. He is shrewd, like the beaver or the possum: knows how to find a shelter for his hide, and can find, by instinct, where the corn and acorn may be gathered. He will house and hive, while I should freeze and starve, perhaps. It is his misfortune that his sharpness has stimulated his self-esteem, as is usually the case with persons of his class who prove success-ful. If, for example he should drive a great bargain in rice or butter, he would just as lief explain the law to Cotesworth Pinckney, as to Tom, my cook. Ten to one should he see you at the harpsichord, he will give you a lesson in music."

"I shall be careful how I afford him the chance."

"He is only a grub, a human grub, with a monstrous instinct for acquisition and saving; no more; but withal useful, and to be cherished —at a distance. I have suffered him to come too near, and familiarity has somewhat blunted me to his obtrusiveness. I see the evil of it only when he comes in contact with others. He has been faithful, however, and I can not cast him off. As long as I have a home, he must share it."

"Fordham tells me that he is to be your overseer."

"He volunteered; insists that he knows all about it; and has set his heart so completely upon it, that, even if I wished it otherwise, I could not well deny him. At all events, I will give him a fair trial this season."

"Fordham will cheerfully assist him."

"Oh! bless you, he fancies he can teach Fordham his business. I tell you he is a simpleton."

"But he must not be suffered to ruin your crop."

"Fordham shall assist *me*, with a hint, should there be any reason to suspect this danger. Meantime, dear madam, please give the fellow no heed. He will say many things that will startle, if not offend. But the blockhead means no evil.—Will you take my arm?"

The lady and her guests proceeded to the dining saloon, which was in the "basement."

The widow took her seat at one end of the table; her son at the other; Porgy occupied a side to himself, while the lieutenant and ser-geant took the other. A couple of liveried servants were in waiting. The lady herself pronounced a grace, and the proceedings began. Porgy was in good spirits. His mind was somewhat relieved of its troubles, and the sight of dinner was calculated always to give it animation. The re-turn to well-known aspects of civilization, so different from his camp experience, was also a source of unspeakable satisfaction.

"Ah! madam!" said he, "I feel, as I look around me, that I may once more become a gentleman. I have been little more than a savage for the last five years. The camp makes sad havoc in the tastes of a gentleman. Rough fare, rough usage, the bare earth for a table, lean beef, bad soup, no bread, frequently no salt, and bad cooking—these are enough to endanger any man's humanity. Talk of patriotism as you will, but, truth to speak, we pay a monstrous high price for it in such conditions as we have been subjected to in this warfare."

Millhouse rattled along in praise of the food and the cook, a good one "for a woman," but said she could learn much from "our Tom."

Mrs. Eveleigh smiled as she answered—

"Old Peggy would scarcely tolerate being sent to school at this time of day, even to such a proficient as the captain's Tom. She has as rare an opinion of her own merits as a cook, as if she had graduated with all the honors fifty years ago. But I have no doubt of Tom's superior merits. Colonel Singleton has been frequent in his praises, and Cotesworth Pinckney insists upon him as beyond all comparison in a terrapin stew."

"Pinckney knows," said Porgy, "if any man. He has a proper taste for the creature comforts, and has done me the honor, frequently, to discuss with me Tom's performances in this preparation. But 'old Peggy' needn't fear comparison with anybody. This beef is excellent. Pray, Mrs. Eveleigh, how did you save your cattle from the marauders."

It was "by having friends on both sides of the question." The whigs were friendly; her husband had a high rank in the British army, and was intimate with General Leslie. She had sold cattle and rice to the British, thus making a profit. It was better, she argued, than refusing and having her cattle stolen and her houses burnt.

The sergeant seized the opportunity to say that she needed now a "man-body" to guard her holdings; and that a woman who refused to marry should have a husband selected for her by the governor or general.

Mrs. Eveleigh at this smiled, and her "blue eyes twinkled merrily," and Porgy "unable to control the sudden impulse, laid down knife and fork, and burst into an uncontrollable fit of laughter. The widow felt the contagious influence and yielded to it. She laughed with the frank, hearty impulsive spirit of girlhood." Arthur was bewildered, but Lance quietly chuckled. Millhouse was immensely astonished, even to delaying the entry of a "huge gobbit of beef" into "the opening doorways of his jaws."

He asked what the fun was about; restated his belief that a woman needed a guardian; said he "meant no offence"; and thought she couldn't understand because women were inferior to men. Mrs. Eveleigh said she was not offended, indeed actually "pleased at the novelty of" his suggestions. Millhouse took the bait, and even said he had never met anyone who "knowed quite as much as me," and as much about the limitations of women.

Porgy saw her eyes sparkling with "mischievous merriment," realized she was leading the loquacious sergeant on to greater follies. Sensing this was a bit painful to the captain, she intentionally miscalled the sergeant "Miller," and suggested he would "join Lieutenant Frampton"— the young man apparently having left the table. Millhouse was obtuse to this hint, saying he preferred her company. He rattled on to indicate she needed a guardian with an army background. Mrs Eveleigh by now was only too cognizant of the sergeant's game. That he should "have annoyed and mortified" his captain, never occurred for a single moment to Millhouse. Porgy was groaning. It became too much when the sergeant started on the merits of Jamaica as a cure for nearly all diseases.

"Sergeant Millhouse!" cried Porgy, in a voice of thunder.

"Cappin!"

"Silence in the ranks, sir!"

"I'm shet up!" At last the sergeant realized his adjurations had not pleased his employer. Porgy must indeed have been greatly disturbed, and had lost his appetite! The widow certainly had a sense of humor, as she "was half tempted by the spirit of mischief" to provoke the sergeant "to further revelations of his peculiar philosophy." She desisted, however, as she felt poor Porgy had been annoyed enough. In leaving the table, Millhouse praised the dinner, and apologized for eating so much, but not for what he had said.

The day was over before the guests left. Porgy was alone with the widow part of the time. Lance and Arthur made plans for a deer hunt together. Millhouse conferred with Fordham.

On the way home the irrepressible Millhouse was telling Porgy he held good cards in this game of courting, but Porgy replied severely, "I suppose, Sergeant Millhouse, that you fancy you have helped this game wonderfully. . . . Hereafter . . . let me play my own game, if you please; I need no assistance." And Porgy spurred his horse ahead.

Then Lance told Millhouse that if the captain "had snapped off your *head, he'd have served you right. What business have you to be meddling with his courtings, if so be it's that he's after . . . I don't know much about women folks, but I'm pretty sure, any woman of sense, will be mighty apt to sicken of a man if she sees he gits his courting done by another."*

The impossible sergeant rejoined that no women had sense; and that he could have married any woman whatever if he had asked her.

Lance derogated his extreme conceit, saying his talk today was "just such foolishness as ought to hang a man. Even her son, Arthur, thought you was insulting to his mother, and I had to tell him that you was a very foolish sort of person, and that it was a fool way you had of talking about things you don't understand, and he musn't mind you."

" 'Me a fool!' muttered Millhouse, but the captain's manner and Frampton's suggestions had opened his eyes.

At home, "by the time supper was ready, Porgy had recovered his good humor." He told his household of the financial arrangements he had accepted from Mrs. Eveleigh.

Tom was the first to speak, praising her for her sense, and saying she had respect for gentlemen, as she had respect for "me, Tom." She had shaken hands with Tom, saying she had heard about Tom, that his "maussa" was her friend. She was "ebbry inch" a lady.

Lance, not speaking, rose and "wrung" Tom's hand "warmly." Millhouse lauded the lady immensely, and was off again on his fixed idea that she should have an army man as guardian. Then Porgy, at last, "with great composure" put the sergeant in his place, saying "there are a few subjects upon which you had better not expend your time and labor," and gave a picture of Millhouse in heaven. Millhouse said he was in no hurry to leave this earth.

"In your own time, sergeant; but when you do go, I think it will not be altogether proper to undertake to show the angels, Gabriel, Michael, Raphael, or any others with whom you may become familiar, in what way they ought to use their wings. I have no doubt you have some very wise notions as to how birds and beasts may fly; but the angels, perhaps, have more experience than you, if not more wisdom, and it will require that you should see much flying done among them, before you can venture to give them any lessons."

"Why, cappin, I reckon you're jest a-laughing at me now, out of the corner of your eye. I ain't sich a bloody fool as to do them things."

"Perhaps not! But when a man is so wise as you are on so many subjects, he is apt to think himself wise in all."

"Well, that's nateral and reasonable too, I'm a-thinking."

"Natural enough, no doubt, but not so certainly reasonable, my good fellow. If you were suddenly to find yourself among bears and buffaloes, you might reasonably undertake to show them how to find their food or prey; if among snakes, I have no doubt you could teach them superior modes of beguiling young frogs into their jaws; as a dweller among hawks and owls, or minks and weasels, you might open new views to them of the processes by which they might empty all the hen-houses in the country; and, teaching squirrels, they might be grateful to you for new lessons in the art of gathering corn out of the fields, and cracking hickory-nuts;—but I doubt if these capacities of yours should entitle you to think yourself appointed to teach young oysters how to swim, or young angels how to fly; and I am even doubtful how far they should justify you in an endeavor to set yourself up as a teacher of love and courtship. Of one thing let me assure you, before I stop, that if ever you undertake to make love to any woman on my account, again, and in my presence, by the Lord that liveth, sergeant, I will fling you from the windows, though the house were as high as the tower of Babel. Be warned in season;—and now let us have a sup of Jamaica, before sleeping for the night."

"I told you so,—" said Frampton, brushing by the sergeant as the latter stood up, in silence, to drink with his superior.

"Well, thar's no *on*derstanding it," muttered the sergeant, after the captain had retired. "Thar's some people so cross-grained in the world, they won't let you make 'em smooth."

Tom, the cook, had his comment also.

"Hah! mass Millhouse, you yer! Look out! when maussa talk so, he's in dead airnest! Ef he tell you he guine fling you out de window, he do 'em for true. And you know, for all you see 'em look and walk so lazy, he strong as a harricane when he git in a passion. He will, sure as a gun, brek' you neck out de window, ef he promise!"

"Thar's no onderstanding it!" was the only response of the sergeant to those suggestions. "And all the time I was a-doing the best,—jest a making his wheel run smooth!"

During the next few weeks "Captain Porgy, charged with his letters of credit and introduction, visited Charleston; obtained the five hundred guineas of the widow; has executed to her a mortgage of all his negroes, with the exception of Tom; has procured . . . all necessary supplies; has conferred with . . . Pinckney; received his counsel; endeavored, but in vain, to see his creditor, M'Kewn, who was absent from the city, no one knew where; and returned to his plantation" and stayed there.

Meanwhile "his subordinates have not been idle . . . Millhouse . . . as overseer, and Lance Frampton, as a temporary assistant, have . . . done wonders. The lands have been broken up for planting. . . ." Negro houses have been built, rail fences raised, and several months work done in "as many weeks. The negroes, glad once more to find themselves in possession of a homestead, certain provisions, and the protection of a white man, have worked with a hearty will and cheerfulness which have amply made up for lost time." Millhouse was not without good reasons for being "vain of his prowess as an overseer."

Lance took "special charge of the buildings," including erecting stables; and, with Porgy's assistance, did the hunting. It was rare "that the family lacked fresh meat." Young Eveleigh found Porgy and Frampton good company, and hunted with them every other day, to the great satisfaction of Millhouse.

"Porgy rode over to the widow's . . . twice a week, dining there usually. . . ." He did not ask his followers to go, "nor did they receive any more invitations from the lady." Millhouse was content not to go, since he was not to be permitted to "assist in the courtship."

At the widow Eveleigh's, Porgy was received on the most friendly and familiar footing. He was well read, of contemplative mind, had been trained in good society, and, though somewhat wanting in the precision of the courtier, in consequence of the loose, free and easy manner which he had acquired in camp, he was yet capable of curbing himself, when the impulse strove within him; and this done, he could minister to the social tastes of his fair companion, with an ease, grace, and vivacity, that made him always a very grateful visiter. Mrs. Eveleigh was almost wholly free from affectations; was frank and ever gay of mood; always cheerful; always ingenuous, and never labored at the concealment of her sympathies. She laughed at the good things of the captain and freely pardoned his familiarities. There was a freshness and a saliency about his peculiar humor which pleased her, and when he chose to be serious, he could rise into provinces of thought, generalizing from the abstract to the familiar, and thus coupling the most remote affinities and associations, in a strain of expression at once graceful and expressive. He quickly discovered in what respects he could most successfully address her ear, and he naturally availed himself of his discovery. Porgy, before entering the army, was well read in Shakspere, Milton, Dryden, and the best of the then current English writers. It must be admitted, we fear, that he had also drank freely of fountains less undefiled; had dipped largely into the subsequent pages of the Wycherlys, the Vanbrughs, the Congreves, the Wilmots, Ethereges, and Rochesters, of a far less intellectual, and therefore less moral, period. But the taste of the latter had not spoiled him for the just appreciation of the former; had perhaps heightened his estimate of them by force of contrast; and the fruit of his familiarity with both classes of writers, was a knowledge, not then commonly possessed—scarcely now, indeed,—of materials for graceful conversation, illustrated with frequent happy quotations, which particularly commended him to a woman who was, herself, at once refined and intellectual. We can readily understand how interesting was the intercourse between the parties, in a region which sparsely settled, and wanting in books, left so many wearisome hours, and wanting moods, which no plantation employments could satisfy or supply.

We do not mean to say that the widow regarded Porgy in any other aspect than that of a very agreeable companion. But we are constrained to admit on behalf of the captain, that he soon became seriously interested in the widow. That he should respect her heart, and love it, because of the liberality she had shown him, was natural enough;—but when he came to know her mind; the sweet graces of her intellect; her quiet, gentle, always just and wholesome habit of thought; the pleasant animation of her fancies; the liveliness of her conversation, enriched by the anecdotes of a very large and varied experience, as well in England as America, he began to admire her on other grounds, so that frequent association with her became almost a necessity. Still, there was a something wanting to the perfect sway of the widow over her admirer; something which he felt, but could not explain, or account for, to himself. She was a fine-looking woman, "fair, fat, and forty,"—but he found himself occasionally objecting to "the fat." The very fact that he was, himself, too much so, was enough to make him quarrel with her possessions of the same sort. He asked himself repeatedly the question: "Do I—can I love this woman?—as a woman *ought* to be loved; as a man ought to love;—as she deserves to be loved by any husband, and especially by me?"

Millhouse, could he have heard this question, would have answered it without a moment's hesitation; but Porgy never broached the subject in his ears, and now, studiously, since the memorable dinner, checked every approach to it which the former made.

"Yet," quoth the soliloquizing captain, "am I not shaping this passion of love into a bug-bear for my own fright and disappointment? Does it need that either the widow or myself should experience all the paroxysms and fancies of eighteen, in order to feel secure of the force of our attachment. Is it natural or reasonable, that, at forty-five, I at least, should need, or expect, to recall my youthful frenzies, before venturing upon the married condition? Is not the sort of love which we require now, that which belongs rather to the deliberate consent of the mind than the warm impulses of the blood and fancy? Is it necessary with us, that, in addition to the cool conviction of the thought, in favor of the propriety of this union, there should be a nervous and excitable upspringing in the heart, of tumultuous emotions, indefinable, intense, passionate, eager—which reject reason, which baffle thought, which seem to be guided rather by dreams than by right reason—and which ask none of the securities, by which thought would shelter faith—which is, in fact, a faith itself, beyond any of the help or the convictions of the understanding? My judgment is perfectly satisfied with the widow Eveleigh. She is vastly superior, as a lady—as a woman of sense and sweetness—grace and intelligence—to any that I know. She thinks well and kindly of me, that is evident. We harmonize admirably together. She listens with pleasure to my speech, and I am willing to listen gladly when she speaks in turn. She is a noble-looking woman—a little too stout, I admit—but of fine figure nevertheless, and a face that is at once sweet and commanding. She has wealth; but, by Jupiter, I reject that as a consideration. Her money shall not enter into the estimate. Her other attractions are surely quite sufficient. Yet, *are* they sufficient? *Am* I satisfied? Why do I ask myself so doubtingly whether I can bind myself to her for life, and feel no lack, no deficiency—no weight in the bonds I carry?"

The captain ended the soliloquy with a sigh. He strode the chamber impatiently, and paused finally before the fireplace, in which the fire smouldered rather than gave forth light and heat. At that moment the form of the widow Griffin rose vividly before his eyes.

"Why is it?" he muttered to himself, "that, whenever I try to meditate this question of the widow Eveleigh, the image of Mrs. Griffin starts up before me. *She* is a fine woman undoubtedly; good, gentle, humble, affectionate; and has no doubt been very beautiful;—is still very sweet to look upon;—but she can not compare with the widow Eveleigh! She is not wise, not learned; is really very ignorant; has no manners, no eloquence; is simply humble and adhesive;—*she* is rather thin than stout, that is true, her figure is good;—she has still a face of exquisite sweetness, but she is no associate for me;—she has no resources, no thoughts, no information; has seen nothing, knows nothing! They are not to be spoken of in the same moment. The widow Eveleigh is far superior in *all* but simply personal respects! Yet, Griffin does move about with a delightful grace; so soft, so modest. In household affairs she is admirable. I don't know that I ever saw Mrs. Eveleigh attending to household affairs at all. Her servants are numerous and well trained. She has only to command. Yet, on a small scale, considering her inadequate resources, it is wonderful with what skill Griffin manages; with how little noise, how little effort. Poor woman, what a lonesome life she leads. It is abominable that I have only been to see her once since I have been from town. I will certainly ride over to-morrow."

And he did so; and he dined with Mrs. Griffin; and a very nice extempore dinner did she give him. There were some cold baked meats; there was a beautiful broiled steak, a stripe from a quarter of beef which she had received as a present the day before from Mrs. Eveleigh; the breadstuffs of Mrs. Griffin were inimitable; her butter was the best in the parish; and a cool draught of her buttermilk, fresh from the churn, was welcomed by Porgy with all the enthusiasm of a citizen escaping, for the first time, from dusty walks and walls, to the elysium of green fields and forest shelter.

Notions of arcadian felicity crept into Porgy's mind. Everything seemed perfect, and perfectly delightful about the humble cottage of the widow Griffin. The trees had a fresher look; the grounds seemed to shelter the most seductive recesses; even the dog lying down in the piazza, and the cow ruminating under the old Pride of India before the door, seemed to enjoy dreams of a happier sort than usually come to dog and cow in ordinary life. The skies above the cottage appeared to wear looks of superior mildness and beauty, and to impart a something kindred to the looks of the beings who dwelt under their favoring auspices. What a sweet, smiling, modest creature was Ellen Griffin, whom our Lieutenant Frampton was shortly to take to his bosom. And how like her still—how nearly as youthful—how quite as meek, and gentle, and devoted—was the mother.

Porgy was delighted with the part of the day spent with this little family. His incertitude, in matrimonial respects, increased the more he surveyed her. Griffin made her impressions, differing much from those of the widow Eveleigh, but in their way not less strong; perhaps, stronger, since it was certain that Captain Porgy showed himself much more at ease with the one lady than the other. There was no doubt, indeed, that the superior social position of Mrs. Eveleigh, her equal grace and dignity of bearing, the calm, natural manner with which she met his approaches, all joined, in some degree, to restrain our hero—to lessen, somewhat, his own ease! to make him less assured on the subject of his own dignity. He was sometimes warned by the lady, that the *brusquerie* of his army habits, would not altogether answer—that he must be on the watch against himself, to check his involuntary *escapades,* and never to be forgetful of the fact that the time had come when, to play somewhat with the language of the poet—"arms must give way to the *gown!*"

It was this feeling of constraint which chiefly qualified the pleasure of his intercourse with the widow Eveleigh; which made him hesitate to give her the preference and which, on the other hand, assisted to increase the favorable impressions which a previous association had given him of the fair widow Griffin. With her, easily awed, conscious of social inferiority, looking up with great reverence to the captain of partisans, as her late husband's superior, he felt under few restraints of mere language and deportment. He did not dare to swear in the presence of Mrs. Eveleigh; that would have been a terrible violation of the rules of good society in that day. Yet our captain had an infirmity of this sort, and so inveterate was his habit, that he had only been able to check himself, at times, when in the widow's presence, by arresting the unlucky oath upon his lips by a manual operation; by clapping his broad palm entirely over his own mouth. Now, he did not feel the same sort of necessity when in the presence of the widow Griffin. Her social standards were less exacting. Her social experiences were more adapted to his own later habits, and the feeling of ease which he enjoyed in her presence, was such, that, without deliberately weighing the claims of the two ladies against each other, he rated it as a something almost compensative for the surrender of the graceful, intellectual attractions of the wealthy widow. He could smoke his pipe in the presence of the widow Griffin, which he had not dared to do at Mrs. Eveleigh's. The former when he had dined with her, filled his pipe, herself, from a store of tobacco which might have been a hoard of her late husband, and dropped, with her own hands, the little coal of fire, from the tongs, into it. It was like a coal from the altars of Cupid, upon the heart of the partisan; and while he sat in the piazza, after dinner, his chair resting solely on its hind legs, his own thrown over the bannisters, his head thrown back, at a declination almost the proper one for sleep, and sent up cloud after cloud, by way of tribute to the heavens, his half-shut eyes watched with a growing sense of the grace and beauties of the widow, her gliding and unobtrusive figure, as she busied herself about the hall and table; assisted Ellen to move the table back, brushed up her hearth with a fairy-like besom of broom straw, and finally drew her knitting to the doorway, and sat down in silent and submissive companionship. Porgy mused and said to himself:—

"One does not want an equal, but an ally in marriage. A man ought to be wise enough for his wife and himself. To get a woman who shall best comprehend one is the sufficient secret; and no woman can properly comprehend her husband, who is not prepared to recognise his full superiority. When it is otherwise, there are constant disputes. The woman is for ever setting up for herself. She is not only unwilling that you should be her master, but she sets up to be your mistress. Why, if she has the mind, should she not use it; and if she has mind enough for the household, what's the use of yours? Clearly, there can not be peace in any planet which acknowledges two masters."

How long the pleasant surveys and soliloquies of the captain might have continued, it is not possible to say. They were interrupted by the sudden riding up of Mr. Fordham, the overseer of Mrs. Eveleigh. He made a respectful bow to the captain, taking off his hat, and offering his hand as he did so; and entered the house, shaking hands with the widow and daughter with all the frankness of an old acquaintance. After a while, the captain's horse was brought out, Fordham volunteering to do the service. Porgy left the overseer behind him. As he rode off, the thought suddenly occurred to him—

"Can it be possible that this fellow, Fordham, is thinking of the widow?—Humph!"

And the suggestion led to a prolonged fit of musing which was only arrested when he found himself within his own avenue.

Next day Porgy rode over to see Mrs. Bostwick and Dory, from whom he had received stockings and cloth they had made. It was fortunate that Millhouse did not know he dropped not one but three guineas into little Dory's hands. "While sitting in the porch . . . with Dory quietly nestling in his lap, he was surprised to see" *Mrs. Eveleigh and her* "son ride up on horseback." *The interview was pleasant, although Porgy was a bit embarrassed at being caught in such a paternal position with the little girl.*

Mrs. Eveleigh reported that she had a call yesterday from M'Kewn, who owned a plantation next to hers, and that Porgy could expect a visit soon. "If I could recover that box—" *she added. Mrs. Bostwick had heard nothing from her husband.*

Mrs. Eveleigh's invitation to Dory to spend a week at her house was accepted. Porgy "accompanied the widow and her son, when they took their departure" *part way home.*

He had heard that M'Kewn was nearby; and knew that the legal danger could not long be evaded. "Our partisan would greatly have relished any circumstances which would authorize a transfer of the proceedings from the courts of law to those of arms."

The very next day M'Kewn rode up to Glen-Eberley, as Porgy was alone on his piazza. He "had been smoking, and the pipe was still in his mouth. . . . As soon as M'Kewn was recognized by our partisan," *the latter* "betrayed his emotions" *by shivering his pipe* "over the railing of the piazza." *Porgy rose, greeted him by name with courtly gravity, and asked him to take a seat, after he had ascended to the piazza.*

The Scotchman did so, "laid his hat down . . . drew off his gloves, rubbed his hands," *and seemed resolved to put* "himself on the easiest possible terms with his host." *Porgy* "looked on with stern calmness." *After becoming impatient of the caller's* "commonplace preliminaries" *about the ending of the war, Porgy* "himself broke ground" *on the* "subject of real interest" *between them, by saying that he owed him a* "considerable amount of money," *which he, no doubt, wanted him to pay.*

M'Kewn acknowledged this was true; that his mortgage covered the lands of Glen-Eberley, but if these "were all sold to-morrow, at present prices," they wouldn't pay one half of the debt for which they are bound." There was some thousand pounds of additional unliquidated debt.

"Ah! yes! Well, Mr. M'Kewn, you certainly do not expect that I should have any money so soon after the war. You sufficiently appreciate the patriotism which called us into the field and kept us in the ranks for so many years, without any compensation."

M'Kewn replied that no one appreciated more such patriotism; but he too had lost a great deal. Porgy said that under the circumstances a credit of five years was no credit at all; and that "You can not possibly suppose that I have money."

M'Kewn rejoined that it had been reported that he did have money, that he had been purchasing largely, and the rumor went that "Captain Porgy, returning from the field of Mars with Laurels, has been welcomed to those of Love—" Porgy was roused at this, and even more when M'Kewn began to refer to "a certain wealthy widow."

"Enough, Mr. M'Kewn," said Porgy, arresting him—with a stern aspect, and warning finger uplifted. "You have said what you have heard, I suppose, and now hear what I say. If, hereafter, I hear any man repeating this story, I shall slit his tongue for him. The lady in question is one whom I greatly honor, and of whom I will not hear anybody speak in disparagement. There was that in your tone and manner, Mr. M'Kewn, just now, which I did not relish. Be pleased to take warning."

M'Kewn was taken aback at this threat of violence, yet said he saw no harm in the report about the favor of the widow.

"There is harm, sir, because there is great indelicacy and great injustice in it. I am the proper authority in this matter, and I tell you, sir, in answer to this rumor, that the intercourse between Mrs. Eveleigh and myself is that simply of friendship, occasioned perhaps, wholly, by a service which I had the good fortune to render."

"Well, but, captain, there is no good reason why friendship, in such a case, should not ripen into—"

"No more, sir! The subject is one upon which I can suffer no jesting. That upon which we have to speak simply concerns money. I owe you money;—you want your money you say."

As the Scotchman said he did indeed want it, Porgy demanded a full statement of their accounts, completely itemized. When M'Kewn said such a statement was not needed in case of a mortgage, Porgy rejoined that it might come in handy when the mortgage had been signed under circumstances of error or fraud. With some fierceness, M'Kewn asked if Porgy meant to impute fraud to him.

"And if I did, sir, do you suppose I should value a fig your hectoring looks? Keep your temper within bounds, Mr. M'Kewn; for you would try to bully me in vain; and to let you understand this more fully, let me tell you that I *do* impute fraud to you—"

"Ha!" rising from his seat.

"Yes, sir! I think you at once a great and a little rascal. Since you demand my opinion, you shall have it. I believe you have cheated me in these accounts, for the satisfaction of which, in my blind confidence and folly, I gave you a lien upon my property. I shall require a thorough overhauling of your accounts, from the beginning, sir, and fancy that I shall be able to find, in some process of law, a means by which to arrive at the awards of justice!"

"Very well, sir; very well, sir," gathering up hat and gloves—and shaking them in both hands with nervous fury—"If it's law you want, sir, you shall have it. You shall have enough to remember it all your life."

And he wheeled about to descend the steps. Here he encountered Millhouse, at whose back stood Tom, the cook, and Pomp, the fiddler.

"Say the word, cappin," quoth Millhouse, "and I'll give the fellow a h'ist."

"Say de wud, maussa; da's all," echoed Tom, his sleeves already rolled up; while Pomp threw himself into an attitude, claws extended as if about to grapple with a bear. M'Kewn looked at the enemies in his path, and drew up with recovering dignity.

"Am I to be assaulted in your house, Captain Porgy?"

"Let him go, Millhouse! Let him pass."

As M'Kewn "dashed up the avenue at full gallop," he was followed by various very derogatory jibes from Porgy's loyal retainers.

As for Porgy, "while he reflected, felt that he had perhaps brought on the conflict of strength rather prematurely, and that prudence should have prompted more forbearance; but whenever he recalled the refer-

ences made by M'Kewn to the widow Eveleigh, he became reconciled to his own rashness."

"No! d—n the fellow! Whatever happens I shall never regret what I said to him."

The news soon got abroad of what had taken place at Glen-Eberley, between its proprietor and creditor. *M'Kewn's "own rage" led him to talk; and Millhouse told Fordham.* Mrs. Eveleigh asked Porgy to visit her.

Porgy had become a good friend of Arthur, who *"had learned to relish the eccentricities of his senior, particularly as he always found something in his conversation which"* stimulated thinking. *"Porgy loved the society of the young and framed his conversation to suit their tastes and impulses."* Indeed, *"the veteran and the youth were on terms of the most cordial intimacy,"* and he even whispered to Millhouse that he would be willing to volunteer to serve in any fighting for Porgy, if his difficulties could thus be solved.

Mrs. Eveleigh had called Porgy over to tell him he should have restrained his anger and tried to conciliate M'Kewn so as to gain time. Porgy *"could not venture"* to tell her the references to her had been the great provocation. They agreed, however, that M'Kewn could do little until the courts opened their sessions in the fall.

In the presence of Arthur *"she proceeded to tell of the papers she had from the desk of Moncrieff,"* and of their being in the missing box. Porgy saw at once the power these papers could give them. Porgy knew Bostwick was involved. (M'Kewn had so far managed to conceal his part in the ambuscade.) Little Dory came in, a veritable Cinderella converted into a princess by a long visit as house guest.

On his way to call on the widow, M'Kewn met Arthur. To curry favor with the lad he urged him to hunt on his own plantation. He got from Arthur an admission that Porgy was a frequent visitor at his home, and told of Porgy's wanting to fight it out.

Later M'Kewn gave his version of the altercation with Porgy to Mrs. Eveleigh, and informed her he knew of her *"friendly loans."* She replied that she had *"a mortgage on all his negroes."* M'Kewn rejoined that the five hundred guineas did not cover their value.

Her disapprobation of him had been aroused: *"Captain Porgy is a gentleman by birth and education who has been doing good service to his country for several years, without pay or reward, and to the grievous*

injury of his own fortune. It seems to me that he deserved every indul-
gence . . . by those who are grateful to heaven for those blessings of
independence which he has helped to win."

The Scotchman replied that he "should have been pleased to in-
dulge" Porgy if he had not resorted to personal insolence.

She gave him a stinging rebuke in the terms of the "code". Was
his "mode of resenting a personal injury" to clothe himself "with the
terrors of the creditor, instead of—"? She paused, thinking she had gone
too far in thus suggesting a "duello," and contented herself with sug-
gesting he might be wiser in showing forbearance toward "such a general
favorite."

Sneeringly, M'Kewn implied Porgy was a particular *favorite with*
her. Now fiercely indignant, she rose. "Let me say, sir . . . that I have
been a soldier's wife; and I have learned lessons from" him. "I am a
woman, sir . . . but if it needs . . . that I should lift the weapon of the
man, I shall feel no womanly fears in doing so. If you have any scruples,
sir, in resenting personal indignities as men are apt to do, I have none."
She had friends who would volunteer to "do battle in her cause," but
would not want them to experience danger while "I am able to stand and
confront the insolent myself. . . . Here, if you please, our conference
must end."

Her dignity and indignation . . . recalling that of Boadicea or Zenobia
awed him. Yet she had one final question. It was a mere savage instinct
that prompted her to "send a shaft at random" which hit its mark. "Do
you know, sir, what has become of that man, Bostwick?" He was al-
most paralyzed, but was able to gasp a denial. He realized she had seen
the rascally squatter at Moncrieff's.

As the summer passed, Porgy continued his inner debate as to which
of the two widows he preferred. Now his attention was more centered
on their faults, or rather on the one outstanding fault of each as a
prospective wife. He feared that, in the case of the wealthy one, he
could not maintain that lordship which a husband should have. (Inter-
estingly enough, a vivid sidelight on the status of women in Simms's
South—at least as he saw it—is his comment that Porgy's ideas were
those of "a period when the sex had not yet determined to set up for
itself. . . .") Mrs. Eveleigh was "quite too masculine." Her wealth
deterred him, as it humbled him before her. (During this summer Lance
married Ellen and moved to the Griffin farm as manager.)

On the other hand, he was disquieted by Mrs. Griffin's "intellectual inferiority"! She had "no intelligent conversation," no wit. The struggle affected his appetite, and he lost weight, even to taking in several inches in his belt. Porgy ascribed it to the heat of the summer; but Millhouse, to the lack of a rich wife to drive off the sheriff.

Meanwhile M'Kewn, like "some great political spider" bided his time, though he was really at work. Porgy received and wrote letters to lawyers.

Crops were good on all three plantations, M'Kewn's, Mrs. Eveleigh's, and Porgy's. "Never had such a crop been seen at Glen-Eberley." Indeed it was the best of the three, and Millhouse's boasting can be well imagined. He had been efficient, but owed much to the fact that the Glen-Eberley fields "had been so long rested." Even his pride and pleasure were nothing to that of the Negroes, who took all the credit, and vaunted over those of the "rival plantations." Porgy gave them a great pork supper after the harvesting. . . ."

The wily M'Kewn set himself to win over young Arthur Eveleigh. He appealed to the "vanities of youth" by his extreme deference. He gave him "a beautiful English pointer." His mother "could not venture to convey all her suspicions to him, of M'Kewn's agency with the outlaws, and with the robbery of the negroes. . . ." (Frankly, I do not see why she could not tell her son her "suspicions"—as that was all they were— even if she had not yet the proof. Arthur would surely have been much easier to dissuade from the influence of M'Kewn. Her not doing so, seems to me a flaw in the book—perhaps a carelessness.)

M'Kewn gradually poisoned the boy's mind with insistence on Porgy's faults—his debts, his recklessness, his enormous appetite and size. Then he artfully conveyed the idea that Porgy was seeking to marry his mother, and that she was encouraging him, an idea the youth "found insupport- able." The moment this fear was forced on him, he rushed home to find the supposed suitor closeted at length with the lady.

What were they conferring about? The fatal "Fall term" was now at hand, and Porgy had been warned by his lawyers that "judgment could not long be averted." He told Tom to dress up, and as they together rode over to see Mrs. Eveleigh, he said, that as Tom was still quite young, he hoped for him marriage and a long happy life.

"But, Tom, if I am to see you live as the slave of that scoundrel, M'Kewn, I should rather you were dead. Now, Tom, I must either sell you to Mrs. Eveleigh, or shoot you."

"Shoot me Tom! Oh! git out, maussa, da's all only you' ole foolish talk. Tom aint for shoot."

"Then I must sell you, Tom, or M'Kewn will have you."

"Ha! I tek' de swamp fuss! I nebber guine lib wid dat crook-eye Scotchman."

"Better live with Mrs. Eveleigh."

"I no so much lub for lib wid woman, nodder, maussa. Woman, maussa, is a most too hard 'pon nigger. Wha' for I must be sell?"

"I owe M'Kewn money—the sheriff will seize you if you belong to me. I wish Mrs. Eveleigh to buy you, to keep you out of his clutches; and if I am ever able to buy you back from her, I will do so. Meanwhile, I will hire you from Mrs. Eveleigh."

When Porgy arrived at Mrs. Eveleigh's, he took Tom with him to see the lady. After Porgy explained his proposal more fully, with the added arrangement that meanwhile he was to hire Tom from the widow, Tom, who had been reluctant, expressed his willingness and promised to be a good servant to the lady. Tom asked God to bless her; and cantered back to Glen-Eberley. Porgy gave her the bill of sale, and received a draft for a hundred guineas.

Arthur "bounced into the room," and spoke with "bare civility" to his old friend, the captain. Porgy, seeing the boy had a fowling piece with him, asked him why he had not during the last month looked for birds at Glen-Eberley. Arthur replied that he could find them at home or at Mr. M'Kewn's. His mother expressed her wish that he would find his birds elsewhere than at the latter place; but he appeared not disposed to defer to his mother simply because she had expressed such a wish, and looking at Porgy said that Mr. M'Kewn seemed "quite as much of the gentleman as most men I've seen."

Porgy at this moment rose. His manner was mild, calm, and dignified; a little touched with sorrow. He felt that he was in at the beginning of something like a scene, and he had no taste for it, or curiosity to witness its close.

"Mrs. Eveleigh, suffer me once more to thank you for your kindness. I shall remember with gratitude what you have done for me. I will trespass no longer. Good-by, ma'am—good-by;" and he shook her hand warmly. "Arthur, I am half tempted to regret that you can find your birds at any other point than Glen-Eberley. We can afford you *friends* there as well as birds; and such friends as will never desert you when the battle's coming on."

To this the youth had no answer. He gave his hand sullenly to the captain, who looked at him kindly and curiously, but with a smile that seemed to say, "I understand all your difficulty, my boy," but, beyond his farewell, he had no more words to say. . . . Riding out of the avenue, he muttered to himself—"That foolish boy; that scoundrel, M'Kewn, has been poisoning his ears. I should not be surprised if the rascal had been telling him that I was courting his mother."

He meditated sadly as he rode. "What a pitfall, what a thing of snares, of serpents, and sorrows, is this miserable life. How the devil hangs upon the footsteps of innocence, turn whither it will, ready to delude, to defraud, to degrade, to destroy. Here is this youth, just as he begins to drink of the better and purer sweets of life, the fiend drops his malignant poison into the bowl; embittering the taste as well as the draught—and shaping the whole future career for sin and sorrow. I had taken a great liking to that boy. He could have made a noble fellow. But, he looks upon me as an enemy. He looks upon his own mother with suspicion. It has needed but a mean cunning on the part of this miserable wretch, M'Kewn, to make him turn upon his natural and best allies. Heaven help us, for with the devil at our elbow, with foes among those who surround us, and the vices and vanities at our own hearts to second their labors, unless Heaven help us in season, and with all its angels, hope and humanity stand but a poor chance for happiness."

Alone with her son, Mrs. Eveleigh began to remonstrate with him for his cold treatment of Captain Porgy. She described him as "a very pleasant associate. I know few gentlemen whose conversation is so sensible and interesting." Arthur replied sarcastically that he looked indeed like a "gentleman with that paunch of his, large as a rice-barrel."

With some feeling she reminded him that Porgy had saved her from "indignity and possibly from death. . . ." She explained that her loans to Porgy were secured by a mortgage.

Pointing to a splendid portrait of Major Eveleigh which hung on the wall, Arthur cried out passionately, "That is my father. . . . Can it be possible you mean to fill his place with such a person as this Captain Porgy?"

With impetuous anger, she accused her son of listening to "that devil of mischief, M'Kewn," and permitting him to whisper to him scandal about his mother; that he had been used by him "as a despicable tool against friend and mother."

Fearfully aroused (it is her most human moment) she defended her right to take another husband if she wished and to consult her own will if she did so. She concluded that Arthur must make his choice between "this evil genius M'Kewn and his mother."

Sobbing, Arthur embraced her, pleading for forgiveness. Little Dory came in and asked what was the matter. After his mother left, Arthur, now ashamed, told the child he was "Very sorry, very."

Meanwhile Porgy was sinking into a kind of apathy of despair. Pinckney wrote him "an affectionate letter full of sympathy, but cutting him off from all further escape" from the sheriff; but did try to persuade the sheriff to be as indulgent as possible.

Porgy read this letter to Millhouse, who, entirely on his own, summoned Lance to a council of war. Lance came to Glen-Eberley armed "cap a pie," and prepared to settle there for the time being. The two made plans to protect the plantation and the Negroes against the "inimy." Porgy pronounced absurd the sergeant's project of resorting to force of arms, but did not actually stop it. The sergeant seized the opportunity to harp on his pet solution, the marriage.

"Hush up, Millhouse. No more of that. It must not be thought of. How will it look for me—I who have been borrowing the widow's money—to propose to pay my debts to her, by making her my wife?"

"And the most ixcellentest way for settling a debt that ever was invented on this airth."

"Why, man, I've gone to her as a beggar. I owe her six hundred guineas. Shall I go to her and offer her payment in a bankrupt husband?"

Millhouse pictured the widow as so eager for the match as to be on the verge of popping the question herself, and declared Porgy must save himself from such an embarrassment, as her heart was actually breaking at the delay. Tom now said that he too favored the marriage, and even Lance suggested it diffidently.

The irrepressible sergeant began to envision a Christmas marriage, with a big "blow-out," and himself giving the "sheriff or M'Kewn or

*any other varmint" who came sharking around "a h—l of a licking."
He was even able to convince himself he had at last made progress in
persuading Porgy, but Lance knew better, for his sympathies had taught
him more about seeing "into the captain's heart."*

*"The next morning at sunrise found the two subordinates astir."
Porgy "expressed no surprise to see Frampton linger away from his
young wife." Lance "quietly assumed that air and attitude of one on
duty . . . accustomed to military authority, and trained up in great
measure by Porgy," he "was prepared to obey at every peril. Of law he
had only vague notions." His only experience, his only education was
his army service. He had come to stand up beside, and for, his feudal
lord—such was really "the relationship," and to break spear for him, and
peril life against all comers. He and the sergeant "mounted guard
alternately." Porgy, however, paid little heed to these militant preparations.*

*That afternoon, the posted Negro scouts brought news of the ap-
proach of a "very stylish looking gentleman, in black habit, driving a
'chaise.' This was the sheriff, the gracious "Colonel———," (For convenience I shall call this person Colonel Blank.) His "solicitude to do an
unpleasant task pleasantly, had prompted him to undertake a task which
is now-a-days commonly confided to a deputy." At the gate of the avenue, he found himself suddenly arrested, a "huge horseman's pistol"
clapped to his head by the uniformed Lance, who announced they were
ready to protect Captain Porgy against his enemies, who were trying to
take his property—"enemies, and varmints, sheriffs, and such like people!" "Frampton's mode of cataloging, showed considerable inexperi-
ence, by which the sheriff was amused, rather than annoyed." He denied
he was the sheriff, introducing himself simply as Colonel Blank.*

*Lance warned him that if he drove up the avenue except under his
charge, he was likely to receive a bullet. Now the sheriff saw approaching the remarkable apparition of the sergeant, who ordered him to take
off his hat, and made various threats. A note from the visitor was carried
in by Lance on the point of Millhouse's sword, to Porgy, who was
inside. The sheriff was beginning to be frightened, and certainly wished
himself out of his "present predicament."*

*All the Negroes except Tom had run off into the swamp. When
Porgy received the note brought in by Lance, his sense of humor got*

the better of him. He looked out the window, and "burst into an uncontrollable fit of laughter."

"Ha! ha! ha! Good, i'faith! excellent! The captor in captivity! Ha! ha! ha! Well, this is promising! The game begins well. We shall have a laugh on our side, at least, whether we lose or not in the long run. Ha! ha! ha!"

The captain made the lieutenant repeat the details—the dialogue—every particular; and the merriment of the captain was renewed. The whole thing struck him amusingly. It appealed to his leading passion for practical jokes. He determined to humor it to the end.

"So, you thought Col. —— the sheriff did you? Ha! ha! ha! admirable! What a story to tell! But, I will go out to him. I must only put a few extra dishes on the table. Here, Tom!—And now, Lance, step out to the sergeant; tell him to watch his prisoner closely. I will come out and see if he is really the colonel, whom I know very well! We must not be imposed upon, Lance! By no means! Ha! ha! ha! The captor in captivity! Very good, by Mercury, very good!"

Lance was now convinced that the captain approved of his proceedings. With Tom's assistance, Porgy "put himself in caparison of war. His uniform was put on, "his belt girded about his waist, sword slung at his side, pistols stuck in his belt, and in his hand he carried a long rifle." Tom also armed himself, with tomahawk, hunting knife, and horseman's pistol.

The sheriff had begun to consider "declaring his indignation, in very strong language." But when he saw Porgy coming out from the house, he wondered whether the captain was crazy, and whether he really meant "to defy the laws." He decided it was prudent to "temporize." Porgy asked Millhouse whom he had in the chaise. The "sheriff cried out—"

"What, Capt. Porgy, don't you know me?"

"Bless me, so it is! It is Col.——. My dear colonel, I am truly rejoiced to see you, and greatly regret that my fellows should have subjected you to 'durance vile' for a single moment. It was all a mistake. Get out, if you please. They took you for some d——d harpy of the law—the sheriff or some one of his vile myrmidons. Get out, my dear fellow, and let us hurry in to dinner. You are just in pudding-time."

"He evidently does not know that I have been made sheriff," was the silent whisper of the colonel to himself, as, accepting the invitation, he descended from the vehicle, which Porgy immediately told Frampton to drive up to the house.

"We have but one single negro on the place," said Porgy; "at sight of you, supposing you the sheriff, every two-legged animal, of dark complexion, took to the swamp. You gave them a scare, I assure you. But come, I am really glad to see you at Glen-Eberley, and just at this moment."

And he shook hands with the sheriff, with the cordial army shake, which threatened to dislocate a member in order to compel remembrance. The sheriff felt a little relieved, even while the usage was so rough. They walked toward the house arm in arm.

"Let me carry your rifle, captain," said the sheriff.

"My rifle! No, indeed, colonel, no! I never part with it. I know not at what moment I may have to use it. There is a skunk of a Scotchman in my neighborhood, who may cross my path some day, and, as I tell you, I am in momentary expectation of the visits of the sheriff, or some of his satellite harpies."

"But you certainly would not draw trigger upon an officer of the law?"

"Would I not!" exclaimed the captain, suddenly stopping in his march, withdrawing his own arm from that of the other, and confronting him with a stern expression. "Would I not?—Will I consent, after fighting the battles of my country for seven years, to be driven from my estate by a d——d civilian—a fellow, probably, who never smelt gunpowder in his life. No! indeed! I will die in harness and in *possession!* They may conquer me—I suppose they will, in time; but I will hold on while I can, do battle to the last, and when they do take possession, they shall walk into it only over my dead body."

"And here's the man to baick you, cappin, by the Lord Harry!"

Such was the speech, delivered with stentor-lungs, from the rear; the sergeant at the same moment amusing himself with thrusting back his sabre into the steel sheath, with such an emphasis, as to make it ring again. The sheriff was startled from his propriety, for a moment, by the sudden illustration which followed the captain's fierce determination.

"They are all mad together," he again whispered to himself; and it might be observed that his deportment became more conciliatory than ever.

"Come, colonel, let us in, now, and see what dinner we shall find awaiting us. A stoup of Jamaica will refresh you after your ride, and me after my scare. The very idea of a sheriff makes me thirst; and to be relieved of this idea, I must drink. Come! In!"

And the captain seized his guest good-naturedly by the arm, and the two ascended to the piazza, the sergeant thundering with heavy tread behind, his sabre sheath rattling against the steps at every stride, and reminded the sheriff, momently of the military nature of the escort. When in the house, he threw off his hat, and Porgy discarded his military cap; the squirrel-skin covering of Millhouse was doffed also, and the three joined in a devout draught of Jamaica.

Dinner was announced, and Porgy seated the sheriff at one end of the table, and himself at the other, and the sergeant and Lance on opposite sides. Porgy and his men kept their weapons at hand. With his borrowed money, Porgy had managed to refurnish his house comfortably and elegantly. On the table, though there was no display of plate, there were fine linen, imposing china, and cut glass.

When the dishes were uncovered, it was with increasing surprise that the sheriff beheld one, within reach of Porgy, containing a pair of highly-polished pistols. He attempted something of a jest when he saw them.

"Really, captain, you can not design that dish for the digestion of any visiter."

"The digestion must depend upon himself," was the cool reply; "but there *are* parties, who might sometimes intrude upon me, for whose special feeding they are provided."

"What! the sheriff, eh?" with a faint chuckle.

"Exactly! Shall I help you to soup, colonel?"

"If you please."

"Bouillé?"

"Thank you—a little."

"You will find it more manageable than bullet."

"Yes, indeed!"

"Try a little of that Madeira with your soup. It improves it wonderfully to my taste. Tom!"—tasting—"you have not put quite enough salt in your soup?"

"Who say so? Enty I know? Tas'e 'em 'gen, maussa! I 'speck you fin' salt 'nough in 'em next time."

The dinner featured "a round of beef" and "a pair of wild ducks." The sheriff began to recover his confidence with his appetite, and to praise Tom's cooking. The sergeant was somewhat mystified by the captain's conduct. The inoffensive guest was surely not the sheriff—yet Porgy seemed to be "playing out a game upon him." The sheriff was impressed by the sergeant's air of fierce suspicion, and also by the quiet manner of Lance. "In this young man he beheld a fixed confidence in his superior, and a readiness to obey orders, which showed that, at a wink, he would be prepared to act, without regard to responsibilities."

Dessert was Tom's rice pudding, voted good by all, followed by raisins, peanuts, and black walnuts, with more Madeira. There was varied conversation. The sheriff still declared it seemed incredible to him "that you are all armed and equipped here to resist the operations of the law."

"Indeed!" said Porgy, looking grave. "You find it difficult to understand, and why? Is it so strange that I should be unwilling to surrender all my possessions, at the first demand, and without a struggle."

"But you could scarcely expect to make resistance to the laws of the land. The sheriff is armed with a sovereign power for the time. How would you hope to hold out against him?"

"You mean to say that he would overwhelm me with the *posse comitatus?*"

"Ay, and if need, call out the military!"

"To be sure he may, and certainly there is a power to which my own must succumb. What then? If I am to yield up all the goods of life, why not life also? What is life to me? You know my tastes and habits. You know how I have lived and how I still live. Some men will tell you that I am a glutton, others, that I imbue my appetites equally with my taste and philosophies; all agree that I am, essentially, a good deal of an animal—that I was profligate in youth that I might enjoy life, and that in the good things of this life, I find life itself. I won't deny the charge. Be it so. Am I to survive the good things, and yet cherish the life? Wherefore? What does Shylock say—whom by-the-way, I take to be a very shrewd and sensible fellow, and a greatly ill-used rascal—

——'You take my life
When you do take the means whereby I live!'

And, when I have perilled my life a thousand times for the benefit of other people's goods, shall I not venture it for the protection of my own?"

"But, my dear captain there is a material difference between doing a thing with the sanction of the law, and in defiance of it."

"None to me! Don't you see, my dear colonel, that I am prepared to sacrifice my life with my property, and that law can in no way, exact a higher forfeit? But d—n the law! We've had enough of it for the present. Fill up your glass. You will find that Madeira prime. It is from an ancient cellar!"

"Thank you! [Fills.] Well, my dear captain, suffer me to hope for you an escape from the clutches of the law by legitimate means!"

"I'm obliged to you, my dear colonel; but we army men don't care much about the means, so that we effect the escape. I am for stratagem or fight, sap or storm, just as the best policy councils. Life, after all, is a constant warfare. Rogues are only enemies in lambskins, or ermine. They do not care to cut my throat so long as I have a purse to cut; they will not care to drive me to desperation, so long as it is profitable to them that I should live. I know them! I defy them! I can die without a grunt to-morrow. I have neither wife, nor child, nor mother, nor sister, to deplore my fate, or to profit by my departure. I am, with the exception of these two faithful comrades of mine, utterly alone in the world. They shall live with me while I live. They would die for me to-morrow. Were a man but to lift a finger against me, to assail my life, or my meanest fortunes, they would be into him with bullet and bayonet, and need not a signal from me."

"That's a rightious truth, by the Hokies!" exclaimed the sergeant, with his one fist thundering down upon the table. The lieutenant's eyes brightened keenly, and he looked to the captain, but he said nothing.

"I have no doubt they are true and faithful friends, captain," said the sheriff; "but suppose now, only suppose, I say, the sheriff was suddenly to appear among you, just as I am here now, and were to—"

He was stopped! Stopped in an instant, as by a thunderbolt, by the prompt reply and action of Porgy.

"Suppose the sheriff in you! Ha! suppose the rest for yourself.—See!"

And with the wild but determined look and action of a desperate man, he seized both pistols lying in the dish before him, stood up, reached as far over the table as he could, and covered the figure of the amiable but indiscreet sheriff with both muzzles cocking the weapons as he did so. The sheriff involuntarily dodged and threw up his hands. At the same instant, and as soon as the purpose of the superior had been understood by Millhouse and the lieutenant, they were both upon their feet—the sergeant swinging his sabre over the head of the supposed offender; while Frampton, more silent, but quite as decided, while he swung his sword aloft with one hand, grasped with the other the well-powdered shock of the sheriff, in an attitude very like that which we see employed by the ferocious Blue Beard in the opera, when the poor wife is tremblingly crying out for her brother. Here was an unpremeditated *coup de theatre!* Two swords crossed in air above the victim,—two pistols, with each broad muzzle almost jammed against his own; every eye savagely fixed upon him, and all parties seeming to await only the farther word of provocation from his lips. Nothing had been more instantaneous. The subordinates were machines, to whom Porgy furnished all the impulse. Their action followed his will, as soon as it was expressed. There was no questioning it, and the amiable sheriff was so much paralyzed by the display, that it was only with much effort that he could cry out— "But, my dear captain, don't suppose me the enemy—the assailant—the d——d sheriff or any of his myrmidons."

"By no means, colonel; but you supposed a case in order to see whether, and how, we were prepared for it; and it was essential that you should have a proper demonstration. You have seen; be easy; fill up your glass, my dear sir, and forgive my merry men here for the earnestness with which they performed their parts. They had no reason, indeed, to suppose that I was not serious. You see what chance a *bona-fide* sheriff would stand, if he aimed at any showing here!"

Porgy had resumed his seat, and restored the pistols to the dish as coolly as the actor, who takes his brandy and water, equal parts, after strangling his wife, stabbing the traitor, and dying famously in the person of Othello. It was not so easy for Millhouse to throw off his tragic aspect.

The excellent sheriff no longer felt any call to trespass in experiments upon the legal antipathies of the captain of partisans and his observant followers. He steered wide of all allusions from thenceforth to the officer of the law, and his possible appearance in the precincts. He felt really impressed with the danger of any one who should, with *malice prepense,* do so, in the evidently diseased condition of mind and mood prevailing at Glen-Eberley. That he should thus forbear, however, was by no means agreeable to his self-esteem or his sense of duty. He was uncomfortable when he thought of his official station, and the sealed documents in his pockets. He had come there to make a levy on land and negroes, without dreaming that he should encounter any opposition. Resistance, with force of arms, was entirely beyond his imaginings; and to depart, having done nothing was at once a *lachesse* of duty and a personal mortification. More than once he felt like plucking up his drowning courage, and perilling his life upon his manhood—boldly challenging the danger, and facing it with folded arms of defiance; but, on all such occasions, as if Porgy and his followers knew, by instinct, his emotions, there would occur some explosion, or some symptom of explosion, which would remind him vividly of the smouldering volcano upon which he sat. For example, he once made an allusion, deliberately designed, to M'Kewn; and Millhouse flared up, and fumbled his sabre, and gnashed his teeth, even as the Frenchman when he cries, "Sacre!" through his mustache, or the Spaniard when he growls "Demonios!" and flourishes his dagger. Frampton showed similar signs of impatience —while Porgy exclaimed aloud, striking his fist down upon the table:—

"Don't mention that scoundrel's name in my hearing, colonel! I feel wolfish when I hear of him. Let him but cross my path; let any of his myrmidons but put themselves in my way, and if I do not crop their ears, close to the head, then there's no edge to any weapon in my household."

"But is he not a neighbor, captain?"

"Neighbor! Well, sir, I suppose you may call him a neighbor, even as the devil is a neighbor, and is said to take free lodgings in every man's dwelling; but such neighborhood does not prevent us from flinging the wretch out of the windows, whenever our good saints give us the necessary succor. Don't speak of such a scoundrel to my ears, or I may do you the injustice to suppose you are his friend."

The sheriff took the warning, and M'Kewn was dropped, and all subjects were dropped which were likely to stir up the bile and black blood in the bosoms of the host and his companions. The sheriff resigned himself to his fate, and to the policy of doing nothing with as much grace as possible. He was not only frightened from the purpose for which he came, but the feeling of good fellowship momently grew stronger with the circulation of the wine, and the excellent spirits of the captain. The latter, in all respects, except the one, was on his best behavior, and in most amiable temper. He never showed himself more really humorous and delightful as a companion in all his life. The sheriff was charmed and listened. He was soothed and satisfied. His philosophy came into the support of his necessity. He reasoned thus, accordingly:—

"There is no need to push the matter! Porgy's estate is good, at any moment, for this debt. Every day increases the value of both lands and negroes. Were I to seize and sell now, the property would be sacrificed. It would pay the debt, but leave nothing over to the good fellow, who has been serving his country in a long and honorable warfare. D—n the fellow! I like him, and he shall have indulgence as long as I can grant it!"

As soon as he had thus "resolved that his visit should no longer have a professional object, the play was easy. . . . He felt the charm of his host's fun and philosophy; and he, too, had good things in his keeping. When he had once resolved to sink the sheriff, he . . . let himself out, and became, what he was known to be in the army, a really good fellow, of no savage inclinations, fond of a jovial circle, and capable of making himself the life of it. . . . The day passed, and the party of four had not left the table." All smoked but Lance; coffee, Jamaica, and Madeira were served. Cards followed, and at midnight, when the sheriff rose, he had lost thirty shillings to Millhouse, who "became more reconciled to the suspicious guest" with every shilling he won from him.

When next morning, after the colonel's departure, "—which took place soon after an early breakfast—" Millhouse was praising "his good qualities and companionable virtues," the "captain of partisans laid his hand on his shoulder—"

"Ah! Millhouse, but you don't know the man."

"What! he's Col. ———, aint he?"

"Yes."

"And a main good fellow, I say."

"Well enough;—well enough; but—your ear, sergeant."

The latter yielded it; the captain stooped as if to whisper—then in deep, solemn accents, as if drawn up from immeasurable depths, he cried out:—

"THE COLONEL IS THE SHERIFF!"

The sergeant made but one bounce, and was across the room; his countenance wo-begone with surprise amounting to terror. His involuntary utterance, occasioned equally by what he had heard, and the tone of voice employed in telling it, was characteristic of his early attention when at church service.

"Hairk from the tombs! The sheriff, cappin!"

"The sheriff!"

"What! *our* sheriff, what's a-coming a'ter *our* goods and chattels."

"The same!"

"Oh! ef I'd ha' knowed it!—I'll be a'ter him!—Lance!"

"No! Do nothing of the kind! We've got off, thus far, very well. The joke is a good one, upon which I can feed fat with laughter for a month. I must ride over and tell the widow. How her sides will shake!"

After Porgy had pointed out that the colonel's civility resulted partly from the brandishing of the weapons, Millhouse made the house "shake with his wild yells of laughter." Lance quietly chuckled. Porgy had his horse saddled and rode over to Mrs. Eveleigh's. "The widow did laugh; dignity, in those days, did not deny the privileges of an honest cachination even to nobility . . . her sides did shake: but not vulgarly. . . . It was a lady-like show of shaking. . . ."

When she had recovered, she asked whether he had not been "flying in the face of the law"; but Porgy argued he had done nothing illegal, because the sheriff had "never showed himself in that character." She warned him that, nevertheless, the sheriff would come again.

"I shall play out the play, my dear Mrs. Eveleigh, as it has begun. I must have the fun in full; and for the rest,—why, I will content myself with the proverb of the patriarch—'Sufficient for the day is the evil thereof.' It will be time enough to look out for the bolt when we hear the thunder."

"Too late—the flash!"

"Precisely, my dear widow, precisely that! It is because the case is one against which no precautions can avail, that I choose to look out for the bolt after it strikes and not before. But, good-by, I must ride back and write to Pinckney all about this matter. He must share the fun.

He will relish it, I know. I would he had been a spectator! The thing
is indescribable;—only to be seen in the visages of Millhouse, Lance, and
the sheriff, as the two crossed weapons over his head, and I faced him
out of countenance with my unmuzzled bull-dogs. My dear widow,
would you believe it, the innocent pups that looked so fiercely in the
eyes of the sheriff, were toothless. There was no load in either. But,
good-by; God bless you! I must get back in a hurry. I rode over only
that you should enjoy the story."

*The story spread. That very night Millhouse entertained Fordham
and M'Kewn's overseer by narrating it at length. "M'Kewn's man
relished it quite as much as did Fordham," and enlightened his employer
next morning.*

*The next day M'Kewn put pressure on the sheriff to effect the fore-
closure. That official, rather shamefacedly, pleaded leniency for Porgy,
but was induced to send his deputy Absalom Crooks at once on the
business. Crooks was in the sheriff's office, and was known by M'Kewn
to be "one of the very best bull-terriers of the law—a broad shouldered,
stout, short little fellow, with no crook about him, except in his "bowed
legs, while his arms hung out from his body at large range. He had a
red head, red face, red whiskers, red waistcoat, and was tolerably well
read in the law." M'Kewn promised the man a fine guinea tip, and
warned him he would be dealing with cunning fellows who would try
to scare him. Crooks was very belligerent at any suggestion that Porgy's
men could frighten him.*

*Crooks set off for Glen-Eberley, the documents in his pockets. He
felt adequately armed with the "formidable parchment," with its "terrific
seals of state." He had never served in the wars, though pugnacious . . .
and he had no notion of any power which . . . could gainsay or run
counter to that of the law." A judge was, for him, the most potent of
personages. "He was yet to become familiar with a feudal baron, and
to comprehend the extent of his authority."*

*At the entrance to the avenue at Glen-Eberley, he was knocked out
of his saddle by Lance, who confronted him with pistols, and told him
he was a prisoner, but should have a fair trial at the hands of Porgy.
Lance allowed him to proceed, but he next had to get by the formidable
Millhouse. Crooks, furiously indignant, stated boldly he was there to
make the levy on the plantation in satisfaction of the judgment in the*

*case. Millhouse erupted with choice epithets, such as "mean little copper-
headed son of a skunk." The deputy cried that the sergeant would
"sweat for all this"; but he was forced into the hall and into a seat.*

"We've got him, cappin!" cried out Millhouse to Porgy in his chamber. The captain of partisans had been reaping the stubble field, the
autumnal harvests of his chin, which were quite too grisly to be suffered
to offend his own or other eyes. He came with coat off, sleeves rolled
up, neck bare, and razor in his grasp. The moment he beheld the
deputy, he cried out—

"Heavens! What a monster! What a horrible looking creature!
What a beard. Coppery-red; a perfect jungle, and full, no doubt, of all
sorts of diminutive beasts. Sergeant, we must have that fellow's beard
off."

Millhouse absolutely shouted at the idea.

"Tom!" roared the captain. Tom appeared at the door. "Quick,
Tom, soap and napkin; and take off that horrid beard."

Crooks would have bounded from his seat. He prided himself on his
beard. Its coppery red, apparently so offensive to all about him, was to
him the perfection of beauty. Its red he held to be that of roses, and as
for the amplitude of it, its wild, wide-spread bushy dimensions, these he
stroked a thousand times a day with an affection which may be imagined.
To lose his beard, even in jest, was almost as bad as to lose his scalp.
He now began feverishly to apprehend, that with such companions, he
should lose both. He leaped up, but was immediately thrust back into
his seat by the ready hands of his attendants.

"I won't submit to this. I tell you—I warn you—I am an officer of
justice. I'm here under the great seal of the state. I'm on official duties.
I'm under the sacred protection of the law."

"How horribly he shouts! But, with such a beard, what mortal man
can talk like a human being. You don't understand a word he says,
sergeant?"

"Not a word! I reckon it's a sort of nigger speech from Africa."

"Do you understand the savage creature, Lance?"

"I reckon's he's crazy, captain," answered Lance.

"Truly, I think so. He will need a strait jacket. But there's no judging rightly his condition till we take off that brush."

"Let's burn it off, cappin."

"No! no! he may be human, and that might hurt him. We'll shave it off, and then see what he really is. I suspect he belongs to the monkey species—he's an orang-outang;—you know what that is, sergeant."

"Half man, half horse, and two parts alligator, I reckin."

"You're very nigh the mark. Hurrah, Tom! make haste."

Tom made his appearance with basin, towel, soap, &c. The deputy seeing his danger, and that the affair was looking serious, made another effort to escape from the clutches in which he was held, and accompanied the effort by a fearful outcry, touching the terrors of the law. But in vain.

"Tie him down. Handkerchief, there, Tom. Secure him, so that he may not do himself harm. He is certainly very wild. He must have been only lately caught. Somebody must have put these clothes on him by force."

While the captain thus dilated, his assistants busied themselves in securing the deputy to his seat. His arms were tethered to the back of the chair, which was one of those massive mahogany receptacles so common at that period, and representing a much earlier period in the history of English civilization. The chair was, in fact, modelled upon the times of Elizabeth. Thus secured, with his head held back, the napkin tucked beneath his chin, Tom approached and proceeded to lay on the lather. The thick soapy mass was thrust *ad libitum* into mouth and nostrils. The deputy yelled, but as the soap made fearful progress into his jaws at every opening, he was, perforce, content to sputter, and sneeze, and kick and writhe. All efforts were unavailing. His captors were resolute in their fun. "Law!" he cried. "Lather!" cried Porgy; and Tom obeyed. Half suffocated, though more furious than ever, Crooks finally yielded, and Tom proceeded to apply the razor. Tom had acquired, in camp, the arts of the barber, as well as the cook. He was not so dextrous as determined. Crooks saw that it was at his own peril that he writhed, or twisted, or reared his head, or stuck out his chin unnecessarily. Tom would say quietly:—

"You only guine to wussen youse'f, buckrah—ef you is a buckrah—wid you kickings and cawortings. Better you keep youself easy, ef you don't want me for slice off you nose."

Here was a new peril. Slice off his nose! The loss of the petted beard was a great evil—but to lose his nose also, was such as it made him doubly sweat to meditate.

"Don't cut off his nose, Tom," cried Porgy, with a great air of concern. "This class of animals seldom have much to spare; and the loss of such a member, would really disfigure the face terribly."

"Lord, cappin, nothing could make such a critter more ugly than he is," answered Millhouse; "but he could lose an inch of snout and never miss it. Why, Lord, he's got a nose like a baggonet and a most hafe as long!"

Tom, meanwhile, prosecuted his labor with diligence. He was a bold cutter. It was all army practice with him—swift, slashing, reckless, not easily stopped by trifling impediments. At every swoop, Crooks found a wide waste of forest growth removed; huge tracts of warm furze disappeared, as the prairie grass in autumn, under the fire. Soon, the entire wilderness of brush was cleaned up. The territory was now smooth, and the light let in upon a region that had not seen the day for half a dozen years. Crooks was no longer the same man; he felt cold about the chin; but his chill greatly increased when he heard Tom ask—

"Must tek' off he hair now, maussa? He look berry bad and ugly. I reckin he must be full of warmints."

Porgy seemed for a moment to meditate the matter; but he waived Tom off.

"No! that's enough, Tom, for the present. I think we may now make out the species of the animal."

"I'm the deputy sheriff—my name's Crooks."

"A well-known warmint, cappin. I reckon you mout as well skin him altogether. Jest you take off the scalp now, and we'll be sure to know him next time."

"No! no! It is not so much that we may know him, as that he may know us hereafter. I see what he is. Let him go now. I reckon he's tame enough for the present. Now, let him have a swallow of Jamaica."

"I drink nothing in this house!" cried the deputy rising to his feet.

"Then you lose the taste of a mighty good dram of liquor."

"And I warn you all—all three of you—that you shall answer for this assault and battery. You, Captain Porgy—I know you—and you, and you, I will have it all out of you three, if there's any law in the land."

"You won't drink," said Porgy.

"Not a drop with you, or in this house."

"Will you eat?"

"Not a mouthful!"

"Then we've done all we can do for you, unless you desire that Tom should take off that shock. It is unnecessarily thick and long. Can that be hair?"

"Look you, Captain Porgy, I've submitted to your assaults and batteries because I could not help myself."

"A mighty good reason too!"

"But I will have redress. Now, sir, I will do my duty, and here I give you notice, that in the character of the Sheriff of—"

"Boo! woo! woo! woo! Shall I muzzle him, cappin?"

"No! let him go. Depart, my good fellow, while your bones are whole. We have done for you the best we could."

"I'll not go until I have made a levy upon all the lands and negroes, the goods and chattels of this estate of Glen-Eberley, under the authority of the papers which I now carry, and which I will read for the benefit—"

By this time he had drawn the documents out of his pocket.

"Beware how you attempt to read any of those vile heathen documents here," said Porgy, assuming an air of great sternness.

"State of South Carolina!" began the deputy.

"As surely as you attempt to read that paper, I will make you eat it!"

"Eat it! I'll eat nothing in this house!"

"We'll see to that."

"State of South Carolina—" resumed the deputy.

"Seize him," cried Porgy—"seize him!"

And, in the twinkling of an eye, Frampton caught Crooks in his embrace, and Millhouse set his enormous thumb and forefinger about his neck, and the deputy was forced back into his chair. The paper was snatched by the lieutenant from his hand.

"In the name of the state!" screamed the deputy.

"Feed him with it!" shouted Porgy.

"I levy and seize, distrein and take possession—" began the deputy at a rapid rate, but his mouth was suddenly filled with his documents. The execution was crammed into his jaws—a part of it at least; and the voice of the sergeant, in accents too clear and loud to be misunderstood, advised him what to do with it.

"Feed or suffocate, you skunk."

"You're choking me to death!"

"Feed, then! chaw! swallow!" And, at every word, the sergeant plied the unhappy deputy, with a fragment of the execution. It was in vain that he flounced and floundered, strove, kicked, and scuffled with his persecutor. The iron arm of Millhouse was seconded with an equally iron will, and, perforce, the victim was compelled to chew and mouth the musty document.

"My God! do you mean to kill me?"

"Not unless good feeding will do it. You love the law, you live on it, and ought to be able to digest it. Give him another mouthful, sergeant. It must all be eaten. It is not too much for one meal."

With every bit offered, and finally forced upon the deputy, the same struggle followed, the same unavailing resistance. He was compelled to eat. Nothing but the seal remained. This was not then the fiction which it is in recent times. It was not then thought quite sufficient to write *'locus sigilli,'* and withhold the seal itself. In the present case this was a goodly circular plate of red wax, of some dimensions. It was now offered to the unwilling feeder. At the sight of it the fellow cried out with horror—"I can't eat that! It'll be the death of me. It's got poison in it."

"Ah! ha! is it so? And do you bring p'ison into a gentleman's family, and try to sarve it on him. Well, it's only your own medicine, my honey; you must eat it with the rest. The physic of a law paper kaint be good onless the seal goes with it. Bite! Eat! or I'll——"

But for the interposition of the captain, the sergeant would have persisted in testing to the utmost the capacities of Crooks' stomach. Fortunately, the former was disposed to more indulgence.

"Let him off," said he, "he's had enough. Now give him some Jamaica;—or, perhaps, you'll prefer an emetic, my good fellow, to produce reaction. I can have you a little tartar in a second."

"No! no!" cried Crooks with choking accents—"The rum! the rum!"

The liquor was poured out for him, and the glass put into his hands; as he was about to drink, Millhouse exclaimed—

"Ha! ha! I know'd you'd hev' to come to it at last. You swore you wouldn't eat or drink in this house. You've done both!"

The taunt was enough. The deputy dashed down the untasted liquor, smashing the glass upon the floor.

"Curse the house!" he cried, "and all that's in it!" and shaking his hand in fury, he broke through all restraint, and disappeared from the apartment.

"After him, boys, and see that he clears out. Attend him to the out-posts, Lance! He will hardly venture back with other documents."

Very soon, however, the captain began to have second thoughts about the affair. "It was not so much that he had outraged the laws of the land, as that he had violated those of humanity." He "began to feel ashamed," as he was really revolted at any unnecessary brutality. He did not this time go to report the adventure to the widow, but the tale got about.

Crooks, "boiling with fury," rushed over to tell M'Kewn, who was secretly pleased, as the occurrence might fasten odium upon our partisan, whose "patriotic services had otherwise made him so popular." M'Kewn breathed no such thoughts to the deputy, but gave him five guineas, and a peremptory letter to the sheriff.

Pinckney and Parsons, Porgy's sympathetic lawyers, tried to pacify things, and even claimed Crooks's appearance had been greatly improved. General Marion and Colonel Singleton, both fortunately in Charleston, helped persuade the sheriff to delay. Porgy's friends began to pledge funds to satisfy his debt to M'Kewn, and to think of offering hush money to Crooks, although the lawyers surmised the latter would be "unapproachable," until the beard had once more grown "to former ravishing proportions."

Porgy, unlike Millhouse, knew the truce might not last; but mean-while enjoyed the November hunting with Lance and the now recon-ciled Arthur. His sports did not lessen the number of his visits to the two widows, and the indefatigable Millhouse harped again on his pet project of the marriage with the wealthier one, but Porgy clung to his conviction that "as a man of honor, he could not approach her as a suitor, until he had paid her his debt," or at least "extricated himself from the meshes of the law." Then—perhaps. . . .

Meanwhile M'Kewn had greatly prospered. He felt he had ensnared Porgy and other victims. He had a good crop of rice; he had made great profits by buying African slaves from a "virtuous puritan captain, of Rhode Island." He had begun to take his pleasures, and to think of marriage, though he knew he had no chance with Mrs. Eveleigh.

After a big dinner, served with much wine, for bachelor friends, M'Kewn was sitting alone by his fireside, sipping from a big silver pitcher of whiskey-punch, and gloating over his prospective triumph over Porgy. He was awakened from a pleasant half-sleep to see the grinning face of—Bostwick. Was it a ghost? Had the seas thrown up their victim? A hand on his shoulder, and a voice demanding "that hundred guineas" made him realize Bostwick was only too much alive.

Bostwick averred M'Kewn really owed him thousands for all he had done to him. The squatter had, on arriving in Barbados, contrived to blow up the ship with M'Kewn's friends aboard. Bostwick thoroughly enjoyed vaunting his power over M'Kewn, who began to maneuver to try to get Bostwick to bring him the papers *which were in the widow's box. Bostwick extracted one hundred guineas then, with promise of another hundred when he brought the papers, but made no promise that even then M'Kewn would be rid of him.*

Bostwick indeed did find the box with the papers *in the hollow of the cypress where he had hidden it. On his way to his home, he saw Arthur Eveleigh kissing Dory as they were getting water at a spring. After Bostwick reached home, he began to realize he was sick. After several days of lying in pain, he sent Dory for M'Kewn, and making a supreme effort, rose from his sick bed to go and get the box and bring it to his cabin, meanwhile dreaming to do great things for Dory and his other children with the money he would extort from the Scotchman.*

The sheriff had now planned to take extreme measures, and Porgy learned that he was coming with his posse comitatus *to take Glen-Eberley. Millhouse, as can well be imagined took charge of making the mansion into a veritable defended castle. Lance was delegated to take the Negroes and hide them in the swamp, and then to act as a scout to forestall any invaders before these actually reached the mansion. Who should come along but the lank Dr. Oakenburg and the good-looking George Dennison, old cronies, it will be remembered, of Porgy? Lance met them, and they were willing to aid in the defense, despite the doctor's timidities.*

Porgy ordered that "none of the weapons should be charged with ball"; his aim was only to frighten the invaders, and to avoid all casualties. As the party of the sheriff approached, they were attacked from behind by Lance and the two newly-come followers of Porgy, and by Millhouse and Tom coming out from the house. Tom made the sheriff a prisoner, as Millhouse did the fiercely struggling Crooks. Porgy prevented Tom from stripping off the sheriff's clothes, although he was usually allowed to possess himself of the garments of enemies. Porgy

made something in the way of apology; the sheriff suggested a duel;
but was gradually mollified by Porgy's geniality.

Pinckney had come out from the city to prevent the arrest, but the
sheriff had got a head start and attempted to storm Porgy's mansion.
Abetted by Pinckney, Porgy was able to persuade the sheriff to accept
both his genial hospitality and his apologies. Jamaica was being served,
and Pinckney was apparently preparing to arrange some sort of possible
settlement, when Lance rushed in to report that Bostwick had managed
to come home, and had sent for M'Kewn. Lance thought it was a
chance at last to get the box.

Bostwick was very ill, but kept declaring that gold would cure him,
and now demanded five hundred guineas, dreaming such money would
enable Dory to marry young Eveleigh. M'Kewn suspected that a pile
of bed clothes was suspiciously large—indeed the box was under them.
The two criminals were grappling, when Porgy entered with his group,
Pinckney, and the sheriff, who arrested M'Kewn. Bostwick turned
state's witness, and under oath administered by Pinckney, gave a full
account of M'Kewn's Negro-stealing and other villainies. Pinckney now
saw that Bostwick was dying of the smallpox.

Bostwick, in a dying delirium, confessed his own evil doings, but all
the time clinging to his vision of Dory having all the money. Fortunate-
ly no one caught the dread disease, some having been inoculated, and
every precaution being taken for the others.

M'Kewn was imprisoned, and confessed all. There was ample evi-
dence, however, to convict him in any case. M'Kewn, full of Jamaica,
began to rave about being dragged to the gallows by Bostwick—as the
squatter had more than once predicted—and blew out his brains with a
pistol.

Glen-Eberley . . . was made secure to its proprietor. Our captain of
partisans was relieved of all his embarrassments. His debt to Mrs. Eveleigh was not of this order. The profits of the plantation were quite
adequate, with a few years of indulgence, to liquidate this, and all other
obligations of a pecuniary nature. Porgy, at last, found shelter beneath
his fig-tree, with none to make him afraid. He had his friends about
him, his singing-bird, and his puzzle in a bottle. George Dennison and
Doctor Oakenburg, much to the disquiet of Millhouse, became portions
of the establishment. The one furnished the ballads for the evening

fireside; the other was content to provoke the wit of others, without possessing a spark of it himself. The sergeant still delivered the law from his self-established tripod. He was still an oracle who suffered no dog to bark. Lance Frampton was a frequent visitor, and so once more, was Arthur Eveleigh, satisfied to seek good fellowship, and piquant matter of remark, though still occasionally suspicious of the captain's inclinations to his mother. On this subject, however, he no longer ventured to exhibit his boyish petulance. The one stern rebuke of his otherwise gentle and affectionate mother, had proved quite sufficient to curb, at least for the present, the young tiger striving within him; and, to sum up in a word, Glen-Eberley presented to the eye the condition of a well-managed household, in which the parties were all at peace with themselves and one another.

The same thing might be said of the neighborhood. The genial moods prevailing in the one household radiated in all directions. Glen-Eberley became a sort of center for the parish civilization. The charm was great—a sort of salient attraction—which drew the gentry, all around, within the sphere of its genial, yet provocative influences. Free of anxiety, Porgy resumed his ancient spirit. The piquancy of his society, was everywhere acknowledged; and, with the sergeant and Doctor Oakenburg as his foils, the humor of our captain of partisans was irresistible. Fun and philosophy were strangely mingled in him, and they wrought together in unison. To rise from a practical jest into fields of fanciful speculation, was an habitual exercise with our camp philosopher. To narrate the experiences through which he had gone, delivering history and biography, anecdote and opinion, with the ease of a well bred gentleman over his wine and walnuts, was to him an art familiar as the adjustment of his neck-cloth.—And these things were all delivered with a spirit and a quaintness giving them wonderful relish, and which was peculiarly his own. Thus the days glided by as if all were winged with sunshine—Thus the nights escaped all efforts to delay them, too brief for the enjoyment which they brought. It may be that we shall some days depict these happy times, the "Humors of Glen-Eberley," even as they were well remembered by many, thirty years ago, in all that cluster of parishes which lie between the Ashley and the eastern margin of the Savannah; but, at present, we can refer to them only. Enough, that peace reigned in the household, under the strong will, and the happy temperament of its chief; that the dangers which threatened from without, were all overcome, in consequence of the events already recorded; the sheriff had been soothed by ample apologies from Porgy, to which Pinckney easily persuaded him; and Crooks, the deputy, seasonably sauced with good words and hush-money, was easily persuaded to believe that his digestion was totally unhurt by the unnatural sort of repast which he had been made to swallow by the lawless partisans. Tom, we may here mention, was bought back from the widow Eveleigh, and received a gift of himself, from Porgy, which he cunningly rejected.

"No! no! maussa," he cried, with a sly shake of the head, "I kain't t'ink ob letting you off dis way. Ef *I* doesn't b'long to *you, you* b'longs to *me!* You hab for keep dis nigger long as he lib; and him for keep you. You hab for fin' he didner, and Tom hab for cook 'em. Free nigger no hab any body for fin' 'em he bittle [victuals]; and de man wha' hab sense and good maussa, at de same time, he's a d — n pertickilar great big fool, for let he maussa off from keep 'em and fin' 'em. I no guine to be free no way you kin fix it; so maussa, don't you bodder me wid dis nonsense t'ing 'bout free paper any more. I's well off whar' I is, I tell you; and I much rudder [rather] b'long to good maussa, wha' I lub, dan be my own maussa and quarrel wid mese'f ebbery day. Da's it! You yerry now? I say de wud for all! *You* b'longs to *me* Tom, jes' as much as me Tom b'long to *you;* and you nebber guine git *you* free paper from me long as you lib."

Thus the matter was settled, and Tom continued to the end of the chapter, the cook and proprietor of his master.

It was probably three months after his emancipation from the bond of the sheriff, that Captain Porgy, one morning, made his appearance at breakfast in full dress. His toilet had been prepared with a much nicer care than usual. His beard, which, we shame to confess, was sometimes allowed to grow wild for a week, was now carefully pruned down, leaving the smoothest possible surface of chin and cheek. He wore his buff small clothes, and his new blue coat, with great shining buttons. His neck-cloth was a sky blue silk, which had before been worn. His silk stockings were of the most irreproachable flesh color, and Pompey had done his best to polish his shoes, so as to make them emulate, in some degree, the glittering shine of the fine patent leather of the present day. The whole appearance of our captain was so fresh and so unique, that his presence caused an immediate sensation. The improvement in his toilet struck all parties. Millhouse could not forbear an exclamation, and even Oakenburg opened his eyes as he might have done at the discovery of a new and hitherto unsuspected species of rattlesnake or viper. Dennison only smiled, and said something touching the premature coming of the spring.

"We shall soon be looking for the swallows, captain."

"One would think that we had them here already," replied the captain, glancing obliquely at the enormous bowls of coffee which Pomp was pouring out at the moment.

After breakfast Porgy ordered his horse and rode away. Millhouse announced to Dennison and Oakenburg that "He's gone a-courting," and, certain of the outcome, began to gloat over having so many "niggers" under his direction. He predicted that the new wife would clean house, and sweep out "you idle fellers." Dennison only laughed.

Meanwhile, Porgy pursued his way, as the sergeant had truly conjectured, to the dwelling of the widow Eveleigh. The sergeant had no less truly divined his object in the visit. For some time past, the captain had been meditating the obligations which he owed the widow. He reflected upon what Millhouse had repeatedly suggested to him, in respect to the tender sort of interest which she was supposed to feel for himself. This might be a well-founded suggestion. Repeated examinations of the matter, in his own mind, had not persuaded him that the interest of the widow was anything more than that of a friend. Still, it was possible; and if it were really the case that she entertained any stronger sentiment in his favor, it would certainly, as the sergeant had said—"be a most cruelsome thing that she shouldn't hev' the man she wanted, pretickilarly when she had done so much for his sarcumstances." Porgy felt the ingratitude of any such neglect, on his part, supposing any such feeling on hers, and gratitude furnished a crutch where love might have faltered lamely and failed in his approaches. Repeated meditations had brought the captain to a definite conclusion; and he had armed himself to "come to the sticking point," in other words, to make her a formal offer, of hand and heart and household.

Fortunately for his purposes he found her at home and alone. Dory had gone on a visit to her mother—Arthur had set forth on a deer hunt with Frampton and some other young men. This was probably known to Porgy when he chose this day for his demonstrations. He found the widow as kind and frank, lively and agreeable, as ever; and after chatting

on a variety of topics, he gradually brought the one subject in particular
to bear. He was very nice, and as he thought, very judicious in his preliminaries. He discoursed of marriage in the abstract as a beautiful and
admirably-conceived condition for human beings; he discoursed of his
own wants in particular. Of course, he forebore any allusion to what
might be supposed her wants also. He was pleading and humble and
solicitous, and reasonable and reverential, and touching and truthful;—
and, in short, without throwing himself absolutely at her feet, he declared himself so, and without actually taking her in his arms, he avowed
his great anxiety to do so;—and this, we are bound to say, in the best
possible style with proper modesty and misgiving.

The widow, with a sweet smile, laid her hand upon his own, and
said as gently and tenderly, but as calmly as possible:—

"My dear captain, why is it that men and women can not maintain
an intercourse, as friends, without seeking any other relation. Is it not
astonishing that such a thing should seem impossible to everybody?
Now, why should not you and I be true friends, loving friends, trusting
each other with the utmost confidence, coming and going when we
please—welcomed when we come, regretted when we have to depart—
and never perilling the intimacy of friendship by the fetters of matrimony. Can't it be so with us, my dear captain—and why not? I confess
I think—I feel—that we may be very dear friends, captain, for all our
lives; glad in each other's society, doing each other kindly and affectionate offices—faithful always and always confiding, as friends, and—
nothing more."

The captain answered confusedly. The widow proceeded.

"The fact is, captain, if you look at the matter properly, you will see
that it is quite impossible that we should marry. We should risk much
and gain little by such a tie. I confess to you that were I again to
marry, I know no person to whom I should be more willing to trust my
happiness than yourself."

The captain squeezed her hand.

"But, captain, I am willing to trust myself to nobody again. I have
been too long my own mistress to submit to authority. I have a certain
spice of independence in my temper, which would argue no security for
the rule which seeks to restrain me; and you, if I am any judge of men,
have a certain imperative mood which would make you very despotic,
should you meet with resistance. There would be peace and friendship

between us, my dear captain—nay love—so long as we maintain our separate independence; and, in this faith, I am unwilling to risk anything by any change in our relations. Let there be peace, and friendship, and love between us,—but never a word more of marriage. There is my hand, captain, in pledge of my good faith, my friendship, my affectionate interest in yourself and fortunes—my pleasure in your society—and you must be content with that. Will you, captain? For my sake, let me entreat, and please say no more of other matters."

Porgy took her hand and carried it to his lips.

"God bless you, my dear widow, and believe me grateful for what you are willing to bestow. I must be content—will be—assured of such a friendship as your heart is capable of. You are right, perhaps, and yet—"

"No doubt I am right. We know each other, and there shall be no misunderstanding between us. You must stay to dinner with me today, that I may be sure you feel no impatience with me."

And he stayed.

But the idea of marriage had, for the time, taken particular possession of the brain of our captain. Three days after, he rode over to see the widow Griffin; but on this occasion, he did not take the same pains with his costume as when he visited the other widow. His dress was less pretending, and more somber of hue. The captain knew, before he started, that the widow was alone. Lance Frampton had gone on a visit with his wife to Dorchester, the scene of some of his own exploits during the war, and where he had some relatives. Porgy found the widow in good health and trim, and especially in good spirits. Her welcome was always genial, and she looked particularly charming, though in ordinary household gear. She was at her spinning-wheel when he came. A basket of carded cotton stood beside her, and as she drew off the threads from the wheel, approached it and retired, he thought her as graceful as a young damsel of sixteen. For the first time in his life, he fancied that spinning was a particularly picturesque performance, and wondered that he had not seen it more frequently delineated in pictures.

Mrs. Griffin was very lively and good-humored, and the captain gradually became more and more gallant. After awhile, he officiated somewhat in her operations. Now, he drew the basket of cotton to her side. Anon, when she desired to move the wheel, he caught up one end of it, while she took the other. It was thus borne into the piazza, the better to afford room for her proceedings. In the obscure situation of the cottage, off the public road, and surrounded by great shady evergreens, the piazza was scarcely less private than the hall. The feeling of privacy had its effect on Porgy. Soon, he became more frequent in the little helps he gave the widow, and, at length, when putting aside her spinning, she proceeded to reel off a pile of yarn, the captain forced away the reel, and gallantly thrust his own arms through the hanks. It was in vain that the good, simple Griffin, wondering in discomfiture at this self-humiliation on the part of the captain, strove against it. He gave her a fierce smack upon the lips with his own, and thus put an end to all her efforts to repossess herself of the thread.

Then he placed himself before her in a great chair, his arms extended to the uttermost, his eyes surveying her tenderly, while she, with downcast looks, proceeded, as the sultan ruled, to reel off the threads as well as she might from the digits of her awkward auxiliary. The picture was a sufficiently ludicrous one, but it may be better fancied than described. Griffin might have seen—probably did see,—the grotesque absurdity of the scene; but Porgy was in his Arcadian mood, and certain feelings which he had in reserve, made him obtuse in respect to the queer figure which he cut in this novel employment.

He was startled into a full consciousness of his ridiculous situation, by the sudden appearance, in front of the house, on horseback, of the widow Eveleigh and her son Arthur. In the chat which the captain had kept up, tender and sentimental, and perhaps a little saucy, neither Griffin nor himself had heard the sound of the horses, until escape was impossible. The parties were fairly caught. The first thought of the captain, when he looked up at the sudden noise and saw who were the visiters, was to fling the yarn over Griffin's head; at all events to fling it from his arms; but the mischievous threads adhered tenaciously to the broadcloth, and caught upon the buttons at his wrist, and tangled itself about his fingers, as if each thread were a spirit of disorder, sent especially for his discomfort and defeat. When he sought to rise, it fell in a mass upon his feet, and when he strove to kick it off, the feet got involved within the meshes, so that he dared not take a step forward lest he should lay himself out, at full length, along the piazza. As for the yarn, before he got out of its meshes, it was one inextricable mass of disorder, which filled the eyes of Griffin with consternation to behold.

The pair were really in most pitiable plight; an awkward consciousness of the ludicrousness of the picture they afforded to the new-comers, striking them both irresistibly for the first time. But Porgy's consciousness was particularly vexing upon other grounds. To be seen in such a relation to the one widow, after seeking *such* a relation with the other! As the poor captain meditated upon the matter, which he did in a single instant of time, his face streamed with perspiration, though the month of March, when the event happened, is considered a tolerably cool one, even in a Carolina climate.

Porgy hardly dared encounter the eye of the widow Eveleigh, who had alighted with her son, and now entered. But he strove to pluck up courage, and, in seeking to appear lively, he simply showed himself nervous. When he did catch the eyes of the widow, he saw them filled with a significantly smiling speech, which added to his confusion. She gave him her hand, however, very frankly observing, as she did so—

"What, in our times, Hercules subdued to the distaff!"

"Ah! my dear widow, it is only woman that finds the hero weak. That *you* should have seen me at this folly!"

This was said in something of a whisper.

"Do not count it folly," answered the widow. "It is through the weakness of the man that we know his proper strength. That one is able to forget his dignities, only shows that his heart has not been forgotten. But, truth to speak, my dear captain, the picture was an amusing one."

"Funny! very! It must have been." This was said with a ludicrous attempt to smile, which resulted in a grin. Porgy's plan of courtship was exploded for that day, and for a goodly week afterward. But the purpose was not abandoned.

It was about ten days after, when the captain took occasion to revisit the widow Griffin. Frampton and his wife were still absent. Millhouse, Arthur Eveleigh, and George Dennison, were off on a deer hunt somewhere down the river; and Porgy having smoked his after-dinner pipe, and feeling dull, if not drowsy, having dined alone, resolved briefly the desolateness of his state, and, under a sudden call to change it, ordered his horse, determined to woo the widow Griffin after the most lion-like fashion. To confess another of our captain's weaknesses, he had but little doubt of success in his present quest. Griffin had been so docile, so gentle, so solicitous of his ease and comfort, that he really persuaded himself he had but to seek to secure. And so he rode.

A pretty smart canter soon brought him to her door, where the spectacle that confounded him was even more astonishing to his sight, than the situation could have been to the widow Eveleigh, when she caught himself. He could scarce believe his eyes. There, in the piazza, stood the fair Griffin, clasped close in the arms of the overseer, Fordham, and that audacious personage was actually engaged in tasting of her lips, as a sort of dessert after dinner. The situation was as apparent as the noonday sun. The facts were beyond all question or denial. The parties were fairly caught, and so conscious was the wicked widow of the sinfulness of suffering herself to be caught, that, not able to face the captain she broke away from the arms of Fordham, and rushed headlong into the house. Porgy was swallowed up in astonishment. He was about to wheel his horse around, and ride off, at greater speed than that which brought him, when Fordham sallied out, and asked him to alight, and with the coolest manner in the world said—

"Well, cappin, you've caught us at it; but no harm done, I hope. The widow and me hev' struck hands on a bargain, and I reckon we'll be mighty soon man and wife; and I hope, cappin, to see you at the wedding."

"The d—l you do!" was the only response of the captain, as, looking fiercely indignant at such cold-blooded audacity, he wheeled his horse, clapped spurs to his sides, and sent him homeward at full gallop.

"Mighty strange!" quoth Fordham. "The cappin doesn't seem to like it!"

Simple-minded Fordham, to suppose that a man should like to see his neighbor feeding on the very fruit he had thought to gather for himself.

With the defeat of these attempts, Captain Porgy gave up all notion of marriage.

"Woman!" quoth he, "woman!" and there his soliloquy ended; but the one word, repeated, was full of significance. When at length his comrades were again assembled about the board, and the cheerful fires were blazing on the hearth, and the philosophic cloud wreaths floated about the apartment, and the tankards were filled with potent floods of sunny liquor, Porgy said suddenly to his companions—

"My good fellows, there have been moments when I thought of deserting you,—that is, I sometimes meditated bringing in upon you a fearful influence, which might have lessened your happiness, and destroyed the harmony which prevails among us. I have had various notions of taking a wife—"

"A wife!" cried Dennison. "Oh, hush, captain, and don't frighten a body so! A wife! What madness prompted such a thought?"

"A wife!" cried Oakenburg,—"the Lord deliver us!"

"Ef she'd ha' come, she'd ha' delivered you mighty soon," quoth Millhouse; "I don't see what's to skear a body in a wife, pervided she's in proper sarcumstances, and is kept strik, by a man usen to army rigilations."

"Maussa better widout 'em," quoth Tom; "I nebber kin 'tan for be happy in house whar woman's is de maussa."

"Well, you will all be pleased to hear, then, that I have determined to live a bachelor for your sakes. I sacrifice my happiness for your own. I renounce the temptations of the flesh. It has been a pang to me, gentlemen, to do so, for beauty is precious in my sight. There are women whom I could love. There are charms which persuade my very eyes to sin. There are sweets which make my mouth water. But, for your sakes, I renounce them all. I shall live for you only. You could not well do without me; I will not suffer myself to do without you. You shall be mine always—I shall be yours. To woman, except as friend or companion, I say depart! I renounce ye! Avoid, ye sweet tempters to mortal weakness—ye beguile me with your charms no more! For your sakes, dear comrades, there shall be no mistress, while I live, at Glen-Eberley."

"And may you live for ever!" was the cry from all but Millhouse. He only muttered in the ears of Dennison—

"I sees it all! He disowns the women bekaise he kaint help himself. The grapes is sour!"

THE END

www.ingramcontent.com/pod-product-compliance
Lightning Source LLC
Chambersburg PA
CBHW020653110726
47901CB00001B/174